Just One Night

TRISH MOREY
HELEN BROOKS
ANNA CLEARY

MILLS &
BOON

First Published in Great Britain 2016
By Mills & Boon, an imprint of HarperCollins*Publishers*
1 London Bridge Street, London, SE1 9GF

JUST ONE NIGHT © 2016 Harlequin Books S. A.

Fiancée For One Night, *Just One Last Night* and *The Night That Started It All* were first published in Great Britain by Harlequin (UK) Limited.

Fiancée For One Night © 2011 Trish Morey
Just One Last Night © 2012 Helen Brooks
The Night That Started It All © 2013 Ann Cleary

ISBN: 978-0-263-92059-8

05-0416

Our policy is to use papers that are natural, renewable and recyclable products and made from wood grown in sustainable forests.The logging and manufacturing processes conform to the legal environmental regulations of the country of origin.

Printed and bound in Spain
by CPI, Barcelona

FIANCÉE FOR ONE NIGHT

BY
TRISH MOREY

Trish Morey is an Australian who's spent time living and working in New Zealand and England. Now she's settled with her husband and four young daughters in a special part of South Australia, surrounded by orchards and bushland, and visited by the occasional koala and kangaroo. With a lifelong love of reading, she penned her first book at the age of eleven, after which life, career, and a growing family kept her busy until once again she could indulge her desire to create characters and stories—this time in romance. Having her work published is a dream come true. Visit Trish at her website: www.trishmorey.com.

This book is dedicated to you, the reader,
the person this book was written for.

Please enjoy FIANCÉE FOR ONE NIGHT.

Much love, as always,
Trish x.

CHAPTER ONE

LEO ZAMOS loved it when a plan came together.

Not that he couldn't find pleasure in other, more everyday pursuits. He was more than partial to having a naked woman in his bed, and the more naked the woman the more partial he was inclined to be, and he lived for the blood-dizzying rush from successfully navigating his Maserati Granturismo S at speed around the sixty hairpin turns of the Passa dello Stelvio whenever he was in Italy and got the chance.

Still, nothing could beat the sheer unmitigated buzz that came from conceiving a plan so audacious it could never happen, and then steering it through the ensuing battles, corporate manoeuvrings and around the endless bureaucratic roadblocks to its ultimate conclusion—*and his inevitable success.*

And right now he was on the cusp of his most audacious success yet.

All he needed was a wife.

He stepped from his private jet into the mild Melbourne spring air, refusing to let that one niggling detail ruin his good mood. He was too close to pulling off his greatest coup yet to allow that to happen. He sucked in a lungful of the Avgas-flavoured air and tasted only success as he headed down the stairs to the waiting car. The Culshaw Diamond Corporation, owner and producer of the world's finest pink diamonds and a major powerhouse on the diamond market, had been in the hands of the one big Australian diamond dynasty for ever. Leo had been the one to sense a change in the dynamic of those heading up the business, to detect the hairline cracks that had been starting to show in the Culshaw brothers' management team, though not even he had seen the ensuing scandal coming, the circumstances of which had made the brothers' positions on the board untenable.

There'd been a flurry of interest from all quarters then, but Leo had been the one in pole position. Already he'd introduced Richard Alvarez, head of the team interested in buying the business, to Eric Culshaw senior, an intensely private man who had been appalled by the scandal and just wanted to fade quietly into obscurity. And so now for the first time in its long and previously unsullied history, the Culshaw Diamond Corporation was about to change hands, courtesy of Leo Zamos, broker to billionaires.

Given the circumstances, perhaps he should have seen this latest complication coming. But if Eric Culshaw, married nearly fifty years to his childhood sweetheart, had decreed that he would only do business with people of impeccable family credentials and values, and with Alvarez agreeing to bring his wife along, clearly Leo would just have to find himself a wife too.

Kind of ironic really, given he'd avoided the institution with considerable success all these years. Women did not make the mistake of thinking there was any degree of permanence in the arrangement when they chanced to grace his arm or bed.

Not for long anyway.

But a one-night wife? That much he could handle. The fact he had to have one by eight p.m. tonight was no real problem.

Evelyn would soon find him someone suitable.

After all, it wasn't like he actually needed to get married. A fiancée would do just fine, a fiancée found after no doubt long years of searching for that 'perfect' soulmate—Eric Culshaw could hardly hold the fact they hadn't as yet tied the knot against him, surely?

He had his phone in hand as he nodded to the waiting driver before curling himself into the sleek limousine, thankful they'd cleared customs when they'd landed earlier in Darwin to refuel, and already devising a mental list of the woman's necessary attributes.

Clearly he didn't want just any woman. This one had to be classy, intelligent and charming. The ability to hold a conversation desirable though not essential. It wouldn't necessarily matter if she couldn't, so long as she was easy on the eye.

Evelyn would no doubt be flicking through her contacts, turning up a suitable candidate, before she hung up the phone. Leo allowed himself a flicker of a smile and listened to the burr of a telephone ringing somewhere across the city as his driver pulled effortlessly into the endless stream of airport traffic.

Dispensing with his office two years ago had been one of the best decisions he had ever made. Now, instead of an office, he had a jet that could fly him anywhere in the world, a garage in Italy to house his Maserati, lawyers and financiers on retainer, and a 'virtual' PA who handled everything else he needed with earth-shattering efficiency.

The woman was a marvel. He could only applaud whatever mid-life crisis had prompted her move from employment in a bricks and mortar office to the virtual world. Not that he knew her age, come to think of it. He didn't know any of that personal stuff, he didn't have to, which was half the appeal. No more excuses why someone was late to work, no more hinting about upcoming birthdays or favourite perfumes or sultry looks of availability. He had to endure none of that because he had Evelyn at the end of an email, and given the references she'd proffered and the qualifications and experience she'd quoted in her CV, she'd have to be in her mid-forties at least. No wonder she was over life in the fast lane. Working this way, she'd be able to take a nanna nap whenever she needed it.

The call went to the answering-machine and a toffee butler voice invited him to leave a message, bringing a halt to his self-congratulations. He frowned, not used to wondering where his PA might be. Normally he'd email Evelyn from wherever he happened to be and not have to worry about international connections or time differences. The arrangement worked well, so well in fact that half the time he'd find her answering by return email almost immediately, even when he was sure it must be the middle of the night in Australia. But here in her city at barely eleven in the morning, when she'd known his flight times, he'd simply expected she'd be there to take his call.

'It's Leo,' he growled, after the phone had beeped for him to leave his message. Still he waited, and kept waiting, to see if that announcement would make his virtual PA suddenly pick up. When it was clear no one would, he sighed, rubbed his forehead with his other hand and spat out his message. 'Listen, I need you to find me a woman for tonight...'

'*Thank you for your call.*'

Leo swore under his breath as the butler terminated the message. Come to think of it, there was a damn good reason he usually emailed.

Eve Carmichael dropped the third peg in as many pairs of leggings and growled in frustration as she reached down to scoop up the offending article and fix the final item on the line. She'd been on tenterhooks all day. *All week more like it.* Ever since she'd known *he* was coming to Melbourne.

She looked up at the weak sun, willing it to dry her washing before Melbourne's notoriously fickle weather suddenly changed seasons on her, and shivered, a spidery shiver that descended down her spine and had nothing to do with the weather and everything to do with the fact Leo Zamos was coming.

And then she glanced down at her watch and the spider ran all the way up again.

Wrong. Leo Zamos was *here.*

It made no difference reminding herself that it was illogical to feel this way. She had no reason, no reason at all, to feel apprehensive. It wasn't like he'd asked her to meet his plane. In fact, it wasn't like he'd made any arrangements to see her at all. Logically, there was no reason why he should—she was his virtual PA after all. He paid her to run around on his behalf via the wonders of the world wide web, not to wait on him hand and foot.

Besides, there was simply no time to shoehorn her into his busy schedule even if he did have reason. She knew that for a fact because she'd emailed him the latest version this morning at six, just before she'd got into the shower and worked out her hot water service had chosen today of all days to die, not twenty-four hours after her clothes line had turned up its toes. A sign? She sure hoped not. If it was, it wasn't a good one.

No wonder she was edgy.

And no wonder this strange sense of foreboding simmered away inside her like a pot of soup that had been on the boil so long that it had thickened and reduced until you could just about stand a spoon in it.

Damn.

She shot a warning look at a cloud threatening to block out the sun and gave the old rotary clothes hoist a spin, hoping to encourage a breeze while cursing the fact that right now she probably had more hope of controlling the weather than she did reining in her own illogical thoughts, and there was no chance of controlling Melbourne's changeable weather.

And then she stiffened her jittery spine and headed back to the house, trying to shake off this irrational urge to do a Rip Van Evelyn and go to sleep until Leo Zamos was safely and surely out of her city.

What the hell was her problem?

Simple, the answer came right back at her, catching her so unawares she forgot to open the back door and almost crashed into it instead.

You're afraid of him.

It stopped her for a moment. Stilled her muscles and cemented her bones with the certainty of someone who had good reason to fear.

Ridiculous, she chided, her mind swiftly writing off the possibility, her breath coming short as she finally forced her fingers to work enough to turn the door handle and let herself in. Leo Zamos was nothing to her but the best hourly rate she'd ever been paid. He was a meal ticket, the ticket to renovating her late-nineteenth-century bungalow she affectionately referred to as the hovel, a ticket to something better in her life and getting it a hell of a lot sooner than it would ever happen otherwise. She just wished she didn't have to spend her renovation money on appliances now, before she even had an idea of what she'd need when the final plans came in.

She glanced upward at the strips of paint shredding from the walls of the laundry and the ivy that was creeping inside through the cracks where sixty years ago her grandfather had tacked it onto the back of the bungalow, and told herself she should be grateful for Leo's business, not a jittery bundle of nerves just because he was in town. Their arrangement worked well. That was all that mattered. That's what she had to concentrate on. Not some long-ago dusty memory that she'd managed to blow out of all proportion.

After all, Leo Zamos certainly wasn't wasting any time fretting about her. And in less than forty-eight hours he'd be gone. There was absolutely nothing at all to be afraid of.

And then she pulled open the creaking laundry door and heard a deep rich voice she recognised instantly, if only because it instinctively made her toes curl and her skin sizzle, *"...find me a woman for tonight..."* and the composure she'd been battling to talk herself into shattered into a million pieces.

She stood there, rooted to the spot, staring at the phone as the call terminated, emotions warring for supremacy inside her. Fury. Outrage. Disbelief. All of them tangled in the barbed wire of something that pricked at her skin and deeper, something she couldn't quite—*or didn't want to*—put a name to.

She ignored the niggling prickle. Homed straight in on the fury.

Who the hell did Leo Zamos think he was?

And what did he think she was? Some kind of pimp?

She swooped around the tiny kitchen, gathering dishes and piling them clattering into the sink. Oh, she knew he had his women. She'd arranged enough Tiffany trinkets and bottles of perfume to be sent to his countless Kristinas and Sabrinas and Audrinas over the last two years—and all with the same terminal message—

Thanks for your company.
Take care.
Leo

—to know he'd barely survive a night without a bedwarmer. But just because he was in her home town it didn't mean he could expect her to find him one.

Pipes groaned and hammered as she spun the hot water tap on fruitlessly, until she realised she needed to boil the kettle first to have any hope of hot water. But finally the sink was filled with suds and the tiny room was full of steam. She shoved her hands into rubber gloves and set upon attacking the stack of dishes and plastic cups, all but hidden under the froth and bubbles.

It had been lucky the machine had cut him off when it had or she might have been forced to pick up the receiver and tell him exactly what he could do with his demands—and that would be one sure way to terminate an income flow she had no way of replacing any time soon.

But, then, did she really want to work with a man who seemed to think it was perfectly acceptable asking his PA to organise him a night-time plaything? Maybe she should just call him herself. Remind him of the duties she had agreed to undertake.

Except that would require talking to him…

Oh, for heavens sake! On impulse she swiped at a tea towel and dried her gloves as she crossed the small living area towards the answering-machine, jabbing at a button before she could change her mind, her brain busy being rational. She dealt with his correspondence all the time, even if mostly by email. Surely she wasn't about to go weak at the knees at the sound of his voice?

And then the message replayed and she heard the weight of expectation in his pause as he waited for her to pick up—expected her to pick up—before his message. *"Listen, I need you to find me a woman for tonight…"*

And this time her outrage was submerged in a tremor that started in a bloom of heat that radiated across her chest and down her belly, tingling as it shot down her arms and legs. Damn. She shook her hands as if to rid herself of the unwelcome sensations, and headed back to finish the dishes.

So nothing had changed. Because his voice had had the same unsettling effect on her from the very first time she'd heard him speak more than three years ago in a glass-walled boardroom fifty floors above Sydney's CBD. She recalled the way he'd swept out of the lift that day, the air shifting in currents around him in a way that had turned heads and caused more than one woman to stumble as she'd craned her head instead of looking where she was going.

He'd seemed oblivious to his impact, sweeping into the boardroom like he owned it, spicing the air with a mix of musk and wood and citrus and radiating absolute confidence in himself and his role. And no wonder. For whether by sheer force of his personality or acute business acumen, or maybe the dark chocolate over gravel voice that had soothed everyone into submission, he'd successfully brought that deal to a conclusion that day, bringing together an over-eager buyer and a still unconvinced seller, and had had them both smiling as if they'd each got the better part of the deal.

She'd sat in the far corner of the room, taking minutes for her lawyer boss, while another part of her had been busy taking inventory of the man himself even as his rich voice had rippled through her and given birth to all kinds of wayward thoughts she had no business thinking.

Was there anything the man lacked?

Softness, she'd decided, drinking in the details, the thick black hair, the dark-as-night eyes, the strong angles of jaw and nose and the shadowed planes and recesses of his face. No, there was nothing soft about his looks, nothing at all. Even the lips that gave shape to that smooth-as-sin voice were fiercely masculine, a strong mouth she'd imagined as capable of both a smile as a cruel twist.

And then she'd looked up from her notebook to see him staring at her, his eyes narrowing, assessing as, without a move in his head, their focus moved down, and she'd felt his gaze like the touch of his long-fingered hand down her face and throat until with burning cheeks she'd wrenched her eyes away before she felt them wander still lower.

The rest of the meeting had passed in a blur and all she remembered was that every time she had looked up, it had seemed as though he was there, waiting to capture her eyes in his simmering gaze. And all the while the discussions had gone on around her, the finer points of the agreement hammered out, and all she'd been able to think about was discovering the sinful pleasures promised in his deep, dark eyes.

And when she'd gone to help organise coffee and had met him on the way back, she'd felt warmth bloom in her chest and pool in her belly when he'd smiled at her, and let him draw her gently aside with no more than a touch of his hand to her elbow that had almost had her bones melt.

'I want you,' he'd whispered, shocking her with his savage honesty, thrilling her with his message. 'Spend the night with me,' he'd invited, and his words had poured into all the places that had been empty and longing all her life, even the tiny crevices and recesses she'd never known existed until then.

And she, who had never been noticed in her life by anyone with such intensity, let alone a powerhouse of masculine perfection like this man, had done the only possible thing she could do. She'd said yes, maybe a little too breathlessly, a little too easily, for he'd growled and pulled her into a room stacked high with row upon row of files, already pulling her into his kiss, one hand at her breast, another curving around her behind even as he manoeuvred her to the furthest corner of the room.

Blown away by the man, blown away by the red-hot magma of sensations surging up inside her, she hadn't made a move to stop him, hadn't entertained the possibility until, with one hand under her shirt and his hard thighs wedged between hers, the door had opened and they'd both stilled and waited while whoever it was searched a row of files, pulling one out with a swish and exiting the room. And he'd pulled her shirt down and pushed the hair back from her face from where he'd loosened it from the coil behind her and asked her name, before he'd kissed her one more time. 'Tonight, Eve,' he'd said, before he'd straightened his tie and gone.

Cups clunked together under the suds and banged into the sides of the tiny sink, a sound reassuringly concrete right now. For this was her reality—a ramshackle bungalow it would cost a fortune to tear down and rebuild and probably more if she decided to renovate and try to preserve what original features might be worth saving.

She finished up the dishes and pulled the plug, letting the water go. She had commitments now. Obligations. A glimpse at her watch told her that her most important obligation would be waking up any minute now.

Would her life be any different if she had spent the night with Leo that night, if he hadn't been called away with barely a hurried goodbye to sort out a hiccup in the next billionaire deal he had been brokering somewhere halfway around the world, and if they'd actually finished what they'd started in that filing room?

Or given how she'd been incapable of saying no to him that day, maybe her child might simply have been born with skin even more olive, hair a little thicker?

Not that Leo would make those kind of mistakes, she was sure.

No, it was better that nothing had happened that night. He wouldn't be her client now if it had.

Besides, she knew what happened to the women Leo bedded. She could live without one of those terse thank-you notes, even if it did come attached to some pretty piece of bling.

The room darkened and she looked out the window in time to see the first fat drops fall from the dark clouds scudding across the sky and splatter against the glass.

'I thought I warned you,' she growled at the sky,

already making for the back door and forgetting all about Leo Zamos for one short moment.

Until the phone rang again.

CHAPTER TWO

SHE stood there, one hand on the door handle, one thought to the pattering rain growing louder on the tin lean-to roof, and yet Eve made no move towards the clothesline as the phone rang the requisite number of times before the machine cut in, inviting the caller to leave a message.

'Evelyn, it's Leo.'

Redundant really. The flush of heat under her skin told her who it was, and she was forced to admit that even when he sounded half-annoyed, he still had the most amazing voice. She could almost feel the stroke of it across her heated skin, almost feel it cup her elbow, as his hand once had.

'I've sent you an email,' Leo continued, 'or half of one, but this is urgent and I really need to speak with you. If you're home, can you pick up?'

Annoyance slid down her spine. Of course it was urgent. Or it no doubt seemed urgent to Leo Zamos. A night without a woman to entertain him? It was probably unthinkable. It was also hardly her concern. And still the barbed wire prickling her skin and her psyche tangled tighter around her, squeezing her lungs, and she wished he'd just hang up so she could breathe again.

'Damn it, Evelyn!' he growled, his voice a velvet

glove over an iron fist that would wake up the dead, let alone Sam if he kept this up. 'It's eleven a.m. on a Friday. Where the hell are you?'

And she realised that praying for the machine to cut him off was going to do no good at all if he was just going to call back, angrier next time. She snatched the receiver up. 'I didn't realise I was required to keep office hours.'

'Evelyn, thank God.' He blew out, long and hard and irritated, and she could almost imagine his free hand raking through his thick wavy hair in frustration. 'Where the hell have you been? I tried to call earlier.'

'I know. I heard.'

'You heard? Then why didn't you pick up? Or at least call me back?'

'Because I figured you were quite capable of searching the *Yellow Pages* yourself.'

There was a weighted pause and she heard the roar of diesel engines and hum of traffic, and she guessed he was still on the way to the hotel. 'What's that supposed to mean?'

'I mean, I'll do all manner of work for you as contracted. I'll do your correspondence and manage your diary, without issue. I'll set up appointments, do your word processing and I'll even flick off your latest girlfriend with some expensive but ultimately meaningless bauble, but don't expect me to act like some kind of pimp. As far as I recall, that wasn't one of the services I agreed to provide.'

This time the pause stretched so long she imagined the line would snap. 'Is something wrong?'

God, everything was wrong! She had appliances to replace that would suck money out of her building fund, she had a gut that was churning so hard she couldn't think straight, and now she was expected to find this man a sleeping partner. 'You're the one who left the message on my machine, remember, asking me to fix you up with a woman for the night.'

She heard a muttered curse. 'And you think I wanted you to find me someone to go to bed with.'

'What else was I supposed to think?'

'You don't think me perfectly capable of finding my own bedtime companions?'

'I would have expected so, given…' She dropped her forehead in one hand and bit down on her wayward tongue. Oh, God, what was she thinking, sparring with a client, especially when that client was almost single-handedly funding her life and the future she was working towards? But what else could she do? It was hard to think logically with this churning gut and this tangle of barbs biting into her.

'Given what, exactly?' he prompted. 'Given the number of "expensive but ultimately meaningless baubles" I've had you send? Why, Evelyn, anyone would think you were jealous.'

I am not jealous, she wanted to argue. *I don't care who you sleep with.* But even in her own mind the words rang hollow and she could swear that the barbed wire actually laughed as it pulled tighter and pressed its pointed spines deeper into her flesh.

So, okay, maybe she had felt just a tiny bit cheated that nothing had happened that night and she hadn't ended up in his bed, but it was hardly wrong to wonder, surely? It was curiosity, more than anything. Naturally she'd had plenty of time since then to count herself lucky she had escaped that fate, after seeing how efficiently and ruthlessly he dispensed with his women, but it didn't stop her wondering what it would have been like…

She took a deep, calming breath, blew it out slowly and cursed whatever masochistic tendencies had made her pick up the phone in the first place when it would have been far more productive to rescue her washing than risk losing the best client she was ever likely to have. 'I'm sorry. Clearly I misunderstood your message. What is it that I can do for you?'

'Simple.' His liquid voice flowed down the line now she was so clearly back on task. 'I just need you to find me a wife.'

'Are you serious?'

So far this call was going nothing like he'd anticipated. It wasn't just her jumping to the wrong kind of conclusion about his earlier call that niggled at him, or her obvious disapproval of his sleeping habits—most PAs he'd met weren't that openly prudish; in fact, most he'd encountered had been too busy trying to get into his pants—but there was something else that didn't sit right about his indignant PA. She didn't sound at all like he'd expected. Admittedly he was out of practice with that demographic, but since when did middle-aged women— any woman for that matter—ask their employer if they were serious?

'Would I be asking if I weren't? And I need her in time for that dinner with Culshaw tonight. And she probably doesn't have to be a pretend wife—a pretend fiancée should do nicely.'

There was silence on the end of the line as the car climbed the sweeping approach to the Western Gate Bridge and for a moment he was almost distracted by the view of the buildings of Melbourne's sprawling CBD to his left, the port of Melbourne on his right. Until he realised they'd be at his hotel in Southbank in a matter of minutes and he needed to get things moving. He had to have tonight's arrangements squared away before he got tied up with his lunchtime meeting with the government regulators due to sign off on the transfer of ownership when it went ahead. He'd dealt with those guys before and knew it was likely to be a long lunch. 'Evelyn?'

'I'm here. Although I'm still not quite sure I understand.'

He sighed. What was so hard to understand? 'Culshaw's feeling insecure about the deal. Wants to be sure he's dealing with solid family people and, given the circumstances, maybe I don't blame him. Culshaw and Alvarez are both bringing their wives to dinner tonight, and I don't want to do anything to make Culshaw more nervous by having me turn up alone, not when we're so close to closing the deal. So I want you to increase the number at dinner to six and find me someone who can play my fiancée for a night.'

'I can certainly let the hotel know to cater for six,' she said, sounding like she meant to go on before there the line went quiet again and he sensed a 'but' coming.

'Well?' he prompted, running out of time and patience.

'I can see what you're trying to do.' Her words spilled out in a rush. 'But is taking along a pretend fiancée really wise? I mean, what if Culshaw finds out? How will that look?'

Her words grated on both his senses and his gut. Of course it was a risk, but right now, with Culshaw feeling so vulnerable, so too was turning up alone. 'Choose the right woman,' he said, 'and that won't be an issue. It's only for a night after all. Are you anywhere near your email? I sent you an idea of what I'm looking for.'

'Look, Mr Zamos—'

'Leo.'

'Okay, so, Leo, I appreciate that I got the wrong end of the stick before, but finding you someone to play fiancée, that's not exactly part of the service I offer.'

'No? Then let's make it part of them.'

'It's not actually that simple.'

'Sure it is. Find an acting school or something. Tell whoever you find that I'm willing to pay over the odds. Have you got that email yet?'

'I'm opening it now,' she said with an air of resignation, her Australian accent softened with a hint of husky sweetness. He decided he liked it. Idly he wondered what kind of mouth it was attached to. 'Charming,' she read from the list of characteristics he'd provided, and he wondered. Surprisingly argumentative would be a better way to describe his virtual PA right now.

'Intelligent. Classy.' Again he mused. She was definitely intelligent, given the calibre of work she did for him. Classy? Maybe so if she'd worked as a corporate PA for several years. It wasn't a profession where you could get away with anything less than being impeccably groomed.

'And I've thought of something else.'

'Oh, goodie.'

Okay, so maybe charm wasn't her strong point, but so long as she got him the perfect pretend fiancée, he would overlook it for now. 'You might want to brief her on both Culshaw and Alvarez. Only the broad-brush stuff, no details. But it would be good if she wasn't completely ignorant of the players involved and what they do and can at least hold a conversation. And, of course, she'll need to know something about me as well. You know the kind of stuff…'

And then it suddenly occurred to him what had been bothering him. She said stuff like 'Are you serious?' and 'goodie' in a voice threaded with honey, and that put her age years younger than he'd expected. A glimmer of inspiration told him that if she was, maybe his search for the perfect pretend fiancée was already over…

'How old are you, Evelyn?'

'Excuse me?'

'I had you pegged for middle-aged, but you don't sound it. In fact, you sound much younger. So how old are you?'

'Is that entirely relevant right now?'

'It could be.' Though by the way she was hedging, he was pretty certain his question was unnecessary. At a guess he'd say she wasn't a day over thirty-five. It was perfect really. So perfect he was convinced it might have occurred to him earlier if he hadn't assumed his virtual PA was a good ten years older.

'And dare I ask…?' Her voice was barely a whispered breath he had to search for over the sounds of the city traffic. 'Why would that be?'

And he smiled. 'Because it would be weird if my fiancée looked old enough to be my mother.'

There was silence on the end of the line, a silence so fat with suspicion that it almost oozed out of the handset. Then that husky, hesitant Aussie drawl. 'I don't follow you.'

'It's quite simple,' he said, his blood once again fizzing with the heady buzz of a plan coming together beautifully. 'Are you doing anything for dinner tonight?'

'No. Leo—Mr Zamos. No!' This could not be happening. There was no way she was going to dinner with Leo Zamos and pretending to be his fiancée. No way!

'Excellent,' she heard him say through the mists of her panic. 'I'll have my driver pick you up at seven.'

'No! I meant yes, I'm busy. I meant no, I can't come.'

'Why? Is there a Mr Carmichael I need to smooth things over with? '

'No, but—'

'Then what's the problem?'

She squeezed her eyes shut. Tried to find the words with which to give her denial, words he might understand, before realising she didn't have to justify her position, didn't have to explain she had an infant to consider or that she didn't want to see him or that the idea simply sat uncomfortably with her. She simply had to say no. 'I don't have to do this. And neither do you, for that matter. Mr Culshaw knows you've only just flown in from overseas. Will he really be expecting you to brandish a fiancée at a business dinner?'

'But this is why it's so perfect, Evelyn. My fiancée happens to be Australian and she's already here. What could be better?'

She shook her head. For her own benefit maybe, but it made her feel better. 'It won't work. It can't. This is artifice and it will come unstuck and in grand style.'

'Evelyn,' he said measuredly, 'it can work and it will. If you let it.'

'Mr Zamos—'

'One evening, Evelyn. Just one dinner.'

'But it's not honest. We'd both be lying.'

'I prefer to think of it as offering reassurance where reassurance is needed. And if Culshaw needs reassurance before finalising this deal, who am I to deny him that?'

But making out we're engaged? 'I don't know.'

'Look, I haven't got time for this now. Let's cut to the chase. I said I was willing to pay someone above the odds and that goes for you too. This dinner is important to me, Evelyn, I don't have to tell you how much. What do you think it's worth for a few hours' work?'

'It's not about the money!'

'In my experience, it's always about the money. Shall we say ten thousand of your Australian dollars?'

Eve gasped, thinking of new clothesdryers and new hot water services and the cost of plumbers and the possibility of not dipping into her savings and still having change left over. And last but by no means least, whether Mrs Willis next door might be able to babysit tonight...

'You're right,' he said. 'Let's make it twenty. Would that be enough?'

Eve's stomach roiled, even as she felt her eyes widening in response to the temptation. 'Twenty thousand dollars,' she repeated mechanically, 'For one evening.'

'I told you it was important to me. Is it enough, do you think, to entice you to have dinner with me?'

Twenty thousand dollars enough? It didn't matter that his tone told her he was laughing at her. But for someone who had been willing to spend the night with him for nothing, the concept that he would pay so much blew her away. Did tonight really mean so much to him? Was there really that much at stake?

Really, the idea was so bizarre and ridiculous and impossible that it just might work. And, honestly, what were the chances he would recognise her? It had been almost three years ago and in a different city, and beyond heated looks they'd barely communicated that day and she doubted he even remembered her name, let alone what she looked like. And since then he'd met a thousand women in a thousand different cities, all of them beautiful, plenty of whom he'd no doubt slept with.

And since then she'd let her coloured hair settle back closer to its natural mousy colour and her body had changed with her pregnancy. Now she had curves that hadn't been there before and maybe wouldn't be there if she'd returned to work in that highly groomed, highly competitive office environment. One of the perils of working from home, she mused, was not having to keep up appearances.

Which also meant she had one hell of an afternoon in front of her if she was to be ready before seven. A glance at the wall clock told her she had less than eight hours to find a salon to squeeze into on the busiest day of the week, and find an outfit somewhere. Still assuming her neighbour could babysit tonight.

A thud came from the nursery, followed by a squeal and gurgles of pleasure, and she swung her head around. Sam was awake and busy liberating his soft toys from the confines of the cot. That meant she had about thirty seconds before he was the last man left standing and demanding to be released from jail the way he knew best. The loud way.

'There's a couple of things I have to square away,' she said, anxious to get off the phone before Sam decided to howl the place down. 'Can I call you back in a few minutes to confirm?'

'Of course,' he said, in that velvet-rich voice that felt like it was stroking her. 'Call me. So long as it's a yes.'

Leo slipped his phone into his pocket as the car came to a smooth halt outside his hotel. A doorman touched his gloved fingers to his hat as he pulled open the door, bowing his welcome. 'We've been expecting you, Mr Zamos.' He handed him a slim pink envelope that bore

his name and a room number on the front. 'Your suite
is ready if you'd like to go straight up.'

'Excellent,' he said, nodding his thanks as he strode
into the hotel entry and headed for the lifts, feeling more
and more confident by the minute. He'd known Evelyn
would soon have that little problem sorted, although
maybe he hadn't exactly anticipated her sorting it so
quickly and efficiently.

What was she like? he wondered as the lift whisked
him soundlessly skywards. Was he wrong not to insist
on a photo of her to be safe? Originally he'd had looks
on his list of requirements, on the basis that if he had to
act as someone's fiancé, he'd expected it would be one
hell of a lot easier to be act the part if he didn't have
to force himself to smile whenever he looked at her or
slipped his arm around her shoulders. But maybe someone more ordinary would be more convincing. Culshaw
didn't strike him as the sort of man who went for looks
over substance and, given his circumstances, he'd be
looking for a love match in the people he did business
with. In which case, some nice plain girl might just fit
the bill.

It was only for one night, after all.

The lift doors whooshed open on the twenty-fourth
floor onto a window with a view over the outer city that
stretched to the sea and air faintly scented with ginger
flower.

Other than to get his bearings, he paid scant attention
to the view. It was success Leo Zamos could smell first
and foremost, success that set his blood to fizzing as he
headed for his suite.

God, but he loved it when a plan came together!

CHAPTER THREE

EVE had some idea of how Cinderella must have felt on her way to the ball. Half an hour ago she'd left her old world behind, all tumbling-down house and broken-down appliances and baby rusks, and was now being whisked off in a silken gown to a world she had only ever dreamt of.

Had Cinderella been similarly terrified on her way to the ball? Had she felt this tangle of nerves writhing in her stomach as she'd neared the palace on that fairy-tale night? Had she felt this cold, hard fear that things would come terribly, terribly unstuck before the night was over? If so, she could well empathise.

Not that her story was any kind of fairy-tale. There'd been no fairy godmother who could transform her into some kind of princess in an instant with a touch of her magic wand for a start. Instead, Eve had spent the afternoon in a blur of preparations, almost spinning from salon to boutiques to appliance stores, in between packing up tiny pots of yoghurt and Sam's favourite pasta so Mrs Willis wouldn't have to worry about finding him something to eat. There had been no time for reflection, no time to sit down and really think about what she was doing or why she was even doing it.

But here, sitting alone against the buttery-soft

upholstery of an entire limousine, she had no distractions, no escape from asking herself the questions that demanded to be answered. Why was she doing this? Why had she agreed to be Leo's pretend fiancée, when all her instincts told her it was wrong? Why hadn't she insisted on saying no?

Sure, there was the money. She wouldn't call herself mercenary exactly, but she was motivated at the thought of getting enough money together to handle both her renovations and taking care of Sam. And how else would she so quickly gather the funds to replace a hot water service that had inconsiderately died twelve months too early and buy a new clothesdryer so she could keep up with Sam's washing in the face of Melbourne's fickle weather?

What other reason could there be?

Because you're curious.

Ridiculous. She thrust the suggestion aside, determined to focus on the view. She loved Melbourne. After so many years in Sydney, it was good to be home, not that she got into the city too often these days.

But the annoying, niggling voice in her head refused to be captivated or silenced by the view.

You want to see if he has the same impact on you that he had three years ago.

You want to know if it's not just his voice that makes your stomach curl.

You want to know if he'll once again look at you with eyes filled with dark desire and simmering need.

No, no and no! She shuffled restlessly against the leather, adjusting her seat belt so it wasn't so tight across her chest and she could breathe easier.

Dark desire and simmering need were the last things she needed these days. She had responsibilities now. A child to provide for. Which was exactly what she was doing by coming tonight, she acknowledged, latching onto the concept with zeal. She was providing for her child. After all, if she didn't, who would? Not his father, that was for sure.

She bit down on her lip, remembering only then that she was wearing lipstick for a change and that she shouldn't do that. It had been harder than she'd imagined, leaving Sam for an evening—the first time she'd ever left him at night—and it had been such a wrench she'd been almost tempted to call Leo and tell him she'd changed her mind.

But she hadn't. And Sam had splashed happily in an early bath and enjoyed dinner. She'd read him a story and he'd already been nodding off when she'd left him with Mrs Willis, his little fist clenched, his thumb firmly wedged between cupid bow lips. But what if he woke up and she wasn't there? What if he wouldn't settle back down for Mrs Willis?

God, what the hell had she been thinking, agreeing to this?

Outside the limousine windows the city of Melbourne was lighting up. It wasn't long after seven, the sky caught in that time between day and night, washed with soft shadows that told of the coming darkness, and buildings were preparing, showing their colours, strutting their stuff.

Just like she was, she thought. She wore a gown of aqua silk, which had cost her the equivalent of a month's salary in her old office job, but she figured the evening called for something more grand than her usual chain-store purchases. Leo would no doubt expect it, she figured. And she'd loved the dress as she'd slipped it over her head and zipped it up, loved the look of it over her post-baby curves and the feel of it against her skin, and loved what it did to accentuate the colour of her eyes, but the clincher had been when her eighteen-month-old son had looked up at her from his pram, broken into an enormous grin and clapped his pudgy hands together.

And she must look all right in her new dress and newly highlighted hair because her neighbour had gasped when she'd come to the door to deliver Sam and insisted she cover herself with an apron in case she inadvertently spilled anything on it before she left.

Dear Mrs Willis, who was the closest to a grandparent that Sam would ever know, and who had been delighted to babysit and have Eve go out for a night for a change, no doubt in the hope that Eve would find a nice man to settle down with and provide a father to Sam. And even though Eve had explained it was a work function and she'd no doubt be home early, her neighbour had simply smiled and taken no notice as she'd practically pushed her out the door to the waiting car. 'Have a lovely evening and don't rush. If it's after ten when you get home, I'll no doubt be asleep, so you can come and pick Sam up in the morning.'

And then they were there. The driver pulled into a turnaround and eased the car to a stop. He passed her a keycard as a doorman stepped forward to open her door. 'Mr Zamos says to let you know he's running late and to let yourself in.' She smiled her thanks as he recited a room number, praying she'd manage to remember it as the doorman welcomed her to the hotel.

Deep breath.

Warily she stepped out of the car, cautious on heels that seemed perilously high, where once upon a time she would have thought nothing of sprinting to catch a bus in even higher. Strange, what skills you forgot, she thought, when you don't use them. And then she sincerely hoped she hadn't forgotten the art of making conversation with adults because a few rounds of 'Open, shut them, open, shut them,' was going to get tired pretty quickly.

And then she stepped through the sliding doors into the hotel and almost turned around and walked straight back out again. It was little more than the entrance, a bank of grand elevators in front of her and a lift lobby to the left, but it was beautiful. A massive arrangement of flowers sat between the escalators, lilies bright and beautiful, palm leaves vivid green and all so artfully arranged that it looked too good to be real.

Just like her, she thought. Because she did so not belong here in this amazing place. She was a fake, pretending to be something she was not, and everyone would see through her in an instant.

She must have hesitated too long or maybe they recognised her as a fraud because someone emerged from behind the concierge desk and asked if she needed assistance. 'I'm to meet Mr Zamos in his suite,' she said, her voice sounding other-worldly in the moneyed air of one of Melbourne's most prestigious hotels, but instead of calling for Security, like she half expected, he simply led her to the lift lobby and saw her safely inside a lift, even smiling as he pressed Leo's level on the floor selection so she could make no mistake.

Oh, God, she thought, clutching her shawl around her as the lift door pinged open on the chosen floor, the keycard clenched tightly in her fingers, this is it.

One night, she told herself, it's just one night. *One evening*, she corrected herself, *just a dinner*. Because in just a few short hours she would be home and life could get back to normal and she could go back to being a work-from-home mum in her trackpants again.

She could hardly wait.

She stepped out into the lift lobby, drinking deeply of the hotel's sweetly spiced air, willing it to give her strength as she started on the long journey down the hall. Her stomach felt alive with the beating of a thousand tiny wings, giving flight to a thousand tiny and not so tiny fears and stopping her feet dead on the carpet.

What the hell was she doing? How could she be so sure Leo wouldn't recognise her? And how could she bear it if he did? The shame of knowing how she'd acted—like some kind of wanton. How could she possibly keep working for him if he knew?

Because she wasn't like that. Not normally. A first date might end with a kiss if it had gone well, the concept of a one-night stand the furthest thing from her mind, but something about Leo had stripped away her usual cautiousness, turning her reckless, wanting it all and wanting it now.

She couldn't bear it if he knew. She couldn't bear the aftermath or the subsequent humiliation.

Would he terminate her contract?

Or would he expect to pick up where he'd left off?

She shivered, her thumping heart beating much too loud for the hushed, elegant surroundings.

Lift doors pinged softly behind her and she glanced around as a couple emerged from the lift, forcing her to move both her feet and her thoughts closer to Leo's door.

Seriously, why should he remember her? A rushed grope in a filing room with a woman he hadn't seen before or since. Clearly it would mean nothing to a man with such an appetite for sex. He'd probably forgotten her the moment he'd left the building. And she'd been Eve then, too. Not the Evelyn she'd reverted to when she'd started her virtual PA business, wanting to sound serious and no-nonsense on her website.

And it's only one night, she told herself, willing herself to relax as she arrived at the designated door. Just one short evening. And then she looked down at the keycard in her damp hand and found she'd been clenching it so tightly it had bitten deep and left bold white lines across her fingers.

Let herself in when it was the last place she wanted to be? Hardly. She rapped softly on the door. Maybe the driver was wrong. Maybe he wasn't even there...

There was no answer, even after a second knock, so taking a fortifying breath she slid the card through the reader. There was a whirr and click and a green light winked at her encouragingly.

The door swung open to a large sitting room decorated in soft toffee and cream tones. 'Hello,' she ventured softly, snicking the door closed behind her, not game to venture yet beyond the entryway other than to admire the room and its elegant furnishings. Along the angled wall sat a sofa with chairs arranged around a low coffee table, while opposite a long dresser bore a massive flatscreen television. A desk faced the window, a laptop open on top. Through the open door alongside, she could just make out the sound of someone talking.

Leo, if the way her nerves rippled along her spine was any indication. And then the voice grew less indistinct and louder and she heard him say, 'I've got the figures right here. Hang on...'

A moment later he strode into the room without so much as a glance in her direction, all his focus on the laptop that flashed into life with just a touch, while all her focus was on him clad in nothing more than a pair of black silk briefs that made nothing more than a passing concession to modesty.

He was a god, from the tips of his damp tousled hair all the way down, over broad muscled shoulders that flexed as he moved his hand over the keyboard, over olive skin that glistened under the light, and over the tight V of his hips to the tapered muscular legs below.

And Eve felt muscles clench that she hadn't even known she'd possessed.

She must have made some kind of sound—she hoped to God it wasn't a whimper—because he stilled and glanced at the window in front of him, searching the reflection. She knew the instant he saw her, knew it in the way his muscles stiffened, his body straightening before he slowly turned around, his eyes narrowing as they drank her in, so measuredly, so heatedly she was sure they must leave tracks on her skin.

'I'll call you back,' he said into the phone, without taking his eyes from her, without making any attempt to leave the room or cover himself. 'Something's come up.'

She risked a glance—*there*—and immediately wished she hadn't, for when she looked back at him, his eyes glinted knowingly, the corners creasing, as if he'd known exactly what she'd been doing and where she'd been looking.

'Evelyn?'

He was waiting for an answer, but right now her tongue felt like it was stuck to the roof of her mouth, her softly fitted dress seemed suddenly too tight, too restrictive, and the man opposite her was too big and all too obviously virile. And much, much too undressed. The fact he made no attempt to cover himself up only served to unsettle her even more.

He took a step closer. 'You're Evelyn Carmichael?'

She took a step back. 'You were expecting someone else?'

'No. Nobody else—except...'

'Except what?' she whispered, wondering if spiders' eyes glinted the same way his did as they sized up their prey.

'I sure as hell wasn't expecting anyone like you.'

She felt dizzy, unbalanced and unprepared, and there was absolutely no question in her mind what she had to do next, no wavering. She turned, one hand already fumbling for the door handle, her nails scratching against the wood. 'Clearly you're not ready,' she said, breathless and panicky and desperate to escape. 'I'll wait outside.'

But she'd barely pulled it open an inch before a hand pushed it closed over her shoulder. 'There's no need to run away.'

No need? Who was he trying to kid? What about the fact a near-naked man was standing a bare few inches away from her and filling the air she breathed with a near-fatal mix of soap and citrus and pure, unadulterated testosterone? A man she'd once been prepared to spend the night with, a lost night she'd fantasised about ever since. A man standing so close she could feel his warm breath fanning the loose ends of her hair, sending warm shivers down her neck. What more reason did a girl need to flee?

Apart from the knowledge that it wasn't the beast she had to be afraid of after all. It wasn't the beast she couldn't trust.

It was her own unquenched desires.

'Stay. Help yourself to something from the minibar while I get dressed next door. I promise I won't be long.'

'Thanks,' she whispered softly to the door, not sure if she was thanking him for the offer of a drink or for the fact he was intending to put some clothes on. But she was sure about not turning around before he removed his arm from over her shoulder and moved away. Far, far away with any luck. 'I'll do that.'

And then the arm withdrew and she sensed the air shift and swirl as he departed, leaving her feeling strangely bereft instead of relieved, like she'd expected. Bereft and embarrassed. God, she must seem so unsophisticated and gauche compared to the usual kind of woman he entertained, practically bolting from the room with her cheeks on fire like some schoolgirl who'd wandered into the wrong loos by mistake!

She could actually do with a stiff drink right now, she mused, still shaky as she pulled open the minibar fridge, assuming she could open her throat wide enough to drink it. Then again, tonight would be a very good night not to drink alcohol, and not just because she probably had no tolerance for it these days. But because drinking anything with anaesthetic qualities in this man's presence would be a very, very bad idea.

Especially given she was already half-intoxicated just being in his presence.

True to his word, he was already returning from the room beyond by the time she'd made her selection, a pair of slim-fitting black trousers encasing those powerful-looking legs and a crisp white shirt buttoned over his broad chest. Even dressed, he still looked like a god rather than any mere mortal, tall, dynamic and harshly beautiful, and yet for one insane, irrational moment her eyes actually mourned the loss of naked skin to feast upon, until he joined her at the minibar and it occurred to her that at least now she might be able to speak coherently.

'Did you find something?' he asked, as she moved aside to give him room as he pulled a beer from the fridge.

'Yes, thanks,' she said, twisting the cap from a bottle of mineral water and grabbing a glass, still discomfited by his presence. Then again, it was impossible to see him clothed and not think about those broad shoulders, the pebbled nipples and the cluster of dark hair between them that swirled like storm fronts on a weather map, before heading south, circling his navel and arrowing still downwards…

She sucked in a rush of air, cursing when it came once again laced with his tell-tale scent. Distance was what she needed and soon, and she took advantage of his phone ringing again to find it. She did a quick risk assessment of the sitting room and decided an armchair was the safest option. She needed to stop thinking about Leo Zamos with no clothes on and start thinking about something else. Something that didn't return the flush to her skin and the heat to her face.

Like the decor. Her eyes latched onto a triptych set above the sofa. Perfect. The three black and white prints featured photographs of Melbourne street-scapes from the Fifties and Sixties, their brushed gold frames softening their impact against the cream-coloured wall. Understated. Tasteful. Like the rest of the furnishings, she thought, drinking in the elegant surrounds of the sitting area and admiring how the decorator had so successfully combined a mix of fabrics, patterns and textures. Maybe she should try for something similar…

And then Leo finished the call and dropped onto the sofa opposite, scuttling every thought in her head.

He stretched one arm out along the top of the cushions, crossed one long leg over the other and took a swig from his beer, all the while studying her until her skin prickled with the intensity of his gaze and her heart cranked up in her chest till she was afraid to breathe.

'It's a pleasure to meet you, Evelyn Carmichael, my virtual PA. I have to say I'm delighted to find you're very much real and not so virtual after all.' And then he shook his head slowly and Eve's lungs shut down on the panicked thought, *He knows*! Except his mouth turned up into a wry smile. 'Why did I ever imagine you were middle-aged?'

And breath whooshed from her lungs, so relieved she even managed a smile. 'Not quite yet, thankfully.'

'But your credentials—your CV was a mile long. What did you do, leave school when you were ten?'

The question threw her, amazed he'd remembered the details she'd supplied when he'd first sent his enquiry through her website. But better he remember those details rather than a frenetic encounter in a filing room with a PA with a raging libido. 'I was seventeen. I did my commercial degree part time. I was lucky enough to make a few good contacts and get head-hunted to a few high-end roles.'

His eyes narrowed again and she could almost see the cogs turning inside his head. 'Surely that's every PA's dream. What made you leave all that and go out on your own? It must have been a huge risk.'

'Oh, you know...' she said, her hands fluttering around her glass. 'Just things. I'd been working in an office a long time and...'

'And?'

And I got pregnant to one of the firm's interstate consultants...

She shrugged. 'It was time for a change.'

He leaned forward, held out his beer towards her in a toast. 'Well, the bricks and mortar office world's loss is my gain. It's a pleasure meeting you at last after all this time, Evelyn. You don't know how much of a pleasure it is.'

They touched drinks, her glass against his bottle, his bottomless eyes not leaving hers for a moment, and now she'd reeled in her panic, she remembered the heat and the sheer power of that gaze and the way it could find a place deep down inside her that seemed to unfurl and blossom in the warmth.

'And you,' she murmured, taking a sip of her sparkling water, needing the coolness against her heated skin, tempted to hold the glass up to her burning cheeks.

Nothing had changed, she thought as the cooling waters slid down her throat. Leo Zamos was still the same. Intense, powerful, and as dangerous as sin.

And it was no consolation to learn that after everything she'd been through these last few years, everything she'd learned, she was just as affected, just as vulnerable.

No consolation at all.

She was perfect. Absolutely perfect. He sipped his beer and reflected on the list of qualities he'd wanted in a pretend fiancée as he watched the woman sitting opposite him, trying so hard to look at ease as she perched awkwardly on the edge of her seat, picking up her glass and then putting it down, forgetting to drink from it before picking it up again and going through the same nervous ritual before she excused herself to use the powder room.

She'd been so reluctant to come tonight. What was that about when clearly she ticked every box? She was intelligent, he knew that for a fact given the calibre of the work she did for him. And that dress and that classically upswept hair spoke of class, nothing cheap or tacky there.

As for charming, he'd never seen anything as charming as the way she'd blushed, totally mortified when confronted by his state of undress before she'd tried to flee from the room. He'd had no idea she was there or he would never have scared her like that, but, then, how long had it been since a woman had run the other way when they'd seen him without his clothes on? Even room service the world over weren't that precious, and yet she'd taken off like the devil himself had been after her. What was her problem? It wasn't like he was a complete stranger to her after all. Then again, she'd made plain her disapproval of his long line of companions. Maybe she was scared she might end up on it.

Now, there was a thought...

He discounted the idea as quickly as it had come. She was his PA after all, even if a virtual one, and a rule was a rule. Maybe a shame, on reflection, that he'd made that rule, but he'd made it knowing he might be tempted from time to time and he'd made it for good reason. But at least he knew he wouldn't have to spend the night forcing himself to smile at a woman he wasn't interested in. He found it easy to smile at her now, as she returned from the powder room, coyly avoiding his eyes. She was uncannily, serendipitously perfect, from the top of her honey-caramel hair to the tips of the lacquered toenails peeping out of her shoes. And he had to smile. To think he'd imagined her middle-aged and taking nanna naps! How wrong could a man be? He would have no trouble at all feigning interest in this woman, no trouble at all.

He rose, heading her off before she could sit down, her eyes widening as he approached and blocked off the route to her armchair so she was forced to stop, even in heels forced to tilt her head up to look at him. Even now her colour was unnaturally high, her bright eyes alert as if she was poised on the brink of escape.

There was no chance of escape.

Oh no. His clever, classy little virtual PA wasn't going anywhere yet. Not before he'd convinced Culshaw that he had nothing to fear from dealing with him, and that he was a rock-solid family man. Which meant he just had to convince Evelyn that she had nothing to fear from him.

'Are we late?' she asked, sounding breathless and edgy. 'Is it time to go?'

He could be annoyed at her clear display of nerves. He should be if her nervousness put his plans at risk. But somehow the entire package was so enticing. He liked it that he so obviously affected her. And so what that she wasn't plain? She wasn't exactly classically pretty either—her green eyes were perhaps too wide, her nose too narrow, but they were balanced by a wide mouth that lent itself to both the artist's paintbrush and to thoughts of long afternoons of lazy sex.

Not necessarily in that order.

For just one moment he thought he'd noted those precise details in a face before, but the snatch of memory was fleeting, if in fact it was memory at all, and flittered away before he could pin it down to a place or time. No matter. Nothing mattered right now but that she was there and that he had a good feeling about tonight. His lips curved into a smile. A very good feeling.

'Not yet. Dinner is set for eight in the presidential suite.'

She glanced at the sparkly evening watch on her wrist and then over her shoulder, edging ever so slightly towards the door, and as much as he found her agitation gratifying, he knew he had to sort this out. 'Maybe I should check with the staff that everything's good with the dinner,' she suggested. 'Just remind them that it's for a party of six now…'

He shook his head benevolently, imagining this was how gamekeepers felt when they soothed nervous animals. 'Evelyn, it's all under control. Besides, there's something more important you should be doing right now.' He touched the pad of his middle finger, just one finger, to her shoulder and she jumped and shrank back.

'And what might that be?' she asked, breathless and trembling and trying to mask it by feigning interest in the closest photographic print on the wall. A picture of the riverbank, he noticed with a glance, of trees and park benches and some old man sitting in the middle of the bench, gazing out at the river. That wouldn't hold her attention for long. Not when he did this…

'You're perfect,' he said, lifting his hand to a stray tendril of hair that had come loose and feeling her shudder as his fingertips caressed her neck. 'I couldn't have asked for a better pretend fiancée.'

Her eyelids fluttered as he swore she swayed into his touch until she seemed to snap herself awake and shift the other way. 'I sense a "but" coming.'

'No buts,' he said, pretending to focus on the print on the wall before them. 'We just have to get our stories straight, in case someone asks us how we met. I was thinking it would make sense to keep things as close to the truth as possible. That you were working as my PA and one thing led to another.'

'I guess.'

'And we've been together now, what, two years? Except we don't see each other that often as I'm always on the move and you live in Australia.'

'That makes sense.'

'That makes perfect sense. And explains why we want to wait before making that final commitment.'

'Marriage.' She nodded. 'We're taking our time.'

'Exactly,' he said, slipping a tentative arm around her shoulders, feeling her shudder at the contact. 'We want to be absolutely sure, which is hard when we only get to see each other a few snatched times a year.'

'Okay. I've got that.'

'Excellent.' He turned towards her. Put a finger under her chin and lifted it so that she had no choice but to look into his eyes. 'But there's one thing you don't get.'

'I knew there was a but coming,' she said, and he would have laughed, but she was so nervous, so on edge, and he didn't want to spook her. Not when she was so important to him tonight.

'This one's simple,' he said. 'All you have to do is relax with me.'

'I'm perfectly relaxed,' she said stiffly, sounding more like a prim librarian than any kind of lover.

'Are you, when my slightest touch...' he ran a fingertip down her arm and she shivered and shied away '...clearly makes you uncomfortable.'

'It's a dinner,' she said, defensively. 'Why should you need to touch me?'

'Because any red-blooded man, especially one intending to marry you and who doesn't get the chance to see you that often, would want to touch you every possible moment of every day.'

'Oh.'

'Oh, indeed. You see my problem.'

'So what do you suggest?'

Her eyes were wide and luminous and up close he could see they were neither simply green nor blue but all the myriad colours of the sea mixed together, the vibrant green where the shallow water kissed the sand, the sapphire blue of the deep water, and everything in between. And even though she was supposed to be off limits, he found himself wondering what they'd look like when she came.

'I find practice usually makes perfect.'

She swallowed, and he followed the movement down her slender throat. 'You want to practise touching me?'

Fascinated, his thumb found the place where the movement had disappeared, his fingers tracing her collarbone and feeling her trembling response, before sliding around her neck, drawing her closer as his eyes settled on her too-wide lips, deciding they weren't too wide at all, but as close to perfect as they could get.

'And I want you to practise not jumping every time I do.'

'I…I'll try,' she said, a mist rolling in over her eyes, and he doubted she even realised she was already swaying into his touch.

He smiled as he tilted her chin with his other hand, his thumb stroking along the line of her jaw. 'You see, it's not that hard.'

She blinked, looking confused. 'I understand. I…I'll be fine.'

But he had no intention of ending the lesson yet.

Not when he had such a willing and biddable pupil. 'Excellent,' he said, tilting her chin higher, 'and now there's just one more thing.'

'There is?' she breathed.

'Of course,' he said, once again drawing her closer, his eyes once again on her lips. 'We just need to get that awkward first kiss out of the way.'

CHAPTER FOUR

She barely had time to gasp, barely had time to think before his lips brushed hers, so feather-light in their touch, so devastating in their impact that she trembled against him, thankful for both his solidity and his strength.

More thankful when his lips returned, this time to linger, to play about her mouth, teasing and coaxing and stealing the air from her lungs.

She heard a sound—a mewl of pleasure—and realised it had emanated from the depths of her own desperate need.

Realised she was clinging to him, her fingers anchored in his firm-fleshed shoulders.

Realised that either or both of these things had triggered something in Leo, for suddenly his kiss deepened, his mouth more punishing, and she was swept away on a wave of sensation like she'd only ever experienced once before. He was everywhere, his taste in her mouth, his hot breath on her cheek, his scent filling the air she breathed.

And the feel of his steel-like arms around her, his hard body plastered against her, was almost too much to comprehend, too much to absorb.

It was too much to think. It was enough to kiss and be

kissed, to feel the probing exploration of his tongue, the invitation to tangle and dance, and accept that intimate invitation.

How many nights had she remembered the power of this kiss, remembered what it felt like to be held in Leo's arms? It had been her secret fantasy, fuelled by one heated encounter with a stranger, but even she had not recalled this utter madness, this sheer frantic expression of need.

It was everything she'd ever dreamed of and more, that chance to recapture these feelings. And then he shifted to drop his mouth to her throat and she felt him, rock hard against her belly, and she shuddered hard against him, a shudder that intensified as he skimmed his hands up her sides and brushed peaked nipples in achingly full breasts with electric thumbs.

She groaned as his lips returned to her mouth, a feather-light kiss that lasted a fraction of a second before the air shifted and swirled cold around her and he was gone.

She opened her eyes, breathless and stunned and wondering what had just happened. 'Excellent,' he said thickly. 'That should do nicely. Wait here. I've got something for you.' He turned and disappeared into the other room. She slumped against the credenza behind her, put her hands to her face and tried not to think about how she'd responded to his kiss exactly like she had the first time. Drugged stupid with desire, shameless in her response to him.

Excellent? Hardly. Not when in another ten seconds he could have had her dress off. Another twenty and she would probably have ripped it off herself in desperation to save him the trouble. And all because he didn't want her to be nervous around him! God, how was she supposed to be anything but, especially after that little performance? Had she learned nothing in the intervening years?

She'd barely managed to catch her breath when Leo returned, a tie looped loosely around his collar, a jacket over his arm, and an expression she couldn't quite read on his face. Not the smug satisfaction she'd expected, but something that looked almost uncomfortable. When she saw the two small boxes in his hand, she thought she knew why and she didn't feel any better.

'Try these on,' he said, offering the boxes to her. 'I borrowed them for the night. Hopefully one should fit well enough.'

'You borrowed them?' she said, considering them warily, knowing what came in dangerous-looking little blue boxes like those. And if his words were a hint that whatever sparkly bauble she would wear on her finger wouldn't be hers to keep, it wasn't terribly subtle. But that wasn't what bothered her. Rather, it was the artifice of it all, like they were gilding the lie, layering pretence upon pretence. 'Is this strictly necessary?'

He lifted her hand, dropped the boxes on her palm. 'They'll notice if you don't wear an engagement ring.'

'Can't I simply be your girlfriend?'

'Fiancée sounds much better. All that added commitment.' He winked as he shrugged into his jacket. 'Besides, I've already told them. Go on, try them on.'

Reluctantly she opened the first. Brilliant light erupted from the stone, a huge square-cut diamond set in a sculpted white-gold band, inlaid with tiny pink diamonds. She couldn't imagine anything more stunning.

Until she opened the second and imagination took a back seat to reality. It was magnificent, a Ceylon sapphire set with diamonds either side. She had never seen anything so beautiful. Certainly had never imagined wearing anything as beautiful. She put down the box with the white-gold ring, tugged the other ring free and slipped it on her finger, hoping—*secretly praying*—that it would fit, irrationally delighted when it skimmed over her knuckle and nestled perfectly at the base of her finger.

She looked down at her hand, turning it this way and that, watching the blue lights dance in the stone. 'They must be worth a fortune.'

He shrugged, as if it was no matter, using the mirror to deftly negotiate the two ends of his tie into a neat knot. 'A small one, perhaps. It's not like I'm actually buying them.'

'No. Of course not.' He was merely borrowing them for a night to help convince people he was getting married. Just like he was borrowing her.

But even his ruthless designs couldn't stop her wondering what it must be like to be given such a ring, such an object of incredible beauty, by the man you loved? To have him slide that ring on your finger to the sound of a heartfelt 'I love you. Marry me,' instead of, *'Go on, try them on'*.

The sapphire caught the light, its polished facets throwing a dozen different shades of blue, the diamonds sparkling, and she felt her resistance wavering.

With or without the ring, she was already pretending to be something she was not. Could she really make the lie worse than it already was?

'Very nice,' he said, lifting her fingers. 'Have you tried the other one?'

She looked down at the open box, and the pale beauty that resided there. 'No real need,' she said, trying to sound like she didn't care as well as make out that she wasn't bothered by his proximity, even though her fingers tingled and her body buzzed with his closeness. 'This one fits perfectly.'

'And it matches your eyes.'

She looked up to see him studying her face. 'You know you have the most amazing eyes, every shade of the sea and more.'

'Th-thank you.'

He lifted a hand to her face and swiped the pad of his thumb at the corner of her mouth. 'And you have a little smudge of lipstick right here.' He smiled a knowing smile. 'How did that happen, I wonder?'

Instinctively she put a hand over her mouth, backing away. 'I better repair my make-up,' she said, sweeping up her evening purse from the coffee table and making for the powder room. How had that happened indeed. She really didn't need to be reminded of that kiss and how she'd practically given him a green light to do whatever he wanted with her. It was amazing it was only her lipstick that had slipped. Well, there would be no more smudged lipstick if she had any say in it. None at all.

He watched her go, his eyes missing nothing of her ramrod-straight spine or the forced stiffness that hampered her movements. She hadn't been stiff or hampered a few moments ago, when she'd all but rested her cheek against his hand. She hadn't been stiff or hampered when he'd held her in his arms and kissed her senseless.

'Evelyn,' he called behind her, and she stopped and turned, gripping her purse tightly in front of her chest. 'Something that might make you feel more relaxed in my company...'

'Yes?' She sounded sceptical.

'As much as I enjoyed that kiss, I have a rule about not mixing business with pleasure.'

She blinked those big blue eyes up at him and he could tell she didn't get it. 'I don't sleep with my PA. Whatever I do tonight, a touch, a caress, a kiss, it's all just part of an act. You're perfectly safe with me. All right?'

And something—he'd expected relief, but it wasn't quite that—flashed across her eyes and was gone. 'Of course,' she said, and fled into to powder room.

There. He'd said it. He blew out a breath as he picked up the leftover ring from the coffee table, snapped the box shut and returned it to the safe. Maybe it was, as he had said, to put her at her ease, but there'd also been a measure of wanting to remind himself of his golden rule. Because it had been hard enough to remember which way was up, let alone anything else in the midst of that kiss.

He hadn't intended it to go so far. He'd meant to tease her into submission, give her just a little taste for more, so she'd be more malleable and receptive to his touch, but she'd sighed into his mouth and turned molten and turned him incendiary with it.

And if he hadn't frightened her away by the strength of his reaction, he'd damned near frightened himself. He'd had to leave the room before she could see how affected he was, and before he looked into her ocean-deep eyes and decided to finish what he'd started.

He ached to finish what he'd started.

Why did he have that rule about not sleeping with his PAs? What had he been thinking? Surely this was a matter that should be decided on a case-by-case basis.

And then he remembered Inge of the ice-cool demeanour and red hot bedroom athletics and how she'd so neatly tried to demand a chunk of ice for her finger by nailing him with her alleged pregnancy.

There was good reason for his self-imposed rule, he reluctantly acknowledged. Damn good reason.

If only he could make himself believe it.

She didn't recognise herself in the powder-room mirror. Even after repairing her make-up and smoothing the stray wisps of her hair back into its sleek coil, she still looked like a stranger. No amount of lipstick could disguise the flush to her swollen lips. And while the ring on her finger sparkled under the light, it was no match for the lights in her eyes.

Not when all she could do was remember that kiss, and how he had damn near wrenched out her mind if not her soul with it.

It was wrong to feel excited, even though its impact had so closely mirrored that of the first. But he'd simply been making a point. He'd been acting. He'd said as much himself. It had meant nothing. Or else why could he so easily have turned and walked away?

Yet still she trembled at the memory of his lips on hers. Still she trembled when she thought of how he'd felt, pressing hard and insistent against her belly, stirring secret places until they blossomed and ached with want.

Want that would go unsatisfied. Cheated again. Just an act. *'I don't sleep with my PA.'*

And part of her had longed to laugh and tell him that he'd had his chance, years ago, and blown it then. Another part had wanted to slump with relief. While the greater part of her had wanted to protest at the unfairness of it all.

Damn. She'd known this would be difficult. She'd known that seeing him again would rekindle all those feelings she had been unable to bury, unable to dim, even with the passage of time.

She dragged air into her lungs, breathed out slowly and resolutely angled her chin higher as she made one final check on her appearance. For surely the worst was over. And at least she knew where she stood. She may as well try to enjoy the rare evening out.

How hard could it be?

'Remember,' Leo said, as they made their way to the presidential suite, 'keep it light and friendly and whatever you do, avoid any talk of family.'

Suits me, she thought, knowing Leo would be less than impressed if she started telling everyone about Sam. 'What is it exactly that their sons are supposed to have done?'

'You didn't see the articles?'

She shook her head. 'Clearly I don't read the right kind of magazine.'

'Or visit the right websites. Someone got a video of them at a party and posted it on the web.'

'And they were doing something embarrassing?'

'You could say that. It was a wife-swapping party.'

'Oh.'

'Oh, indeed. Half the board were implicated and Culshaw couldn't stand seeing what he'd worked for all his life being dragged through the mud.' He stopped outside the suite. 'Are you ready?'

As ready as I'll ever be. 'Yes.'

He slipped her hand into his, surprising her but not so much this time because it was unexpected but because it felt so comfortable to have his large hand wrapped around hers. Amazing, given the circumstances, that it felt so right. 'You look beautiful,' he whispered, so close to her ear that she could feel his warm breath kiss her skin, setting light to her senses and setting flame licking at her core.

It's make-believe, she warned herself as he tilted her chin and she once more gave herself up to his kiss, this time a kiss so tender and sweet that the very air seemed to shimmer and spin like gold around her. She drew herself back, trying to find logic in a sea of sensation and air that didn't come charged with the spice of him.

It meant nothing, a warning echoed as he pressed the buzzer. It was all just part of the act. She could not afford to start thinking it felt right. She could not afford to think it was real.

She had just one short evening of pretending this man loved her and she loved him, and then the make-believe ended and she could go home to her falling-down house and her baby son. Alone. That was reality. That was her life.

She should be grateful it was so easy to pretend…

A butler opened the door, showing them into an impressive mirror-lined entry that opened into the massive presidential suite, Eve's heels clicked on the high gloss parquet floor. Floor-to-ceiling mirrors either side reflected their images back at them, and Eve was struck when she realised that the woman in that glamorous couple, her hand in Leo's and her eyes still sparkling, was her. Maybe she shouldn't feel so nervous. Maybe they could pull this off. It had seemed such a crazy idea, and questions remained in her mind as to the ethics of the plan, but maybe they could convince his business colleagues they were a couple. Certainly she had twenty thousand good reasons to try.

'Welcome, welcome!' An older man came to meet them and Eve recognised him from the newspapers. Eric

Culshaw had aged, though, she noticed, his silvering hair white at the temples, his shoulders a little stooped as if he'd held the weight of the world on them. Given the nature of the scandal that had rocked his world, maybe that was how he felt. He pumped Leo's hand. 'Welcome to you both,' he said, smiling broadly.

'Eric,' Leo said, 'allow me to introduce my fiancée, Evelyn Carmichael.'

And Eric's smile widened as he took her hand. 'It is indeed a pleasure, Evelyn. Come over and meet everyone.'

Eve needed the few short seconds to get over the scale of the suite. She'd arranged the bookings for all the rooms, similar corner spa suites for Leo and the Alvarezes, and the presidential suite for the Culshaws, but she'd had no idea just how grand they were. Leo's suite had seemed enormous, with the separate living area, but this suite was more like an entire home. A dining room occupied the right third of the room, a study opposite the entry, and to the left a generous sitting area, filled with plump sofas and welcoming armchairs. Doors hinted at still more rooms, no doubt lavish bedrooms and bathrooms and a kitchen for the dining room, and all along one side was a wall of windows to take in the view of the Melbourne city skyline. The others were sipping champagne in the living room, admiring the view, when they joined them.

Eric made the introductions. Maureen Culshaw was a slim sixty-something with a pinched face, like someone had pricked her bubble when she wasn't looking. Clearly the scandal had hurt both the Culshaws deeply. But her grey eyes were warm and genuine, and Eve took to her immediately, the older woman wrapping her hands in her own. 'I'm so pleased you could come, Evelyn. Now, there's a name you don't hear terribly often these days, although I've met a few Eves in my time.'

'It was my grandmother's name,' she said, giving the other woman's hands a return squeeze, 'and a bit of a mouthful, I know. Either is perfectly fine.'

Maureen said something in return, but it was the movement in Eve's peripheral vision that caught her attention, and she glanced up in time to see something skate across Leo's eyes, a frown tugging at his brow, and for a moment she wondered what that was about, before Eric started introducing the Alvarezes, snagging her attention.

Richard Alvarez looked tan and fit, maybe fifteen years younger than Eric, with sandy hair and piercing blue eyes. His wife, Felicity, could have been a film star and was probably another ten years younger than he, dark where he was fair, exotic and vibrant, like a tropical flower in her gown of fuchsia silk atop strappy jewel-encrusted sandals.

Waiters unobtrusively brought platters of canapés and more glasses of champagne, topping up the others, and they settled into the lounge area, Leo somehow managing to steer them both onto the long sofa where he sat alongside her, clearly part of the act to show how close they were.

Extremely close apparently.

For he stretched back and looped an arm around her shoulders, totally at ease as he bounced the conversation between Eric and Richard, though Eve recognised it for the calculated move it was. Yet still that insider knowledge didn't stop her catching her breath when his fingers lazily traced a trail down her shoulder and up again, a slow trail that had her senses humming and her nipples on high alert and a curling ribbon of desire twisting and unfurling inside her. A red ribbon. Velvet. Like the sound of Leo's voice...

'Evelyn?'

She blinked, realising she'd been asked a question that had completely failed to register through the fog of Leo's sensual onslaught. She captured his wandering fingers in hers, ostensibly a display of affection but very definitely a self-defence mechanism if she was going to be able to carry on any kind of conversation. 'Sorry, Maureen, you were asking about how we met?' She turned to Leo and smiled, giving his fingers a squeeze so he might get the message she could do without the manhandling. 'It's not exactly romantic. I'm actually his PA. I was handling all his paperwork and arrangements and suddenly one day it kind of happened.'

'That's right,' Leo added with his own smile, fighting her self-defence measures by putting a proprietorial hand on her leg, smoothing down the silk of her gown towards her knee, bringing his hand back to her thigh, giving her a squeeze, setting up a sizzling, burning need. It was all Eve could do to keep smiling. She put her glass down and curled her fingers around the offending hand, squeezing her nails just a tiny bit too hard into his palm, just a tiny warning.

But he only looked at her and smiled some more. 'And this was after I'd sworn I'd never get involved in an office romance.'

Maureen clapped her hands together, totally oblivious of Eve's ongoing battle. 'Did you hear that, Eric? An office romance. Just like us!'

Eric beamed and raised his glass. 'Maureen was the best little secretary I ever had. Could type a hundred and twenty words a minute, answer the phone and take shorthand all at the same time. I could hardly let her go, could I?'

'Eric! You told me you fell in love with me at first sight.'

'It's true,' he said, with a rueful nod. 'Her first day in the job and the moment I walked in and saw the sexy minx sitting on her little swivel chair, I was toast. I just can't have that story getting around business circles, you understand.'

The men agreed unreservedly as Maureen blushed, her eyes a little glassy as she reached across and gave Eric's hand a squeeze. 'You're an old softie from way back, Eric Culshaw, and you know it.' She dabbed at her eyes with a lace handkerchief, and Eve, thinking she must look like she was shackled to Leo, shifted away, brushing his hand from her leg as she reached for her champagne. He must have got the message, because he didn't press the issue, simply reached for his own drink, and part of her wondered whether he thought he'd done enough.

Part of her hoped he did.

The other part already missed his touch.

'Felicity, how about you?' she said, trying to forget about that other wayward part of her. 'How did you and Richard meet?'

'Well…' The woman smiled and popped her glass on the table, slipping her hand into her husband's. 'This might sound familiar, but I'd been out with a friend, watching the sailing on Sydney Harbour. It had been a long day, so we stopped off to have a drink in a little pub on the way home, and the next thing I know, this nice fellow came up and asked if he could buy us both a drink.' She turned to him and smiled and he leaned over and kissed her delicately on the tip of her nose. 'And the rest, as they say, is history.'

'That's just like Princess Mary and Prince Frederik of Denmark,' said Maureen. 'Don't you remember, everyone?' Eve did, but she never had a chance to say anything because Leo chose that precise moment to run his finger along the back of her neck, a feather-light touch that came with depth charges that detonated deep down inside her as his fingertips drew tiny circles on her back.

'It wasn't the same hotel, was it?' Maureen continued.

'No. But it's just as special to us. We go every year on the anniversary of that first meeting.'

'How special,' said Maureen. 'Oh, I do love Sydney and the harbour. I have to say, the warmer weather suits me better than Melbourne's, too.'

And Eve, lulled by the gentle touch of a master's hand, and thinking of her never-ending quest to get the washing dried and not looking forward to cold showers and boiling kettles so Sam could have a warm bath, couldn't help but agree. 'Sydney's wonderful. I used to work there. I spent so many weekends at the beach.'

The fingers at her neck stilled, a memory flickering like the frames of an old black and white movie in the recesses of his mind. Something about Sydney and a woman he'd met years ago so briefly—too briefly—*a woman called Eve.*

CHAPTER FIVE

WHAT was it Maureen had said? *'Most people would shorten it to Eve.'* And she'd said something like, *'Either is fine.'* The exchange had niggled at some part of him when he'd heard it, although he hadn't fully understood why at the time, but then the mention of Sydney had provided the missing link, and suddenly he'd realised that there could be no coincidence—that bit had provided the missing piece and the jigsaw had fitted together.

He thought back to a day that seemed so long ago, of flying into Sydney in the early morning, recalling memories of a whirlwind visit to rescue a deal threatening to go pear-shaped, and of a glass-walled office that had looked over Sydney Harbour and boasted plum views of both the Harbour Bridge and the Opera House. But the view had faded to insignificance when his eyes had happened upon the woman sitting in the opposite corner of the room. Her hair had been streaked with blonde and her skin had had a golden tan, like both had been kissed by the sun, and her amazing eyes had looked deeper and more inviting than any famous harbour.

And endless meetings and time differences and jet-lag had all combined to press upon him one undeniable certainty.

He'd wanted her.

'Eve,' she'd told him when he'd cornered her during a break and asked her name. Breathless Eve with the lush mouth and amazing eyes and a body made for sin, a body all too willing to sin, as he'd discovered in that storeroom.

And he'd cursed when he'd had to leave all too suddenly for Santiago, cursed that he'd missed out on peeling her clothes from her luscious body, piece by piece. He'd had half a mind to return to Sydney after his business in Chile concluded, but by then something else had come up. And then there'd been more business in other countries, and other women, and she'd slipped from his radar, to be loosely filed under the-ones-that-got-away.

It wasn't a big file and as it happened she hadn't got away after all. She'd been right there under his nose, answering his emails, handling his paperwork, organising meetings, and she'd never once let on. Never once mentioned the fact they'd already met.

What was that about?

His hand drifted back to his pretend fiancée's back, letting the conversation wash over him—something about an island the Culshaws owned in the Whitsundays—his fingertips busy tracing patterns on her satiny-soft skin as he studied her profile, the line of her jaw, the eyes he'd noticed and should have recognised. She was slightly changed, the colour of her hair more caramel now than the sun-streaked blonde it had been back then, and maybe she wasn't quite so reed thin. Slight changes, no more than that, and they looked good on her. But no wonder he'd thought she'd looked familiar.

She glanced briefly at him then, as the party rose and headed for the dining area, a slight frown marring an otherwise perfect brow, as if she was wondering why he'd been so quiet. He smiled, knowing that the waiting time to meeting her again had passed; knowing that her time had come.

Knowing that for him the long wait would soon be over. She'd been like quicksilver in his arms that day, so potent and powerful that he hadn't been able to wait the few hours before closing the deal to sample her.

There was no doubt in his mind that the long wait was going to be worth it.

So what, then, that he had a rule about not sleeping with his PA? Rules were made to be broken after all, some more than others. He smiled at her, taking her arm, already anticipating the evening ahead. A long evening filled with many delights, if he had anything to do with it. Which of course, he thought with a smile, he did.

Maybe it was the fact everyone so readily accepted Evelyn as his fiancée. Maybe it was the surprising re-alisation that playing the part of a fiancé wasn't as ap-palling or difficult as he'd first imagined that made the evening work.

Or maybe it was the thought of afterwards, when he would finally get the opportunity to peel off her gown and unleash the real woman beneath.

But the evening did work, and well. The drinks and canapés, the dinner, the coffee and dessert—the hotel catering would get a bonus. It was all faultless. Culshaw was beaming, his wife was glowing and the Alvarezes made such entertaining dinner companions, reeling out one amusing anecdote after another, that half the time everyone was laughing too much to eat.

And Evelyn—the delectable Evelyn—played her part to perfection. Though he frowned as he caught her glancing at her watch again. Perfect, apart from that annoying habit she had of checking the time every ten minutes. Why? It wasn't like she was going anywhere. Certainly not before they'd had a chance to catch up on old times.

Finally coffee and liqueurs had been served and the staff quietly vanished back into the kitchen. Culshaw stifled a yawn, apologising and blaming his habit of going for a long early walk every morning for not letting him stay up late. 'But I thank you all for coming. Richard and Leo, maybe we can get those contract terms nutted out tomorrow— what do you think?'

The men drew aside to agree on a time to meet while the women chatted, gathering up purses and wraps. They were nice people, Eve thought, wishing she could have met them in different circumstances, and not while living this lie. She knew she'd never meet them again, and maybe in the bigger scheme of things it made no difference to anything, as they would all go their separate ways in a day or so, but that thought was no compensation for knowing she'd spent the evening pretending to be someone and something she was not.

'Shall we go?' Leo said, breaking into her thoughts as he wrapped his big hand around hers and lifted it to his mouth, and Eve could see how pleased he was with himself and with the way things had gone.

The final act, she thought as his lips brushed her hand and his eyes simmered with barely contained desire. A look filled with heated promise, of a coming night filled with tangled limbs in tangled sheets. The look a man should give his fiancée before they retired to their room for the night. The final pretence.

No pretence necessary when her body responded like a woman's should respond to her lover's unspoken invitation, ripening and readying until she could feel the pulse of her blood beating out her need in that secret place between her thighs, achingly insistent, turning her thoughts to sex. No wonder everyone believed them to be lovers. He acted the part so very well. He made it so easy. He made her body want to believe it.

A shame, she thought as they said their final good-byes and left the suite. Such a shame it was all for nothing. Such a waste of emotional energy and sizzling intensity. Already she could feel her body winding down, the sense of anticlimax rolling in. The sudden silence somehow magnified it, the hushed passage devoid of other guests, as empty as their pretend relationship.

'Will the car be waiting for me downstairs?' she asked, glancing at her phone as they waited in the lift lobby. No messages, she noticed with relief, dropping it back into her purse. Which meant Mrs Willis had had no problems with Sam.

'So anxious to get away?' the man at her side said. 'Do you have somewhere you're desperate to get to?'

'Not really. Just looking forward to getting home.' And she wasn't desperate. There no point rushing now, Eve knew. She'd been watching the time and chances were Mrs Willis was well and truly tucked up in bed by now, which meant no picking up Sam before morning. But equally there was nothing for her here. She'd done her job. It was time to drop the make-believe and go home to her real life.

'No? Only you kept checking your watch every five minutes through dinner and you just now checked your phone. I get the impression I'm keeping you from something—or someone.'

'No,' she insisted, cursing herself for being so obvious. She'd gone to the powder room to check her messages during the evening, not wanting to be rude or raise questions. She hadn't thought anyone would notice a quick glance at her watch. 'Look, it's nothing. But we've finished here, haven't we?'

'Aren't you forgetting something?'

'What?' He took her hand and lifted it, the sapphire flashing on her finger. 'Oh, of course. I almost forgot.' She tried to slip her hand from his so she could take it off, but he stilled her.

'Not here. Wait till we get to the suite.' And she would have argued that it wasn't necessary, that she could give it to him in the lift for that matter, only she heard voices behind them and the sound of the Alvarezes approaching and knew she had no choice, not when their suites were on the same floor and it would look bizarre if she didn't accompany Leo.

'Ah, we meet again,' Richard said, coming around the corner with Felicity on his arm as the lift doors whooshed open softly behind them. 'Great night, Leo, well done. Culshaw seems much more comfortable to do business now. He agreed to call to arrange things after his walk in the morning.'

Leo smiled and nodded. 'Excellent,' he said, pressing the button for the next floor as they made small talk about the dinner, within seconds the two couples bidding each other goodnight again and heading for their respective suites.

And, really, it wasn't a problem for Eve. Leo had told her his rule about not mixing business with pleasure. So she knew she had nothing to fear. She'd give him back the ring, make sure the coast was clear, and be gone. She'd be in and out in two minutes, tops.

He swiped a card through the reader, holding the door open so she could precede him into the room. She ignored the flush of sensation as she brushed past him, tried not to think about how good he smelt or analyse the individual ingredients that made up his signature scent, and had the ring off her finger and back in its tiny box before the door had closed behind her. 'Well, that's that, then,' she said brightly, snapping the box shut and setting it back on the coffee table. 'I think that concludes our business tonight. Maybe you could summon up that car for me and I'll get going.'

'You said you didn't have to rush off,' he said, busy extracting a cork from what looked suspiciously like a bottle of French champagne he'd just pulled from an ice bucket she was sure hadn't seen before, and felt her first shiver of apprehension.

'I don't remember that being there when we left.'

'I asked the wait staff to organise it,' he explained. 'I thought a celebration was in order.'

Another tremor. Another tiny inkling of...*what*? 'A celebration?'

'For pulling off tonight. For having everyone believe we were a couple. You had both Eric and Maureen, not to mention Richard and Felicity, eating out of your hand.'

'It was a nice evening,' she said warily, accepting a flute of the pale gold liquid, wishing he'd make a move to sit down, wishing he was anywhere in the suite but standing right there between her and the door. Knowing she could move away but that would only take her deeper into his suite. Knowing that was the last place she wanted to be. 'They're nice people.'

'It was a perfect evening. In fact, you make the perfect virtual fiancée, Evelyn Carmichael. Perhaps you should even put that on your CV.' He touched his glass to hers and raised it. 'Here's to you, my virtual PA, my virtual fiancée. Here's to...us.'

She could barely breathe, barely think. There was

no *us*. But he had that look again, the look he'd had before they'd left the presidential suite that had her pulse quickening and beating in dark, secret places. And suddenly there was that image back in her mind, of tangled bedlinen and twisted limbs, and a strange sense of dislocation from the world, as if someone had changed the rules when she wasn't looking and now black was white and up was down and nothing, especially not Leo Zamos, made any kind of sense.

She shook her head, had to look away for a moment to try to clear her own tangled thoughts.

'Oh, I don't think I'll be doing anything like this again.'

'Why not? When you're so clearly a natural at playing a part.' He nodded in the direction of her untouched glass. 'Wine not to your taste?'

She blinked and took a sip, wondering if he was ever going to move away from the minibar and from blocking the door, moving closer to the wall at her back in case he was waiting for her to move first. 'It's lovely, thank you. And the Culshaws and Alvarezes are lovely people. I still can't help but feel uncomfortable about deceiving them that way.'

'That's something I like about you, Evelyn.' He moved at last, but not to go past her. He moved closer, touching the pad of one finger to her brow, shifted back a stray tendril of hair, a touch so gentle and light but so heated and powerful that she shivered under its impact. 'That honest streak you have. That desire not to deceive. I have to admire that.'

Warning bells rang out in her mind. There was a calm, controlled anger rippling through the underbelly of his words that she was sure hadn't been there before, an iron fist beneath the velvet-gloved voice, and she wasn't sure what he thought he was celebrating but she did know she didn't want to be any part of it.

'I should be going,' she said, searching for the nearest horizontal surface on which to deposit her nearly untouched drink, finding it in the credenza at her side. 'It's late. Don't bother your driver. I'll get myself a cab.'

He smiled then, as lazily and smugly as a crocodile who knew that all the efforts of its prey were futile for there was no escape. a smile that made her shiver, all the way down.

'If you'll just move out the way,' she suggested, 'I'll go.'

'Let you go?' he questioned, retrieving her glass and holding it out to her. *When she was so clearly leaving.* 'When I thought you might like to share a drink with me.'

She ignored it. 'I had one, thanks.'

'No, that drink was a celebration. This one will be for old times' sake. What do you say, Evelyn? Or maybe you'd prefer if I called you *Eve.*'

And a tidal wave of fear crashed over her, cold and drenching and leaving her shuddering against the wall, thankful for its solidity in a world where the ground kept shifting. *He knew!* He knew and he was angry and there was no way he was going to move away from that door and let her calmly walk out of here. Her tongue found her lips, trying valiantly to moisten them, but her mouth was dry, her throat constricted. 'I'm good with either,' she said, trying for calm and serene and hearing her voice come out thready and desperate. 'And I really should be going.'

'Because I met an Eve once,' he continued, his voice rich and smooth by comparison, apparently oblivious to her discomfiture, or simply enjoying it too much to put an end to it, 'in an office overlooking Sydney Harbour. She had the most amazing blue eyes, a body built for sinful pleasures, and she was practically gagging for it. Come to think of it, she *was* gagging for it.'

'I was not!' she blurted, immediately regretting her outburst, wishing the shifting ground would crack open and swallow her whole, or that her pounding heart would break the door down so she could escape. Because she was kidding herself. Even if it hadn't been how she usually acted, even if it had been an aberration, he was right. Because if that person hadn't interrupted them in the midst of that frantic, heated encounter, she would have spread her legs for him right there and then, and what was that, if not gagging for it?

And afterwards she'd been taking minutes, writing notes, even if she'd found it nearly impossible to transcribe them or remember what had actually been said when she'd returned to her office because of thoughts of what had almost happened in that filing room and what would happen during the night ahead.

He curled his fingers under her chin, forced her to look at him, triumph glinting menacingly in his eyes. 'You've been working with me for more than two years, sweet little Miss Evelyn don't-like-to-deceive-anyone Carmichael. When exactly were you planning on telling me?'

She looked up at him, hoping to reason with him, hoping that reason made sense. 'There was nothing to tell.'

'Nothing? When you were so hot for me you were practically molten. And you didn't think I might be interested to know we'd more than just met before?'

'But nothing happened! Not really. It was purely a coincidence that I came to work for you. You wanted a virtual PA. You sent a query on my webpage. You agreed the terms and I did the work you wanted and what did or didn't happen between us one night in Sydney was irrelevant. It didn't matter.' She was babbling and she knew it, but she couldn't stop herself, tripping over the words in the rush to get them out. 'It wasn't like we ever had to meet. If you hadn't needed a pretend fiancée tonight, you would never have known.'

'Oh, I get it. So it's my fault, is it, that all this time you lied to me.'

'I never lied.'

'You lied by omission. You knew who I was, you knew what had so very nearly happened, and you failed to tell me that I knew you. You walked in here and hoped and prayed I wouldn't recognise you and you almost got away with it.'

'I didn't ask to come tonight!'

'No. And now I know why. Because you knew your dishonesty would come unstuck. All that talk about not deceiving people and you've happily been deceiving me for two years.'

'I do my job and I do it well!'

'Nobody said you didn't. What is an issue is that you should have told me.'

'And would you have contracted me if I had?'

'Who knows? Maybe if you had, we might be having great sex right now instead of arguing.'

Unfair, she thought as she sucked in air, finding it irritatingly laden with his testosterone-rich scent. So unfair to bring up sex right now, to remind her of what might have been, when she was right here in his suite and about to lose the backbone of her income because she'd neglected to tell him about a night when nothing had happened.

'Let me tell you something, Evelyn Carmichael,' he said, as he trailed lazy fingertips down the side of her face. 'Let me share something I might have shared with you, if you'd ever bothered to share the truth with me. Three years ago, I was aboard a flight to Santiago. I had a fifty-page report to read and digest and a strategy to close a deal to work out and I knew what I needed to be doing, but hour after hour into the flight I couldn't concentrate. And why couldn't I concentrate? Because my head was filled with thoughts of a blonde, long-limbed PA with the sexiest eyes I had ever seen and thinking about what we both should have been doing right then if I hadn't had to leave Sydney.'

'Oh.' It had never occurred to her that he might have regretted his sudden departure. It had never occurred to her that she hadn't been the only one unable to sleep that night, the only one who remembered.

'I felt cheated,' he said, his fingers skimming the line of her collarbone, 'because I had to leave before we got a chance to…get to know each other.' His fingers played at her shoulder, his thumbs stroking close to the place on her throat where she could feel her pulse beat at a frantic pace. 'Did you feel cheated, Evelyn?'

'Perhaps. Maybe just a little.'

'I was hoping maybe more than just a little.'

'Maybe,' she agreed, earning herself a smile in return.

'And now I find that I have been cheated in those years since. I never had a chance to revisit what we had lost that night, because you chose not to tell me.'

She blinked up at him, still reeling from the impact of his words. 'How could I tell you?'

'How could you not tell me, when you must know how good we will be together. We knew it that day. We recognised it. And we knew it earlier when I kissed you and you turned near incendiary in my arms. Do you know how hard that kiss was to break, Evelyn? Do you know what it took to let you go and take you to dinner and not take you straight to my bed?'

She shuddered at his words, knowing them to be true, knowing that if he'd taken her to bed that night, she would have gone and gone willingly. But he'd left her confused. He'd been angry with her a moment ago, yet now the air vibrated around them with a different tension. 'What do you want?'

'What I have always wanted ever since the first time I saw you,' he said, his eyes wild with desire and dark promises that kept those dark, secret places of her humming with sensation and aching with need. 'I want you.'

CHAPTER SIX

'This won't work,' she warned weakly, her hands reaching for the wall behind her as his mouth descended towards hers. 'This can't happen.'

He brushed her lips with his. 'Why not?'

'You don't sleep with your PAs. You don't mix business with pleasure. You said so yourself.'

'True,' he agreed, making a second pass over her mouth, and then a third, lingering just a fraction longer this time. 'Never mix business with pleasure.'

'Then what are you doing?' she asked, her senses buzzing. He slipped his hands behind her head, his fingers weaving through her hair as he angled her mouth higher.

'Unfinished business, on the other hand,' he murmured, his eyes on her mouth. 'That's a whole different rule book.' He moved his gaze until dark eyes met her own, gazing at her with such feverish intensity that she felt bewitched under their spell. 'Do you want to open that book, Evelyn? Do you want to dip into its pages and enjoy one night of pleasure, one night of sin, to make up for that night we were both cheated out of?'

This time he kissed her eyes, first one and then the other, butterfly kisses of heated breath and warm lips that made her tremble with both their tenderness and their devastating impact on her senses. 'Or do you still wish to leave?'

He kissed her lips then before she could respond, as if trying to convince her with his hot mouth instead of his words, and she could feel the tension underlining his movements, could tell he was barely controlling the passion that bubbled so close below the surface as he tried to be gentle with her. He was offering her a night of unimaginable pleasure, a night she'd thought about so many times since that ill-fated first meeting.

Or he was offering her escape.

She was so, so very tempted to stay, to stay with this man who'd invaded her dreams and longings, the man who'd taken possession of them ever since the day they'd first met. The man who had made her want and lust and feel alive for the first time in her life. She wanted to stay and feel alive again.

But she should go. The sensible thing would be to go. She was no longer a free agent, able to do as she pleased when she pleased. She had responsibilities. She was a mother now, with a child waiting at home.

His kisses tortured her with their sweetness while her mind grappled with the dilemma, throwing out arguments for and against. The decision was hers and yet she felt powerless to make it, knowing that whatever she decided, she would live to regret it.

But it was just one night.

And her child was safely tucked up in bed, asleep.

But hadn't her child resulted from just one such night? One foolish wrong decision and she would live with the consequences for ever. Did she really want to risk that happening again? Could she afford to?

Could she afford not to?

Did she really want to go home to her empty bed

and know that she'd turned her back on this chance to stop wondering what if, the chance to finally burn this indecent obsession out of her system?

And didn't she deserve just one night? She'd worked hard to make a success of her business and to provide for Sam. Surely she deserved a few short hours of pleasure? Maybe then she could stop wondering, stop imagining what it would have been like to have made love that night, to have finished what they'd started. And maybe he was a lousy lover and this would cure her of him for ever, just like one night with Sam's father had been more than enough.

Hadn't she already paid the price?

His mouth played on hers, enticing her into the dance, his tongue a wicked invitation, his big hands skimming her sides so that his thumbs brushed the undersides of her breasts, so close to her aching nipples that she gasped, and felt herself pushing into his hands.

A lousy lover? *Not likely.*

'What's it to be?' he said, pulling back, his breathing ragged, searching her eyes for her answer. 'Do I open the book? Or do you go? Because if you don't decide now, I promise you, there will be no going anywhere.'

And his words were so hungry, the pain of his restraint so clearly etched on his tightly drawn features, that she realised how much power she really held. He wanted her so much, and still he was prepared to let her walk away. Maybe because he sensed she was beyond leaving, maybe because he knew that his kisses and touches had lit a fire inside her that would not be put out, not be quenched until it had burned itself to ash. But he was giving her the choice.

When really, just like that first time, there was none.

'Maybe,' she ventured tentatively, her voice breathy as she wondered whether in wanting to make up for a lost opportunity she was making the mistake of her life, 'we could at least check out a page or two.'

He growled his approval, a sound straight from the Stone Age, a dark, deep sound that rumbled into her very bones and shook them loose. She would have fallen then, if he hadn't pulled her into his kiss, his hot mouth explosive on her lips, on her throat, as he celebrated her acquiescence, his arms like steel crushing her to him, his hands on her back, on her shoulders, capturing a breast and sweeping his thumb over her peaked nipple, sending sensation spearing down to that hot place between her thighs and making her mewl into his mouth.

'God, I want you,' he said, echoing the only words she was capable of thinking, as she pushed his jacket off his shoulders and he shucked off his shoes. He released her for only a moment, shrugged the jacket off and let it drop to the floor while she worked desperately at his buttons and his tie, and he turned his attentions to her zipper. She felt the slide down her spine and the loosening of fabric, the electric touch of his hands at the small of her back. Impatient to similarly feel his flesh under her hands, she ripped the last few buttons of his shirt apart, scattering them without regard.

Finally she had him, her hands on his firm chest, her fingers curling through the wiry thatch of hair, lingering over the hard, tight nubs of his nipples, relishing all the different textures of him, the hard and the hot, the wet and the insistent, and if she'd had any doubt at all that he wanted her, it was banished by the bucking welcome of that rigid column as her hand slid down to cup his length. He groaned and pushed her back hard against the wall as she grappled with his belt.

He was everywhere then, his taste in her mouth, his hands separating her from the dress, slipping the straps from her shoulders, letting it slip between them as he took her breasts, the scrap of lace no barrier against the heat from his hands. And then even that was gone, replaced by his hot mouth, devouring her, lapping and suckling at her flesh until she cried out with the agony and the ecstasy of it all. It was everything she had imagined in dreams spun in hot, torrid nights alone and more, and still it was not enough.

She clung to his shoulders as he laved her nipples, gathering her skirt as his hands skimmed up her legs, not taking his time but still taking so much longer than she wanted.

'Please,' she pleaded, clutching at his head, gasping as he cupped her mound, his long fingers stroking her through panties wet for him, needing him, hot and hard, inside her. Needing him now, before she came with just one more touch. *'Please!'*

'God, you're so hot,' he said, dispensing with her underwear, pulling free his belt with damn near the same frenetic action.

She saw him then. Her first glimpse of him unleashed and hungry and pointing at her, a compass needle finding true north. Once she might have wanted to believe it. But she was wiser than to believe such fantasies these days, and much wiser to the consequences. Which reminded her...

'Protection,' she muttered through the fog of need, but he was already ripping open a sachet with his teeth, rolling it on before pulling her back into his kiss. Her breasts met his chest, the feel of skin against skin taking her breath away, or maybe it was what he was doing with his hands and clever fingers.

Her dress bunched at her waist, his hands kneading her behind, fingers teasingly close to the centre of her, driving her insane with need, as he lifted her, the wall at her back, still kissing her as he urged her legs around him until she felt him, thick and hard, nudging, testing, at her entrance.

She cried out, something unintelligible and primal, lost in an ocean of sensation, drowning under the depths. It was almost too much and yet it was nowhere near enough and she only knew that if she didn't get him inside her she would surely die of need.

He didn't keep her waiting. With a guttural cry of his own he lowered her, meeting her with his own thrust, until he was lodged deep inside her.

A moment in time. Just a moment, a fraction of a second perhaps, but Eve knew it for a moment about which she would always remember every single detail, the salt of his skin and the smell of his shampoo, the feel of his big hands paused at her hips, and the glorious feeling of the pulsing fullness inside her.

Could it get any better than this?

And then he moved, and it did, and flesh against flesh had never felt so good, every new moment giving her treasures to secrete away, to add to a store of memories she would take from this night, of sensations she would never forget. Sensations that built, one upon another, layer upon layer, higher and higher, fed by each calculated withdrawal, each powerful thrust.

Until there was no place to go, no place higher or brighter or more wondrous as the sensation, the friction, the furious rhythm of his pounding body all melded together into a cataclysm, taking her with it.

She screamed her release, throwing her head back

against the wall, her muscles clamping down hard as he shuddered his own frenetic release.

She didn't know how long they stood together that way, she couldn't tell, too busy trying to replace the oxygen consumed in the fire of their coupling while her body hummed its way down from the peak. But slowly her feet found the floor, slowly her senses and sensibility returned. To the knowledge she was standing barely dressed between a wall and a near naked man she barely knew but with whom she'd just had mind-blowing sex.

'Wow,' she said, embarrassed in the aftermath as he dispensed with the condom and she remembered her own wantonness. Had she really pulled his shirt apart in her desperation to get inside it? Had she really cried out like a banshee?

And he laughed, a low rumble in a velvet coat. 'Evelyn Carmichael,' he told her with a chaste kiss to her lips, 'you are just one surprise package after another.'

He didn't know the half of it. She found the straps of her dress, pulling it up to cover herself before she started looking for her underwear.

'Leave it,' he said, his hand around her wrist. 'There's no point. It's only coming off again.'

'Again?'

His eyes glinted. 'This book I was telling you about. It's a long book,' he said. 'That was only chapter one.'

She blinked up at him, her dress gathered in front of her, and he pulled her arm away, letting the dress drop to her waist, then slide over her hips in a whisper of silk to pool like a lake on the floor.

And even though they'd just had sex, she felt nervous standing there before him wearing nothing more than lace-topped stockings and spiky sandals. She hadn't been with anyone since Sam's father. She didn't have the body she'd once had, her belly neat but traced with tiny silvery lines and softer than it had been before bearing a child.

She held her breath. Could he tell? Would it matter?

'You look,' he said, 'like a goddess emerging from the sea.' And some tiny, futile creature somewhere deep inside her grew wings and attempted a fluttery take-off.

'And you look like a pirate,' she countered, reminding herself it was just a game. It wasn't real and that pointless tiny creature inside her would soon die a rapid death, its gossamer wings stilled. 'Ruthless and swashbuckling.'

'Uncanny,' he said, his lips turning in a half-smile as he swung her into his arms. 'However did you know?'

'Know what?' she asked, feeling a secret thrill as he carried her into the next room.

'The goddess of the sea and the swashbuckling pirate.' He winked at her and he laid her gently on the king-sized bed. 'That's the title of chapter two.'

It was a long and detailed chapter. There were passages Eve found agonising going, like when the pirate sampled the goddess, tasting every last inch of her except *there*, where she craved his detailed attentions the most, and then there were the passages that moved at what felt like breakneck speed, where he feasted on her until she was bucking on the bed.

And even when she lay, still gasping, after her latest orgasm, the chapter didn't end and he joined her in savouring the final few pages together until that final breathtaking climax.

Outside the lights of Melbourne winked at her, the

skies unusually clear, a heavy full moon hanging above the bridge over the Yarra.

Inside the suite, Eve's breathing slowly returned to normal as she savoured the feel of Leo's arm lying pro-prietorially over her stomach as he lay face down along-side her, his eyes closed, his lips slightly parted, his thick black hair mussed into bed-head perfection by her own hands. He wasn't asleep, she knew, but it was a wonder given the energy he'd used tonight. Definitely a pirate, she thought. And very definitely a magic night. But it was late and magic nights had to end, just as goddesses had responsibilities too.

Oh, my, he'd actually called her a goddess! And she felt that tiny winged creature launch itself for another lurching spin around her stomach.

'I should go,' she said, with a wistful sigh for the ill-fated beast before she returned to sensible Evelyn Carmichael again and considered the practicalities of not having a functioning hot water service. 'Do you mind if I take a shower before I go?'

And his eyes blinked open, the arm around her waist shifting, scooping higher to capture a breast. A smile played on his lips while he coaxed a nipple into unex-pected responsiveness. 'I've got a much better idea.'

She swallowed. Surely it wasn't possible? But still her body hummed into life at the thought. 'Chapter three?'

He nodded, his busy fingers hard at work on the other nipple, adding his hot mouth to the mix, guarantee-ing the result. 'The goddess returns to the sea only to find the pirate lurking in the depths, waiting to ambush her.'

'That's a long title.'

'It's a long chapter,' he said, rolling off the bed and scooping her up into his arms. 'In which case, we should get started.'

An hour later Eve had bubbles up to her chin and warm jets massaging all those newly found muscles of hers she hadn't realised would so appreciate the attention. From the bedroom came the sound of Leo's voice on the phone as he arranged her car. In a moment she'd have to prise herself from the bath and shower off the bubbles but for the moment she lingered, her limbs heavy, feeling languorous and spoilt and thoroughly, thoroughly spent.

It was easy to feel spoilt here, she thought, quietly reflecting on her opulent surroundings, committing them to memory as part of the experience. For if the size and scale of the suites had amazed her, the sheer lavishness of the bathroom had taken her breath away.

Marble in muted tones of sun-ripened wheat and golden honey lined the floor and walls, the lighting low and warm and inviting, the spa and shower enclosure—a space as big as her entire bathroom at home—separated from the long marble vanity by heavy glass doors. It was utterly, utterly decadent.

And if there hadn't been enough bubbles, he'd found champagne and ripe, red strawberries to go with it. He'd turned what she'd intended simply as a shower into another erotic fantasy.

What a night. Three chapters of his book, all of them different, every one of them a complete fantasy. If chapter one had been desperate and frenetic, and chapter two slow to the point of torture, chapter three had showed the pirate at his most playfully erotic best. The slip of oils on skin, the play of the jets on naked flesh and the sheer fun of discovering what lay beneath the foam.

She closed her eyes, allowing herself just a few snatched seconds of imagining what it would be like if this was her life, all posh hotels with views of city lights and an attentive lover like Leo to make her feel the most special woman alive, with no worries about broken-down appliances and falling-down houses.

But then there was Sam.

And she felt guilty for even thinking of a world that didn't include him—that couldn't include him. For Sam was her life, whereas this was a fantasy that had no other course but to end and end soon.

She slipped under the water one last time, letting her hair fan out around her head, relishing the big wide bath, before she sat up, the water sluicing from her body. No regrets, she told herself as she squeezed the water from her hair, she wouldn't allow it. She'd made her choice. She would live with it. And whatever happened in her life after this, whatever her everyday suburban life might hold, she knew she would have this one secret night of passion to look back on.

'The car will be waiting in half an hour,' Leo said, returning to the bathroom, a white towel slung perilously low over his hips, and even though she knew what lay beneath, even though she knew what that line of dark hair leading down from his navel led so tantalisingly and inexorably to, she couldn't look away. *Or maybe because of it.* 'Will that give you enough time for that shower you wanted and get dressed?'

And even though she knew this moment was coming, Eve still felt a pang, the fabric of her fantasy starting to unravel, as already she started counting down the minutes. Just thirty of them to go before she turned from one-night lover to a billionaire into long-term single mother. But there was nothing else for it. She nodded. 'Plenty of time,' she said.

He offered her his hand rather than the towel she would have preferred and she hesitated, before realising that after the things they'd done together this night, there was no point in being coy. So she rose, taking his hand to prevent her slipping as she stepped out, and taking half the foam with her. Something about the way his body stilled alerted her. She was taller than him now, standing in the raised bath like this, and his eyes drank her in. 'What is it?' she said, looking down to see patches of foam sliding down her body and clinging to her breasts, the pink nub of one nipple peeping through. And she looked back to him to see him shaking his head, his dark eyes hot and heavy with desire. 'Suddenly I'm not so sure it will be anywhere near enough time.'

Something sizzled in her veins, even while her mind said no. 'You can't be serious.'

He gave a wry smile as he reached out to brush the offending nipple with the pad of one finger, sending tremors through her sensitive flesh, and he smoothed away more of the suds to reveal patches of skin, piece by agonising piece. 'It's still early.'

'Leo,' she said, ignoring the pleas her body was making to stay right where she was and stepping out to snap on the shower taps before she could take his words seriously. A torrent rained down from the cloudburst showerhead and she stepped into it, determined to be rid of the bubbles regardless of the water temperature. 'It's three o'clock in the morning. I'm going home.'

He peeled the towel from his hips, turned on his own shower. 'We have all night.'

'No. I have to go.' She turned her face away from the sight of his thickening member and up into the stream of water, relishing the drenching. It was cooler than she would normally prefer, but it was helping to clear her mind, helping cool her body down. And very definitely she needed to cool down. What kind of man could make love so many times in one night and still come back for more? When had fantasy ever collided so perfectly with reality? Well, that was apart from the reality she would no doubt be exhausted tomorrow while Sam would be his usual bundle of energy. *Today*, she reminded herself. He'd be up in a few short hours. She really needed to get home if she was to get any sleep tonight. 'Besides, you have an important deal to close.'

'So maybe I can give you a call, pick you up afterwards?'

Her heart skipped a beat and she paused, soap in hand, feeling only the pounding of the cascading water, the thudding of her heart and the flutter of those damned tiny wings. Without turning around, she said, 'I thought you were planning on leaving for London the minute you concluded the Culshaw deal.'

His mouth found her shoulder, his arms wrapping around her belly, and there was no missing that growing part of him pressing against her back, no missing the rush of blood to tissues already tender. And even though she knew his words meant nothing, nothing more anyway than him wanting a repeat performance in bed, it was impossible not to lean her head back against his shoulder just one last sweet time. 'I don't think that would be wise.' She turned off the water and peeled herself away, reaching for a towel as she exited the shower. 'We both agreed this was just one night. And while it's been good, I think, given our working relationship, that it's better left that way.'

'Only good?' he demanded, and she rolled her eyes.

Trust the man to home in on the least important detail of the conversation. He followed her from the stall, swiping his own towel from the rack and lashing it around his hips, not bothering to wipe the beads of water from his skin so that his chest hair formed scrolls like an ancient tattoo down his chest to his belly and below.

Oh, my…

She squeezed her eyes shut. Grabbed another towel and covered her head with it, rubbing her hair frantically so she couldn't see him, even if she opened her eyes. 'All right. The sex was great. Fabulous.'

The towel blinding her eyes was no defence against the electric touch of his fingers at her shoulders. 'Then why shouldn't we meet again? It's not as if I'm asking for some long-term commitment.'

That's just it, she yearned to say. There's no future in it. There's nothing but great sex and the longer that happens, the greater the risk that I start to believe it's about more than that, and I can't afford to let that happen.

Not when she had Sam…

One night of sin was one thing. But she could not contemplate any kind of affair. What Sam needed was stability, not his mother embarking on a series of meaningless one-night stands, passing him off to whoever could look after him. She shook her head, heading for the bedroom, her clothes and a return to sanity. 'I can't sleep with you and work with you at the same time.'

'So become my mistress instead of my PA.'

She blinked, blindsided once again by the night's increasingly insane developments, pulling on her underwear in a rush, slipping off the towel to fix her bra, needing the shelter of her dress.

'Are you kidding?'

'You're right,' he said, without a hint of irony. 'Who could I get to replace you? So why can't you be both?'

'Perfect.' She slipped into her dress, retrieved her stockings and sat on the end of the bed, hastily rolling them up her legs. 'I thought you'd never ask. And when you get sick of me being your mistress, you can get me to send myself one of those trinkets you're so fond of sending to your ex-playmates. I already know where to send it. How efficient would that be?'

'Evelyn?'

She was busy in her purse, searching for a comb in order to slick back and twist up her wet hair and not finding one. 'What?'

'Anyone might think you were jealous.'

'Jealous? Me?' She scooted past him back into the bathroom. Pulled a comb from the complimentary supplies boxed up on the vanity, raking it through her hair before twisting it up and securing it with a clip. It was rough but it would do until she got home. She certainly wasn't going to hang around here, styling her hair or trying to reapply make-up that would just have to come off at home anyway. 'Jealous of what?'

He leaned an arm up against the door, muscles pulling tight under his skin, making the most of the posture, and she cursed the fact he hadn't thought to put on anything more than a towel yet. Or maybe that was his intention. To remind her what she'd be missing out on. Well, tough. After tonight she knew what she'd be missing out on. Of course, he was tempting, but there came a time where self-preservation came first.

'You did make a point about having to send out those gifts to…my friends.'

'Your ex-lovers, you mean.'

'You *are* jealous.'

She shrugged. 'No. I've had my one night with you. Why should I be jealous?'

'Well, something's bugging you. What is it?'

She turned toward him then, wishing she could just walk away, sensitive to the fact that she could still be at risk of losing her contract if she angered him but still bothered enough by the riddle that was Leo Zamos to ask. 'You really want to know?'

'Tell me.'

'Okay,' she started, her eyes taking this last opportunity to drink in the glorious definition of his body, wanting to imprint all she could upon her memory before she left, because after tonight her memories would be all she had. 'What I don't understand is you.'

He laughed, a rich, deep sound she discovered she liked too much. 'What's so hard to understand?'

'Everything. You're confident and successful and ultra-rich—you have your own plane, for heaven's sake!—and you're a passionate lover and clearly have no trouble finding women willing to share your bed...' She paused for a moment, wondering if she'd said enough, wondering if she added that he was drop-dead gorgeous and had a body that turned a woman's thoughts to carnal acts, she would be saying more about herself than about him.

He smiled. 'That's it? I'm not actually sure where your problem lies.'

'No, that's not it. You know there's more. People are drawn to you, Leo, you know it. And it's just that, with everything you have going for you, I don't understand how it can be that when you feel the need to play happy families, you have to pay someone to pretend to be your fiancée.'

'You would have done it for free?' He gave a wry smile. 'I'll remember that for next time.'

'No!' she said, knowing she was making a hash of it, knowing he was laughing at her. 'That's not my point at all. I just don't understand why you're in the situation where you need to pretend. How is it that a man with clearly such great appeal to women hasn't got a wife or a fiancée or even a serious girlfriend? How is that possible?'

The smile slipped as he pushed away from the wall, moving closer, the menacing glint in his eyes putting her on sudden alert. 'Maybe,' he said, drawing near, touching his fingers to her brow, tracing a line south, 'it's because there is no lack of women willing to share my bed. What is that delightful saying? Why buy a book when you can join a library?'

She stood stock-still, resisting the tremors set off by his merest touch, hating the smug look on his face, forcing a smile to hers. 'Well, the loan on this particular book just expired. Goodnight, Leo.'

He let her go, at least as far as the door.

'Evelyn.'

She halted, put her hand on the doorframe to stop herself swaying, and without turning around said, 'Yes?'

'Something I tell all the women I spend time with. Something I thought you might have understood, although, given your questions, maybe you need to hear it too.'

She looked over her shoulder, curious about what it was he told his 'women', what he thought she needed to hear. 'Yes?'

'I like women. I like sex. But that's where it starts and finishes. Because I don't do family. It's not going to happen.'

This time she took a step towards him, stunned by his sheer arrogance. 'You think I was on some kind of fishing expedition to work out what my chances were of becoming Mrs Leo Zamos for real?'

'You were the one asking the questions.'

'And I also said I don't want to see you again. Which part of "I don't want to see you again" equates to "Please marry me" exactly?'

'I was just saying—'

'And I'm saying you needn't have bothered. I'm not in the market for a husband as it happens, but even if I were, I'm certain I'd prefer someone who didn't profess to liking women and sex quite so much!' She turned on her heel and strode through the bedroom, slipping on her heels and picking up her purse, scanning the room for anything she might have left.

'Evelyn!'

But she didn't stop until she was through the living room then, turned, one more question to be answered before she left. 'I'll understand if you no longer want to retain me as your PA.'

'Don't be ridiculous. Of course I want to keep you.'

She nodded, relieved, suddenly realising how perilously close she'd come to blowing things. 'All right. All the best with the deal tomorrow. I guess I'll be hearing from you in due course.' She offered him her hand, back to brisk, businesslike efficiency, even if she was dealing with a man wearing nothing more than a towel. 'Thank you for a pleasant evening, Mr Zamos. I'll see myself out, under the circumstances.'

One eyebrow quirked at the formality but he took her hand, squeezing it gently. 'It was my pleasure, Evelyn. My pleasure entirely.'

Minutes later, she sank her head back against the

plush leather headrest and sighed as the limousine slipped smoothly from the hotel. Better to end this way, she reflected; better that they had argued rather than agreeing to meet again. Better that it had ended now when anything else would merely have been putting off the inevitable.

For it would have ended, nothing surer, and probably as soon as their next meeting. And then Leo would take off in his jet and find another convenient Evelyn somewhere else in the world, and she would be forgotten.

But now they'd claimed their stolen night, the night they'd been cheated out of by conspiring circumstances those years ago, and it had been an amazing night and she'd managed to survive with both some degree of pride and her job intact. But it was for the best that it had ended on a sour note.

Now they could both put it behind them.

CHAPTER SEVEN

SHE grappled with the front-door key, her baby growing heavier by the minute. That or her night of sinful and unfamiliar pleasures had taken it out of her, but the child dozing on her shoulder felt like he'd doubled in size and weight overnight. Then again, maybe he'd just had one too many pancakes. She knew she had. She'd woken this morning after too few hours' sleep almost ravenous.

She was barely inside the door when the phone started ringing and she picked it up more to shut it up than any desire to talk to whoever was calling. She had less desire to talk when she found out who it was.

'Evelyn, it's Leo.'

The sound of his voice sent ripples of pleasure through her, triggering memories formed all too recently to not remember every single sensual detail. She sucked in air, but Leo was the last person she'd expected to call and there was nothing she could think of to say. Hadn't they said everything that needed to be said last night?

'Evelyn?'

She squeezed her eyes shut, trying to ignore the snatches of memory flashing through her mind, the rumble of his murmured words against her thigh, the brush of his whiskered cheek against her skin, his clever tongue…

'I...I didn't expect to hear from you.'

'I didn't expect to be calling. Look, Evelyn, there's been a development. Culshaw wants to move the contract discussions to somewhere where the weather suits Maureen better. He suggested we reconvene on his island off North Queensland.'

With the dead-to-the-world weight of her toddler on her shoulder, she battled to work out what it was Leo actually wanted. 'So you need me to make some bookings? Or do I have to rearrange your schedule?'

'Neither.' A pause. 'I need you to come.'

Sam stirred on her shoulder, his head lolling from one side to the other, and she kissed his head to soothe him. 'Leo, you know that's not possible.'

'Why isn't it possible?'

'You said our deal was for one night only and I already told you I wouldn't meet you again.'

'But that was before Culshaw came up with this idea.'

'That's too bad. I did what we agreed.' And then, thinking he might better understand it in business-speak, 'I fulfilled the terms of the contract, Leo, and then some.'

'So we make a new deal. How much this time, Evelyn?' he asked, sounding angry now.

'I told you before, it's not about the money.'

'Fifty thousand.'

'No. I told you, they're nice people. I don't want to lie to them any more.'

'One hundred thousand.'

She looked up at the ceiling, cursing under her breath, trying not to think about what a sum like that would mean to the timing of her renovation plans. She could engage a decent architect, get quotes, maybe landscaping so Sam had a decent play area outside. But it was impossible. 'No!'

'Then you won't come?'

'Absolutely not.'

'So what am I supposed to tell Culshaw?'

'It's your lie, Leo. Tell him what you like. Tell him it's family reasons, tell him I'm sick, tell him I never was and never will be your fiancée. It's your call.' On her shoulder her son grew unsettled, picking up on the vibe in the air, butting his head from side to side against her shoulder, starting to grizzle.

'What was that?' Leo demanded.

'Me about to hang up. Are we finished here? Only it's not really a convenient time to call.' Please, God, can we be finished here? she prayed as her muscles burned under Sam's weight.

'No. I need...I need some documents to take with me!'

'Fine,' she said, sighing, wondering which documents they could possibly be when she was sure she'd provided him with everything he needed already and in triplicate. 'Let me know which ones and I'll email them straight away.'

'No. I need them in hard copy. All originals. You have to bring them to the hotel, as soon as you can.'

If she'd had a free hand, it would have gone to her head. 'I've always emailed documents to you before. It's never been a problem.'

'I need those documents delivered to me personally this afternoon!'

She sucked in a breath. 'Okay. I'll get them couriered over as soon as I can.'

'No. Definitely not couriered. You need to deliver them personally.'

'Why?'

'Because I need them immediately and they're commercial-in-confidence. I'm not about to entrust them to someone else, not at this crucial stage. You'll have to bring them yourself.'

When she made no response, she heard, 'You did say you wanted to keep working with me.'

Bastard! She could take a veiled threat just as well as she could take a hint. She was damned if she'd take more of Leo's money to pretend to be his fiancée, but right now she couldn't afford to ditch him as a client. 'Of course. I'll bring them over myself.'

'Good. I'll be in my suite.'

'Not there.'

'What?'

'I won't bring them to your suite. I won't go there again. Not after…'

'You think I'd try something?'

Hardly, after the way they'd parted last night. But she didn't trust herself not to be tempted, there in that room where they'd done so many things… How could she be in that room and see that wall and know how it felt to have her back to it and have him between her legs and driving into her? How could she calmly pretend nothing had happened? How could she not want it to happen again?

She swallowed, trying not to think of all the reasons she didn't want to be in that room. 'I just don't think it would be wise.'

She heard his rushed expulsion of air. 'Okay,' he said. 'Let's play it your way. Culshaw's taking Maureen out to visit friends so we should be safe to meet in the bar. I'll buy you a coffee—is that permissible?'

She nodded into the phone, relieved at least they'd

be meeting somewhere public. Sam settled back on her shoulder. 'A coffee would be fine.'

He clicked off his phone, cursing softly. So she wouldn't come to the room. But she had agreed to come. Of course she could have emailed the documents, but then he'd have no way of convincing her to come to the island with him. He could convince her, he had no doubt. Look at how she had all but melted in his arms last night with just one kiss! And once she was back in his bed, she'd get over whatever hang-up she had about coming with him. He was already looking forward to it.

Because while sex was easy to come by, great sex wasn't, and last night had definitely registered right up there with the best. And while he'd been content for it to end last night the way it had—it would have ended some time anyway—the opportunity to have her in his bed for another couple of nights held considerable appeal. He could do much worse than sharing his bed with Evelyn.

He'd soon make it happen. Once she was here, he'd just have to come up with a way to get her up to his suite and convince her how much she wanted to come with him. He'd think of something.

His phone rang, a glance at the caller ID assuring him it wasn't Evelyn calling back to change her mind about meeting him.

'Eric,' he said, relieved, his mind already working on a plan to get Evelyn up to his suite. 'What can I do for you?'

But relief died a quick death as Culshaw explained how Maureen was looking to book a day in the island resort's spa for the women and wanted to know if Evelyn might be interested. Leo knew he had to say something now, in case she refused to change her mind.

'Look, Eric, about Evelyn, you might want to warn Maureen. It seems there's a slight chance she might not be able to make it after all…'

'I wish I could help, lovey,' Mrs Willis said, when Evelyn nipped over to ask if she would mind babysitting again, this time only for an hour or so, 'but my brother Jack's just had an episode and I promised to go and help Nancy with him. He gets terribly confused, poor love. I was going to pop by and tell you, because I might be away for a few days.' She stopped folding clothes for a moment, her creased brow folding along time worn lines. 'I hate leaving you, though, with the hot water not working and no family to help out. Such a tragedy to lose your parents so young and then your granddad. They've all missed out on so much, watching you grow up and now Sam.' She shook her head. 'Such a pity.'

'I know,' Eve said softly, feeling a pang of sadness for her grandfather and for parents she could barely remember. 'But don't worry. You do too much for me as it is. We'll be fine. I'll call Emily down the street. She's always on the lookout for some extra cash.'

Except when she called it was to hear Emily was already working a shift at the local supermarket. Which left Evelyn with only one option.

Not such a bad option, she reflected as she turned onto the freeway and pointed her little city commuter towards the city, wondering why it hadn't occurred to her earlier. She hadn't wanted to tell Leo about her child, figuring it was none of his business and that it might prejudice his opinion of her as someone able to handle his workload, but neither did she trust him not to try to change her mind by fair means or foul. And then there was the matter of not trusting her own wayward desires. Look where they'd landed her last night—right in Leo Zamos's bed. Not to mention his spa bath...

She shivered, unable to suppress either a secret smile or the delicious shimmy at the memories of his mouth seeking her breasts as he raised her over him, of his hungry mouth at her nipples as he probed her entrance, of the long, hard length of him filling her as he pulled her down on him inch by glorious inch, a shimmy that radiated out from muscles tender and sore and clearly still far too ready to party.

Oh, no, there was no way she could trust herself with him.

And if there was one certain way to ensure that there would be no repeats of last night's performance, it was to take her child along. Leo didn't do family, and clearly didn't want one. He'd made that abundantly clear and she was grateful he had. For it had put paid to that tiny creature that insisted on fluttering around inside her despite what she'd known in her head all along to be true. That his interest in her began and finished with sex. There could be no future with him. There was no future for them.

And with just one look at Sam he'd forget all about wanting to play make-believe with her. One look at Sam and he'd never want to see her again. Which suited her just fine.

It was foolproof!

Forty minutes later the doorman helped her unload both her baby stroller and a sleeping Sam startled into wakefulness from the car. She settled him, watching his eyelids flutter closed again, still sleepy from the journey, lowering the back and tucking his favourite bear by his side so he would feel secure and snooze on as long as possible. Soon enough he'd be demanding to get out and explore this new world—she just prayed he'd last until she got him out of the hotel. Not that the meeting should take longer than ten minutes when it was only documents she had to hand over. Probably less, she thought with a smile, doubting Leo would stick around long enough for coffee when he saw what else she'd brought with her.

She could hardly wait to see his face.

The subtly lit lounge wasn't busy, only a few tables occupied this time of the day, couples sharing coffee and secrets, family groups gathered around tables enjoying afternoon tea.

She found a hotel phone, asked Reception to let Mr Zamos know she was there, and stopped a while in awe to admire, over the balcony, the amazing sweeping stairway that rose grandly from entry level and the water feature that spilled and spouted between levels of the hotel. She must commit this to memory, she thought. It was the place of fairy-tales, of princes and princesses, and not of the real world, and of ordinary people like her who had blown hot water services and frazzled appliances to replace.

She settled into a booth that offered some degree of privacy, gently rocking the stroller. Sam wasn't buying it, jerking into wakefulness, this time taking in the unfamiliar surroundings with wide, suspicious eyes.

'It's okay, Sam,' she said, reaching for the stash of food she'd brought and had tucked away in the baby bag. 'We're visiting, that's all. And then I'll take you for a walk along Southbank. You'll like that. There's a river and lots of music and birds. Maybe we might even spot you a fish.'

'Fith!' He grinned, recognising the word as she handed him his favourite board book and he reached for a sultana with the other. 'Fith!'

He'd been waiting on the call, all the while working out a strategy that would get her out of the lounge and up into his room. At last he'd hit on the perfect plan, so simple it couldn't fail. He'd play it cool, accept the documents she'd brought without mention of the trip away and without trying to change her mind, and see her to her car, remembering once they'd got to the lifts something he'd meant to bring down for her—it wouldn't take a moment to collect it from his suite…

He hit the second floor with a spring in his step. Oh, he loved it when a plan came together.

He scanned the lounge for her, skipping over the groups and couples, searching for a single woman sitting no doubt nervously by herself. Had she been able to forget about last night's love-making yet? He doubted it. Even though the night had ended on a sour note, those flashbacks had kept him awake thinking about it half the night. When Culshaw had mooted this idea of going away for the weekend, he'd initially been appalled. It was bad enough that the closing of the deal had been held up by last night's dinner, without having to endure still more delays while Culshaw soothed his wife's wounded soul with an impromptu holiday. Until he'd worked out that he could easily endure a couple of more nights like the last. Very easily.

And then he saw her sitting with her back to him in a little booth off to one side, her hair twisted high behind her head, making the most of that smooth column of neck. Just the sight of that bare patch of skin sent such a jolt of pure lust surging through him, such a heady burst of memories of her spread naked on his sheets, that it was hard to think over the pounding of the blood in his veins, other than to want to drag her to his room and prove why she needed to come with him until she begged him not to leave her behind.

In another time, maybe even in another part of this world, he would do exactly that, and nobody would stop him, nobody would think twice.

But there was more reason than the mores of the so-called civilised world that stilled his savage urges. For he knew what he might become if he let the animal inside him off the leash.

Never had he felt so close to that beast. Why now? What was it about her that gave rise to such thoughts? She was the means to an end, that was why he needed her. Nothing more. Great sex was just a bonus.

She turned her head to the side then, her lips moving as if she was talking to someone, but there was nobody there, nothing but a dark shape in the shadowed recess behind the sofa, a dark shape that had him wondering if he'd found the wrong woman the closer he got. Because it made no sense…

She looked around at the exact time his brain had finally come to terms with what his eyes were telling him, at the precise moment the cold wave of shock crashed over him, washing away his well-laid plans and leaving them a tangled and broken mess at his feet.

'Hello, Leo,' she said, closing the picture book she was holding in her hands. 'I've brought those documents you asked for.'

She'd brought a hell of a lot more than documents! In the dark shape he'd worked out was a pram sat a baby—a child—holding onto the rail in front of him and staring wide-eyed and open-mouthed up at Leo like he was some kind of monster. It didn't matter that the kid was probably right. He looked back at Evelyn. 'What the hell is this?'

'Leo, meet my son, Sam.' She turned toward the pram. 'Sam, this is Mr Zamos. If you're very nice, he might let you call him Leo.'

'No!' Sam pushed back in his stroller and twisted his body away, clearly unimpressed as he pushed his face under his bear and began to grizzle.

'I'm sorry,' she said, one hand reaching out to rub him on the back. 'He's just woken up. Don't worry about coffee, it's probably better I take him for a walk.' She picked up a folder from the table and stood, holding it out for Leo. 'Here's all the documents you asked for and I've flagged where signatures are required. Let me know if there's anything else you need. I promised Sam a walk along the river while we're here, but we'll be home in a couple of hours.'

He couldn't say anything. He could barely move his hand far enough to accept the folder she proffered. All he could think of was that she had a child and she hadn't told him. What else hadn't she told him? 'You said there wasn't a Mr Carmichael.'

'There's isn't.'

'Then whose is it?'

'His name is Sam, Leo.'

'And his father's name?'

'Is none of your business.'

'And is that what you told him when he asked you where you were all night?'

She shook her head, her eyes tinged with sadness. 'Sam's father doesn't figure in this.'

His eyes darted between mother and child, noticing for the first time the child's dark hair and eyes, the olive tinge to the skin, and he half wondered if she was bluffing and had borrowed someone else's baby as some kind of human shield. He would have called her on it but for noticing the angle of the child's wide mouth and the dark eyes stamped with one hundred per cent Evelyn, and that made him no happier.

Because someone else had slept with her.

He thought of her in his arms, her long-limbed body interwoven with his, he thought of her eyes when she came apart with him inside her, damn near shorting his brain. And now he thought of her coming apart in someone else's arms...

'You should have told me.'

'Why?'

'Damn it, Evelyn! You know why!'

'Because we spent the night together?' she hissed. Sam yowled, as if he'd been on the receiving end of that, and she leaned over, surprising Leo when she didn't smack him, as he'd half expected, but instead delicately stroked the child's cheek and calmed him with whispered words. Something twisted inside him, something shapeless and long buried, and he had to look away lest the shape take form and he worked out what it was. His gut roiled. What was happening to him? Why did she have this effect on him? She made him feel too much. She made him see too much.

She made him remember things he didn't want to remember.

And none of it made sense. None of it he could understand.

'I'm sorry you feel aggrieved,' she said, and reluctantly he turned back to see her unclipping the child's harness and lifting the child into her arms, where he snuggled close, sniffling against her shoulder as she rubbed his back. 'But what part of our contract did I miss that said I should stipulate whether I should have children or what number of them I should have?'

'Children? You mean there's more?'

She huffed and turned away, rubbing the boy's back, whispering sweet words, stroking away his hiccups, and the gentle sway of her hips setting her skirt to a gently seductive hula.

'Ironic isn't it?' she threw at him over her shoulder. 'Here you are, so desperate to prove to Eric Culshaw that you're some kind of rock-solid family man, and you're scared stiff of a tiny child.'

'I'm not—'

She spun around. 'You're terrified! And you're taking it like some kind of personal affront. But I wouldn't worry. Sam's a bit old for anyone to believe he was conceived last night, so there's no reason to fear any kind of paternity claim.'

'You wouldn't dare!'

'Oh, you do flatter yourself. A woman would have to be certifiably insane to want to shackle themselves to you!'

'Clearly Sam's father was of the same mind about you.'

He knew he'd hurt her. He recognised the precise moment when his words pierced the fighting sheen over her eyes and left them bewildered and wounded. He almost felt regret. Almost wanted to reach out and touch her cheek like she'd touched her child's, and soothe away her pain.

Almost.

But that would mean he cared. And he couldn't care about anyone. Not that way.

And just as quickly as it had gone down, the armour

was resurrected and her eyes blazed fire at him. 'I have a child, Mr Zamos. It's never affected the quality of my work to date and it's my intention that it never will, but if you can't live with that then fine, maybe it's time we terminated our agreement now and you found someone else to look after your needs.'

Bile, bitter and portentous, rose in the back of his throat. She was right. There was no point noticing her eyes or the sensual sway of her hips. There was no point reliving the evening they'd had last night. She couldn't help him now and it was the now he had to be concerned with. As to the future, maybe it was better he found someone else. Maybe someone older this time. It wasn't politically correct to ask for a date of birth, but he'd never been any kind of fan of political correctness. Especially not when it messed with his plans. He huffed an agreement. 'If that's what you want.'

She stood there, the child plastered against her from shoulder to hip, his arms wound tightly around his mother's neck, the mother so fierce he was reminded of an animal fighting to protect its litter that he'd seen on one of those television documentaries that appeared when you were flicking through the channels on long-haul flights. The comparison surprised him. Was that how all mothers were supposed to be?

'In that case,' she said, 'I'll burn everything of yours onto disk and delete it from my computer. I'll send it to you care of the hotel. You can let them know your forwarding address.'

His hands clenched at his sides, his nails biting into his palms. 'Fine.'

'Goodbye, Mr Zamos.' She held out her hand. 'I hope you find whatever it is you're looking for.' Her words washed over him, making no sense as he looked down at her hand. The last time he would touch her. The last time they would meet skin to skin.

How had things gone so wrong?

He wrapped his hand around hers, her hand cool against his heated flesh, and he felt the tremor move through her, saw her eyelids flutter closed, and despite the fact she represented everything he didn't want in this world, everything he hated and despised and had promised himself he would never have, still some strange untapped part of him mourned her loss.

Maybe that was how it started, though, with this strange want, this strange need to possess.

Maybe it was better to let her go now, he thought, while he still could. While she was still beautiful.

But still it hurt like hell.

Unable to stop himself, unable to let her go just yet, his other hand joined the first, capturing her hand, raising it to his mouth for one final kiss.

'Goodbye Evelyn,' he said, his voice gravel rich, tasting her on his lips, knowing he would never forget the taste of her or the one night of passion they'd shared in Melbourne.

'Leo! Evelyn!' came a voice from over near the bar. 'There you are!'

CHAPTER EIGHT

EVE gasped, tugging to free her hand, the fight-or-flight instinct telling her to get out while she still could, but Leo wasn't about to let her go, his grip tightening until she felt her hand was encased in steel. 'This is your fault.' He leaned over and whispered in her ear as Eric Culshaw bounded towards them, beaming from ear to ear. 'Remember that.' And then he straightened and even managed to turn on a smile, although his eyes were anything but relaxed. She could almost hear the brain spinning behind them.

'Eric,' Leo said, his velvet voice all charm on the surface, springloaded with tension beneath. 'What a surprise. I thought you were taking Maureen out.'

He grunted. 'She spotted some article in a woman's magazine—you know the sort of thing—and grew herself a headache.' He shook his head. 'Sordid bloody affair. You'd think the reporters could find something else to amuse themselves with by now.' And then he huffed and smiled. 'Which makes you two a sight for sore eyes.' His eyes fell on the dozing child in her arms. 'Although maybe I should make that three. Who's this little tacker, then?'

Almost as if aware he was being discussed, Sam

stirred and swung his head round, blinking open big dark eyes to check out this latest stranger.

'This is Sam,' Eve said, her tongue feeling too big for her mouth as she searched for things she could tell him that wouldn't add to the lie tally. 'He's just turned eighteen months.'

Culshaw grinned at the child and Sam gave a wary smile in return before burying his head back in his mother's shoulder, which made the older man laugh and reach out a hand to ruffle his hair. 'Good-looking boy. I thought you two were playing things a bit close to the chest last night. When were you going to tell us?'

Eve felt the ground lurch once more beneath her feet. Eric thought Sam was *theirs*? But, then, of course he would. They were supposed to have been a couple for more than two years and Sam's father was of Italian descent. It would be easy to mistake Sam's dark eyes and hair for Leo's. Why would they question it?

But she couldn't let them keep thinking it. Weren't there enough lies between them already?

'Actually,' she started, 'Sam—'

Her efforts earned her a blazing look from Leo. 'Eve doesn't like to give too much away,' he said, smiling at Eric, glancing back in her direction with a look of cold, hard challenge.

Suddenly Maureen was there too, looking pale and strained, her mood lifting when she saw Sam, clucking over him like he was a grandchild rather than the child of someone she'd only just met.

'You didn't tell us you had such an adorable little boy,' she admonished, already engaging Sam in a game of peek-a-boo before holding out her hands to take him.

'Some people wouldn't approve,' Eve offered stiffly, ignoring Leo's warning glare as she handed Sam over, then adding because of it, 'I mean, given the fact we're not married and all.'

'Nonsense,' Eric said, pinching Sam's cheek. 'There's no need to rush things, not these days.'

Leo smiled, his eyes glinting triumphantly as Maureen settled into a chair and jogged Sam up and down on her knees, making him chuckle.

'So,' said Eric, following his wife's lead and pulling up a chair, and soon demanding equal time with Sam, 'I assume Sam explains the "family reasons" you weren't going to be able to join us on the island?'

Eve dropped into a chair, feeling like she was being sucked deeper and deeper into a web of deceit. Leo must have warned them she might not be coming and used one of the excuses she'd suggested.

'That was my fault, Eric,' he said coolly. 'I figured that a toddler was hardly conducive to contract deliberations.'

'He can be very disruptive,' she added. 'Especially when he's out of his routine. You wouldn't believe what a handful he can be.'

'What, this little champion?' Bouncing the laughing toddler on his knee with such delight until it was impossible to work out who was laughing the most, Eric or Sam, as the toddler got the horsy ride of his life. 'You must come,' he said, slowing down to take a breather.

'More,' demanded Sam, bouncing up and down. 'More!'

Culshaw laughed and obliged, though at a much gentler pace. 'You will come, won't you? After all, it's hardly fair to keep you two apart when you barely get to see each other as it is. You will love it, I promise. Tropical island paradise. Your own bungalow right on the beach. We'll organise a cot for Sam and a babysitter to give you a real break. I imagine you don't get too many of those, working for Leo and looking after this little chap. How does that sound?'

Eve tried to smile, not sure she'd succeeded when the ground beneath her felt so unsteady. 'It does sound lovely.' And it did. A few days on a tropical island paradise with nothing more to do than swim or read or sip drinks with tiny umbrellas. The bungalow probably even had hot running water. Except she'd be sharing that bungalow with *him*. 'It's just that—'

'Oh, please,' Maureen added, putting her hand on Eve's arm. 'Last night was the best time I've had for ages. I know it's asking a terrible lot of everyone and disrupting everyone's schedules, but right now it would mean so very much to me.'

'Of course they'll come,' she heard Leo say, 'won't you, Eve?'

And finally the unsteady ground she'd felt shifting under her feet the last few days opened up and swallowed her whole.

A smiling flight attendant greeted them, cooing over Sam, as Eve carried him on her hip into the jet. Eve just nodded in return, weariness combining with a simmering resentment. As far as she was concerned, this was no pleasure trip and she certainly wasn't happy about how she'd been manipulated into coming.

And then she stepped into the plane and found even more reason to resent the man behind her. It looked more like a luxury lounge room than any plane interior she'd ever seen before, the cabin filled not with the usual rows and rows of narrow seats and plastic fittings and overhead lockers but a few scattered wide leather armchairs with timber cabinet work trimmed with bronze. Beyond the lounge area a door led to what must be more rooms and Eve caught a glimpse of a dining table with half a dozen chairs in a recessed alcove.

So much wealth. So much to impress. Leo Zamos seemed to have everything.

Everything but a heart.

Maybe that's how you got to be a billionaire, she mused as another attendant showed her to a pair of seats where someone had already fitted her child restraint to buckle Sam in more securely. She helped settle the pair in and to stow their things, chattering pleasantly all the time while Eve stewed as she stashed books and toys close by and missed every word.

It all made sense. No wonder Leo Zamos was the success he was. Being ruthless in business, ruthless in the bedroom, taking what you wanted when you wanted—a heart would surely get in your way if you had one.

And while Eve simmered, Sam, on the other hand, was having the time of his tiny life, relishing the adventure and the attention, his dark eyes filled with glee as he pumped his arms up and down and made a sound like a war cry.

'I think someone approves,' Leo said from the seat alongside when the attendants had gone to fetch pre-flight drinks.

'His name is Sam,' she hissed, her resentment bubbling over at how she'd been trapped into this weekend away, a weekend of continued pretence with people who didn't deserve to be lied to. The only bright spots she could see were that the Culshaws and the Alvarezes were travelling together on the Culshaws' jet, and that they would all have private quarters, which meant she didn't have to pretend being madly in love with Leo twenty-four seven. She couldn't have stood the strain of it all if she had. As it was, she didn't know now how she was going to keep up the charade.

The attendant brought their drinks, advised there were two minutes until departure and discreetly disappeared.

What a mess. Eve poured a box of juice into a two-handled cup and passed it to a waiting Sam, along with a picture book to occupy him for a few minutes. How was she expected to act like Leo's loving fiancée now? It had been so much easier last night when there had been so much sexual tension and simmering heat sparking between them. Now the tension and the heat had more to do with anger.

All to do with anger, she corrected herself with a sigh. She was over him, even if he did have a velvet voice and the body of a god.

Across the aisle, the subject of her dark thoughts raised his drink. 'You sound like you have a problem.'

'Funny you should mention that.'

'You could have said no.'

'I did say no, remember? And then you turned around and said yes, of course we would come!'

He shrugged, as if it didn't matter, and if they'd been on any normal kind of plane, Eve could have given in to the desire to smack him. 'What can I say? Maureen likes you. It means the world to her that you can go.'

'You don't care about Maureen,' she said, keeping her voice low so she didn't alarm Sam. 'You don't care about anyone. All you care about is yourself and what you want, and you'll do anything to keep this deal from going off the rails, even if it means lying to people.'

'You don't know anything.'

'I know you made the right decision to never get married. Because I understand you now, and I understand what makes you tick, and you might have a fortune and a private jet and do okay in the sack with women, but you have a stone where your heart should be.'

His dark eyes glinted coldly, his jaw could have been chiseled from the same hard stone from which his heart was carved. 'Thank you for that observation. Perhaps I might make my own? You seem very tense, Evelyn. I think you might benefit from a couple of days relaxing on a tropical island.'

Bastard! Eve turned away, checking on Sam as the cabin attendant collected their glasses and checked all was ready for take-off.

The jet engines wound up as the plane taxied to the runway and Sam looked up in wonder at her, excited but looking for reassurance at the new sounds and sensations. She stroked his head. 'We're going on a plane, Sam. We're going on a holiday.'

And Sam squealed with delight and the plane raced down the runway and lifted off. *Good on you, Sam,* Eve thought, finding the book she'd hoped to read a few pages of as the plane speared into the sky, *at least one of us might as well enjoy the weekend.*

She must have dozed off. Bleary eyed, she found her book neatly placed by her side, while beside her Sam was grizzling softly but insistently, unable to settle.

'What's wrong?' Leo asked, putting aside the laptop he was working on as she unbuckled Sam from his seat and brought him against her chest.

'It's his nap time. He might settle better on my lap.' She searched for the chair's controls, although it was hard to manoevre with Sam's weight on her chest. 'Does this seat recline?'

'I've got a better idea. There's still a couple of hours'

flight time to go. You might both be more comfortable in the bedroom. Let me show you the way.'

And the idea of a real bed in which to cuddle up and snooze with Sam sounded so wonderful right now, she didn't hesitate.

Maybe if she hadn't been so bone-weary. Maybe in an ordinary airline seat, by holding onto the back of the seat in front of her to pull herself up, she could have managed it. Then again, she realised, maybe if she'd thought to undo her seat belt she could have done it. Damn.

'What is it?' he said, when she didn't follow him.

'Can you take Sam for a moment? My seat belt's still done up.'

Leo turned into a statue right before her eyes, rigid and unblinking as he stared down at her restless child. And if she wasn't mistaken, that look she saw in his eyes was fear.

'Take him?'

'Yes,' she said, her hands under his arms, ready to hand him over. 'Just for a second. I just need to undo my seat belt.'

'I…'

'I'll give you a hand,' said one of the cabin attendants, slipping past the stunned Leo. 'I've been secretly hoping for a cuddle of this gorgeous boy.'

She took Sam from her and swung him around, jogging him on her hip so that he stopped grizzling, instead blinking up at her with his big dark eyes, plump lips parted. 'You are gorgeous, aren't you? You're going to be a real heartbreaker, I can tell.' And then to Eve, 'How about I carry him for you? I'm probably more used to the motion of the plane.' Eve smiled her thanks, retrieving Sam's bear from the seat as Leo remembered how to move and led the way.

'There you go,' the attendant said a few moments later, as she peeled back the covers and laid the drowsy child down. 'Press this button,' she said, pointing to a console on the side table, 'if there's anything else I can help you with.' And with a brisk smile to them both and one last lingering look at Sam, she was gone.

'Thank you for thinking of this,' Evelyn said, sitting down alongside her son and tucking his bear under his arm. And then, because she felt bad about the things she'd said to him earlier and without taking her eyes from Sam, she said, 'I'm sorry for what I said earlier. I had no right.'

'Forget it,' he said, his velvet voice thick with gravel. 'For the record, you were probably right. Now, there's an en suite through that door,' he continued, and she looked over her shoulder, surprised to see a door set so cleverly into the panelling that she'd missed it as she'd looked around.

'Oh, I thought that was the bathroom we passed on the way. Next to the galley.'

'That serves the other suite.'

'Wow,' Eve said, taking it all in—the wide bed, the dark polished timber panelling and gilt-edged mirror and adding it to what she'd already seen, the dining table and spacious lounge. 'Incredible. A person could just about live in one of these things, couldn't they?'

'I do.'

Her head swung back. 'When you're travelling, you mean?'

'You know my diary, Evelyn. I'm always travelling. I live either in the plane or in some hotel somewhere.'

'So where's home?'

He held out his arms. 'This is home. Wherever I am is home.'

'But you can't live on a plane. Everyone has a home. You must have family somewhere.' She frowned, thinking about his voice and the lack of any discernable accent. Clearly he had Mediterranean roots but his voice gave nothing away. 'Where do you come from?'

Something bleak skated across his eyes as he looked at his watch. 'You're obviously tired and I'm keeping you both. Have a good sleep.'

He turned to leave then, turned back, reaching into his pocket. 'Oh, you'd better have this back.' He set the tiny box on the bedside table. Eve blinked at it, already knowing what it held.

'They extended the loan?'

He gave a wry smile. 'Not exactly. But it's yours to keep afterwards.'

'You bought it?'

'It looks good on you. It matches your eyes.'

She looked from the box to the man, still stroking her son's back, aware of his soft breathing as he settled into a more comfortable sleep. Thank heavens for the reality of Sam or she could easily think she was dreaming. 'What is this?' she said, mistrustful, the smouldering sparks of their earlier confrontation glowing brightly, fanned by this latest development. 'Some kind of bribe so I behave properly all weekend?'

'Do I need it to be?'

'No. I'm here, aren't I? And so I'm hardly likely to make a scene and reveal myself as some kind of fraud. But I'm certainly not doing it for your benefit, just like I'm not doing it for any financial gain. I just don't want to let Maureen down. She's had enough people do that recently, without me adding to their number.'

'Suit yourself,' he said, his voice sounding desolate and empty. 'But if you change your mind, feel free to consider it your parting trinket. And just like you said, you won't even need to post it to yourself. So efficient.'

And then he was gone, leaving only the sting of his parting words in his wake. She kicked off her shoes and crawled into the welcoming bed, sliding her arm under Sam's head and pulling him in close. She kissed his head, drinking deeply of his scent and his warm breath in an attempt to blot out the woody spice of another's signature tones.

She was so confused, so tired. Sleep, she told herself, knowing that after a late night of sexual excesses followed by today's tension, what she really needed was to sleep. But something tugged at her consciousness and refused to let go as his words whirled and eddied in her mind, keeping her from the sleep she craved so much as she tried to make sense of what Leo had said.

A heart of stone she'd accused him of, and when she'd apologised, he'd told her she was probably right. She shivered just thinking how forlorn he'd looked. How lost.

A man with a stone for a heart. A man with no home.

A man with everything and yet with nothing.

And a picture flashed in her mind—the photographic print she'd seen in Leo's suite before dinner last night.

She'd been looking for a distraction at the time, looking for something to pretend interest in if only so she didn't have to look at him, so her eyes would not betray how strongly she was drawn to him. Only she hadn't had to feign interest when she'd seen it, a picture from the 1950s, a picture of a riverbank and a curving row of trees and a park bench set between.

Something about the arrangement or the atmosphere

of that black and white photograph had jagged in her memory at the time, just as it struck a chord now. It was the old man sitting all alone on that park bench, hunched and self-contained, and sitting all alone, staring out over the river.

A lonely man.

A man with no family and nowhere to call home.

A man with nothing.

And it struck her then. Twenty or thirty years from now, that man could very well be Leo.

It was just a hiccup, Leo told himself as he considered the task ahead, just a slight hitch in his plans. Only a weekend, three nights at most, and the deal would be wrapped up once and for all. After all, Culshaw knew that even though they all called the shots in their respective businesses, none of them could just drop everything and disappear off the face of the earth—not for too long anyway. Neither could he risk them walking away. It had to be tied up this weekend.

He sighed as he packed up his laptop. He'd got precious little done, not that he'd expected to, with a child running riot. Only this one he'd barely seen and still he'd got nothing done.

Maybe because he couldn't stop thinking about her.

What was it about the woman that needled him so much? She was so passionate and wild in bed, like a tigress waiting to be unleashed, waiting for him to let her off the chain. Wasn't that enough? Why couldn't she just leave it at that? Why did she have to needle him and needle him and lever lids off things that had been welded shut for a reason? All her pointless questions.

All working away under his skin. And why did she even care?

Two days. Three nights. So maybe extending his time in her presence wasn't his preferred option, but he could survive being around Evelyn that long, surely. After all, he'd had mistresses who'd lasted a month or two before he'd lost interest or moved cities. Seriously, what could possibly happen in just a weekend?

Hopefully more great sex. A sound sleep would do wonders to improve her mood, and a tropical island sunset would soon have her feeling romantic and back in his arms. Nothing surer.

And in a few short days he'd have the deal tied up and Evelyn and child safely delivered home again.

Easy.

'Mr Zamos,' the cabin attendant said, refreshing his water, 'the captain said to tell you we'll be landing in half an hour. Would you like me to let Ms Carmichael know?'

He looked at his watch, rubbed his brow, calculating how long she'd slept. If his theory was right, her mood should be very much improved already. 'Thank you,' he said, 'but I'll do it.'

There was no answer to his soft knock, so he turned the handle, cracked open the door. 'Evelyn?'

Light slanted into the darkened room and as his eyes adjusted he could make her out in the bed, her caramel hair tumbling over the pillow, her face turned away, her arm protectively resting over her child's belly.

Mother and child.

And he felt such a surge of feeling inside him, such a tangle of twisted emotions, that for a moment the noise of that blast blotted everything else out, and there was nothing else for it but to close his eyes and endure the rush of pain and disgust and anger as it ripped through him.

And when he could breathe again, he opened his eyes to see another pair of dark eyes blinking up at him from the bed. Across the sleeping woman, the pair considered each other, Leo totally ill equipped to deal with the situation. In the end it was Sam who took the initiative. He pulled his teddy from his arms and offered him to Leo. 'Bear.'

He looked blankly at the child and immediately Sam rolled over, taking his toy with him, then promptly rolled back and held his bear out to Leo again. 'Bear.'

And Leo felt—he didn't know how he felt. He didn't know what was expected of him. He was still reeling from the explosion of emotions that had rocked through him to know how to react to this.

'Bear!'

'Mmm, what's that, Sam?' Eve said drowsily, and she looked around and saw Leo. 'Oh.' She pushed herself up, ran a hand over her hair. 'Have I overslept?'

Her cheek was red where it had lain against the pillow, her hair was mussed and there was a smudge of mascara under one eye, but yet none of that detracted from her fundamental beauty. And he felt an insane surge of masculine pride that he was the one responsible for her exhaustion. And a not-so-insane surge of lust in anticipation of a repeat performance in his near future.

'We'll be landing soon. You don't want to miss the view as we come in. It's pretty spectacular, they tell me.'

It *was* spectacular, Eve discovered after she'd freshened herelf up and changed Sam before joining Leo back in the cabin. The sea was the most amazing blue, and she could make out in the distance some of the islands that made up the Whitsunday group. From here they looked like jewels in the sea, all lush green slopes and white sand surrounded by water containing every shade of blue. The sun was starting to go down, blazing fire, washing everything in a golden hue.

'That's Hamilton Island,' he said, indicating a larger island as they circled the group for their approach. 'That's where we'll land before transferring to the helicopter for Mina Island.'

'It's beautiful,' she said, pointing over Sam's shoulder. 'Look, Sam, that's where we're going for a holiday.' Sam burst into song and pumped his arms up and down.

It did look idyllic, she thought. Maybe a couple of days relaxing on a tropical island wouldn't be such a hardship. She glanced over at the man beside her, felt the familiar sizzle in her veins she now associated with him and only him, and knew she was fooling herself.

With Leo around things were bound to get complicated. They always did.

Which meant she just had to establish a few ground rules first.

CHAPTER NINE

'I'M NOT sleeping with you.'

They'd landed on Hamilton Island and made the helicopter transfer to Mina without incident, arriving to be greeted by Eric just as the sun was dipping into the water in a glorious blaze of gold. Eric had laughed, secretly delighted she could tell, when they'd all stood and watched the spectacle, telling them they'd soon get used to 'that old thing', before dropping them off at their beachside bure to freshen up before dinner.

And now, after a tour of the timber and glass five-star bungalow, their eyes met over the king-sized bed. The *only* bed, aside from the cot set up for Sam in the generous adjoining dressing room.

She wasn't about to change her mind. 'You'll just have to find yourself somewhere else to sleep.'

'Come on, Evelyn,' he said, sitting down on the bed and slipping off his shoes, peeling off his socks, 'don't you think you're being just a little melodramatic? It's not like we haven't slept together before.'

'That was different.'

He looked over his shoulder at her, one eyebrow raised. 'Was it?'

Her arms flapped uselessly at her sides. From outside she could hear Sam laughing as Hannah, the young woman who had been sent to be his babysitter, fed him his dinner. At least that part of the arrangements seemed to be going well.

'I'm not sharing a bed with you,' she said. 'And I certainly don't have to sleep with you just because we happen to be caught in the same lie.'

He stood, reefing his shirt from his pants as he started undoing the buttons at his cuffs. 'No? Even though you know we're good together?'

She blinked. 'What are you doing?'

He shrugged. 'Taking a shower before dinner,' he said innocently enough, although she saw the gleam in his eyes. 'Care to join me?'

'No!'

But she couldn't resist watching his hands moving over the buttons, feeling for them, pushing them through the holes. Clever hands. Long-fingered hands. And as he tweaked the buttons she was reminded of the clever way he'd tweaked her nipples and worked other magic... She looked away. Looked back again. 'There's no point. No point to any of it.'

'It's only sex,' he said, finishing off the rest of the buttons before peeling off his shirt. 'It's not like we haven't already done it—several times. And I know for a fact you enjoyed it. I really don't know why you're making out like it's some kind of ordeal.'

'It was supposed to be for just one night,' she said, trying and failing not to be distracted by his broad chest and that line of dark hair heading south. 'A one-night stand. No strings attached.'

'So we make it a four-night stand. And I sure as hell don't see any strings.'

She dragged her recalcitrant eyes north again, wondering how he could so easily consider making love to a person like they had for not one but four nights, and not want to feel some kind of affection for the other party. But, then, he had a head start on her. He had a heart of stone. 'It was nice, sure. But that doesn't mean we have to have any repeat performances.'

'There's that word again.' His hands dropped to the waistband of his pants, stilled there. '"Nice". Tell me, if you scream like that for nice, what do you do for mind-blowing? Shatter windows?'

She felt heat flood her face, totally mortified at being reminded of her other wanton self, especially now when she was trying to make like she could live without such sex. 'Okay, so it was better than nice. So what? It's not as if we even like each other.'

'And that matters because…?'

She spun away, reduced to feeling like some random object rather than a woman with feelings and needs of her own, and crossed to the wall of windows that looked out through palm trees to the bay beyond. It was moonlit now, the moon dusting the swaying palm leaves with silver and laying a silvery trail across the water to the shore, where tiny waves rippled in, luminescent as they kissed the beach. It was beautiful, the air balmy and still, and she wished she could enjoy it. But right now she was having trouble getting past the knowledge that she'd spent an entire night, had bared herself, body and soul, to a man who treated sex as some kind of birthright.

And if it wasn't bad enough that he'd not so subtly pointed out she'd been vocally enthusiastic, now he'd as much as agreed that he didn't even like her. Lovely.

And that was supposed to make her happier about sleeping with him?

Fat chance.

She felt his hands land on her shoulders, his long fingers stroking her arms, felt his warm breath fan her hair. 'You are a beautiful woman, Evelyn. You are beautiful and sexy and built for unspeakable pleasure. And you know it. So why do you deny yourself that which you so clearly desire?'

Self-preservation, she thought, as his velvet-coated words warmed her in places she didn't want warmed and stroked an ego that wanted to be liked and maybe, maybe even more than that.

'I can't,' she said. *Not without losing myself in a place I don't want to be. Not without risking falling in love with a man who has no heart.* 'Please, just believe me, I'll pretend to be your fiancée, I'll pretend to be your lover. But, please, don't expect me to sleep with you.'

The big house, as the Culshaws referred to it, was exactly that. Not flashy, but all spacious tropical elegance, the architecture, like that of the bures, styled to bring the outside in with lots of timber and glass and sliding walls. Outside, on an expansive deck overlooking the bay and the islands silhouetted against the sky, a table had been beautifully laid, but it was the night sky that captured everyone's attention.

'I don't think I've ever seen so many stars,' Eve confessed, dazzled by the display as they sat down for the meal. 'It's just magical.'

Eric laughed. 'We think so. This island takes its name from one of them but don't ask me to point out which one.'

Maureen continued, 'When we first came here for a holiday about thirty years ago, we got home to Melbourne and wanted to turn right back round again.

We've been coming here every year since. Hasn't been used much lately, not since—'

Eric cut in, saving her from finishing. 'Well, it's good to have guests here again, that's for sure. So I'd like to propose a toast. To guests and good friends and good times,' he said, and they all raised their glasses for the toast.

'Now,' Eric said, from alongside Leo, 'how's that young man of yours settling in?'

'He's in his element,' Eve replied. 'Two of his favourite things are fish and boats. He can't believe his good fortune.'

'Excellent. And the babysitter's to your satisfaction? Did she tell you she's hoping to study child care next year?'

'Hannah seems wonderful, thank you.'

Maureen distracted her on the other side, patting her on the hand. 'Oh, that reminds me, I've booked the spa,' she started.

But Eve didn't hear the rest, not when she heard Eric ask Leo, 'How old did you say Sam was again?'

She froze, her focus on the man beside her and how he replied to the question, the man stumbling with an answer, seemingly unable to remember the age of his own supposed child.

'Ah, remind me again, Eve?' he said at last. 'Is Sam two yet?' Eve excused herself and smiled, forcing a laugh.

'You go away much too much if you think Sam's already had his birthday. He's eighteen months old. How could you possibly forget?'

Leo snorted and said, 'I never remember this milestone stuff. It's lucky Evelyn does,' which earned agreement from Eric at least.

'It must be hard on you, though, Evelyn, with Leo always on the move,' Maureen said. Eve wanted to hug the woman for moving the conversation along, although a moment later she wished she'd opted for a complete change of topic. 'Do you have family nearby who help out?'

She smiled softly, looking up at the stars for just a moment, wondering where they were amidst the vast array. Her grandfather had held her hand and taken her outside on starry nights when she hadn't been able to stop crying and had told her they were up there some-where, shining brightly, keeping her grandmother company. And now her grandfather was there too. She blinked. 'I have a wonderful neighbour who helps out. My parents died when I was ten and—I hate to admit it—I don't remember terribly much about them. I lived with my grandfather after that.'

'Oh-h-h,' said Felicity. 'They never got to meet Sam.'

'No, and I know they would have loved him.' She took a breath. 'Oh, I'm sorry for sounding so maudlin on such a beautiful night. Maybe we should change the topic, talk about something more cheerful.'

'I know,' said Eric jovially. 'So when's the happy day, you two?'

Eve wanted to groan, until she felt Leo's arm around her shoulders and met his dazzling smile. 'Just as soon as I can convince her she can't live without me a moment longer.'

Somehow they made it through the rest of the evening without further embarrassment but it was still a relief to get back to their bure. The long day had taken its toll, the stress of constantly fearing they would be caught out weighing heavily on Eve, and even though she'd slept on the plane, she couldn't wait to crawl into bed. *Her bed*, because after their earlier discussion, Leo had offered to sleep on the sofa. Hannah was sitting on it now, watching music television on low. She stood and clicked the remote off as they came in.

'How was Sam?' Eve asked, looking critically at the sofa, frowning at its length. Or lack of it. How the hell did Leo think he was going to fit on that?

'Sam's brilliant. I let him stay up half an hour longer, like you suggested, and he went down easy as. I checked him the last time about five minutes ago, and he hadn't stirred. I don't think I've ever looked after such a good baby.'

Eve smiled, relieved. 'Lucky you didn't meet him last week when he was teething—you might have had a different opinion.' She opened her purse to find some notes and Hannah waved her away. 'No. It's all taken care of. It's my job to look after Sam while you're here.' She headed for the door, gave a cheery wave. 'I'll see you in the morning, then.'

Eve met Leo coming out of the bedroom with an armful of pillows and linen. 'Goodnight,' he said, heading for the sofa maybe a little too stoically.

She watched him drop it all on the sofa, measured the height and breadth of man against length and width of sofa and realised it was never going to work. It should be her sleeping on the sofa. Except Sam's room was beyond the bedroom and it would be foolhardy if not impossible to move him now.

She watched him for a while try to make sense of

the bedding, as if he was ever going to be comfortable there.

And suddenly she was too tired to care. It wasn't like they were strangers after all. They had made love and several times. And even if they didn't like each other, surely they could share two sides of a big wide bed and still manage to get a good night's sleep?

'Stop it,' she said, as Leo attempted to punch his pillow into submission at one end, one bare foot sticking out over the other. 'This is ridiculous.'

'You don't say.'

'Look, it's a big bed,' she said reluctantly, gnawing her lip, trying not to think of the broad, fit body that would be taking up at least half of it. 'We can share it.' Then she added, 'So long as that's all we share. Is that a deal?'

He sat up on a sigh, clearly relieved. 'It's a promise. I promise not to share anything, so long as you don't jump me first.'

'Ha. And I thought you were awake. Now I know you're dreaming. I'm going to have a shower—alone. You'd better be in bed and asleep when I get there, or it's straight back to the sofa for you.'

And he was asleep when she slipped under the covers, or he was good at pretending. She clung close to her edge of the bed, thinking that was the safest place, yet she could still feel the heat emanating from his body, could hear his slow, steady breathing, and tried not to think about what they'd been doing twenty-four hours ago, but found it hard to think of anything else. Especially when she was so acutely aware of every tiny rustle of sheets or shift in his breathing.

Twenty-four hours. How could so much have happened in that time? How could so much change?

Outside the breeze stirred the leaves in the trees, set the palm fronds rustling, and if she listened hard, she could just hear a faint swoosh as the tiny swell rushed up the shore. But it was so hard to hear anything, so very hard, over the tremulous beating of her heart…

It was happening again. He buried his head under the blanket and put his hands over his ears but it didn't stop the shouting, or the sound of the blows, or the screams that followed. He cowered under the covers, whimpering, trying not to make too much noise in case he was heard and dragged out too, already dreading what he'd find in the morning at breakfast. If they all made it to breakfast.

There was a crash of furniture, a scream and something smashed, and the blows continued unabated, his mother's cries and pleas going unheard, until finally, eventually, he heard the familiar mantra, the mantra he knew by heart, even as his mother continued to sob. Over and over he heard his father utter the words telling her he was sorry, telling her he loved her. 'Signome! Se agapo. Se agapo poli. Signome.'

Sam! Eve woke with a mother's certainty that something was wrong, bolting from the bed and momentarily disoriented with her new surroundings, only to realise it wasn't Sam who was in trouble. For in the bed she'd so recently left, Leo was thrashing from side to side, making gravel-voiced mutterings against the mattress, rantings that made no sense in any language she knew, his body glossy with sweat under the moonlight.

He cried out in his sleep, a howl of desperation and helplessness, anguish clear in his tortured limbs and fevered brow as he twisted and writhed. Eve did the only thing she could think of, the only thing she knew helped Sam when he had night terrors. She went to Leo's side of the bed and sat down softly. 'It's okay, Leo,' she said, sweeping a calming hand over his brow, finding it burning hot. He flinched at her touch, resisting it at first, so she tried to soothe him with her words. 'It's okay. It's all right. You're safe now. Leo, you're safe.'

He seemed to slump under her hands, his body slick with sweat, his breathing still hard but slowing, and Eve suspected that whatever demons had invaded his midnight hours had now departed. She went to leave then, to return to her side of the bed, but when she made a move to leave, a hand locked around her wrist and she realised that maybe there were still some demons hanging on.

And just as she would do and had done with Sam when he needed comfort, she slid under the covers alongside the hot body of Leo, putting her arm around him, soothing him back to sleep with the gentle reassurance of another's touch and trying not to think of the heated presence lying so close to her or the thud of his heart under her hands.

Five minutes should be enough, she figured, until he had settled back into sleep. Five minutes and she'd escape back to her edge of the mattress. Five minutes would be more than enough…

Something was different. She woke to the soft light of the coming dawn, filtering grey through the shutters, and to the sound of birdsong coming from the palms

outside. And she woke to the certain knowledge that she
had stayed far, far too long. Fingers trailed over her back,
making lazy circles on her skin through her thin cotton
nightie and setting her skin to tingling, and warm lips
nuzzled at her brow as the hand between them somehow
managed to brush past her nipples and send spears of
electricity to her core.

And she was very, very aroused.

She was also trapped, his heavy arm over her, one leg
casually thrown over hers. She tried to wiggle her way
out but the movement brought her into contact with a
part of him that told her he was also very much aroused.
He growled his appreciation, shifted closer, and she tried
not to think about how good that part of him had felt
inside her.

'Leo...' she said, conflicted, her mind in panic, her
body in revolt, turning her face up to his, only to be met
by his mouth as he dragged her into his long, lazy kiss,
a kiss she had no power or intention to cut short even
though she knew it was utter madness.

Utter pleasure.

Her senses soared, her flesh tingled and breasts ached
for the caress of his clever hands and hot mouth, and arguments that things were complicated enough, that there
was no point, that this must end and end badly made
little impression against this slow, sensual onslaught.

'I see you changed your mind,' he murmured, a brush
of velvet against her skin.

'You had a nightmare.'

'This,' he said, sliding one long-fingered hand up the
back of her leg, kneading her bottom in his hand, 'is
no nightmare.'

'Don't you—' His mouth cut her off again as his hand

captured her breast, working at her nipple, plucking at her nerve endings, making her groan into his mouth with the exquisite pleasure of his caress, emerging breathless and dizzy when it ended so that she almost forgot what she wanted to say. 'Don't you remember?'

'Maybe…' he said, rolling her under him, pinning her arms to the bed above her head as his head dipped to her throat, 'maybe right now I'd rather forget.'

She moaned with the wicked pleasure of it all, his hot mouth like a brand against her skin. But this wasn't supposed to happen. She hadn't wanted this to happen. But as he lowered his head to her breast and drew in one achingly hard nipple to his mouth, laving it with his hot tongue, blowing on the damp fabric and sending exquisite chills coursing through her, she couldn't, for the life of her, remember why. Her body was alive with wanting him, alive with the power that came from him and that she craved, and there was no way she could stop.

He let her wrists go, his hands busy at her nightie. She felt the soft fabric lifting as he skimmed his hands up her sides, before skimming down again, taking her underwear with them. 'You're beautiful,' he growled, his voice like a brush of velvet over her bare skin as he pulled it over her head. And yet he was the magnificent one, broad and dark, his erection swaying and bucking over her, a pearl of liquid glistening at its head. Transfixed, unable to stop herself, she reached out her hand and touched it with the pad of her thumb. He uttered something urgent, his dark eyes flared, wild and filled with the same dark need that consumed her as he swiped up his wallet, found what he needed and tossed the wallet away in his rush to be inside her.

He dragged in air, forced himself to slow. 'You do this to me,' he accused her softly as he parted her thighs with his hand and found her slick and wet and wanting. 'You make me rock hard and aching,' he continued, his fingers circling that tiny nub of nerve endings, a touch so delicious she mewled with pleasure, writhing as sensation built on the back of his words, fuelling her need, fuelling her desperation.

Until at last she felt him nudge her *there*, hot and hard and pulsing with life as he tensed above her for one tantalising moment of anticipation.

And then joyfully, blissfully, he entered her in one magical thrust and she held him there, at her very core, welcoming him home, tears squeezing from her eyes at the sheer ecstasy of it all.

So much to feel. So much to experience and hold precious. And still the best was to come. The dance, the friction, the delicious moment of tension when he would sit poised at her entrance, before slamming back inside.

She went with him, matched him measure for measure, gasp for gasp as the pace increased, their bodies slick and hot as the rhythm increased, faster, more furious, the climb too high until this thing building inside her felt too big for her chest, her lungs too small.

Until with one final thrust, one final guttural roar, he sent her shattering, coming apart in his arms, falling, spinning weightless and formless and satisfied beyond measure.

'So beautiful,' he said, as he smoothed her hair from her damp brow, kissing her lightly on her eyes, on her nose, on her gasping lips.

And you're dangerous, she thought as he disappeared

to the bathroom, as her brain resumed functioning and a cold and very real panic seized her heart. So utterly, utterly dangerous.

And I am so in trouble.

What should one say now? What would an army do, its defences stripped bare, the castle walls well and truly breached? Try to hastily rebuild them? Call for reinforcements?

Or surrender?

She squeezed her eyes shut, trying not to think about the sizzle under her skin where his fingers had stroked her shoulder.

As if she had a choice. She would no sooner patch up her defences and he would have them down again. One silken touch, one poignant kiss, and he would have those walls tumbling right down.

But she was kidding himself. There was no point rebuilding walls or calling for reinforcements. No point trying to save herself from attack from outside the castle walls.

Not when the enemy was already within.

Tears sprang to her eyes and she swiped them away. Damn. What was she doing? What was she risking? 'I can't afford to get pregnant again,' she said when he returned, putting voice to her greatest fear.

'I wouldn't let you.'

'But Sam's father—'

He rose over her, cutting her off with his kiss. 'I would never do that to you.'

'How do I know that? And I would have two babies from two different fathers. How could I cope with that?'

'Believe me. It won't happen but even if it did, I would not abandon you as he has done.'

'But you wouldn't marry me either.'

He searched her eyes and frowned and she thought it was at her words, until he used the pad of his thumb to wipe away the moisture there.

'I thought I heard you say any woman would be certifiably insane to want to get shackled to me.'

'I'm sorry,' she whispered, remembering the scene in the bar. 'I was angry.'

'As was I. I should never have said what I did about Sam's father thinking the same of you. But you're right. Marriage is not an option, which means the best thing for everyone is to ensure we're careful. All right?'

She wished he wouldn't be like this. She wished he could go back to being ruthless and hard, because when he was tender and gentle with her, she could almost, *almost*, imagine he actually cared.

And she could almost, *almost*, imagine that she cared for him. She couldn't afford to care for him. She couldn't afford to read anything into his apology for what he'd said about Sam's dad when it was plain he wasn't lining up to marry her himself.

But she could enjoy him.

Two more nights in Leo's bed. Why was she fighting it when it was where she so wanted to be? Why not treat it as the holiday it really was? Time spent in a tropical paradise with a man who knew how to pleasure a woman. No ties, no commitments and a promise not to let her down.

Was she mad to fight it?

And was it really surrendering, to take advantage of what she'd been offered on a plate?

His hand cupped her breast, feeling its weight, stroking her nipple and her senses until it peaked hard and plump under his fingers while his lips worked their heated way along her jaw towards her mouth. 'Evelyn?'

A woman would have to be mad to want to give this up, she reasoned, leaning into his ministrations, giving herself over to the sensations. Two nights to enjoy the pleasures of the flesh. It was more than some people had in a lifetime.

It would be enough.

It had to be enough.

'All right,' she whispered, giving herself up to his kiss.

CHAPTER TEN

SAM'S morning chatter roused them, as he tested all the sounds in his vocabulary in one long gabble, then she heard a tell-tale bump on the floor, followed by a squeal. 'That's Sam,' she said unnecessarily, locating her nightie and snatching up her balled-up underwear and a robe and making for the bathroom for a quick pit stop, wanting to ensure she looked maternal rather than wanton when she greeted her son. Not that he was old enough to notice anything amiss, she thought, giving thanks for his innocence.

Sam was hanging onto the rails and bouncing on the mattress and greeted her with a huge grin followed by 'mumumumumum', which warmed her heart. Unconditional love. There was nothing like it. She changed him on the table provided and equipped for the task before popping his wriggling body down on the floor. 'Bear!' he shouted, gleefully scooping up the toy and running with his wide toddler gait out of the room before her, looking a little bit lost at the new surroundings for just a moment, before running full pelt and colliding with the bed.

Dark eyes blinked up at Leo, openly curious. He blinked back, wondering what one was supposed to say to a child. Sam looked around at his mother, who was pulling milk from the fridge in the small kitchenette and pouring it into a jug. 'It's okay, Sam, you remember Leo,' she said reassuringly as she put the jug in the microwave, and Sam turned and careened straight into his mother's legs, hiding his face between them.

'I'm sorry,' she said, hoisting him to her hip in one efficient movement, although it wasn't so much the efficiency that impressed Leo but the unexpected way the sudden angle of her hip displayed the long line of her legs. His mouth went dry, his blood went south. Strange really, for here she was, dressed in a cheap cotton nightgown, a toweling robe sashed at her waist and with a baby at her hip, and maybe it was her tousled hair, or the jut of that damned hip, or even the fact she'd just blown his world apart in bed—twice—but suddenly he was thinking about a third time.

The microwave pinged.

'Ping,' cried Sam, holding his hands out. 'Ping!'

One-handed, she poured the milk into some kind of cup, fixing on a spout before passing it to the boy. 'Here's your ping, Sam.' Leo watched her, admiring the way she looked so at ease working one-handedly. Sam dropped his bear to clasp the cup in his pudgy hands, gulping deep. 'Sam's used to joining me in bed in the morning,' she said, bending over to retrieve the bear and giving his sex a hell of a jolt in the process. Until, through the fog of rising testosterone, it occurred to him that she was about to bring Sam back to bed.

'Although, admittedly,' she added, already on her way, 'he's not used to finding someone else there.'

He tucked that piece of information away in a file that came marked with a tick, even as he gladly took her hint and pulled on a robe to vacate the bed. He liked the knowledge she didn't often entertain at home. Sam was evidence she'd been with someone, and that wasn't something he wanted to contemplate. He didn't want to think there had been or were others.

'I didn't mean you had to run away,' she said, settling Sam between the pillows. 'It's still early.'

'I think I'll go for a run.'

'You haven't had that much to do with babies or children, have you?'

'Does it show?'

'Blatantly. You might want to do something about that if you want people to believe you're actually Sam's father. The fact you're travelling most of the year is no excuse for not knowing how to deal with the child who's supposed to be your own.'

He shrugged, knowing he'd handled things badly last night, not even remembering his supposed son's age, but uncomfortable with where the conversation was headed. 'What do you suggest?'

'Maybe you should try holding him from time to time. Even just hold his hand. Engage with him.'

'Engage with him?'

'He's a person, Leo, just like anyone else. Maybe try directing all that animal magnetism you have at him instead of every woman you happen to meet.'

He looked at the child. Looked back at her, not sure who was making him feel more uncomfortable now. 'But can he even understand what I say?'

She laughed. 'More than you know.'

He sat down awkwardly on the side of the bed, watching Sam, Sam watching him as he swigged at his milk, his teddy tucked securely once again under his arm.

And Sam guzzled the last of his milk and held out his toy. 'Bear!'

He looked on uncertainly, not sure what was expected

of him, unfamiliar with this role. 'I'm not sure I can do this.'

'He's offering it to you. Try taking it,' she suggested.

He put out his hand toward the bear and Sam immediately rolled over, giggling madly, the toy wedged tightly beneath him.

He looked over at her. 'I don't get it.'

'It's a game, Leo. Wait.' And sure enough the arm shot out again.

'Bear.'

This time Leo made a grab for it. A slow lunge, and way too slow for Sam, but he loved it anyway, squealing with glee as he hid his teddy.

The next time was nearly a draw, Sam winning by a whisker, and he was in stitches on the bed, his body curved over his prize, and even Leo was finding it amusing. 'He's quick,' he said, and he looked at Evelyn, who was smiling too, although her eyes looked almost sad, almost as if...

'I'll go take a shower,' he said, standing abruptly, not interested in analysing what a look like that might mean. He didn't do family. He'd told her that. And if the shadowed remnants of last night's nightmares had reminded him of him anything, it was that he could never do family. He dared not risk it. He was broken, and that was just the way it was.

So she could look at him any damned way and it would make no difference. Because after two more nights with her, he would let her go for ever.

He didn't want anything more.

And he definitely didn't want her pity.

They were all meeting after breakfast at the dock, ready for a day's adventure. A morning sail, and then a helicopter trip over the more far-flung sights of the islands and the reef. Hannah had already collected Sam and taken him up to the main house where there was a large playroom filled with toys and games and all surrounded by secure fences so he couldn't get into trouble if he wandered off. Which meant Eve had a rare few hours without Sam, not to work but to enjoy her beautiful if temporary surroundings, and the heated attention of a man just as beautiful and temporary, if a lot more complex.

He held her hand as they wended their way along the palm-studded sand toward the dock on the bay, the whispering wind promising a day of seductive warmth, the odd scattered white cloud offering no threat, and the man at her side promising days and nights filled with sinful pleasures.

Now that she had made her decision, and had Leo's commitment that he wouldn't abandon her if the worst happened, as Sam's father had done, she was determined to enjoy every last moment of it. Maybe she was crazy, but she trusted him, at least on that score. And there was no question that he didn't lack the means to support a child.

The morning sun kissed her bare arms where it infiltrated the foliage, the air fresh with salt and the sweet scent of tropical flowers. Ten whole degrees warmer up here than Melbourne's showery forecast, Eve had heard when she'd flicked on the weather channel while feeding Sam his breakfast. She could think of worse ways to spend the time waiting for a new hot water service to be installed.

She glanced up at the man alongside her, his loose white shirt rolled up at the cuffs, with designer stubble adding to his pirate appeal, and with one look the memories of their love-making flooded back, warming her in places the sun did not reach. Oh, no, she would have no trouble enjoying her nights with him either.

'You look pleased with yourself.'

'Do I?' Only then did she realise she'd been smiling. 'It must be the weather.'

'Good morning!' Maureen said, greeting them, looking resort elegant in linen co-ordinates in taupe and coffee colours. 'How was the bure? Did you all sleep well?'

Eve smiled. 'It's just beautiful. I love it here.'

'Everything is perfect,' Leo added, slipping an arm around Eve's shoulders, giving her arm a squeeze. 'Couldn't be better.'

'And Sam's okay with Hannah? You're not worried about leaving him, are you?'

Eve shook her head. 'Hannah's wonderful. He's having the time of his life.'

The older woman looked from one to the other and smiled knowingly. 'I hope you understand why we were so keen to drag you away from Melbourne. And there's just so much more to share with you.'

'All aboard!' called Eric, appropriately wearing a captain's cap over his silvering hair, and Leo handed both women onto the yacht where Richard and Felicity were already waiting. There was a distinct holiday mood in the air as they set off, the boat slicing through the azure waters, the wind catching in the flapping sails, the magnificent vistas ever-changing, with new wonders revealed around every point, with every new bay. 'Isn't it fabulous?' Felicity said, leaning over the railing, looking glamorous in a short wrap skirt and peasant top, and Eve could't help but agree, even though she felt decidedly designer dull in her denim shorts and chain-store tanktop. Motherhood in Melbourne, she reflected, didn't lend itself to a vast resort wardrobe.

Decidedly dull, that was, until Leo slipped an arm around her waist and pressed his mouth to her ear. 'Did I tell you how much I love your shorts,' he whispered, 'and how much I can't wait to peel them off?'

And she shuddered right there in anticipation of that very act. But first there were other pleasures, other discoveries. They discovered secret bays and tiny coves with sheer cliff walls and crystal-clear waters. They found bays where inlets carved dark blue ribbons through shallow water backed by pure white sand, a thousand shades of blue and green against the stark white beach and the lushly vegetated hills rising above.

They stopped for a swim at that beach, followed by a picnic comprising a large platter of antipasto and cold chicken and prawns, with Vietnamese cold rolls with dipping sauce all washed down with chilled white wine or sparkling water.

After lunch, the Alvarezes went for a stroll along the beach and Maureen took a snooze while Eric and Leo chatted, no doubt about business, a little way away. And Eve was happy to sit right there on the beach in her bikini, taking in the wonders of the scenery around her, the islands and the mountains, the lush foliage and amazing sea and above it all the endless blue sky. And she felt guilty for not sharing it with Sam, even though she knew that if he had come, none of them would have been able to relax for a minute. One day, when he was older, she would love to show him.

Leo dropped down on his knees behind her, picked up her bottle of lotion and squeezed some into his hand, started smoothing it onto her shoulders and neck until she almost purred with pleasure. She didn't think it necessary to inform him she'd just done that. 'You look deep in thought.'

'I was just thinking how much Sam would love this. I'll have to try to bring him one day.'

His hands stilled for a moment, before they resumed their slippery, sensual massage. 'Don't you love it?' she said. 'Can you believe the colour of that sea?'

'I've seen it before.'

'You have?' But of course he would have. Leo had been everywhere. 'Where?'

'In your eyes.'

The shiver arrowed directly down her spine. She snapped her head round. 'What?'

He squeezed more lotion, spread it down her arms, his fingertips brushing her bikini top as he looked out at the bay. 'When I first saw them, they reminded me of the Aegean, of the sea around the islands of Santorini and Mykonos, but I was wrong. For every colour in your eyes is right here, in these waters.'

And that battle scarred never-say-die, foolish, foolish creature inside her lumbered back into life and prepared for take-off once more. 'Leo…'

He looked down at her upturned face, touched one hand to the side of her face. 'I don't know how I'm ever going to forget those eyes.'

Then don't! she almost blurted, surprising herself with her vehement reaction, but he angled her shoulders and invited her into his kiss, a heart-wrenching bitter-sweet kiss that spoke of something lost before it had even been found, and she cursed a man with a stone for a heart, cursed her own foolish heart for caring.

'Come on, you two lovebirds,' Eric yelled along the beach. 'We've got a seaplane to catch!'

* * *

If the Whitsundays had been spectacular from the boat, they were breathtaking from the air in the clear afternoon light. Island after island could be explored from the air in the tiny plane, each island a brilliant green gem in a sapphire sea. And just when Eve thought it couldn't possibly get any better, they headed out over the Coral Sea to the Great Barrier Reef. The sheer scale of the reefs took everyone's breath away, the colours vivid and bright, like someone had painted pictures upon the sea, random shapes bordered in snowy white splashed with everything from emerald green and palest blue to muted shades of mocha.

And then they landed on the water and transferred to a glass-bottomed boat so they could see the amazing Technicolor world under the sea together with its rich sea life. 'I am definitely coming back one day to show Sam,' she told Maureen as they boarded the seaplane for the journey back to Mina. 'Thank you so much for today. I know I'll treasure these memories for ever.'

And from the back seat Eric piped up, 'You just wait. We saved the best till last!'

They had. They were heading back over a section he identified as Hardy Reef, one part of a network of reefs that extended more than two thousand kilometres up the north Queensland coastline, when she saw something that didn't fit with the randomness of the coral structures.

She pointed out the window. 'That looks like… Is that what I think it is?' Eric laughed and had the pilot circle around so they could all see.

'That's it. What do you think of that?'

It was incredible and for a moment her brain had refused to believe what her eyes were telling her. For in the middle of a kind of lagoon in the midst of a coral reef where everything appeared random, there sat a reef grown in the shape of a heart, its outline made from coral that looked from above like milk chocolate sprinkles on a cake, the inside like it was covered in a soft cream-cheese frosting, all surrounded by a sea of brilliant blue.

And little wonder she thought in terms of frostings and cakes, because it reminded her so much of the cake she'd made for Sam for his first birthday, knowing that as he got older he'd want bears or trains or some cartoon character or other. She figured that for his first, before he had a say, she could choose, and she'd made a heart shape, because that was what Sam meant to her.

'Look, Richard,' Felicity said, clasping his hand as they circled around. 'It's a heart. Isn't that amazing?'

'It magical,' Eve said, gazing down in wonder at the unique formation below. 'This entire place is just magical. Thank you.' The Culshaws laughed, delighted with the reactions of their guests as Leo took her hand and pressed it to his lips. She turned to him, surprised at the tenderness of the gesture, finding his eyes softly sad, feeling that sense of loss again, for something she had not yet quite gained. 'What is it?' she asked, confused.

'You are magical,' he told her, and his words shimmied down her spine and left her infused with a warm, golden glow and a question mark over her earlier accusation. A heart of stone? she wondered.

But there was definitely something magical in the air.

They dined alfresco that evening, an informal barbecue held early enough that Sam could join them, happily showing off his new toy collection to anyone who displayed an interest. Luckily nobody seemed to mind and Sam was in his element, lapping up the attention. When he yawned, there was general consensus amongst the couples. It had been a fabulous day, but exhausting, and tomorrow there was serious work to be done, an agreement to finally be hammered out between the men, a morning at the spa on a neighbouring island for the women.

And before that a night of explosive sex. Eve felt the tension change in the man alongside her, the barely restrained desire bubbling away so close to the surface she could just about smell the pheromones on the fresh night air. She sensed the changes in her own body, the prickling awareness, the mounting heat. It distracted her.

Sam, sensing the party winding up around him, found his second wind and made a dash for the toy room. Eve was too slow, caught unawares, and surprised when it was Felicity who snatched up the squirming child. 'Gotcha!' she said, swinging him in the air and tickling his tummy before, breathless and red cheeked, she passed him to his mother.

He was asleep before they reached the bure. She put Sam down, emerging from his small room to a darkened bedroom, lit only by the moonlight filtering through the glass windows. Leo had left the blinds open. She liked that; liked the way the shadows of the palms swayed on the breeze; liked the way the room glowed silver.

'Come to bed,' came the velvet-clad invitation.

And that was the part she liked best of all.

She was screaming again, crying out in pain as the blows rained down, as the bad words continued. 'Stomato to!' *he cried from his bed.* 'Stop it!' *But it*

*didn't stop, and in fear and desperation he crept to the
door, tears streaming down his face, afraid to move,
afraid not to move, afraid of what he would find when
he opened the door. So he did nothing, just curled up
into a ball behind the door and covered his ears and
prayed for it to stop.*

'Leo, it's okay.'

He sat bolt upright in bed, panting, desperate for air,
burning up. He put his hands to his head, bent over his
knees.

'You had a nightmare again.'

God, it wasn't a nightmare. *It was his life.* He swept
the sheet aside, stormed from the bed, pacing the floor,
circuit after circuit.

Twenty years ago he had escaped. Twenty years ago
he had made his own way. But he had always known it
was there, always known it was lurking. Waiting.

But it had never been this close. This real.

He felt cool hands on his back. 'What is it?'

He flinched, jumping away. 'Don't touch me! You
shouldn't touch me!'

'Leo?'

'I have to go for a walk.' He pulled open a drawer,
pulled out a pair of cotton pants and shoved his legs into
them.

'It's two o'clock in the morning.'

'Let me go!'

The night air fanned around him, warming against
his burning skin, the shallows sucking at his feet. There
was a reason he didn't get close to anyone. Good reason.
He was broken. Twisted. Made to be alone.

Couldn't she see that?

And yet she kept looking at him that way with those

damned blue eyes and even had him wishing for things that could never be. It was his fault. When had he stopped acting a part? When had he forgotten that this weekend was about pretence, that it wasn't real?

When she'd bucked underneath him in bed, her body writhing in its sweat-slicked release? Or when she'd talked about her parents and made him want to reach out and soothe her pain?

He stopped where the beach turned to rock, looked out over the sea to the looming dark shapes of the nearest islands.

One more day. One more night. And he would take her home before he could hurt her and there would be no more dreams.

It was as easy and as hard as that.

CHAPTER ELEVEN

SHE needed this. Eve lay on the massage table, scented candles perfuming the air, skilful hands working the knots out of her back and neck. She only wished someone would work out the knots in her mind, but that was impossible while Leo Zamos was at their core.

He'd been so desperate to get away, bursting from the bure this morning like the devil himself was after him. She'd watched him go, lit by moonlight as he'd moved through the trees towards the beach. Watched him and waited for him to come back. But eventually she'd gone back to bed and when she'd woken, he'd been sitting, having coffee on the deck.

She didn't know what it was, only that something was terribly, desperately wrong and that if he only opened up and shared what was troubling him, maybe she could help.

She sighed, a mixture of muscular bliss and frustrated mind, as the masseuse had her roll over, readying her for her facial. What was the point of wanting to help? He didn't want it and tomorrow she would go home, and all of this would be nothing more than a memory.

She couldn't afford to care. She mustn't, even when he told her she was magical. Even when he tugged on her heart and her soul with his kiss.

Even though she so very much wanted to believe it.

Thoroughly pampered after their hours at the spa, the three women enjoyed a late lunch at the big house, on the terrace overlooking the pool. The men were still in conference apparently, although Maureen suggested that might just mean they'd popped out in the boat for a spot of fishing while the women weren't looking. Not that it mattered. After they'd been massaged until their bones had just about melted, they were more than content to sit and chat in the warm, balmy air of tropical North Queensland. After all, they were going home tomorrow. Soon enough real life would intrude.

Sam was once again more than happy to provide the entertainment if they weren't up to it. He tottered between the three women, perfectly at ease with them all now, sharing around building blocks he'd taken a shine to, taking them back and redistributing them as if this was all part of some grand plan, happily chattering the whole time. Eve watched him, so proud of her little man, knowing that at least when Leo walked out of her life, she would still have Sam. He'd surprised her too. Instead of providing a disruptive force, as she'd expected, it seemed that, at least in some part, he seemed to pull them together. He definitely kept them amused.

And Felicity surprised her again, playing his games, picking him up when he passed, giving him hugs and raspberry kisses on his cheek to his squeals and giggles of delight before he scampered off on his toddler legs.

'I always wanted a child,' she said wistfully, her eyes following his escape. 'In fact, I always imagined myself surrounded by children. And when I met Richard and thought he was the one, I thought it might happen, even though it was already getting late...' Then she blinked and looked around. 'I guess things sometimes turn out differently to what we expect.'

And the other two women nodded, each wrapped in their own separate thoughts and experiences.

'It seemed easier to give up and pretend it didn't matter. But meeting you and seeing you with Sam makes me realise how much it means to me. I want to try again. At least one more time.' Tears made her eyes glassy. 'You're so lucky to be able to give Leo a child, Evelyn. I really wish I could do the same for Richard.' Her voice hitched. 'Damn! I'm so sorry.' She fled inside.

Eve felt sick, a hand instinctively going to her mouth. And all the good feelings, all the positive goodwill she'd been stashing away in her memory while she was determined to enjoy this weekend were for nothing. They meant nothing if her deceit led someone else to want what she was having. A wish based on a lie.

She rose to follow and tell her exactly that when Maureen stopped her. 'Let her go.'

'But she thinks—'

Maureen nodded. 'I know what she thinks.'

'But you don't understand.' She slumped back in her chair, feeling the weight of the lie crushing down on her, feeling her heart squeezed tight, knowing she couldn't go home without admitting the truth. 'I hate this! I hate the pretence. I'm so sorry, Maureen.' She shook her head, and still couldn't find a nice way to say it. 'Look, Leo's not really Sam's father.'

She heard a sharp intake of air, followed by an equally sharp exhalation. But then, instead of the censure she'd expected, or the outrage, she felt a gentling hand over her own. 'I wondered when you were going to feel able to share that.'

Warily, feeling sicker than ever, Eve looked up. 'You knew?'

'From the moment I met you in that bar in Melbourne. Of course, Sam could have passed for Leo's son, but it was crystal clear to anyone who had ever been a mother that Leo had no idea about being a father. And then his awkwardness at dinner, not knowing his own son's birthday, only reinforced that impression, at least to me.' She shrugged. 'Though when it comes down to it, does Sam's parentage really matter?'

'But you don't understand. It's not that simple—'

'Of course it's that simple.' Maureen said, cutting her off. 'I saw you and Leo out there yesterday in the boat and on the beach. It's clear to everyone that you love him and he loves you, so why should it matter one bit who Sam's father really is?' she insisted. 'Why should a silly detail like that matter when you are going to marry a man who clearly worships the ground you walk on? Now, I'll go check on Felicity and you stop worrying.'

How could Maureen know so much and yet be so wrong? Eve sat on the sand with Sam, watching him busily digging holes. All those hours of massaging and jet baths and a relaxing facial, all that pampering and all for nothing. Not even the magic of the island itself, the rustle of the palms and the vivid colours, none of it could dispel the tightness in her gut.

She didn't love Leo.

Sure, she was worried about him and whatever it was that plagued his dreams and turned his skin cold with sweat, and she certainly had an unhealthy obsession with the man, one that had started that fateful day three years ago, and which had only gathered momentum after mind-blowing nights of sex.

And maybe she didn't want to to think about going home tomorrow and never seeing him again.

But that was hardly the same as love.

As for Leo, no way did he love her. He was merely acting a part, plying her with attention as a means to an end, certainly not because he loved her. Ridiculous. They'd only been together a couple of days after all. What Maureen was witnessing was pure lust. Leo just had a bit more to throw around than most. He didn't do family and he didn't want her thinking he'd change his mind. Why else would he underline every endearment, every tender moment with a stinging reminder that it would soon end?

Sam oohed and pulled something from the sand then, shaking it, showing her what looked like some kind of shell, and she gave up thinking about questions she had no answers to, puzzles that made no sense. Tomorrow, she knew, she would go home and this brief interlude in her life would be over and she would have to find herself new clients and build a new fee base. And look after Sam. That's what she should be worrying about.

'Shall we see what it is, Sam?' she said to the child, a launch catching her attention for just a moment as it powered past the bay, before taking Sam's hand as they stepped into the shallows to wash this new treasure clean.

'Boat!' he said, pointing.

'It is,' she said. 'A big one.'

Her sarong clung to her where she'd sat in the damp sand, her ankles looked lean and sexy as her feet were lapped by the shallows, all her attention on her child by her side, guiding him, encouraging him with just a touch or a word or a smile, and he knew in that instant he had never seen anything more beautiful or powerful or sexy.

All he knew was that he wanted her. He wanted to celebrate, knowing the deal was finally done, but he wanted something more fundamental too. More basic. More necessary.

Except he also knew he couldn't let that happen. He'd realised that during his walk this morning and as much as he'd tried to find a way around it all day, even when he was supposed to be thinking about the Culshaw deal, he still knew it to be true. He couldn't take the chance.

He watched, as mother and son washed something in the shallows, he couldnt tell what, and she must have sensed his presence because he hadn't moved and she couldn't have heard him, yet she'd turned her head and looked up and seen him. And he'd seen his name on her lips as she'd stood and she'd smiled, only a tentative smile, but after the way he'd abandoned her this morning, he didn't deserve even that much.

And something bent and shifted and warmed inside that he could treat her so badly and still she could find a smile for him. He hoped it meant she liked him, just a little, just enough to one day find a way to forgive him for the way he had no choice but to treat her.

The wash was nothing really. No more than a ripple to any adult, and Leo had no idea it would be any different for a child, until he saw Sam pushed face first into the water with the rolling force of it.

'Sam!' he yelled, crossing the beach and pulling the child, spluttering and then squealing, from the water. 'Is he all right?' he asked, as she collected the wailing child, dropping to her towel, rocking him on her shoulder.

'Oh, my God, I took my eye off him for a second,' she said, her voice heavy with self-recrimination. 'I'm so sorry, Sam,' she said, kissing his head. 'I should have seen that coming.'

'Will he be okay?' Leo asked, but Sam's cries were already abating. He sniffled and hiccuped and caught sight of a passing sail, twisting in his mother's arms as his arm shot out. 'Boat!'

She sighed with relief. 'He sounds fine. He got a shock. I think we all did.'

Leo squatted down beside them and they said nothing for a while, all watching the boat bob by.

'You actually picked him up,' she said. 'Is that the first time you've ever held a child?'

He frowned as he considered her question, not because he didn't already know the answer but because this weekend suddenly seemed filled with firsts: the first time he'd thought a cotton nightie sexy; the first time he'd looked at a woman holding a baby and got a hard on; the first time he'd felt remorse that he'd never see a particular woman again...

But, no, he wasn't going there. What were his nightmares if not a warning of what would happen if he did?

'It's not something my job calls for much of, no.'

'Well, thank you for acting so quickly. I don't know what I was doing.'

He knew. She'd been looking at him with those damned eyes of hers. And he hadn't wanted to let them go.

Sam soon grew restless in his mother's arms and wiggled his way out, soon scouring the sands and collecting new treasure, keeping a healthy distance from the water, his mother shadowing his every movement.

'So how goes the deal?'

'It's done.'

She looked up, her expression unreadable, and he wasn't entirely certain what he'd been looking for. 'Congratulations. You must be pleased.'

'It's a good feeling.' Strangely, though, it didn't feel as good as it usually did, didn't feel as good as he'd expected it would. Maybe because of all the delays.

And then she was suddenly squatting down, writing Sam's name with a stick in the sand while he looked on, clapping. 'So we're done here.'

And that didn't make him feel any better. 'Looks like it. Culshaw is planning a celebratory dinner for tonight and tomorrow we all go home.'

'I thought you didn't have a home.'

There was a lump in the back of his throat that shouldn't have been there. He was supposed to be feeling good about this, wasn't he? He rubbed the back of his neck with his hand, watched her write 'Mum' in the sand. 'Mum,' she said to Sam, pointing.

Sam leaned over with his hands on his pudgy knees and solemnly studied the squiggles she'd made in the sand. 'Mumumumum,' sang Sam.

'That's right, clever clogs, you can read!' And she gave him a big squeeze that he wriggled out of and scooted off down the beach.

'Tell me about Sam's father,' Leo said, as they followed along behind.

She looked up suspiciously, her eyebrows jagging in the middle. Where was this coming from? 'Why?'

'Who was he?'

She shrugged. 'Just some guy I met.'

'You don't strike me as the "just-some-guy-I-met" type.'

'Oh, and you, with your vast experience of women, you'd know about all the different types, I guess.'

'Stop trying to change the subject. This is about you. How did you manage to hook up with such a loser?'

She stopped then, her eyes flicking between Leo and Sam. 'You don't know the first thing about me. And you certainly don't know the first thing about him. He just turned out not to be who I thought he was.'

'I know that he was a fool to let you go.'

Wow, she thought, forced to close her eyes for a second as the tremor rattled through her, *where did that come from*?

'Thanks,' she said, still getting over his last comment. 'But it was me who was the fool.'

'For getting pregnant? You can't blame yourself for that.'

For ever imagining he was anything at all like Leo. 'No. For believing him. He was an interstate consultant who visited every couple of weeks. Always flirting. We worked late one night, he invited me out for a drink afterwards'—*and he had sexy dark hair and olive skin and dark eyes and I wanted to pretend…*

'And?'

She shrugged. 'And the rest, as they say, is history.'

'You told him about Sam—about the pregnancy?'

'I told him. I wasn't particularly interested in seeing him again, but I thought he had a right to know. He wasn't interested as it happened. He was more interested in his wife not finding out.'

'Scum!' he spat, surprising her with the level of ferocity behind the word.

'It's not so bad. At least I've got Sam. And it got me motivated to start my own business.' She caught a flash of movement in the crystal clear water, a school of tiny fish darting to and fro in the shallows. She scooped up her son and ventured to the water's edge, careful not to disturb them. 'Look Sam,' she said, 'fish!'

And Sam's eyes opened wide, his arms pumping up and down. 'Fith!'

She laughed, chasing the fish in the shallows even as she envied her young son his raw enthusiasm. She envied him his simple needs and pleasures. Why did it have to become so hard when you were a grown up, she wondered, when the world spun not on the turns of the planet and shades of dark or light, but on emotions that made a mockery of science and fact and good sense.

Wanting Leo was so not good sense.

Loving him made even less.

Maureen was wrong. She had to be.

The mood at dinner was jovial, the conversation flowing and fun. Only Leo seemed tense, strangely separate from the group, as if he'd already moved on to the next place, the deal. The next woman. 'Are you all right?' she asked, on the way back to their bure, his hand like a vise around hers. 'Do you want to go take a walk first?'

Hannah had taken Sam back earlier and by now he would be safely in the land of Nod. They didn't have to rush back if he had something on his mind.

He blew out in a rush. 'I'll sleep on the sofa tonight,' he said almost too quickly, as if the words had been waiting to spill out. 'It'll be better that way.'

And she stopped right where she was and refused to move on so he had no choice but to turn and face her. 'You're telling me that after three nights of the best sex of my life, on the last night we have together, you're going to sleep on the sofa? Not a chance.'

He tried to smile. Failed miserably. 'It's for the best.'

'Who says? What's wrong, Leo? Why can't you tell me?'

'Believe me,' he snorted, 'you really don't want to know.'

'I wouldn't ask if I didn't want to know. What the hell changes tonight? The fact you don't have to pretend anymore?'

'You think I ever had to pretend about that?'

'Then don't pretend you don't want me tonight.' She moved closer, ran her free hand up his chest, 'We've got just one night left together. We're good together. You said that yourself. Why can't we enjoy it?'

He grabbed her hand, pushed it away. 'Don't you understand? It's for your own good!'

'How can I believe that if you won't tell me? What's wrong? Is it the dreams you're having?'

And he made a roar like a wounded animal in distress, a cry that spoke of so much pain and anguish and loss that it chilled her to the bone. 'Just leave it,' he said. 'Just leave me.'

He turned and stormed off across the sand towards the beach, leaving her standing there, gutted and empty on the path.

Maybe it was better this way, she thought, as she dragged herself back to the bure, forcing herself to put on a bright face for Hannah who wasn't taken in for a moment, she could tell, but she wasn't about to explain it to anyone. Not when she had no idea what was happening herself.

She checked Sam, listening to his even breathing, giving thanks for the fact he was in her life, giving thanks for the gift she'd been given, even if borne of a mistake. He was the best mistake she'd ever made.

And then she dragged bedding to the sofa, knowing from the previous night Leo was more likely to disturb her if he tried to fit onto the sofa than because of any nightmare he might have. At least she knew he would fit on the big king sized bed.

She lay there in the dark, waiting for what seemed like hours, until at last she heard his footfall on the decking outside. She cracked open her eyelids as the sliding door swooshed open and she saw his silhouette framed in the doorway, big and dark and not dangerous, like she'd always seen him, but strangely sad. He crossed the floor softly, hesitating when he got to the sofa. She could hear him at her feet, hear his troubled breathing.

Come to me, she willed, *pick me up and carry me to bed like you have done before and make love to me.*

And she heard him turn on a sigh and move away. She heard the bathroom door snick closed and she squeezed her eyes shut, wondering what he would do if she sneaked into the bed before he came back; knowing it was futile because he would straightaway head for the sofa.

He didn't need her any more. Or he didn't want her. What did it matter which or both it was? They both hurt like hell. They both hurt like someone had ripped out her heart and torn it to shreds and trampled on the pieces.

Could injured pride feel this bad? Could a miffed ego tear out your heart and rip it to shreds? Or had she been kidding herself and it had been Maureen who had been right all along?

Oh god, surely she hadn't fallen in love with Leo?

And yet all along she had known it was a risk, the greater risk; had known the possibility was there, the possibility to be drawn deeper and deeper under his spell until she could not bear the thought of being without him. All along she had known he had a heart of stone and still she had managed to do the unthinkable.

She'd fallen in love with him.

She lay there in the semi-gloom, the once silvery light of the moon now a dull grey, listening to him climb into bed, listening to him toss and turn and sigh, wishing him peace, even if he couldn't find it with her.

The scream woke him and he stilled with fear, hoping he'd imagined it. But then he heard the shouting, his father's voice, calling his mother those horrible names he didn't understand only to know they must be bad, and he cringed, waiting for the blow that would come at the end of his tirade. Then it came with a thump and his mother made a sound like a football when you kick it on the street and he vomited right there in his bed. He climbed out, weak and shaky, to the sound of his mother's cries, the bitter taste of sick in his mouth.

'*Stamata,*' he cried weakly through his tears, knowing he would be in trouble for messing up his bed, knowing his mother would be angry with him, wanting her to be angry with him so that things might be normal again. '*Stamato to tora.*' Stop it now!

And he pulled the door open and ran out, to see his father's fist raised high over his mother lying prostrate on the floor.

'*Stamato to!*' he screamed, running across the room, lashing out at his father, young fists flying, and earning that raised fist across his jaw as his reward, but not giving up. He couldn't stop, he had to try to make him stop hurting his mother.

He struck out again lashing at his father, but it was his mother who cried out and it made no sense, nor the thump of a body hitting the floor and then a baby screamed somewhere, and he blinked into consciousness, shaking and wet with perspiration, and waking to his own personal nightmare.

She was lying on the floor, looking dazed, tears springing from her eyes and her hand over her mouth where he must have hit her. And Sam screaming from the next room.

And he wanted to help. He knew he should help. He should do something.

But the walls caved in around him, his muscles remained frozen. Because, oh god, he was back in his past. He was back in that mean kitchen, his father shouting, his mother screaming and a child that saw too much.

And he wanted to put his hands over his ears and block it all out.

Oh god.

What had he done?

What had he done?

CHAPTER TWELVE

SHE blnked up at him warily, testing her aching jaw. 'I have to get Sam,' she said, wondering why he just sat there like a statue, wondering if that wild look in his eyes signalled that he was still sleeping, still lost in whatever nightmare had possessed him.

'I hit you,' he said at last, his voice a mere rasp, his skin grey in the moonlight.

'You didn't mean to,' she said, climbing to her feet. 'You were asleep. You were tossing and—'

'I hurt you.'

He had, but right now she was more concerned with the hurt in his eyes. With the raw, savage pain she saw there. And with reassuring her son, whose cries were escalating. 'It was an accident. You didn't mean it.'

'I warned you!'

'I have to see to Sam. Excuse me.' She rushed around the bed to the dressing room and her distraught child, his tear streaked face giving licence for her own tears to fall. 'Oh Sam,' she whispered, kissing his tear stained cheek, pushing back the damp hair from his brow and clutching him tightly to her as she rocked him against her body. 'It's all right, baby,' she soothed, trying to believe it. 'It's going to be all right.'

She heard movement outside, things bumping and

drawers being opened, but she dared not look, not until she felt her son's body relax against her, his whimpers slowly steadying. She waited a while, just to be sure, and then she kissed his brow and laid him back down in his cot.

And then she stood there a while longer, looking down at her child, his cheek softly illuminated in the moonlight, while she wondered what to do.

What did you do when your heart was breaking for a man who didn't want family? Who didn't want your love?

What could you do?

'What are you doing?' she asked when she emerged, watching Leo stashing clothes in a bag.

'I can't do this. I can't do this to you.'

'You can't do what to me?'

'I don't want to hurt you.'

'Leo, you were in the midst of a nightmare. I got too close. You didn't know I was there.'

He pulled open another drawer, extracted its contents. 'No. I know who I am. I know what I am. Pack your things, we're leaving.'

'No. I'm not going anywhere. Not before you tell me what's going on.'

'I can't do this,' he said in his frenzied state, 'to you and Sam.'

She sat on the bed and put a hand to her forehead, stunned, while he opened another drawer, threw out more clothes. 'You're not making any sense.'

'It makes perfect sense!'

'No! It makes no sense at all! Why are you doing this? Because of a nightmare, because you accidentally lashed out and struck me?'

He walked stiffly up the bed, his chest heaving. 'Don't you understand, Evelyn, or Eve, or whoever you are, if I can do that to you asleep, how much more damage can I do when I am awake?'

And despite the cold chill in his words, she stood up and faced him, because she knew him well enough by now to know he was wrong. 'You wouldn't hit me.'

'You don't know that!' he cried, 'Nobody can know that,' giving her yet another hint of the anguish assailing him.

And Eve knew what she had to say; knew what she had to do; knew that she had to be brave. She moved closer, slowly, stopping before she reached him, but wanting to be close enough that he could see the truth of her words reflected on her face in the moonlight, close enough that she could pick up his hand and hold it to her chest so that he might feel her heart telling him the same message.

'I know it, because I've been with you Leo. I've spent nights filled with passion in your bed. I've spent days when you made me feel more alive than I have in my entire life. And I've seen the way you pulled my child from the sea when you saw him fall into the surf before I did. I know you would never harm him.'

She shook her head, amazed that she was about to confess something so very, very new; so very, very precious and tender, before she had even time to pull it out and examine it for all its flaws and weaknesses in private herself.

'Don't you see? I know it, Leo, because—' She sucked in air, praying for strength in order to confess her foolishness. Because hadn't he warned her not to get involved? Hadn't he told her enough times nothing could come of their liaison? But how else could she reach him? How else could she make him understand? 'Damn it, I know it because I love you.'

He looked down at her, his bleak eyes filled with some kind of terror before he shut them down, and she wondered what kind of hell she would see when he opened them again.

'Don't say that. You mustn't say that.' His words squeezed through his teeth, a cold, hard stiletto of pain that tore at her psyche, ripping into the fabric of her soul. But while it terrified her, at the same time she felt empowered. After all, what did she have left to lose? She'd already admitted the worst, she'd already laid her cards on the table. There was nothing left but to fight for this fledgling love, to defend it, and to defend her right to it.

'Why can't I say it, when it's the truth? And I know it's futile and pointless but it's there. I love you, Leo. Get used to it.'

'No! Saying I love you doesn't make everything all right. Saying I love you doesn't make it okay to beat someone.'

But he hadn't—

And suddenly a rush of cold drenching fear flooded down her spine along with the realisation that he wasn't talking about what had just taken place in this room. And whatever he had witnessed, it was violent and brutal and had scarred him deeply. 'What happened to you to make you believe yourself capable of these things? What horrors were you subjected to that won't let you rest at night?'

'The nightmares are a warning,' he said. 'A warning not to let this happen, and I won't. Not if it means hurting you and Sam.'

'But Leo—'

'Pack your things,' he said simply, sounding defeated. 'I'm taking you home.'

Melbourne was doing what it knew best, she thought as they touched down, offering up a bit of everything, the runway still damp from the latest shower, a bit of wind to tinker with the wings and liven up the landing and the sun peeping out behind a gilt edged cloud.

But it was so good to be home.

He insisted on driving her—or rather, having his driver drive them—and she wondered why he bothered coming along if he was going to be so glum and morose, unless it was so he could be sure she was gone.

And then they were there. At her house she had until now affectionately referred to as the hovel and never would again, because it was a home, a real home and it was hers and Sam's and filled with love and she was proud of it.

'Let me help you out,' Leo said and she wanted to tell him there was no need, that the driver would help unload and that she could manage, but there were bags and bags and a child seat and a sleeping Sam to carry inside, and it would have been churlish to refuse, and so she let him help.

Except what was she supposed to do with a billionaire in her house?

She had Sam on her hip, heavy with sleep, head lolling and clearly needing his cot while Leo deposited the last of her bags and her car seat, looking around him, looking like the world had suddenly been shrink wrapped and was too small for him. What on earth would he think of her tiny house and eclectic furniture after his posh hotels and private jet?

'Thank you,' she said, her heart heavy, not wanting to say goodbye but not wanting to delay the inevitable as clearly he looked for an exit. 'For everything.'

'It wouldn't work,' he offered, with a thumb to the place he knew he'd hurt her. 'It couldn't.'

She leaned into his touch, trying to hold it for as long as she possibly could, trying to imprint this very last touch on her memory. 'You don't know that,' she said. 'And now you'll never know.'

'There are things—' he started, before shaking his head, his eyes sad. 'It doesn't matter. I know there is no way…'

'You know nothing,' she said, pulling away, stronger now for simply being home, by being back in her own environment, with her own bookshelves and ancient sofa and even her own faded rugs. 'But I do. I know how you'll end up if you walk out that door, if you turn your back on me and my love.

'You'll be like that old man in the picture in your suite, the old man sitting hunched and all alone on the park bench, staring out over the river and wondering whether he should have taken a chance, whether he should have taken that risk rather than playing it safe, rather than ending up all alone.

'You will be that man, Leo.'

He looked at her, his eyes bleak, his jaw set. He lifted a hand, put it one last time to Sam's head.

'Goodbye, Evelyn.'

CHAPTER THIRTEEN

EARLY summer wasn't one whole lot more reliable than spring, Eve reflected, as she looked up at the patchy blue sky, determined to risk the clothes line rather than using the dryer. Any savings on the electricity bill would be welcome. She'd picked up a couple of new clients recently, but things were still tight if she didnt want to dip into her savings.

Although of course, there was always the ring…

She'd taken it off in the plane, meaning to give it back to Leo but she'd forgotten in those gut wrenching final moments and he'd always said it was hers. Every day since then she checked her emails to see if he'd sent her some small message. Every time she found a recorded message, she punched the play button hoping, always hoping.

And after two weeks when he'd made no contact, out of spite or frustration or grief, she'd taken the ring to a jewellery shop to have it valued, staggered when she found out how much it was worth.

She wouldn't have to scrimp if she sold it.

But that had been nearly a month back and she hadn't been able to bring herself to do it.

Six weeks, she thought, as she pegged the first of her sheets to the line. Six weeks since that night in his suite, since that weekend in paradise. No wonder it seemed like a dream.

'Nice day,' called Mrs Willis, from over the fence. 'Reckon it'll rain later though.'

She glanced up at the sky, scowling at an approaching bank of cloud. 'Probably. How's Jack lately?'

'Going okay since they changed his meds. Sister reckons he's on the improve.' Her neighbour looked around. 'Where's Sam?'

'Just gone down for a nap,' Eve said, pegging up another sheet. 'Should be good for a couple of hours work.'

'Oh,' the older woman said. 'Speaking of work, there's someone out the front to see you. Some posh looking bloke in a suit. Fancy car. Says he tried your door, but no answer. I told him I thought you were home though. I told him—'

Something like a lightning bolt surged down her spine. 'What did you say?' But she was already on her way, the sheets snapping in the breeze behind her. She touched a hand to the hair she'd tied back in a rough ponytail, then told herself off for even thinking it. Why did she immediately think it could be him? For all she knew it could be a courier delivery from one of her clients, although since when did courier drivers dress in posh suits and drive flash cars? Her heart tripping at a million miles an hour, nerves flapping and snapping like the sheets on the line, she allowed herself one deep breath, and then she opened the door.

There he stood. Gloriously, absolutely Leo, right there on her doorstep. He looked just as breathtakingly beautiful, his shoulders as broad, his hair so rich and dark and his eyes, his dark eyes looked different, there was sorrow there and pain, and something else swirling in the mix—hope?

And her heart felt it must be ten times its normal size the way it was clamouring around in there. But she'd had hopes before, had thought she'd seen cracks develop in his stone heart, and those hopes had been dashed.

'Leo,' she said breathlessly.

'Eve. You look good.'

She didn't look good. She had circles under her eyes, her hair was a mess and Mrs Willis had been on at her about losing too much weight. 'You look better.' And she winced, because it sounded so lame.

He looked around her legs. 'Where's Sam?'

'Nap time,' she said, and he nodded.

'Can I come in?'

'Oh.' She stood back, let him in. 'Of course.'

He looked just as awkward in her living room. 'I'll make coffee,' she suggested when he grabbed her hand, sending an electrical charge up her arm.

'No. I have to explain something first, Eve, if you will listen. I need you to listen, to understand.'

She nodded, afraid to speak.

He took a deep breath once they were sitting on the sofa, his elbows using his knees for props as he held out his hands. 'I was not happy when I left you. I went to London, threw myself into the contract negotiations there; then to Rome and New York, and nowhere, nowhere could I forget you, nothing I could do, nothing I could achieve could blot out the thoughts of you.

'But I could not come back. I knew it could not work. But there was something I could do.'

She held her breath, her body tingling. Hoping.

'I hadn't seen my parents since I was twelve. I had to find them. It took— It took a little while to track them down, and then it was to discover my father was dead.'

She put a hand to his and he shook his head. 'Don't feel sorry. He was a sailor and a brutal, violent man. Everytime he was on leave he used my mother as a punching bag, calling her all sorts of vicious names, beating her senseless. I used to cower in fear behind my door, praying for it to stop. I was glad he was dead.'

He dragged in air. 'And the worst part of it—the worst of it was that he was always so full of remorse afterwards. Always telling her he was sorry, and that he loved her, even as she lay bruised and bleeding on the floor.'

Eve felt something crawl down her spine. A man who couldn't let himself love. A man who equated love with a beating. No wonder he felt broken inside. No wonder he was so afraid. 'Your poor mother,' she said, thinking, poor you.

He made a sound like a laugh, but utterly tragic. 'Poor mother. I thought so too. Until I was big enough to grow fists and hurt him like he hurt my mother. And my mother went to him. After everything he had done to her, she screamed at me and she went to him to nurse his wounds.' He dropped his head down, wrapped his arms over his head and breathed deep, shaking his head as he rose. 'She would not leave him, even when I begged and pleaded with her. She would not go. So I did. I slept at school. Friends gave me food. I got a job emptying rubbish bins. I begged on the streets. And it was the happiest I'd ever been.'

'Oh, Leo,' she said, thinking of the homeless child, no home to go to, no family...

'I left school a year later, went to work on the boats around the harbour. But I would not be a sailor like him, at that stage I didn't want to be Greek like him. So I learned from the people around me, speaking their languages, and started handling deals for people.

'I was good at it. I could finally make something of myself. But even though I could escape my world, I could not escape my past. I could not escape who I was. The shadow of my father was too big. The knowledge of what I would become…' His voice trailed off. 'I swore I would never let that happen to me. I would never love.'

She slipped a hand into one of his, felt his pain and his sorrow and his grieving. 'I'm so sorry it had to be that way for you. You should have had better.'

'Sam is blessed,' he said, shaking his head. 'Sam has a mother who fights for him like a tigress. His mother is warm and strong and filled with sunshine.' He lifted her hand, pressed it to his lips. 'Not like…'

And his words warmed her heart, even when she knew there was more he had to tell her. 'Did you find her then? Did you find your mother?'

His eyes were empty black, his focus nowhere, but someplace deep inside himself. 'She's in a home for battered women, broken and ill. She sits in a wheelchair all day looking out over a garden. She has nothing now, no-one. And as I looked at her, I remembered the words you said, about an old man sitting on a parkbench, staring at nothing, wishing he'd taking a chance…'

'Leo, I should never have said that. I had no right. I was hurting.'

'But you were right. When I looked at her, I saw my future, and for the first time, I was afraid. I didn't want it. Instead I wanted to take that chance that you offered me, like she should have taken that chance with me and escaped. But my father's shadow still loomed over me.

My greatest fear was turning into him. Hurting you or Sam. I could not bear that.'

'You're not like that,' she said, tears squeezing from her eyes. 'You would never do that.'

'I couldn't trust myself to believe it. Until I was about to leave my mother's side and she told me the truth in her cracked and bitter voice, the truth that would have set me free so many years ago, but I never questioned what I had grown up believing. The truth that my father had come home after six months at sea and found her four months pregnant.'

'Leo!'

His eyes were bright and that tiny kernel of hope she'd seen there while he'd stood on her doorstep had flickered and flared into something much more powerful. 'He was impotent and she wanted a child and I was never his, Eve. I don't have to be that way. I don't have to turn into him.'

Tears blurred her vision, tears for the lost childhood, tears for the betrayal of trust between the parents and the child, the absence of a love that should have been his birthright. 'You would never have turned into him. I know.'

And he brought her hands to his lips and kissed them. 'You do things to me, Eve. You turn me inside out and upside down and I want to be with you, but I just don't know if I can do this. I don't know if I can love the way I should. The way you deserve.'

'Of course you can. It's been there, all along. You knew what was happening was wrong. You tried to save your mother. You tried to save me and Sam by cutting us loose. Because you didn't want to hurt us. You would never have done that if you hadn't cared, if you hadn't loved us, just a little.'

'I think…' He gave her a look that spoke of his confusion and fears. 'I think it's more than a little. These last weeks have been hell. I never want to be apart from you again. I want to wake up every morning and see your face next to mine. I want to take care of you and Sam, if you'll let me.'

She blinked across at him, unable to believe what she was hearing, but so desperately wanting it to be true. 'What are you saying?'

'I can't live without you. I need you.' He squeezed her hands, just as he squeezed the unfamiliar words from his lips. 'I love you.'

And she flew into his arms, big, fat tears of happiness welling in her eyes. 'Oh Leo, I love you so much.'

'Oh my god, that's such a relief,' he said, clutching her tightly. 'I was afraid you would hate me for how I treated you.' He tugged her back, so he could look at her, brushing the hair from her face where it had got mussed. 'Because there's something else I need to know. Eve, will you take a chance on me. Would you consider becoming my wife?'

And her tears became a flood and she didn't care that she was blubbering, didn't care that she was a mess, only that Leo had loved her and wanted to marry her and life just couldn't get any better than that. 'Yes,' she said, her smile feeling like it was a mile wide, 'Yes, of course I will marry you.'

He pulled her into his kiss, a whirlpool of a kiss that spun her senses and sent her spirits and soul soaring.

'Thank you for coming into my life,' he said, drawing back, breathing hard. 'You are magical, Eve. You have brought happiness and hope to a place where there was only misery and darkness. How can I ever repay you?'

And she smiled up at his beautiful face, knowing he would never again live without love, not if she had anything to do with it. 'You can start by kissing me again.'

EPILOGUE

Leo Zamos loved it when a plan came together. He relished the cut and thrust of business, the negotiations, the sometimes compromise, the closing of the deal.

He lived for the adrenaline rush of the chase, and he lived for the buzz of success.

Or at least he had, until now.

These days he had other priorities.

He shook Culshaw's hand, who was still beaming with the honour of walking Eve down the aisle before leaving him chatting to Mrs Willis about the weather. He looked around and found his new bride standing in the raised gazebo where they'd been married a little while ago. She was holding Sam's hand as Hannah jigged him on her hip, the sapphire ring sparkling on her finger nestled alongside a new matching plain band. Evelyn—Eve—he still couldn't decide which he liked best, had always looked more like a goddess than any mere mortal, but today, in her slim fitting lace gown, her hair piled high and curling in tendrils around her face and pinned with a long gossamer thin veil that danced in the warm tropical breeze, she was the queen of goddesses, and she was his. She laughed as her veil was caught in the breeze, the ends tickling Sam's face and making him squeal with delight. And then, as if aware he was watching, as if feeling the tug of his own hungry gaze, she turned her head, turned those brilliant blue eyes on him, her laughter faltering as their eyes connected on so many different levels before her luscious mouth turned up into a wide smile.

And it was physically impossible for his feet not to take the quickest and most direct route through the guests until he was at her side, his arm snaked around her waist pulling her in tight, taking Sam's free hand with the other.

'How is my beautiful new family enjoying today?'

And Sam pulled both hands free and pointed, 'Boat!'

'Sam is beside himself,' Eve said, as Hannah put him down and let him run to the other side of the gazebo to gaze out between the slats at the sailing boat lazily cruising past the bay.

'Culshaw's the same. Asking him to give you away has made his year, I'd say.'

'I like him,' she said, as they watched him animatedly tell Mrs Willis a story. 'He feels like family to me.'

'Canny old devil,' he said as he folded his arms around her. 'Did I tell you what he said when I tried to apologise and tell him that we hadn't really been engaged that weekend in Melbourne? He actually said, "poppycock, everyone knew you were destined to be together",' and Eve laughed.

'Maureen told me the same thing.'

'And they were right,' he said, drawing her back into the circle of his arms, kissing her lightly on the head. 'You are my destiny, Eve, my beautiful wife.'

'Oh,' she said, turning in the circle of his arms. 'Did you hear the Alvarezes' news?'

He frowned, 'I'm not sure I did.'

'Felicity is pregnant. They're both thrilled. I couldn't be happier.'

He nodded. 'That is good news, but at the risk of trying to make you happier, I have a small present for you.'

'But you've already given me so much.'

'This is special. Culshaw's agreed to sell Mina Island. It's yours now, Evelyn.'

'What?' Her eyes shone bright with incredulity. 'It's mine? Really?'

'Yours and Sam's. Everything of mine is now yours, but this is especially for you both. It's a wedding gift and a thank you gift and an I love you gift all rolled into one. And it guarantees you can bring Sam back when he's older any time you want and show him everything he missed out on now.'

'Oh, Leo,' she said, her eyes bright with tears, 'I don't know what to say. It's too much. I have nothing for you.'

He shook his head. 'It's nowhere near enough. It was here that you gave me the greatest gift of all. You gave me back my heart. You taught me how to love. How can I ever repay you for that?'

She cupped his cheek against her palm, her cerulean eyes filled with love, and he took that hand and pressed his lips upon it. 'I love you, Evelyn Zamos.'

'Oh, Leo, I love you so very, very much.'

They were the words he needed to hear, the words that set his newly unlocked heart soaring. He kissed her then, in the white gazebo covered with sweetly scented flowers, kissed her in the perfumed air as the breeze set the palm tree fronds to rustling and the sail boat gracefully cruised by.

'Boat!' yelled Sam to the sound of wobbly footsteps,

suddenly tugging at their legs, pointing out to sea. 'Boat!'

And laughing, Leo scooped the boy up in his arms and they all gazed out over the sapphire blue water to watch the passing vessel. 'How long, do you think,' he whispered to the woman at his side, 'is the perfect age gap between children?'

She looked up at him on a blink. 'I don't know. Some people say two to three years.'

'In that case,' he said, with a chaste kiss to her forehead and a very unchaste look in his eyes, 'I have a plan.'

* * * * *

JUST ONE LAST NIGHT

BY
HELEN BROOKS

Helen Brooks lives in Northamptonshire, and is married with three children and three beautiful grandchildren. As she is a committed Christian, busy housewife, mother and grandma, her spare time is at a premium, but her hobbies include reading, swimming and gardening, and walks with her husband and their two Irish terriers. Her long-cherished aspiration to write became a reality when she put pen to paper on reaching the age of forty and sent the result off to Mills & Boon.

CHAPTER ONE

MELANIE stared at the letter in her hand. The heavy black scrawl danced before her eyes and she had to blink a few times before reading it again, unable to believe what her brain was telling her.

Didn't Forde understand that this was impossible? Absolutely ridiculous? In fact it was so nonsensical she read the letter a third time to convince herself she wasn't dreaming. She had recognised his handwriting as soon as she'd picked the post off the mat and her heart had somersaulted, but she'd imagined he was writing about something to do with their divorce. Instead...

Melanie breathed in deeply, telling herself to calm down.

Instead Forde had written to ask her to consider doing some work for him. Well, not him exactly, she conceded reluctantly. His mother. But it was part and parcel of the same thing. They hadn't spoken in months and then, cool as a cucumber, he wrote out of the blue. Only Forde Masterson could be so spectacularly outrageous. He was unbelievable. Utterly unbelievable.

She threw the letter onto the table and began to open the rest of the post, finishing her toast and coffee as she did so. Her small dining room doubled as her office, an arrangement that had its drawbacks if she wanted to invite friends round for a meal. Not that she had time for a social life anyway. Since leaving Forde a few weeks into the new year, she'd put all her energy into building up the landscape design company she had started twelve months after they'd married, just after—

A shutter shot down in her mind with the inflexibility of solid steel. That time was somewhere she didn't go, had never gone since leaving Forde. It was better that way.

The correspondence dealt with, Melanie finished the last of her first pot of coffee of the day and went upstairs to her tiny bathroom to shower and get dressed before she rang James, her very able assistant, to go through what was required that day. James was a great employee inasmuch as he was full of enthusiasm and a tirelessly hard worker, but with his big-muscled body and dark good looks he attracted women like bees to a honeypot. He often turned up in the morning looking a little the worse for wear. However, it never affected his work and Melanie had no complaints.

Clad in her working clothes of denim jeans and a vest top, Melanie looped her thick, shoulder-length ash-blonde hair into a ponytail and applied plenty of sunscreen to her pale, easily burned English skin. The country was currently enjoying a heatwave and the August day was already hot at eight in the morning.

Before going downstairs again, she flung open her bedroom window and let the rich scent of the climbing roses outside fill the room. The cottage was tiny—just her bedroom and a separate bathroom upstairs, and a pocket-size sitting room and the dining room downstairs, the latter opening into a new extension housing a kitchen overlooking the minute courtyard garden. But Melanie loved it. The courtyard's dry stone walls were hidden beneath climbing roses and honeysuckle, which covered the walls at the back of the cottage too, and the paved area that housed her small bistro table and two chairs was a blaze of colour from the flowering pots surrounding its perimeter. In the evenings it was bliss to eat her evening meal out there in the warm, soft air with just the twittering of the birds and odd bee or butterfly for company. It wasn't too extreme to say this little cottage had saved her sanity in the first crucifyingly painful days after she'd fled the palatial home she'd shared with Forde.

The cottage was one in the middle of a terrace of ten, all occupied by couples or single folk and half of them—like the ones either side of Melanie—used as weekend bolt-holes by London high-flyers who retreated to the more gentle pace of life south-west of the capital, where the villages and towns still retained an olde-worlde charm. It was also sixty miles or so distant from Forde's house in Kingston upon Thames, sufficient mileage, Melanie had felt, to avoid the prospect of running into him by chance.

She had wondered if her fledgling business would survive when she'd moved, but in actual fact it had thrived so well she had been able to take on James within a month or two of leaving the city. The nature of the work had changed a little; when she had been based in Kingston upon Thames she'd been involved with the layout of housing areas with play facilities and general urban regeneration. Now it was mostly public and private garden work, along with forest landscaping and land reclamation. Some of the time she and James worked with members of a team that could include architects, planners, civil engineers and quantity surveyors depending upon what the job involved. On other projects they worked in isolation on private gardens or country estates. Inevitably office work was part of the deal, along with site visits and checking progress of work where other bodies were involved.

Becoming aware she was in danger of daydreaming, Melanie turned away from the window, her mind jumping into gear and detailing what the day involved.

James was due to oversee the bulldozing of a number of ancient pigsties, which the client wanted transformed into a wild flower garden, being concerned about the loss of natural habitats in the countryside in general and in the surrounding area of the old farmhouse he'd bought in particular. Melanie had suggested a meadow effect, created with a profusion of wild flowers growing in turf on soil that was low in fertility, the mowing regime of which had to allow the flowers to seed before being cut.

In stark contrast, she was off to put the finishing touches to a formal garden she and James had been working on for three weeks. It was a place of calm order, expressed in a carefully balanced treatment of space and symmetry, the details of which had been all-important. The retired bank manager and his wife who had purchased the property recently in the midst of a small country town had been delighted with her initial plan of a neat lawn and matching paved areas at either end of the grass, clipped bushes and trained plants—along with fruit trees in restricted shapes—providing a gentle approach to the precise layout they'd first requested.

She loved her job. Melanie breathed a silent prayer of thankfulness. Devising a personal creation for each individual client was so satisfying, along with reconciling their ideas with the practical potential of the available plot. Not that this was always easy, especially if a client had seen their 'perfect' garden in a magazine or brochure, which inevitably was bigger or smaller than the space they had available. But then that was part of the challenge and fun.

Half smiling to herself as her mind skimmed over several such past clients, Melanie made her way downstairs, pausing at the door to the dining room. It was only then she acknowledged that since reading Forde's letter, every single word had been burning in her brain.

Dear Melanie,
I'm writing to ask a favour, not for myself but for Isabelle.

Typical Forde, she thought darkly, her heart thudding as she glanced at the letter lying on the table. No 'how are you?' or any other such social nicety. Just straight to the point.

She hasn't been too well lately and the garden at Hillview is too much for her, not that she would ever admit it. The whole thing needs complete changing with an emphasis on low maintenance now she's nearly eighty. The trouble is she won't even allow a gardener onto the premises so I've

no chance of persuading her to let strangers do
an overhaul. But she'd trust you. Think about it,
would you? And ring me.
Forde

Think about it! Melanie shook her head. She didn't
have to think about it to know what she was going to
do, and there was no way she was going to ring Forde
either. She had insisted on no contact between them
and that still held.

Walking over to the table, she picked up the piece
of paper and the envelope and ripped them into small
pieces, throwing the fragments into the bin. There.
Finished with. She had enough to do today without
thinking about Forde and his ridiculous request.

She stood for a moment more, staring into space.
What did he mean when he'd said Isabelle hadn't been
well? She pictured Forde's sweet-faced mother in her
mind as her heart lurched. It had been almost as bad
walking out of Isabelle's life as that of her son all those
months ago, but she had known all threads holding her
to Forde had to be severed if she had any chance of
making it. She'd written a brief note to her mother-in-
law, making it clear she didn't expect Isabelle to understand but that she'd had good reasons for doing what
she'd done and that it hadn't altered the genuine love
and respect she had for the older woman. She had asked
Isabelle not to reply. When she had, Melanie had returned the letter unopened. It had torn her in two to
do it, but she hadn't doubted it was the right decision.
She wouldn't put Isabelle in the position of piggy-in-
the-middle. Isabelle adored Forde, an only child, and

mother and son were closer than most, Forde's father having died when Forde was in his late teens.

Her mobile ringing brought her out of her reverie. It was James. There had been a bad accident just in front of him and he was stuck in a traffic jam that went back for miles so he was going to be late getting to the site. Was it possible she could go there and detail to the workmen exactly what needed to be done and get them started before she went on to her own job? They had the plan of work on paper but there was nothing like face-to-face instructions…

Melanie agreed. After a disaster on an early job when a perfectly sound conservatory had been demolished and the old ramshackle greenhouse had been left intact, she didn't trust workmen to take the time to read plans, and this was something she'd drummed into James from the start.

Sighing, she mentally revised her morning, decided to leave straight away rather than see to a pile of paper-work she'd hoped to sort out before she left the house, and within a few minutes was travelling towards the farmhouse in her old pickup truck. It was going to be a hectic day but that was good—if nothing else, of neces-sity she wouldn't have time to think about Forde's letter.

It *was* a hectic day. Melanie arrived home in deep twi-light but with a big, fat cheque in her pocket from the re-tired couple who had been thrilled how their garden had come together. After sliding the truck into the parking space reserved for her in the square cobbled yard at one side of the row of cottages, she walked along the narrow pathway that led off the yard and along the back of the cottages, pausing at the small doorway in the long, ivy-festooned wall that led into her tiny garden. Unlocking the door, she stepped into her small haven of peace, breathing in the delicious perfume of the roses adorning the walls. She was home, and she wanted nothing more than a long, hot bath to relax her aching muscles. She had been determined to finish the job on schedule today and hadn't even stopped for a bite of lunch.

Locking the garden door, she entered the house through the kitchen as she did most days, slipping off the thick walking boots she wore on a job and leaving them on the cork mat ready for morning. Barefoot, she padded upstairs, flinging open the bathroom window so the scents of the garden could fill the room, and began to run the bath before going into the bedroom and divesting herself of her clothes.

Two minutes later she was lying in hot, soapy bubbles gazing up at a charcoal sky in which the first stars were peeping. Not for the first time she blessed the fact that the developers who had renovated the string of cottages had had soul. In placing the big, cast-iron bath under the window as they had, it meant the occupier could lie and see an ever-changing picture in the heavens through the clear glass they'd installed. Melanie never closed the blinds until she was ready to get out of the bath and on occasions like tonight, when she was tired and aching, it was bliss to lie in the dark and think of nothing. Although tonight the carefully cultivated trick of emptying her mind and totally relaxing wasn't working…

Melanie frowned, acknowledging Forde had persistently been battering at the door to her consciousness all day, however much she had tried to ignore him. And she had tried. How she'd tried. She didn't *want* any contact with him, however remote. She didn't *want* to have him invading her mind and unsettling her. He, and Isabelle too, for that matter, were the past, there was no place for them in the present and less still in the future. This was a matter of self-survival.

She heard the telephone ring downstairs but let the answer machine take a message. Forcing her tight muscles to relax, limb by limb, she slid further into the silky water, shutting her eyes. After a few minutes her mobile began playing its little tune from the pocket of her working jeans in the bedroom. It was probably James, reporting how his day had gone, but she made no attempt to find out. This was *her* time, she told herself militantly. The rest of the world could take a hike for a while.

It was another half an hour before she climbed out of the bath, and the house phone had taken another two messages by then. After washing her hair and swathing it on top of her head with a small fluffy towel, she slipped on her bathrobe. Her stomach was reminding her she hadn't eaten since the two slices of toast at breakfast, and, deciding food was a priority, she didn't bother to get dressed, making her way downstairs just as she was.

She had reached the bottom step and her tiny square of hall when a sharp knock at the front door caused Melanie to nearly jump out of her skin.

What now? She shut her eyes for an infinitesimal moment. It could only be James reporting some disaster or other after he'd been unable to reach her by phone. And that was fine, she was his boss after all, but she really had wanted to simply crash tonight. It was clearly too much to ask.

Wiping her face clear of all irritation and stitching a smile in place, she tightened the belt of her bathrobe and then opened the door.

The six-foot-four, ruggedly handsome male standing on her doorstep wasn't James.

A bolt of shock shot through her and then she froze.

'Hi.' Forde didn't smile. 'Am I interrupting something?'

'What?' She gazed at him stupidly. He looked wonderful. White shirt, black jeans, a muscled tower of brooding masculinity.

The silver-blue eyes with their thick, short, black lashes flicked to her bathrobe and then back to her stunned face. 'Are you...entertaining?'

As the full import behind his words hit, hot colour surged beneath her high cheekbones along with a reviving dose of adrenaline into her body. Her expression becoming icy, she said slowly, 'What did you say?'

Forde relaxed slightly. OK, so he'd got that wrong, then. But he had been waiting all day for a response to his letter, which had never come, and after ringing several times tonight he'd decided to see if she was ignoring him or wasn't home. There had been lights on—*upstairs*—and then she'd come to the door flustered and dressed like that, or rather *un*dressed like that. What was he supposed to think? 'I wondered if you had visitors,' he said carefully, getting ready to use his shoulder on the door if she tried to slam it in his face. 'You weren't answering the phone.'

'I was late home from work and then I had a bath—' She stopped abruptly. 'What am I explaining to you for?' she added furiously. 'And how dare you suggest I had a man here?'

'It was the obvious answer,' said Forde.

'To you, maybe, but you shouldn't judge everyone by your own standards.' She glared at him angrily.

'I'm suitably crushed.'

His mocking air was the last straw. Forde had always been the only person in the whole world who could make her so mad the cool façade she hid behind normally melted in the heat. Having been brought up in a succession of foster homes, she had learnt early on to keep her feelings hidden, but that had never worked with Forde. 'Will you please leave?' she said tightly, trying to close the door and finding his shoulder was in the way.

'Did you get my letter?' In contrast to her fury he appeared calm and composed, even relaxed. That rankled as much as his outrageous assumption she'd had a man in her bed.

Melanie nodded, giving up the struggle to close the door.

'And?' he pressed with silky smoothness.

'And what?'

He studied her with the silvery gaze that seemed to have the power to look straight into her soul. 'Don't pretend you don't care.'

For a moment she thought he was referring to him and then realised he was talking about her concern for his mother. She blinked, the anger draining away. Quietly, she said, 'How is Isabelle?'

He shrugged. 'As stubborn as a mule, as always.'

Melanie could almost have smiled. Forde's mother was a softer, more feminine version of her strong-willed, inflexible son but every bit as determined. But Isabelle had always been wonderfully supportive and loving to her, the mother she'd always longed for but never had. The thought was weakening, intensifying the ever-present ache in her heart. To combat it her voice was flat and without emotion when she said, 'You said she'd been unwell?'

'She fell and broke her hip in that damn garden of hers and then there were complications with her heart during surgery.'

Melanie's dark brown eyes opened wide. When he'd said in his letter Isabelle had been unwell she'd imagined Forde's mother had had the flu, something like that. But an operation… Isabelle could have died and she wouldn't have known. Her heart thudding, she murmured, 'I— I'm sorry.'

'Not as sorry as I am,' Forde said grimly. 'She won't do as she's told and seems hell-bent on putting herself back in hospital, refusing to come and stay with me or take it easy in a convalescent home somewhere. She was determined to return home as soon as she was discharged and against medical advice, I might add. The only concession she'd make was to let me hire a live-in nurse until she's mobile again, and that was under protest. She's impossible.'

Melanie stared at him. Forde would be exactly the same in those circumstances. He was impossible at the best of times. And easily the sexiest man on the planet.

The last thought caused her to pull the belt of her robe tighter. *Don't let him see how him being here is affecting you,* she told herself silently. *You know it's over. Be strong.* 'I'm sorry,' she said again, 'but you must see me doing any work for your mother is ridiculous, Forde. We're in the middle of a divorce.'

'*We* are. That shouldn't affect your relationship with Isabelle, surely? She was very hurt when you returned her letter unread, by the way,' he added softly.

Unfair. Below the belt. But that was Forde all over. 'It was for the best.'

'Really?' He considered her thoughtfully. 'For whom?'

'Forde, I'm not about to stand here bandying words with you.' She shivered involuntarily although the night air was warm and humid.

'You're cold.' He pushed the door fully open, causing her to instinctively step back into the hall. 'Let's discuss this inside.'

'*Excuse me?*' She recovered her wits enough to bar his way. 'I don't remember inviting you in.'

'Melanie, we've been married for two years and unless you've put on a pretty good act in all that time, you are fond of my mother. I'm asking for your help for her sake, OK? Are you really going to refuse?'

Two years, four months and five days, to be precise. And the first eleven months had been heaven on earth. After that... 'Please go,' she said weakly, much more weakly than she would have liked. 'Our solicitors wouldn't like this.'

'Damn the solicitors.' He took her arm, moving her aside as he stepped into the hall and shut the door behind him. 'Parasites, the lot of them. I need to talk to you, that's the important thing.'

He was close, so close the familiar delicious smell and feel of him were all around her, invoking memories that were seductively intimate. They brought a sheen of heat to her skin, her heartbeat speeding up and beginning to rocket in her chest. Forde was the only man she'd ever loved, and even now his power over her was mesmerising. 'Please leave,' she said firmly.

'Look,' he murmured softly, 'make some coffee and listen to me, Nell, OK? That's all I'm asking. For Isabelle's sake.'

He wasn't touching her now but her whole being was twisting in pain. Nevertheless, the harsh discipline she'd learnt as a child held good, enabling her to control the flood of emotion his old nickname for her had induced and say, a little shakily admittedly, 'This isn't a good idea, Forde.'

'On the contrary, it's an excellent idea.'

She looked at him, big and dark in her little hall, his black hair falling over his brow, and knew he wasn't going to take no for an answer. And considering he was six-feet-four of lean, honed muscle and she was a slender five-seven, she could scarcely manhandle him out of the house. She turned, saying over her shoulder, 'It doesn't seem I've much option, does it?' as she led the way into her pocket-size sitting room.

Forde followed her, secretly amazed he'd been allowed admittance without more of a fight. But, hey, he thought. Go with the flow. The first battle was over but the war was far from won.

His gaze moved swiftly over the small room, which had Melanie's stamp all over it, from the two plumpy cream sofas and matching drapes and the thick, coffee-coloured carpet, to the old but charmingly restored Victorian fireplace, which had a pile of logs stacked against it. Very stylish but definitely cosy. Modern but not glaringly so. And giving nothing of herself away. A beautiful mirror stretched across the far wall making the room appear larger, but not one picture or photograph to be seen. Nothing personal.

'Sit down and I'll get the coffee.' She waved to one of the sofas before leaving, shaking her hair free of the towel as she went.

Forde didn't take the invitation. Instead he followed her into the hall and through to the kitchen-diner. This was more lived in, the table scattered with files and papers and the draining board in the tiny kitchen holding a few plates and dishes. He dared bet she spent most of the time at home working.

Melanie had turned as he'd entered and now she followed his glance, saying quickly, 'I didn't have time to wash up this morning before I left and I was too tired last night.'

Forde pulled up one of the dining chairs, sitting astride it with his arms draped over the back as he said easily, 'You don't have to apologise to me.'

'I wasn't. I was explaining.'

It was curt and he mentally acknowledged the tone. Ignoring the hostility, he smiled. 'Nice little place you've got here.'

Her eyes met his and he could see she was deciding whether he was being genuine or not. He saw her shoulders relax slightly and knew she'd taken his observation the way it had been meant.

'Thank you,' she said quietly. 'I like it.'

'Janet sends her regards, by the way.'

Janet was Forde's very able cook and cleaner who came in for a few hours each day to wash and iron, keep the house clean and prepare the evening meal. She was a merry little soul, in spite of having a husband who had never done a day's honest work in his life and three teenage children who ate her out of house and home. Melanie had liked her very much. Janet had been with her on the day of the accident and had sat and held her until the ambulance had arrived—

She brought her thoughts to a snapping halt. *Don't think of that. Not now.* Woodenly, she said, 'Tell her hello from me.' Drawing in a deep breath and feeling she needed something stronger than coffee to get through the next little while, she opened the fridge. 'There's some wine chilled if you'd prefer a glass to coffee?'

'Great. Thanks.' He rose as he spoke, walking and opening the back door leading onto the shadowed court-yard. 'This is nice. Shall we drink out here?'

She was trying very, very hard to ignore the fact she was stark naked under the robe but it was hard with her body responding to him the way it always did. He'd always only had to look at her for her blood to sing in her veins and her whole being melt. Forde was one of those men who had a natural magnetism that oozed masculinity; it was in his walk, his smile, every move he made. The height and breadth of him were impressive, and she knew full well there wasn't an ounce of fat on the lean, muscled body, but it was his face—too rugged to be pretty-boy handsome but breathtakingly attractive, nonetheless—that drew any woman from sixteen to ninety. Hard and strong, with sharply defined planes and angles unsoftened by his jet-black hair and piercing silvery eyes, his face was sexy and cynical, and his slightly crooked mouth added to his charm.

Dynamite. That was what one of her friends had called him when they'd first begun dating, and she'd been right. But dynamite was powerful and dangerous, she told herself ruefully, taking the opportunity to run her hands through the thick silk of her hair and bring it into some kind of order.

When she stepped into the scented shadows with two glasses and the bottle of wine, Forde was already sitting at the bistro table, his long legs spread out in front of him and his head tilted back as he looked up at the riot of climbing roses covering the back of the house. They, together with the fragrant border plants in the pots, perfumed the still warm air with a sweet heaviness. Another month or so and the weather would begin to cool and the first chill of autumn make itself felt.

It had been snowing that day when she'd left Forde. Seven months had passed. Seven months without Forde in her life, in her bed…

She sat down carefully after placing the glasses on the table, pulling the folds of the robe round her legs and wishing she'd taken the time to nip upstairs and get dressed. But that would have looked as though she expected him to stay and she wanted him to leave as soon as possible.

The thought mocked her and she had to force her eyes not to feast on him. She had been aching to see him again; he'd filled her dreams every night since the split and sometimes she had spent hours sitting out here in the darkness while the rest of the world was asleep after a particularly erotic fantasy that had left her unable to sleep again.

'How are you?' His rich, smoky voice brought her eyes to his dark face.

She reached for her glass and took a long swallow before she said, 'Fine. And you?'

'Great, just great.' His voice dripped sarcasm. 'My wife walks out on me citing irreconcilable differences and then threatens to get a restraining order when I attempt to make her see reason over the next weeks—'

'You were phoning umpteen times a day and turning up everywhere,' she interrupted stiffly. 'It was obsessional.'

'What did you expect? I know things changed after the accident but—'

'Don't.' This time she cut him short by jumping to her feet, her eyes wild. 'I don't want to discuss this, Forde. If that's why you've come, you can leave now.'

'Damn it, Nell.' He raked his hand through his hair, taking a visibly deep breath as he struggled to control his emotions. A few screamingly tense moments ticked by and then his voice came, cool and calm. 'Sit down and drink your wine. I came here to discuss you taking on the garden at Hillview and making it easy for my mother to manage it. That's all.'

'I think it's better you go.'

'Tough.' He eyed her sardonically, his mouth twisting.

Her nostrils flared. 'You really are the most arrogant man on the planet.' And unfortunately the most attractive.

Forde shrugged. 'I can live with that—it's a small planet.' He took a swallow of wine. 'Sit down,' he said again, 'and stop behaving like a Victorian heroine in a bad movie. Let me explain how things stand with

Mother at present before you decide one way or the other, OK?'

She sat, not because she wanted to but because there was really nothing else she could do.

'Along with her damaged hip she's got a heart problem, Nell, but the main problem is Isabelle herself. I actually caught her trying to prune back some bush or other a couple of days ago. She'd sneaked out of the house when the nurse was busy. I've offered to get her a gardener or do the work myself but she won't have it, although under pressure she admits it's getting overgrown and that upsets her. When I suggested it needs landscaping she reluctantly agreed and then flatly refused to have what she called clod-hopping strangers tramping everywhere. You can bet your boots once the nurse is no longer needed in a couple of weeks she'll be out there doing goodness knows what. I shall arrive one day and find her collapsed or worse. There's nearly an acre of ground all told, as you know—it's too much for her.'

He was really worried; she could see that. Melanie stared at him, biting her lip. And she knew how passionate Isabelle was about her garden; when she had still been with Forde she and his mother had spent hours working together in the beautiful grounds surrounding the old house. But what had been relatively easy for Isabelle to manage thirty, twenty, even ten years ago, was a different story now. But Isabelle would pine and lose hope if she couldn't get out in her garden. What needed to be done was a totally new plan for the grounds with an emphasis on low maintenance, but even then, if they were to keep the mature trees Isabelle loved so dearly, Forde's mother would have to agree to a gardener coming in at certain times of the year to deal with the falling leaves and other debris. And she really couldn't see Isabelle agreeing to that, unless...

Thinking out loud, she said slowly, 'I'd obviously need to make a proper assessment of the site, but looking to the future, James, the young man who works for me, is very personable. All the old ladies love him.' The young ones as well. 'If Isabelle got to know him, perhaps she'd agree to him coming in for a day or two once a month to maintain the new garden, which I'd design with a view to minimum upkeep.'

Forde shifted in his seat. 'You'll do it, then?' he said softly. 'You'll take on the job?'

Melanie brought her eyes to his face. There was something in his gaze that reminded her—as if she didn't know—that she was playing with fire. Quickly, a veil slid over her own expression. 'On certain conditions.'

One black eyebrow quirked. 'I might have guessed. Nothing is straightforward with you. OK, so what are these conditions? Nothing too onerous, I trust?'

It was too intimate—the hushed surroundings enclosing them in their own tiny world, the perfumed air washing over her senses, Forde's big male body just inches away, and—not least—her nakedness under the robe. This sort of situation was exactly what she'd strived to avoid by not seeing him over the last torturous months. She really shouldn't have let him in.

She gulped down the last of her wine and poured another for Dutch courage. Forde's glass was half-full but he put his hand over the rim when she went to top it up. 'Driving,' he said shortly, settling back in his seat and crossing one leg over the other knee. 'Spell out your demands,' he added, when she still didn't speak. 'Don't be shy.'

The sarcasm helped, stiffening her backbone and her resolve, but she still felt as though she was standing on the edge of a precipice. One false move and she'd be lost.

'But before you do…' He moved swiftly, taking her hand before she had time to pull away and holding it fast in his own strong fingers as he leaned across the table. 'Do you still love me, Nell?'

CHAPTER TWO

IT WAS so typical Forde Masterson! She should have been expecting it, should have been aware he'd take her off guard sooner or later. His ruthless streak had taken the fledgling property-developing business he'd started in his bedroom at the family home when he was eighteen years old, using an inheritance left to him by his grandmother, into a multimillion-pound enterprise in just sixteen years. His friends called him inexorable, single-minded, immovable; his enemies had a whole host of other names, but even they had to admit they'd rather deal with Forde than some of the sharks in the property-developing game. He could be merciless when the occasion warranted it but his word was his bond, and that was increasingly rare in the cut and thrust of business.

Melanie stared into the dark, handsome face just inches from hers. His eyes shone mother-of-pearl in the dim light, their expression inscrutable. Somehow she managed to say, 'I told you I'm not discussing us, Forde.'

'I didn't ask for a discussion. A simple yes or no would suffice.' Black eyebrows rose mockingly.

She moved her head, allowing the pale curtain of her hair to swing forward, hiding her face as she jerked her hand free. 'This is pointless. It's over—*we're* over. Accept it and move on. I have.' *Liar*.

'You still haven't answered my question.'

'I don't have to.' In an effort to control the trembling deep inside she reached out her hand and picked up her glass of wine, taking several long sips and praying her hand wouldn't shake. 'This is *my* house, remember? I make the rules.'

'The trouble is, you never did believe in happy endings, did you, Nell?' Forde said softly.

Her head jerked up as his words hit home and then he watched a shutter click down over her expression. She had always been able to do that, mask what she was thinking and adopt a distant air, but nine times out of ten he'd broken through the defence mechanism she used to keep people at bay. He knew her childhood had been tough; orphaned at the age of three, she couldn't remember her parents. Her maternal grandmother had taken her in initially but when she, too, had tragically died a year later, none of Melanie's other relations had stepped up to the mark. One foster home after another had ensued and Melanie admitted herself she'd been a troubled little girl and quite a handful. When he had fallen in love with her he had wanted to make that all better. He still wanted to. The only obstacle was Melanie herself, and it was one hell of an obstacle.

'From the first day we met you were waiting for us to fall apart,' he continued in the same quiet tone. 'Waiting for it to all go wrong. I didn't realise that until recently. I don't know why. There were enough indicators early on.'

She spoke through clenched teeth. 'I don't know what you are talking about.'

He studied her thoughtfully as she finished her second glass of wine. Her voice and body language belied her blank face. Underneath that formidable barrier she presented, that of a capable, strong businesswoman and woman of the world, Melanie was scared. Of him. He had acknowledged it at the same time he'd come to the conclusion she had never believed they'd make old bones together. She had loved and trusted him, he knew that, but he also knew now that those feelings had made her feel vulnerable and frightened. She had been on her own emotionally all her life before they'd met—twenty-five years—and that tough shell had been hard to break, but he'd done it. She had let him in. But not far enough, or they wouldn't be in this mess right now.

Following through on his thoughts, he said, 'I blamed myself at first after the accident, you know—for the distance between us, for the way every conversation fragmented or turned into a row. Stupid, but I didn't understand you'd made the decision to shut me out and nothing short of a nuclear explosion could have changed things.'

She didn't say a word. In fact she could have been carved in stone. A beautiful stone statue without feelings or emotion.

'The accident—'

'Stop talking about the *accident*,' she said woodenly. Although she had been the one to insist they called it that. 'It was a miscarriage. I was stupid enough to fall downstairs and I killed our son.'

'Nell—'

'No.' She held up her hand, palm facing him. 'Let's face facts here. That is what happened, Forde. He was born too early and they couldn't save him. Another few weeks and it might have been all right, but at twenty-two weeks he didn't stand a chance. I was supposed to nurture him and keep him safe and I failed him.'

In one way he was glad she was talking about it; she'd refused to in the past, locking her emotions away from him and everyone else. In another sense he was appalled at the way even now, over sixteen months later, she was totally blaming herself. She had been a little light-headed that morning and had stayed in bed late after he'd left for work, Janet having brought her up a breakfast tray some time around ten o'clock. At half-past ten Janet had heard a terrible scream and a crash and rushed from the kitchen into the hall, to find Melanie lying twisted and partially conscious at the foot of the stairs, the contents of the tray scattered about her.

It had been an accident. Tragic, devastating, but an accident nonetheless, but from the time their son had been stillborn some hours later Melanie had retreated into herself. He hadn't been able to comfort her, in fact she'd barely let him near her and at times he was sure she'd hated him, probably because he was a reminder of all they'd lost. And so they'd struggled on month after miserable month, Melanie burying herself in the business she'd started and working all hours until he was lucky if he saw her for more than an hour each night, and he— Forde's mouth set grimly. He'd been in hell. He was still in hell, come to it.

He wanted to say, 'Accidents happen,' but that was too trite in the circumstances. Instead he stood up, drawing her stiff, unyielding body into his arms. 'You would have given your life for his if you could have,' he said softly. 'No one holds you responsible for what happened, Nell, don't you see?'

Melanie drew in a shuddering breath. 'Please go now.'

She felt brittle in his grasp; she was too thin, much too thin, and even as he held her she swayed slightly as though she was going to pass out. 'What's the matter?' He stared into her white face. 'Are you unwell?'

She looked at him, her eyes focusing, and he realised she was holding onto him for support. 'I—I think I must be a little tipsy,' she murmured dazedly. 'I missed lunch and I haven't eaten yet, and two glasses of wine...'

Hence the reason she'd spoken about the miscarriage, but, hell, if he needed to keep her in a permanent state of intoxication to break through that iron shield, he would. He gentled his voice when he said, 'Come indoors, I'll get you something.'

'No, I can manage. I— I'll ring you.'

There was no way on earth he was walking out of here right now, not when they were talking—properly talking—for the first time since Matthew's death. For a second a bolt of pain shot through him as he remembered his son, so tiny and so perfect, and then he controlled himself. He said nothing as he led her into the house and when he pushed her down on one of the dining room chairs and walked into the kitchen, she made no protest. He rifled the fridge before turning to face her. 'OK, I can make a fairly passable cheese omelette—' He stopped abruptly. Tears were washing down her face.

With a muttered oath he reached her side, lifting her against him and holding her close as he murmured all the things he'd been wanting to say for months. That he loved her, that she was everything to him, that life was nothing without her and that the accident hadn't been her fault…

Melanie clung to him, all defences down, drinking in the strength, the hard maleness, the familiar smell of him and needing him as she'd never needed him before. She had never loved anyone else and she knew she never would; Forde was all she had ever wanted and more. At the back of her mind she knew there was a reason she should draw away but it was melting in the wonder of being in his arms, of feeling and touching him after all the months apart.

'Kiss me.' Her voice was a whisper as she raised her head and looked into his hard, handsome face. 'Show me you love me.'

He lowered his mouth to hers, brushing her lips in a tender, feather-light kiss, but as she blatantly asked for more by kissing him back passionately, her mouth opening to him, the tempo changed.

She heard him groan, felt all restraint go and then he was kissing her like a drowning man, ravaging her mouth in an agony of need. When he whisked her off her feet, holding her close to his chest, his mouth not leaving hers, she lay supine, no thought of escape in her head.

Their lovemaking had always been the stuff dreams were made of and she'd been without him for so long, she thought dizzily. She needed to taste him again, experience his hands and mouth on her body, feel him inside her…

She was barely aware of Forde carrying her up the stairs but then she was lying on the scented linen of her bed and he was beside her, the darkness broken only by the faint light from the window. He continued to kiss her as he tore off his clothes in frantic haste, caressing the side of her neck, the hollow under her ear with his burning lips before taking her mouth again in a searing kiss that made her moan with need of him.

Her robe had come undone and now he slipped it off her completely, his voice almost a growl as he murmured, 'My beautiful one, my incomparable love...'

There was no coherent thought in her head, just a longing to be closer still, and the fierceness of his desire matched hers. They touched and tasted with a sweet violence that had them both writhing and twisting as though they would consume each other, and when he plunged inside her she called out his name as her body convulsed in tune with his. Their release was as fierce and tumultuous as their lovemaking, wave after wave of unbearable pleasure sending them over the edge into a world of pure sensation, where there was no past and no future, just the blinding light and heat of the present.

Forde continued to hold her as the frantic pounding of their hearts quietened, murmuring intimate words of love as their breathing steadied. Her eyes closed, she settled herself more comfortably in the circle of his arms as she'd done so many times in the past after a night of loving, her thick brown lashes feathering the delicate skin under her eyes as she sighed softly. Within moments she was fast asleep, a sleep of utter exhaustion.

Forde's eyes had accustomed to the deep shadows and now he lifted himself on one elbow, his gaze drinking in each feature of her face. Her skin was pure milk and roses, her eyelids fragile ovals of ivory under fine, curving brows and her lips full and sensuous. He carefully stroked a strand of silky blonde hair from her brow, unable to believe that what had happened in the last hour was real.

He had had women before he'd met Melanie, and when he'd first seen her at a mutual friend's wedding he'd thought all he wanted to do was possess her like the others, enjoy a no-strings affair for as long as it lasted. By the end of their first date he'd fallen deeply in love and found himself in a place he'd never been before. They had married three months later on her twenty-sixth birthday and taken a long honeymoon in the Caribbean, which had been a magical step out of time.

His body hardened as he remembered the nights spent wrapped in each other's arms. For the first time he'd understood the difference between sex and making love, and he'd known he never wanted to be without this woman again for a moment of time.

They had returned to England where Melanie had spent the next little while giving his house in Kingston upon Thames a complete makeover to turn it into their home, rather than the very masculine bachelor residence he'd inhabited. She had given up her job working for a garden contractor when they'd got married; Melanie had wanted to try for a baby straight away and whatever she'd wanted was fine with him. He knew her history, the fact she'd never had a family home or people to call her own, and had understood how much she wanted her own children, little people who were a product of their love.

He frowned in the darkness, still studying her sleeping face. What he *hadn't* understood, not then, was that her haste to start a family was motivated more by fear than anything else. She'd been like a deprived child in a sweet shop cramming its mouth with everything in sight because it was terrified it would soon find itself locked outside once again in the cold.

And then the miscarriage happened.

He groaned in his soul, shutting his eyes for a moment against the blackness of that time.

And everything had changed. Melanie had changed. He felt he'd lost his wife as well as his child that day. He hadn't doubted at first that he would get through to her, loving her as he did, but as weeks and then months had gone by and the wall she'd erected between them had been impenetrable he'd begun to wonder. When he had returned home one night and found her gone— clothes, shoes, toiletries, every personal possession she had—and read the note she'd left stating she wanted a divorce, it almost hadn't come as a surprise.

He had been so angry that night. Angry that she could leave him when he knew nothing on earth could have made him leave her. And bereft, desperate, frantic with fear for her.

Melanie stirred slightly before curling even closer, her head on his chest and her hair fanning her face. His arms tightened round her; she seemed so small, so fragile, so young, but in part that was deceptive. She had walked away from him and made a new life for herself over the last months, managing perfectly well without him. Whereas he… He had been merely existing.

He hadn't expected this tonight. Hell, the understatement of the year, he thought wryly. Would she regret it in the morning? His chin nuzzled the silk of her hair.

He'd have to make damn sure she didn't, he told himself grimly. He had told her, in one of their furious rows after she had first left him when she had been staying with friends, that he would never let her go, and he meant it. But he'd also seen then that she was at the end of her tether, mentally, physically and emotionally. So he'd drawn back, given her space. But enough was enough. Tonight had proved she still wanted him physically however she felt about their marriage, and that was a start.

He lay perfectly still in the darkness while Melanie slept, the acutely intelligent and astute mind that had taken him from relative obscurity to fabulous wealth in just a few short years dissecting every word, every gesture, every embrace, every kiss they'd shared. When the sky began to lighten outside the window he was still awake, only finally drifting off after the birds had finished the dawn chorus, Melanie still held close to his heart.

CHAPTER THREE

THE sun was well and truly up when Melanie's eyes eased open after the first solid night's sleep she'd had since leaving Forde. She had slept so deeply that for a moment she was only semiconscious, and then memories of the previous night slammed into her mind at the same time as she became aware that she was curled into the source of her contentment.

Forde.

Frozen with horror, she stiffened, petrified Forde would open his eyes, but the steady measured vibration beneath her cheek didn't pause, and after a moment she cautiously raised her head. He was fast asleep.

She disentangled herself slowly, pausing to look into his face. Her gaze took in the familiar planes and hollows, made much more boyish in slumber; the straight nose, high cheekbones, crooked mouth with its hint of sensuality even in repose, and the dark stubble on his chin. A very determined chin. Like the man himself.

How could she have been so unbelievably stupid as to sleep with him again? Her breath caught in her throat as her stomach twisted. And it was no good blaming the wine. She had wanted him last night; she had ached and yearned for him since the time they'd parted, more to the point.

But she didn't *need* him, she told herself stonily. She had proved that; she had lived without him for seven months, hadn't she? And she was getting by.

She had barely survived losing Matthew. She had wanted nothing more than to die, the grief and guilt crucifying. She didn't ever want to be in a place where something like that could happen again. She *wouldn't* be in such a place.

She slid carefully out of bed, the trembling that had started in the pit of her stomach spreading to her limbs. She had to get out of the house before Forde woke up. It was cowardly and mean and selfish, but she *had* to. She loved him too much to let him hope they could make a go of their marriage. It was over, dead, burnt into ashes with no chance of being resurrected. It had died the moment she'd begun to fall down those stairs.

But he *would* be hoping, a little voice in the back of her mind reminded her relentlessly as she gathered her clothes together as silently as a mouse. Of course he would. As mixed messages went, this one was the pièce de résistance.

Once in the kitchen she dressed swiftly, scared any moment there would be movement from upstairs. Then she wrote him a note, hating herself for the cruelty but knowing if she faced him this morning she would dissolve in floods of tears and the whole sorry mess would just escalate.

Forde, I don't know how to put this except that I'm more sorry than I can say for behaving the way

I did last night. It was all me, I know that, and it was inexcusable.

Melanie paused, her stomach in a giant knot as she considered her next words. But there was no kind way to say it.

I can't do the together thing any more and that's nothing to do with you as a person. Again, it's all me, but it's only fair to tell you my mind is made up about the divorce. I'll still do the work for Isabelle if you want me to. Ring me about it tonight. But no more visits. That's the first condition.

Again she hesitated. How did you finish a note like this? Especially after what they'd shared the night before.

Tears were burning at the backs of her eyes but she blinked them away determinedly. Then she wrote simply:

I hope at some time in the future you can forgive me.
Nell

She owed him the intimacy of the nickname at least, she thought wretchedly, feeling lower than anything that might crawl out from under a stone. He had been attempting to comfort her last night when they'd first come into the house, and she had practically begged him to make love to her. She had instigated it all; she knew that.

Creeping upstairs, she placed the note on top of the clothes he'd discarded so frantically the night before but without looking at him again. She couldn't bear to.

It was only when she was driving away from the house that the avalanche of tears she'd been holding at bay burst forth. She managed to find a lay-by that was hidden from the road by a row of trees once she'd entered it, and cut the engine.

Steeped in misery made all the worse by the remorse and self-condemnation she was feeling, she cried until there were no more tears left. Then she wiped her eyes and blew her nose and got out of the car to compose herself in the warm, fresh air. The chirping of the birds in their busy morning activities in the trees bordering the lay-by registered after a minute or two, and she raised her eyes, searching out a flock of sparrows who were making all the noise.

Life was so simple for them, for all the animal kingdom. It was only Homo sapiens, allegedly the superior species, who made things complex.

The fragrance of Forde still lingered on her skin, the taste of him on her lips. Hugging her arms about her, she recalled how it had felt to have him inside her again, taking her to heaven and back. Falling asleep with her head on his chest, close to the steady beat of his heart, had felt like coming home and had been as pleasurable as their lovemaking.

She straightened, her soft mouth setting. She wasn't going to think about this. She was too early to arrive at the farmhouse where she and James would be working for the next week or so, but there was a café on the way that would be open. She'd go and buy herself breakfast.

The café only had one other occupant when she pushed open the door, a lorry driver who was reading his paper while he shovelled food into his mouth. After ordering a round of bacon sandwiches and a pot of tea, Melanie made her way to the ladies' cloakroom, locking the door behind her. The small room held a somewhat ancient washbasin besides the lavatory, and she peered into the speckled mirror above it. She'd looped her hair into a ponytail before leaving the house but it was in dire need of attention. And she hadn't showered or brushed her teeth.

Stripping off her clothes, she had a wash with the hard green soap, which was as ancient as the washbasin, before drying herself with several of the paper towels in the rusty dispenser. Dressing quickly, she brushed her hair and redid her ponytail before applying plenty of the sunscreen she always carried in her handbag. Brushing her teeth would have to wait.

She was about to leave the cloakroom when she glanced at herself in the mirror again and then drew closer, arrested by the look in her eyes. She blinked, unnerved by the haunting sadness. Was that what Forde had seen? Worse, was that why he had stayed and made love to her? He'd stated quite clearly that the only reason he had come to see her was to discuss the work he wanted her to undertake for Isabelle. Had he felt sorry for her? He had left her severely alone since the time she'd threatened to take out a restraining order; maybe he was seeing other women now?

Feeling emotionally sick, she left the cloakroom and

went into the main part of the café. The lorry driver had left but a group of motorbike enthusiasts were clustered around three tables, talking and laughing. She saw them glance her way but, after one swift glance, kept her head down. Dressed in leathers and with tattoos covering most of their visible flesh, they were a little intimidating, as were the huge machines parked outside next to her beaten-up old truck.

The waitress brought her sandwich and tea immediately as she sat down. Aware her eyes were still puffy from the storm of weeping, Melanie forced down the food as quickly as she could and drank one cup of tea before standing up to leave. She had just reached the door when someone tapped her on the shoulder and she turned sharply to find a huge, bearded biker behind her.

'Your bag, love,' he said, holding out her handbag, which she realised she'd left on a chair, the keys to the car being in her pocket. And then, his eyes narrowing, he added, 'You all right?'

'Yes, yes, th-thank you,' she stammered, feeling ridiculous.

'You sure?'

His blue eyes were kind under great winged eyebrows, and, pulling herself together, Melanie managed a smile. 'I'm fine, and thank you for noticing the bag,' she said, silently acknowledging this was an apt lesson in not going by appearances.

He grinned. 'I'm well trained, love. My girlfriend's the same. Forget her head, she would, if it wasn't screwed on.'

Once on the road again, Melanie gave herself a stern talking-to. The biker had asked if she was all right and the honest answer would have been no, she doubted if she would ever be what he termed 'all right' again, but that was nobody's fault but her own. She should have known better than to marry Forde and try to be like everyone else. She *wasn't* like everyone else.

She passed a young mother pushing a baby in a pushchair and bit hard on her lip. It still hurt her, seeing mothers with babies. Like a knife driven straight through her heart.

Throughout her life, every person she had loved had been taken from her in the worst possible way. First her parents, then her grandmother, even her best friend at school—her only friend, come to it, because she hadn't been a particularly sociable child—had drowned while on holiday abroad with her parents. She could still remember the numbing shock she had felt when the headmaster had announced Pam's death in assembly, and the feeling that somehow the tragedy was connected with Pam's friendship with her.

If she hadn't married Forde and wanted his baby, Matthew wouldn't have died. She had tempted fate, thought she could escape the inevitable and because of that Forde's heart had been broken as well as hers. She would never forget the look on his face when he'd held that tiny body in the palms of his hands. That was the moment she had known she had to let him go, make him free to find happiness somewhere else. Forde had said last night that she would have given her life for Matthew's if she could and he was right, but she hadn't been able to. But she could protect Forde from more hurt by exiting his life. Once the divorce was through she would move again, far away, perhaps even abroad, and in time he would meet someone else he could commit to. Women fell over themselves to get his attention and he was a passionate and very physical man. Whatever the cost in the present, this was the right thing to do for the future. *And there could be no more incidents like last night*.

Her mind irrevocably made up, Melanie felt slightly better. She had to be cruel to be kind. It was the only way.

Forde awoke suddenly with the presentiment that something was wrong. For a moment he couldn't reconcile where he was and then he remembered, turning to see that the place next to him in the bed was empty. The house was quiet and still, no sound from the bathroom or downstairs, and he let out a breath he didn't know he'd been holding.

Glancing at his watch, he saw it was gone nine o'clock and he swore softly, cursing the fact he hadn't woken before her as he swung his feet out of bed, running a hand through his sleep-tousled hair. Damn it, this was exactly what he'd wanted to prevent. But maybe she was having breakfast in the tiny courtyard garden they'd sat in the night before?

As naked as the day he was born, he took the stairs two at a time, but even before he opened the back door and looked into Melanie's tiny garden snoozing in the sun he knew she wasn't around. The small house was devoid of her presence, as if the heart of it was missing.

Cursing some more, he retraced his steps, and this time, as soon as he entered her bedroom, he saw the note on top of his clothes, which she had folded neatly for him. It was a single piece of cream-coloured paper and, sitting down on the side of the bed, he began to read it.

His stomach muscles contracted, as though a cold, hard fist was squeezing his gut. So nothing had changed. After all they'd shared last night, the fire, the passion, she was still intent on divorcing him.

Screwing the paper into a ball, he flung it across the room before getting to his feet and reaching for his clothes. He needed to get out of her house fast before he gave in to the crazy urge to break something.

Once downstairs again he relocked the back door and left by the front one, which had a Yale lock, slamming it hard behind him. His Aston Martin was waiting for him in the small car park and after sliding into the car he sat, the door wide open and his hands on the steering wheel.

Where did he go from here? This morning had been a repeat of so many mornings when he'd awakened from erotic dreams of their lovemaking and reached out for her across an empty expanse of bed, only for reality to slam in. But this morning had been different. Last night had been real. She'd been silk and honey in his arms, her body opening to him and accommodating him perfectly as he'd thrust them both to a climax of unbearable pleasure. But it wasn't just his body that burnt for her, hot and fulfilling though their lovemaking had always been. He wanted *her*, his Nell.

He watched a black cat saunter across the car park, stopping for a moment when it noticed him, its green eyes narrowing before it dismissed him as unimportant and continued with its leisurely walk. The cat walked alone, he thought fancifully. Like Nell. She'd come to the same conclusion about him as that damn animal, whereas he needed her in every part of his life. He wanted to share waking up together at the weekend and reading the Sunday papers in bed while they ate croissants and drank coffee, watching TV with a glass of wine after a hard day's work while the dinner cooked, going to the theatre or to a film, or simply taking a long walk in the evening arm in arm. In the early days they'd done all those things and they had talked about anything and everything—or so he'd thought. Now he realised there was a huge part of her psyche she'd kept from him.

He started the car, frowning to himself.

He'd known she'd been damaged by her earlier life when he'd got to know her, of course. He'd just under-estimated the extent of the damage and that had been fatal. Or maybe his ego had ridden roughshod over any concerns he might have had, telling him he would be able to deal with any difficulties in the future.

He nosed the powerful car out of the car park and onto the road beyond, deep in thought. But all that was relative now. One thing was for sure, she wouldn't have responded to him as she'd done last night if she didn't still care for him, deep down somewhere. And when he'd asked her if she loved him she hadn't said no. Admittedly, she hadn't said yes either…

He'd call her tonight, as she'd suggested. Everything in him wanted to come back here and bang on the door till she let him in so he could convince her how much he loved her, but something told him that would accomplish nothing. He'd played the waiting game for months, hadn't he? He could play it a little longer. But this time on his terms. She wouldn't go back on her word, she'd work at Hillview and he knew how fond she was of his mother. That was the reason he'd suggested this in the first place.

Well, he conceded in the next moment. Not the only reason. It was true his mother's heart wasn't good since the hip operation but she hadn't been quite so…difficult about the garden as he'd led Melanie to believe. But Hillview's grounds *did* need a complete overhaul and his mother, albeit with a very pointed glance at his and Melanie's wedding portrait, which still kept pride of place over the mantelpiece in her sitting room, *had* said she wouldn't allow a stranger in to do the work. He knew his mother was with him one hundred per cent; she'd loved Melanie like a daughter and grieved for her daily.

He'd drive back to the house, shower and change his clothes, and go to the office after a pot of strong black coffee, and ring Melanie tonight. And he had no intention of fooling himself the road to getting her back was going to be easy, he just knew it was a road he'd keep walking until… He shook his head. There was no until. He'd walk it. End of story.

CHAPTER FOUR

IT HADN'T been a particularly exhausting day, not compared to some, but when Melanie walked into the cottage that evening she felt bone-weary. Try as she might she'd been unable to think of anything else but Forde all day, endless post-mortems addling her brain until she barely knew which end of her was up. If James had asked her once if she was OK, he'd asked her a dozen times. She wondered what her very able assistant would have said if she'd told him she was verging on a cataclysmic nervous breakdown, she thought wryly, going through the nightly routine of taking off her boots on the mat and then heading for the stairs. Laughed, most likely, because he wouldn't have taken her seriously. James thought she was the ultimate cool, collected, modern woman. Everyone did. Only Forde had ever understood the real her.

She mentally slapped herself for the thought. None of that. If she was going to take up the threads of this new life again—threads that had nearly been broken last night—then she had to control her mind. Simple. Only it wasn't.

After turning on the taps for a warm bath, she went through to the bedroom, steeling herself to glance at the bed. It was rumpled and very, very empty. A shaft of physical pain made her wince. Grimly, she stripped off the covers and dumped them in her linen basket for a wash, opening the windows wide to let in the perfumed night air. It was her imagination that she could still smell Forde's unique scent—a mixture of the expensive aftershave he favoured and his own chemical make-up, which turned into an intoxicating fragrance on his male skin.

It was as she was slipping off her jeans that she noticed the little ball of paper in a corner of the room where it had clearly been thrown. Her note. Oh, Forde, Forde...

She shut her eyes for a moment but tears still seeped beneath her closed lids. What must he have felt like reading it? But she couldn't go there. She mustn't. Walking across the room, she bent and picked it up. She didn't straighten the paper out but held the little ball in one hand, stroking where he'd touched with one finger, guilt and shame washing over her.

She continued to cry all the time she was in the bath, but after she'd washed her hair and dried herself, she splashed her hot face with cold water and took stock. No more crying. She was done.

She pulled on an old pair of comfortable cotton pyjamas and looped her damp hair into a high bun, before going downstairs and fixing herself something to eat with the groceries she'd collected on the way home. It was hard to force the food down; she was on tenterhooks waiting for Forde's call, but she managed to clear her plate and her full stomach helped to quieten her jangling nerves some.

The call came at eight o'clock.

'Hi.' His voice was cool and steady. She expected him to ask how she was or mention her ignominious flight before he awoke that morning, but, Forde being Forde, he didn't do the expected. 'We need to iron out the details for you to work at Hillview. You said you had some conditions?'

'Yes.' Her voice came out as a squeak and she cleared her throat. His rich, smoky tones had brought a whole rush of emotions she could have done without. 'But before I start, are you sure Isabelle will want me around after—after everything?'

'After you walking out and demanding a divorce, you mean?' His even voice belied the content of his words. 'Quite sure. My mother has always taken the view that what goes on between a couple is their business and theirs alone. You know her, you should realise that. Now, your conditions?'

Melanie felt she'd been thoroughly put in her place, and her voice was crisp when she said, 'Firstly, in spite of what you've just said, I shall need to come and see Isabelle and discuss whether she wants me to do the job. If she does, then I'll take it, but all the arrangements will be between myself and your mother. I don't want you involved.'

'Can you see my mother letting me be involved?' he asked drily.

'What I mean is—'

'What you mean is that you don't want me around, popping in for a visit, things like that?'

It was exactly what she meant. 'I can't stop you visiting your mother,' she prevaricated awkwardly, 'but in the circumstances it would be better all round if you tried to avoid doing so when I'm there, I guess.'

'Noted.'

Oh, hell, this was going worse than she'd imagined. 'Of course if there's a crisis of some kind with Isabelle's health—'

'I'll be allowed on the premises,' he finished for her.

'Look, Forde—'

'Next condition,' he said politely.

Melanie took a deep breath. She was *not* going to let him get under her skin. 'James and I are working on a job at the moment and there's another lined up straight afterwards, which cannot wait, but it won't take long. We were due to begin a fairly substantial project mid-September but I've been in touch with the people concerned and they're happy to delay a while. In fact they've said they'd prefer the work doing in the spring because—' She faltered; too late she wished she hadn't begun the sentence. 'Because the lady is expecting a baby at the end of October and hasn't been too well lately. Her husband feels it would have been a little stressful for her. So, we've a space for Isabelle if she wants it.'

'Business is good by the sound of it.'

She swallowed hard. 'Yes, yes, it is.'

'One thing I must make clear, and this isn't to be shared with my mother. I intend to pay for the work, my Christmas present to her, but as she's somewhat proud at the best of times I shan't mention it until the job is finished. With that in mind, there will be no need to worry about getting anything but the best in materials and so on, but you might like to quote her a substantially lower price than is realistic. Once you've priced the job and given me an estimate, you have my word I will pay in full whenever you wish. Understood?'

She took a moment to consider his words. She *had* intended to do the work at the very lowest margin she could manage, but if Forde was paying it would mean she could price it the same way she would do for anyone else. And she could understand why Forde was keeping it a secret until it was a fait accompli. Isabelle was extraordinarily proud of her successful son but had always refused to accept a penny from him, declaring Forde's father's death had left her mortgage free and with a nest egg in the form of a life assurance her husband had taken out some years before he'd died. Having had Forde late in life at the age of forty-three, Isabelle also had a very good pension from the civil service where she'd been employed all her working life before leaving to become a full-time mother when Forde was born.

Melanie cleared her throat. 'I understand. It might be helpful to me if payment for the bulk of the materials I use could be given as the job progresses. Cash flow and so on.'

'Fine. When can you talk to her?'

'Tomorrow evening?' Better to get it over with.

'Good. I'll ring her tonight and tell her I've suggested you for the work and you're agreeable, depending on the job when you assess it, and you'll be in contact tomorrow. OK? Anything else?' he added crisply.

It was totally unfair, not to mention perverse, but his businesslike tone was making her want to scream. Last night they'd indulged in wild, abandoned sex and she'd slept in his arms, and he was talking as though he were discussing a contract with some colleague or other. Keeping her voice as devoid of emotion as his, Melanie said, 'I don't think so at this stage.'

'Goodnight, then.' And the phone went dead.

Melanie stared blankly across the room. 'You pig.' But at least she didn't feel like crying any more. Throwing something, yes, but not crying.

Isabelle picked up the phone on the second ring the next evening, and was as gentle and courteous as she'd always been. So it was, promptly at two o'clock the following Sunday afternoon, normally her housework and catch-up day, Melanie presented herself at Forde's mother's fine Victorian house situated some ten miles or so from the home she and Forde had shared.

She was so nervous she was trembling as she rang the bell, but it was a uniformed nurse who opened the door rather than Isabelle. The woman showed her into Isabelle's comfortable sitting room where a wood fire crackled in the grate despite the warm weather, for all the world as though she were a stranger rather than her patient's daughter-in-law, which led Melanie to believe the nurse wasn't aware she was Forde's wife.

Isabelle confirmed this the moment the nurse had shut the door, leaving them alone. 'Hello, my dear.' Forde's mother was sitting on a sofa pulled close to the fire and she lifted up her face for Melanie to kiss her cheek as she'd always done in the past, before patting the seat beside her. 'Sit down. I didn't tell Nurse Bannister who you were. She's a nosy soul and always poking her nose into this and that. Thank heaven she'll be leaving at the end of next week and not a day too soon. I can't wait to have my house back to myself.'

'Hello, Isabelle.' Melanie's voice was shaky. She'd half expected Forde's mother to look ill and pale, for things to be different somehow, but instead both Isabelle and this room were exactly the same. She had left Forde, then left the city and made a new life for herself, but it was as though the last seven months had never happened and she had been here the day before. The same floor-to-ceiling bookshelves lined with books graced two walls of the somewhat old-fashioned room, the same heavily patterned wool carpet covering the floor and thick embossed drapes at the window... She took a deep breath. 'How are you? Forde told me you've been in hospital recently.' She'd decided to mention his name straight away rather than having him hanging over the proceedings like a spectre at the feast.

Isabelle smiled. 'I was foolish enough to break a hip and then my heart played up a little, but what can you expect at my age? I'm no spring chicken. More to the point, how are *you*, dear?'

'Very well, thank you.' Telling herself she had to say what she'd rehearsed for days, Melanie took the plunge. 'Isabelle, when I returned your letter it wasn't because I didn't want to keep in touch, not really, but because I—I couldn't.'

A pair of silvery-blue eyes very like Forde's smiled at her. 'I know that, dear. It had to be a clean sweep for you to be able to go on. We were too fond of each other for it to be any different.'

She wanted to cry. She wanted to lay her head on Isabelle's lap and cry and cry, as she had done the first time she'd seen Forde's mother after losing Matthew. Isabelle had cried with her then, telling her she would never forget Matthew but there would be other babies to take away the edge of her grief and loss. Frightened by the way she was feeling, Melanie retreated. 'You want the garden replanning, I understand.'

Isabelle accepted the change of conversation with her normal grace. '*Want* is perhaps not the right word. *Need* is better. I have to confess it's become a little too much lately.'

'And you don't want a gardener in to see to things?'

'Occasionally, but not every day. As you know I've put in several hours most days for years—it's my plea-sure. I can still do a little but not all that's required.'

'So if we got it under control, my assistant coming in perhaps once a month for a couple of days wouldn't dis-tress you too much?' Melanie asked gently, feeling for Forde's mother. The grounds were beautiful and they'd been Isabelle's pride and joy. 'You'll like James,' she added. 'I promise.'

'I'm sure I will. Now, Nurse Bannister is bringing us a cup of tea and then I thought we might see the gar-den together?'

Melanie nodded. In truth she wanted to get out of this room. She had noticed at once that Isabelle had kept their wedding picture in its elaborate gold frame exactly where it had always been, and she'd avoided looking at it since. The tall, dark, smiling man and his radiant bride could have been different people, so far removed did she feel from the girl in the photograph.

It was clear Nurse Bannister had made the connec-tion when she returned with the tray of tea a few moments later, her gimlet-hard eyes searching Melanie's face avidly. With no trouble Melanie decided she could quite understand Isabelle's desire to be rid of the companion Forde—for all the right reasons, of course—had thrust upon his mother.

By the time she left Hillview three hours later Melanie felt she had a good idea of what Isabelle would like, and more importantly *not* like, in the new garden. They'd agreed to leave well alone where they could and all the mature trees would remain, but Melanie had encouraged Isabelle to treat the acre of ground as a series of compartments flowing into and round each other to create a whole. Easy maintenance being the prime concern, Melanie had suggested vigorous ground cover in places, evergreen, naturally dense plants planted to form a thatch of vegetation that would give weeds little opportunity to develop. A water feature in the form of a large sunken pool surrounded by a pebble 'beach' to keep down weeds and an area for sitting in one part of the garden, in another a landscaped rockery with helianthemums, verbascums and sisyrinchiums to give vibrant colour, a bed of gravel aiding drainage and avoiding waterlogging.

Isabelle had listened to all her suggestions, welcoming the idea of winding paths leading to arbours and two or three patio areas, along with several chamomile lawns. This aromatic perennial would provide a contrast of texture to other areas of the garden, and when bruised by light treading the leaves would release a pleasant apple-like scent. The main advantage over a grass lawn for Isabelle was that the chamomile only would need very occasional trimming, which James could see to.

An area of decking surrounded by scented shrubs; a sunny, gentle slope adapted to suit sun-loving plants chosen for their rich flowering and compact shape on a bed of tiny, different-coloured pebbles; dramatic island beds of large shrubs surrounded by lavender or ornamental grasses—Melanie had come up with them all, and Isabelle had been remarkably open to the changes.

They had agreed Melanie would go away and make scale drawings recording features of both the present garden and the new proposed changes, so that Isabelle could review the options and make sure she was completely happy. Melanie had told her mother-in-law that, at the initial stage, Isabelle must treat the drawing as a base plan and she could use overlays of tracing paper to test out different ideas. Once Isabelle was sure how she wanted the changes to look, Melanie would make detailed planting plans for particular areas as well as drawing up cross-sections of specific features, like the pool, the arbour and grass walk they'd discussed, the topiary and other ideas. Nothing was definite and Isabelle had the right to change her mind as many times as she wanted to, Melanie had impressed on the old lady, knowing it was a little overwhelming for her.

They parted with a kiss and a hug, Isabelle holding her tight for a little longer than was strictly necessary. Melanie had a lump in her throat as she drove away from the house. It had felt so *right* to be with Isabelle again, but she didn't dwell on her feelings, applying her mind to the drawings she would make on graph paper from her notes and thinking of one or two other ideas as she drove. Softening the stone walls surrounding a patio area by planting vibrant flowers and trailing plants in the top of it, and maybe staggered railway sleepers in the far corner to give a step effect with boulders and varied plants.

She wanted Isabelle's garden to continue to be a sanctuary to be enjoyed by the old lady, a retreat from the world, and to that end she was planning paths that curled from one feature to another, shady corners with trees and shrubs and sunny spots like the rockery and pool. And lots of benches, comfortable wooden ones, she told herself, where Isabelle could sit and rest any time anywhere in the grounds.

The changes were going to take a lot of money but there was no reason why, at the end of it all, Isabelle's original high-maintenance garden, which had always been kept in a state of perfection by the dedicated gardener her mother-in-law had been, couldn't be turned into something just as beautiful but dramatically more labour friendly. In fact she would make sure of it, Melanie determined.

Once home, she made a pot of coffee and began work at the dining table. She was deep into transferring all the measurements she'd taken that afternoon onto her rough plan when the phone rang. Her mind occupied with right angles and base lines and boundaries, she lifted up the receiver and spoke automatically. 'Hello, Melanie Masterson.'

'Hello, Melanie Masterson. This is Forde Masterson speaking.'

Her heart ricocheted off her ribcage and then galloped at twice its speed. Somehow she managed to say fairly normally, 'Oh, hi, Forde. I was working.'

'I won't keep you,' he said, the faintly teasing note that had been in his voice disappearing.

She wanted to say it was OK, that she hadn't meant it like that, as a put-down, but, telling herself it was better to keep things businesslike and formal, she kept quiet.

'I just called to thank you for how you handled my mother. She phoned a while ago and, from being more than a little apprehensive about her beloved garden being chopped about, as she'd put it initially, she came across as actually excited about the changes you'd discussed. I appreciate it, Nell.'

As ever, hearing the special nickname sent a flicker of desire sizzling along her nerve endings. His power over her was absolute, she recognised with a stab of dismay. Nothing had changed. Just hearing his voice made her want him so badly she was trembling with it.

'Nell? Are you still there?'

'Yes, I'm here,' she said quickly, pulling herself together. 'And there's no need to thank me. You do realise it's going to be pretty expensive if we do it properly.'

'Of course.' There was a pause. 'Would it be crass to point out you know what I'm worth and money isn't a consideration? I just want her satisfied at the end of it.'

'She will be.' Melanie found she didn't want him to finish the conversation. She wanted to keep talking to him, hearing those deep, smoky tones. She should never have agreed to do the job, she thought as fear at her vulnerability where Forde was concerned streaked through her. This was crazy, just asking for trouble. 'She'll love it, Forde. I promise.'

'I don't doubt that for a moment,' he said softly. 'I trust you, Nell. I always have.'

Panic gave her the strength to say, 'I have to go now. I'll be in touch once Isabelle's decided exactly what she wants and I've planned and costed everything. Goodbye, Forde.'

'Goodnight, sweetheart. Sweet dreams.'

He'd put the phone down before her stunned mind could compute again. *Sweetheart?* And sweet dreams? What had happened to her conditions? she thought frantically as she went into the kitchen to fix more coffee, needing its boost to calm her shattered nerves. Admittedly she hadn't actually spelled out 'no endearments,' but surely he'd got the message?

She found he had completely ruined her concentration when she tried to work on the drawings again. Eventually she took an aspirin for the pounding headache that had developed in the last hour or so and went to bed, there to toss and turn half the night, and have X-rated dreams in which Forde rated highly for the other half.

Nevertheless, when she awoke early Monday morning her steely resolve was back. The divorce was going through, come hell or high water, she determined as she sat eating her breakfast in the tiny courtyard, feeling like a wet rag. Absolutely nothing could prevent it. *Nothing.* It was the only way she could ever regain some peace of mind again.

CHAPTER FIVE

CONTRARY to what Melanie had expected after Forde's call the day she had visited his mother, the next four weeks passed by without further contact with him. She visited Isabelle twice more during the time she was finishing the other contracts, and they ironed out exactly what was required to their mutual satisfaction.

On her second visit, Melanie took James along with her. He was fully acquainted with the circumstances but—James-like—had taken it all in his stride as though it were the most natural thing in the world for an estranged wife who was seeking a divorce to undertake a major job for her mother-in-law.

Melanie could tell Isabelle was a little taken aback at first when she met James. He *was* something of an Adonis with a smile that could charm the birds out of the trees, but, just so her mother-in-law didn't put two and two together and make ten, she took her aside at one point when James was busy measuring this and that at the other end of the garden and made it clear theirs was a working relationship and nothing more.

'Of course, dear,' Isabelle said sweetly, as though the thought of anything else hadn't crossed her mind, but Melanie noticed her mother-in-law's smile was warmer the next time she conversed with James. For his part, James was his normal, sunny self and by the end of the afternoon he had Isabelle eating out of his hand, which boded well for the future.

The night before they were due to start work at Hillview, Melanie didn't sleep well. The August heatwave had continued into an Indian summer, and it was even hotter in September if anything. Everywhere, the ground was baked dry, and, although this was slightly preferable to working in drenching rain and mud, it wasn't ideal. But it wasn't the pending job that had her giving up all thought of further sleep at four in the morning and going downstairs to make a pot of coffee, which she took outside into the courtyard; it was Forde.

There had scarcely been a waking minute he hadn't invaded her thoughts since the night they'd slept together, and even when she'd fallen asleep he was still there, carving his place in her subconscious. *And she hadn't heard from him.* Not a word. Not a phone call. Nothing. She'd submitted a ridiculously low estimate to Isabelle as he had requested once she'd worked out the pricing of the job, and a realistic one to him via his office rather than his home, thinking this emphasised the businesslike nature of the arrangement. His secretary had called the next day to say that Mr Masterson was happy with the estimate and his confirmation of acceptance would arrive by return of post. Which it had. A signature in the required space. Great.

Melanie wrinkled her nose in the scented darkness. He'd finally cut his losses and moved on, that was plain to see. The last ridiculous scenario when she'd all but begged him to make love to her and then frozen him out the next morning had been too much. She didn't blame him. How could she? Why would any man put his hand up to take on a nutcase like her? And it was what was necessary, what she'd been aiming for, so why did it feel as though her heart were being torn out by its roots?

She sighed heavily, swigging back half a cup of coffee and looking up into the dark velvet sky above, punctured by hundreds of twinkling stars. She had to get a handle on this. Her dream of a happy-ever-after ending had been smashed to pieces months ago so why was she dredging up the past? She wasn't like anyone else—that was what Forde didn't understand. And it wasn't his fault he'd married a jinxed woman. But she would never let herself get close to anyone again; that way she couldn't be hurt and neither could anyone else.

Finishing the last of the coffee, she continued to sit on as the sky lightened and the birds woke up, her limbs leaden. She hadn't really slept well since Forde had come back into her life again—not that he'd ever left, if she was being brutally honest. She might not have spoken to or seen him those seven months before he had written to her, but he'd only been a heartbeat away, nonetheless.

This had to get better, she told herself miserably. It must. She couldn't spend the rest of her life feeling like this. Her grief and remorse about Matthew would always be with her; she had come to terms with that and in a strange way almost welcomed it. If she couldn't do anything else for her darling little boy she could mourn him, and as long as she was alive he would never be forgotten but cherished in her heart. But the sense of loss about Forde was different and much more complicated.

Stop analysing. She shut her eyes, letting the first gentle rays of the sun warm her face. By ten or eleven o'clock it would be baking hot and less of a blessing, but right now it felt comforting. She felt so tired—physically, mentally and emotionally—but she had to keep going. And there were people so much worse off than she was: folk with terminal illnesses or severe health issues. At least she was young and strong and fit. She mustn't turn into a whinger—she'd always hated them.

The silent pep talk helped a little, enough to get her on her feet anyway. After leaving the coffee tray in the kitchen she went upstairs to shower and change, and by seven o'clock was on the road. After picking James up from the house he rented with three friends—it was pointless them both driving the hundred-mile round trip each day—they drove to Hillview on roads not yet traffic logged with morning traffic, arriving at Isabelle's house just after eight.

The first thing Melanie noticed was Forde's Aston Martin parked in the driveway. Her stomach somersaulted, but James was unfurling himself out of the truck and stretching, and didn't glance at her before starting to unload some of the equipment in the back of the pickup. By the time she joined him on the drive she was in command of herself, but angry. Forde had *promised* he'd stay away when she was around, and she didn't believe for a moment he wasn't aware she was starting work today. This was so, so unfair.

She heard the front door open and knew by some sixth sense Forde was standing there, but she didn't glance his way, continuing to help James until they were done. By that time Forde had walked down the drive from the house to where they were parked, some yards from the Aston Martin.

'Good morning.' His voice was cool, clipped, and as she looked at him she saw the silver-blue eyes were cold and he wasn't smiling.

Her anger went up a notch. How dared he look at her like that when he shouldn't be here? Her tone matching his, she said pointedly, 'Good morning, Forde. I'm starting work on the garden today or had it slipped your memory?'

'No, it hadn't slipped my memory,' he said evenly, holding out his hand to James as he added, 'I'm Forde Masterson, Melanie's husband. I take it you're James?'

She'd forgotten she'd employed James after she'd left Forde and the two men hadn't met. She watched James take Forde's hand almost gingerly and she didn't blame him; Forde was making no effort to be friendly, his face straight and his eyes narrowed.

James mumbled a polite hello and then extracted his hand, saying he'd start taking some of the equipment to the back of the house before scampering off with armfuls of tools.

'You spoke about your assistant as though he was a young lad just out of school and wet behind the ears,' Forde said accusingly. 'He's a grown man of what—twenty-four, twenty-five?'

'What?' Why was he talking about James when he knew full well he shouldn't *be* here?

'And he looks to me as though he knows his way about,' Forde added grimly. 'In every sense of the word.'

'James backpacked round the world for three or four years with his friends after leaving uni, and I have never suggested he was a young boy.' Melanie glared at Forde. 'Not that that's any of your business. And why are you here this morning anyway?'

'So I was right. He's twenty-four, twenty-five?'

Why this obsession with James's age? 'He's twenty-six, and, I repeat, why are you here?'

'Answering an early-morning summons by my mother because she thought she had a bird down the chimney,' Forde answered shortly. 'OK? And before you ask, no, there was no damn bird.'

Since an incident some years ago when a large wood pigeon had fallen down Isabelle's chimney and then positioned itself on a ledge a few feet up from the fireplace where it had cooed frantically until Forde had arrived and got it out, along with a cloud of soot and grime that had covered the room in smuts, there had been several such fruitless summonses by Forde's mother. Isabelle lived in horror of inadvertently lighting the fire and burning a bird alive, even though Forde had told her repeatedly that the stainless-steel mesh bird cowl he'd had installed in the top of the chimney to prevent just such a catastrophe made it impossible. When she had still lived with Forde he had been convinced that the wood pigeon he'd rescued took a fiendish delight in sitting on the roof and calling down the chimney to fool his mother and cause him grief.

'Oh.' Melanie nodded, feeling guilty of her suspicions, and—although she would rather die than admit it, even to herself—a little piqued that his presence had absolutely nothing to do with a desire to see her.

'So this James.' Forde raked back his hair with an

impatient hand. 'Is he married? Got a long-term girl-friend? What?'

He was jealous. As the light dawned Melanie stared at him in amazement. He surely didn't think... She didn't know whether to take it as a compliment or an insult that he thought a handsome, virile, young stud like James would bother with a married woman two years older than himself and with enough baggage to fill umpteen football stadiums. She decided on the lat-ter. 'James's personal life is his own business,' she said icily. 'He works for me, that's all, Forde. Got it?'

Forde looked spectacularly unconvinced.

'He favours statuesque brunettes who can play tennis and squash and all the other sports he's mad about as well as he does, and who can stay up all night dancing in clubs and then go sailing after breakfast,' Melanie stated firmly. 'But even if I was his type, and he mine, it still wouldn't be an option. I'm his employer, he's my employee. End of story.'

She watched him expel a silent sigh. It was a com-pletely inopportune moment to feel such a consuming love for him it stopped her breath. She dropped her eyes, scared he might see what he must not see. He clearly hadn't stopped to shave before he'd left home and the black stubble accentuated his rugged good looks ten-fold. Combine that with the casual clothes he was wear-ing—open-necked shirt showing a hint of dark body hair and beautifully cut cotton trousers—and he was any maiden's prayer. Their mother's and grandmother's too.

His voice came low and intense. 'This should be the moment when I say I'm sorry and I have no right to ask, but I'm not sorry and I have every right to ask. You're my wife.'

It was one of the hardest things she'd ever done to raise her gaze to his without betraying herself. 'It's over, Forde.'

'It will never be over,' he said roughly. 'It wasn't a piece of paper that joined us, Nell, or a man of the cloth saying a few words and two gold rings. You're mine, body, soul and spirit. I love you and I know you love me.'

He watched her face as he spoke but all the barriers were up and he couldn't read a thing.

'We can't go back to how it was,' she said with a quietness that was more final than any show of emotion.

'No,' he said softly. 'We can't. We had a son together and he died, and he'll for ever be a part of us and a sadness that's shaped us into the people we are today. But you and I, that is a thing apart. This punishing yourself for something that wasn't your fault has to end.'

'What?' She reared up as though he had slapped her.

'That's what you are doing, Nell, whether you acknowledge it or not, and you're punishing me too,' he said, feeling incredibly cruel to face her with what he believed. But he would lose her if he didn't start to force her to take stock.

'You don't understand anything.'

He flinched visibly, telling himself to keep calm. How she could come out with something like that when all he'd done since Matthew's death *was* understand, he didn't know. 'This is not all about you—have you considered that?' He could hear her damn assistant coming back, whistling some pop tune or other, and wanted—

quite unreasonably—to punch him on the nose. 'I loved Matthew too.'

'But you didn't cause his death.'

'Neither did you, for crying out loud.' He hadn't meant to shout, he'd told himself before he walked out of the house he was going to be calm and rational, but at least the whistling had stopped.

She turned away, her soft mouth pulling tight in a way he knew from past experience meant she was digging her heels in. 'I've work to do.' She glanced up to where James was standing some distance away, clearly uncertain of whether he was welcome in what was obviously a danger zone. 'James, come and help me with the rest of this.'

Knowing if he didn't leave fairly rapidly he was going to say or do something he'd be sorry for, Forde turned on his heel and walked back to the house without another word. His mother was waiting for him in the hall, just inside the open front door.

'I heard you shout.' Isabelle's voice was gently accusing.

He loved his mother. She was a strong-minded, generous soul with the faintly old-world charm and dignity of her generation, and for that reason he bit back the profanities hovering on his tongue and said curtly, 'It was that or strangle her, so be thankful for the shouting.'

Isabelle's eyes widened. She opened her mouth to say something and then clearly thought better of it.

'I'm going.' Forde bent and kissed her forehead. 'I'll ring you later.'

When he left the house again Melanie and James were nowhere to be seen, although he could hear voices beyond the stone wall that separated the drive and the front of the house from the gardens at the rear. He glanced at the side gate for a moment and then decided there was nothing to be gained from saying goodbye. Striding over to the Aston Martin, he opened the door and slid inside, starting the car immediately and swinging it round so fast the tyres screeched.

That hadn't gone at all as he'd intended, he thought, gripping the steering wheel so hard his knuckles showed white. He hadn't expected her assistant to look like a young George Clooney with muscles for one thing, or for Melanie to be so... He couldn't find a word that satisfactorily described her mix of cool hauteur and wariness and gave up trying.

Once he'd reached home he prowled round the house like a restless animal instead of showering and getting changed for the office. Everywhere he looked there were reminders of Melanie; she'd so enjoyed having the team of interior designers in when they'd first got married and stamping her mark on the house. And he loved her taste. In fact he loved everything about her, damn it, although there had been moments after she had left him when the pain had got so bad he'd wished he'd never met her.

He had never imagined there would be a problem in life where he couldn't reach her, that was the thing. He'd been confident whatever befell them he'd be able to protect and nurture her, see her through, that they would face it together. But he had been wrong. And it had cost him his marriage. He walked through to the massive kitchen-cum-breakfast-room at the back of the house and slumped down at the kitchen table.

He was still deep in black thoughts when Janet let herself into the house at gone ten.

'Mr Masterson, what are you doing here at this time in the morning?' She had always insisted on giving him his full title even though he'd told her to call him Forde a hundred times. 'Are you ill?'

He lifted bleak eyes to the round, robin-like ones of the little woman who was a friend and confidante as much as his cook and cleaner. Janet's life was far from easy but you'd never have guessed it from her bright and cheery manner, and in the ten years she'd worked for him since he had first bought the house they'd grown close. She was a motherly soul, and he looked on her as the older sister he'd never had. For her part, he knew she regarded him like one of her sons and she had never been backward in admonishing him, should the situation call for it. He could tell Janet anything, unlike his mother. Not that Isabelle wouldn't have understood or given good advice, but since his father's death he'd always felt he had to shield his mother from problems and worry.

'I saw Melanie this morning,' he said flatly. 'It wasn't an…amicable exchange.'

'Oh, dear.' Janet bustled over to the coffee maker and put it on. 'Have you eaten yet?'

He shook his head.

Once he had a mug of steaming coffee and a plateful of egg and bacon inside him, he felt a little better. Pouring him a second cup and one for herself, Janet plonked herself opposite him at the kitchen table. 'So,' she said companionably. 'What happened?'

He told her the gist of the conversation and Janet listened quietly. After a moment, she said, 'So you think Mrs Masterson is having an affair with her assistant?'

Forde straightened as suddenly as though he'd had an electric shock. 'Of course not.'

'But you're going to give up on her, nonetheless?'

'Of course not,' he said again, getting angry. 'You know me better than that, Janet.'

'Then why are you sitting here moping?' Janet said, giving him one of her straight looks.

The penny dropped and Forde smiled sheepishly. 'Right.'

'I told you when she left like that it was going to be a long job and you needed to be patient as well as persistent, now didn't I?' Janet poured them both more coffee. 'The way she was that day before the ambulance came, it was more than the normal shock and despair someone would feel in the same circumstances. Mrs Masterson really believes there's some sort of jinx on her that touches those close to her.'

Forde stared at her. Janet had mentioned this before but he hadn't given it much credence, thinking that Melanie was too sensible to really believe such nonsense. 'But that's rubbish.'

'You know that and I know it,' Janet said stoutly, 'but as for Mrs Masterson...'

Forde leant back in his chair, his eyes narrowed. 'She's an intelligent, enlightened, astute young woman, for goodness' sake. I don't think—'

'She's a young wife who lost her first baby in a terrible accident and she blames herself totally. Add that to what I've just said, bearing in mind the facts about her parents, grandmother and even a friend at school she mentioned to me, all of whom were taken away from her, and reconsider, Mr Masterson. Melanie had a miserable childhood and became accustomed to keeping everything deep inside her and presenting a façade to the rest of the world. It doesn't come natural for her to speak about her feelings, not even to you. And, begging your pardon, don't forget you're a man. Your sex work on logic and common sense.'

Forde looked down at the gold band on the third finger of his left hand. 'Let me get this right. You're saying she thinks if she'd stayed with me something would happen to me?'

'Mrs Masterson probably wouldn't be able to put it into words but, yes, that is what I think. And there's an element of punishing herself too, the why-should-I-be-happy-after-what-I've-done syndrome.' Janet shrugged. 'In its own way, it's perfectly understandable.'

Forde stared at her. 'Hell,' he said.

'Quite.' Janet nodded briskly. 'So you save her from herself.'

'How?' he said a trifle desperately. 'Exactly how, Janet?'

Janet stood up and began to clear the table. 'Now that I don't know, but you'll find a way, loving her like you do.'

Forde smiled wryly. 'And here was I thinking you had all the answers.'

'She loves you very much, Mr Masterson, that's what you have to remember. It's her Achilles' heel.'

'You really think that? That she still loves me?'

Janet smiled at the man she had come to think of as one of her own brood. As big and as tough as he was, Mr Masterson had a real soft centre and that was what she liked best about him. Some men with his wealth and looks would think they were God's gift to womankind, but not Mr Masterson. She didn't think he wasn't ruthless when it was necessary, mind, but then he wouldn't have got to where he was now without a bit of steel in his make-up. 'Sure she loves you,' she said softly. 'Like you love her. And love always finds a way. You remember that when you're feeling like you did this morning.' She wagged a finger at him. 'All right?'

Forde got up, his silver-blue eyes holding a warmth that would have amazed his business rivals. 'You're a treasure, Janet. What would I do without you?'

'That's what my hubby always says when he rolls back from the pub after one too many,' Janet said drily, 'usually after helping himself to what's in my purse.'

'You're too good for him. You know that, don't you?'

Janet smiled at him as Forde left the kitchen. Be that as it may, and she certainly didn't disagree with Forde's summing up of her Geoff, Mr and Mrs Masterson were a perfect match. She had always thought so.

Her smile faded. She just hoped they could work their problems out, that was all. In spite of her encouraging words to Mr Masterson, she was worried Mrs Masterson would never come home, short of a miracle.

CHAPTER SIX

IT WAS the middle of November. A mild November, thus far, with none of the heavy frosts and icy temperatures that could make working outside difficult. But Melanie wasn't thinking of the weather as she left the doctor's surgery. She walked over to her pickup truck in the car park, but once she was sitting inside she didn't start the engine, staring blindly out of the windscreen.

She hadn't seen Forde since the day she had begun working for Isabelle, although he had phoned her several times, ostensibly with questions about his mother's garden. On learning from her solicitor that they'd been waiting for some time for Forde to sign and return certain documents appertaining to the divorce, she'd called *him* at home two nights ago.

She leant back in the truck's old, tattered seat and shut her eyes. Forde had been cheerfully apologetic about the delay, making some excuse about pressure of work, but what had really got under her skin was the woman's voice she'd heard in the background when she'd been talking to him. She hadn't asked him who he was with, she had no right whatsoever to question him after the way she'd walked out of their home and the marriage, but it had hurt her more than she would have thought possible to think of another woman in their home.

Stupid. Opening her eyes, she inhaled deeply. Forde was at liberty to see whomever he wished. Nevertheless, she hadn't been able to sleep that night. She had arrived at work the next morning feeling ill, and when she'd fainted clean away as she and James had been preparing a gravelled area for a number of architectural and structural plants her assistant had been scared to death.

Poor James. If she weren't so shocked and dazed at what the doctor had found she could have smiled. He'd been beside himself, saying she hadn't been well for weeks and what if she fainted again when she was driving or using some of the equipment they'd hired for the job? She could badly injure herself or worse. In the end, just to appease him, she had promised to call her doctor's surgery and as it happened they'd had a cancellation this morning. She had walked into Dr Chisholm's room explaining she knew she was suffering from stress and all her symptoms could be put down to that, and if she could just have some pills to take the edge off she would be fine. He'd gently reminded her that *he* was the doctor and he'd prefer to give her a thorough examination after asking her a few questions.

Her hands trembling, she forced herself to start the engine. She had to get back to work. There was still plenty to do at Hillview and each day the mild weather continued was a bonus. The old-timers were predicting that a mild October and November meant the country would suffer for it come December and January. They were on target to finish the job mid-December and if any bad weather could hold off till then, it would be a huge benefit.

But she found she couldn't drive. She was shaking too much. She sat huddled in her seat as reality began to dawn on her stunned mind. She was expecting a baby. Forde's baby. That one night in August had had repercussions the like of which she hadn't imagined in her wildest dreams. With hindsight, it was ridiculous she hadn't suspected the non-appearance of her monthlies, the tiredness and queasiness that had developed into bouts of nausea and sickness could be something other than stress. But she hadn't. She really hadn't. Perhaps she'd blanked her mind to the possibility she could be pregnant, but there was no mistaking it now. She was *thirteen weeks* pregnant.

She had fainted a couple of times in the early days when she was carrying Matthew. *Matthew.* Oh, Matthew, Matthew… She began to cry, her mind in turmoil. 'I'm sorry, my precious baby,' she murmured helplessly. 'I never meant for this to happen. I love you, I'll always love you. You know that, don't you?'

How long she sat there she didn't know. She only came to herself when her driver's door was suddenly yanked open and Forde crouched down beside her, his voice agonised as he said, 'Nell? Nell, what is it? What's the matter?'

He was the only person she wanted to see and yet the last person, and she couldn't explain that even to herself. Desperately trying to control herself, she stammered, 'Wh-what are you—you doing here?'

He had closed her door and walked round the bonnet, sliding into the passenger seat and taking her into his arms—in spite of the gear stick—before she knew what was happening. 'My mother realised you weren't with James this morning and asked where you were,' he murmured above her head. 'James said you'd gone to the doctor's, that he was worried about you. Damn it, Nell, I'm your husband. If anyone has the right to be worried about you, it's me. What's wrong?'

She hadn't had time to think about this, to decide what to tell him—if anything. But no, she would have to tell him, she thought in the next moment. He had a right to know. He was the father. *The father.* Oh, hell, hell, this couldn't be happening. And yet in spite of her desperate confusion and the feeling she'd let Matthew down in some way, her maternal instincts had risen with a fierceness that had overwhelmed her.

She thought of all the heavy work she'd done over the past weeks and breathed a silent prayer of thankfulness she hadn't lost this tiny person growing inside her. But now she was scared, *petrified* something would happen to the baby because of her.

'Nell?' Forde's voice was a rumble above her head as he continued to hold her close. 'Whatever this is, whatever's wrong, we'll get through it, OK?'

His words acted like an injection of adrenaline. She pulled away, wiping her eyes with the back of her hand in a childish gesture that belied her words when she said baldly, 'I'm pregnant.'

Forde heard the words but for a moment they didn't register. Since his mother had called him to say Melanie was at the doctor's surgery, that she had been ill for weeks without telling anyone, he'd imagined she was suffering from every terminal illness under the sun.

She had been so thin and fragile-looking the last time he'd seen her, he'd told himself with savage self-condemnation. He should have done something about it. And everyone knew certain diseases and conditions were only successfully treated if you did something about them fast. And it had been weeks, months…

He had driven like a madman to the address of the surgery James had given his mother, one eye on every vehicle coming in the opposite direction in case she had passed him. He'd fully expected she would be gone when he pulled into the doctor's car park and when he'd seen the truck had known a moment's deep relief before he'd realised she was bent over the steering wheel with her head in her hands. Then he'd known a panic he'd never felt before.

His face as stunned as hers had been when Dr Chisholm had given her the news, he said, 'What did you say?'

'I'm—I'm expecting a baby.' Drawing on every scrap of composure at her disposal, she went on, 'The night you came to my cottage in August, it happened then. I'm thirteen weeks pregnant.'

He raked back his hair in the old familiar way. 'But you're on the pill.' It had been one of the things they had argued about in the months following the miscarriage, her insistence that she go on the pill to avoid another pregnancy. He'd been patient at first, understanding her mind as well as her body needed time to get over what had happened, but then after one particularly painful row she had told him she didn't want more children, not ever. And that night he had returned to the house to find her gone.

'After I'd left there was no need to take it,' she said flatly.

He stared at her. There hadn't been much need before she'd left; she had hardly let him near her, even to kiss her. She had withdrawn into herself with a completeness that had baffled him. She still baffled him, but... The wonder began to dawn on him. She was *pregnant*. Pregnant with their baby.

As his face lit up Melanie strained away from him, her back pressing against the driver's door. 'No,' she mumbled, fear in her voice as well as her body language. 'I don't want this—can't you see? This doesn't change anything between us.'

'Are you crazy?' he said huskily. 'Of course it does.' And then, as her words hit home, his eyes widened. 'You're not considering a termination?'

Hurt beyond measure he could think such a thing, she felt anger replace panic. 'Of course I'm not,' she all but spat at him. 'I can't believe you said that.'

There was a stark silence as she watched his face change. 'Let me get this right. You want the baby but you don't want me? Is that what you're trying to say?'

Her face white, Melanie shook her head. 'I don't mean that.'

'Then what the hell *do* you mean?' Knowing his voice had been too loud and struggling for calmness, Forde took a rasping breath. 'Look, let's get out of here and go somewhere for a coffee where we can discuss this.'

'No.'

It was immediate and again the note of fear was there. Forde could feel his control slipping. She was making him feel like some sort of monster, for crying out loud. She was his wife and this was his baby, and she wouldn't even talk to him?

Whether Melanie realised what he was thinking, he didn't know, but in the next instant he saw her take a deep breath before she said, 'I'm sorry, Forde, really, but I have to have time to adjust to this myself and I need to get back to work—'

'The hell you are.' His face darkened. 'You're thirteen weeks pregnant, woman. Think of the baby.'

Baby. Just the sound of the word brought such a rush of emotion she felt dizzy. 'Women the world over work when they are pregnant,' she pointed out with a calmness she was far from feeling, 'and I shall explain the situation to James and tell him I won't be doing any lifting or carrying of heavy bags and things. But I still need to work, Forde. I *want* to work.'

'You're not well enough,' he said stubbornly.

'Now I know why I've been feeling the way I have I can eat little and often and make sure I don't miss meals or get too tired, but normal life *will* continue.' Feeling a compromise was in order, she added, 'I'll phone you tonight, I promise.'

'Not good enough. I want to sit down with you and discuss this properly. You're carrying my child, Nell. I'll take you out for a meal tonight. Be ready about eight.'

She really didn't want to do this. For one thing the complaint she now recognised was morning sickness tended to be more afternoon and evening sickness, and for another being with Forde was painful at the best of times, reminding her of all she'd lost. 'I don't think—'

She found her words cut off as his mouth took hers.

The kiss was a deliberate assault on her senses, she recognised that from the moment his mouth descended, but he'd taken her by surprise and by the time reason was back she was trembling at the sweetness of his lovemaking. He had moved to lean over her, using one hand to steady himself and the other to lightly cup her breast, but immediately his tongue had slid along her teeth and he had probed her lips open.

In spite of herself she gave no resistance as he slowly and voluptuously explored her mouth; she couldn't. He only had to touch her—he'd only *ever* had to touch her—and she melted, turning liquid with desire. Her attraction to him had always been consuming, that was why she had tried to put distance between them after they'd lost Matthew. First by shutting herself away emotionally and mentally, and then by physically removing herself from his orbit. But he had forced his way into her life again, with disastrous results. But no, she couldn't think of their baby as a disaster.

With her guard lowered and her defences down, Melanie kissed him back as she had done on the fateful night in August. His sharp intake of breath told her he'd sensed her capitulation, but his mouth was like a drug and she couldn't break its hold on her.

It was another car drawing alongside them that caused Forde to ease back into his own seat, his mouth reluctantly leaving hers after one last long kiss at the side of her mouth.

To her shame, Melanie knew she wouldn't have been able to show such restraint, regardless of who was around. And that was the trouble, she told herself silently as she smoothed back a strand of hair off one hot

cheek. Forde had been the chink in the armour she'd
worn against the outside world from the day she had
met him. He had made her believe in happy-ever-after
for a while, convinced her that his love was enough to
protect her from anything that might come against them,
from within and without. But he hadn't been able to stop
her hurting Matthew.

A young mother with a toddler climbed out of the car
that had parked next to them, clearly pregnant for the
second time. The girl didn't look a day over eighteen and
she was bright-eyed and bushy-tailed, her long blonde
hair and short miniskirt, which revealed endless legs
clad in leggings, making Melanie feel like an old hag.

That was the sort of woman Forde should have married, she thought miserably. Someone fresh and sparkling without any hang-ups. Someone as far removed
from herself as the man in the moon, in fact. Her
thoughts gave strength to her voice when she said, 'I
have to get back to work, Forde. Now.'

He didn't argue this time. 'OK. But you make sure
you explain this new turn of events to James, Nell. I
have a spy in the camp who'll inform me if you're not
behaving, remember that.'

He had been joking, well, half joking, she surmised,
but the words were like a bucket of cold water poured
over her head. *Isabelle.* This baby was her *grandchild.*
The panic returned but stronger, and she felt she must
know what a fish felt like when caught in a fisherman's
net with no visible source of escape.

'Eight o'clock tonight, OK?'

Forde was looking at her and, seeing in his eyes he
wouldn't take no for an answer, Melanie nodded jerkily.

He gave her one last swift kiss, his uneven mouth quirking. 'Stop looking as though the prospect of dinner with the father of your child is a fate worse than death,' he murmured sardonically. 'My ego has taken enough hits in the last months as it is.'

Afterwards, she wondered what on earth had made her say her next words. Maybe it was because the memory of the woman's voice in the background when she'd been talking to him on the phone still rankled—more than rankled, if she was being honest. Or perhaps it was his assumption that the fact that she was pregnant sorted all the problems? Or that he didn't understand, he simply didn't *get* the torment she'd been going through since Matthew's death because she, and she alone, was responsible for their son's stillbirth and nothing could change that.

'I'm sure there are plenty of willing fingers just itching to stroke that ego though,' she said with deliberate nonchalance.

She watched the beautiful silver-blue eyes turn to crystal hardness. And immediately regretted her rashness.

'Now that was definitely loaded,' he said, searching her face with laserlike intensity. 'Explain.'

She shrugged. 'Nothing *to* explain. I was just saying I'm sure there are more than a few women lined up who are quite happy to keep you company, that's all.' Ecstatically so, no doubt.

'And on what do you base that assumption?' he asked with deceptive mildness.

'Forde, I'm fully aware I have no right to criticise

you seeing other women. You are free to do whatever
you please.'

'Is that so?' It was a snarl. 'And this—' he held up his
left hand with the thick gold wedding band '—means
nothing? Is that it? Well, think again, sweetheart. It
means a great deal to me as it happens.'

The hypocrisy was too much. 'I know someone was
with you the night I phoned about the divorce papers,'
she said stonily.

'What?' His brow wrinkled, then cleared. 'Yes,
you're right,' he said with silky smoothness. 'There were
several people present actually. I was holding a dinner
party for my mother's birthday, just her and several old
friends of hers. I don't know who you heard, Melanie,
but I can assure you every woman present was eighty
years old or above.'

Wonderful, just wonderful. Not only had she forgotten Isabelle's birthday but had revealed herself as a jealous, mean-minded shrew. Gathering the remnants of her
dignity around her, she stared at him, her chin lifting.
'I see, but you don't have to explain to me. I was just
saying you're free to do whatever you please.'

'No, Nell, I'm not.'

The return of his pet name for her after the Melanie
of a few moments ago made her want to sag with relief. But she didn't. Stubbornly, she began, 'I have no
right—'

'You have every right to demand of me the same
faithfulness and honesty I demand of you, Nell. And let
me just say this for the record. When I made my wedding vows I meant every one of them. And they hold
firm. Got it?' Forde was secretly rather pleased at the

jealousy she'd betrayed but knew better than to bela-
bour the point. 'And I'll pick you up at eight tonight.'

She wanted to object but when she looked at him
there was an unsettling blend of concern and tenderness in his face. It wiped away her resolve. Weakly, she
said, 'James should never have said anything to your
mother. I'm not pleased with him.'

'Be as hard on him as you like,' Forde said cheerfully,
'but he *did* say something and I'll be at yours at eight.'
He opened the truck door and then paused, turning to
face her once more. 'You *were* going to tell me about
the baby, weren't you?'

His uncertainty made her feel like the worst sinner
on earth. She answered with obvious sincerity, her voice
soft. 'You would have been the first to know, Forde,
even if you hadn't turned up here this morning.' And
then honesty forced her to continue, 'But it might not
have been for a day or two until I'd adjusted to the idea.'

He stared at her. 'Is it really so bad, being pregnant
with our baby?'

It was the worst thing and the best thing in the world,
but how could she explain that to him when she couldn't
explain it to herself? 'I have to go,' she said tightly.

He nodded. 'Drive carefully.' And then, as an af-
terthought, he added, 'What are you going to tell my
mother? She's worried about you, Nell.'

She bit down hard on her bottom lip. 'The truth, I
guess.' But that was going to be nearly as painful as these
last few minutes with Forde. Isabelle wouldn't understand why, in these new circumstances, they weren't getting back together for a start, and who could blame her?

This was such a mess. *She* was a mess. And things

were going to get even messier in the next days when Forde realised she wasn't going back to him.

Her voice brittle, she said, 'Goodbye, Forde. And— and thank you for coming.'

He smiled. 'You don't have to thank me. I'm your husband, remember?'

He stood and watched her as she drove away, his hands thrust in his pockets and his shoulders slightly hunched. He looked big and solid and very sexy, and she was indisputably pregnant by this wonderful man who was also her husband. She should have been the happiest woman in the world...

CHAPTER SEVEN

ISABELLE must have been by the window looking out for her, because the minute she drove onto the drive and parked the truck, the front door opened. 'Melanie, dear.' Isabelle was leaning on the stick she'd used since the accident with her hip. 'Could you spare a moment or two before you go through to the garden?' she called as Melanie slammed the truck door.

Better to get it straight over with, Melanie told herself as she obediently followed Forde's mother into the house.

'I was just making a pot of coffee and was going to take a cup to dear James with a slice of the fruit cake he likes,' Isabelle said, leading the way into her farmhouse-style kitchen. James had become 'dear James' very quickly, which didn't surprise Melanie in the least. 'Sit yourself down while I see to him, and perhaps you'd like to cut yourself a slice of cake and pour us both a cup while I'm gone?'

Overcome with the strangest urge to burst into tears for the second time that morning, Melanie didn't trust herself to speak, merely nodding and smiling. In the days when she had still been with Forde she had spent many mornings helping Isabelle with something in the

garden, and their eleven o'clock coffee and cake break
had been something she'd looked forward to. A time of
cosy chats and laughter. But she didn't think there'd be
much laughter today.

Isabelle's fruit cake was one of her mother-in-law's
specialities and, in spite of how she was feeling, Melanie
discovered she was ravenously hungry, having skipped
breakfast that morning after oversleeping. She'd done
that more than once recently due to tossing and turning for the first part of the night and then falling into a
deep sleep as dawn began to break. Consequently she
felt tired all the time. Or she'd put down the exhaustion
she felt lately to that, she thought, biting into a hefty
piece of cake. Now, of course, she understood there
was another factor too. In the early days with Matthew
she'd felt drained.

Isabelle came back, beaming as she said, 'Such a
nice boy, that James, but I don't think he eats enough
living with those friends of his. He always wolfs down
his cake as though he's starving.' The silver-blue eyes
fastened on Melanie. 'And you, dear? Are you eating
enough? You've looked a little peaky lately, if you don't
mind me saying so, and James said you'd gone to the
doctor's this morning?'

Melanie swallowed a mouthful of cake and nodded. 'I have been feeling unwell but there's nothing
wrong, not exactly. I—I didn't realise but—' she took
a deep breath; this was harder than she'd expected with
Isabelle's sweet, concerned face in front of her '—I'm
expecting a baby. Forde's baby,' she added hastily, just
in case her mother-in-law got the wrong idea.

Isabelle's face was the third that morning to register stunned surprise, but she recovered herself almost immediately. 'Well, that's wonderful, dear,' she said warmly, reaching out and squeezing Melanie's hand. 'When is the baby due?'

'In the spring, May time.' It was so like Isabelle not to ask the obvious questions, Melanie thought gratefully, but feeling obligated to explain a little, she said, 'Forde came to see me one night in August to discuss— Well, to discuss my doing the work here actually. And—and one thing led to another...' She stopped helplessly.

'Well, I'm thrilled for you both,' Isabelle said briskly. 'Does Forde know?'

Melanie nodded. 'He came to the surgery as I was leaving.' Then quickly, before she lost her nerve, she said, 'This doesn't mean we—we're getting back together, Isabelle.'

There was a moment's silence. Then Isabelle said gently, 'Do I take it you don't love him any more?'

'*No.* I mean, I do love Forde. Of course I do.'

'And I know he loves you. Deeply. So forgive me but I don't quite understand...'

Melanie tried, she really tried to keep back the tears but it was hopeless. And this wasn't polite, ladylike weeping either. She wailed heartbrokenly, her eyes gushing and her nose running, and even when she felt Isabelle's arms go round her with a strength that belied their frailty, she couldn't pull herself together. She was crying for Matthew, for her dear little boy, and for Forde, for the way she had broken his heart when they'd lost their son, for all the smashed dreams and hopes that had turned to ashes. And for this new baby, this tiny, little person who hadn't asked to exist and who was so vulnerable...

When her cries had dwindled to hiccuping sobs, Isabelle fetched a cold flannel and towel and mopped her face as though she were three years old instead of nearly thirty. Utterly spent, Melanie sat quiet and docile, her head aching and her eyes burning as her mother-in-law made a fresh pot of coffee. Once they both had a steaming mug in front of them, Isabelle sat down at the kitchen table with her and took Melanie's hands in her own parchment-like ones. 'Talk to me,' she said softly.

Melanie shook her head slowly. 'Oh, Isabelle, I don't know how to explain.'

The old lady sighed. 'You're the daughter I never had, you know that, don't you? And that will never change, whatever the future holds. But this blaming yourself for something that wasn't your fault has to stop, child.'

Melanie looked at her through tear-drenched eyes. 'I don't feel I have the right to be happy again, not after losing Matthew, and I'm frightened...'

'What?' Isabelle pressed, when Melanie paused.

'I'm frightened something will happen to Forde if I'm with him, and now this baby too.' Instinctively she put a protective hand on her stomach. 'I think I'm perhaps meant to be alone, Isabelle.'

'Nonsense, dear.' Isabelle never minced words. 'You had a terrible and tragic accident, and on top of that woman's curse of hormones came into play, colouring your thinking and causing the depression you're still suffering from. If you had taken the medication the doctor prescribed you might be feeling better by now.'

Melanie's chin came up. 'I didn't want to. Matthew

deserved to have me grieve for him. It was all I *could* do.' She retrieved her hands, wiping her eyes and blowing her nose before she said, 'I know you mean well, Isabelle, but I have to work out what I'm going to do in my own way.'

'Yes, dear, I know that, but will you do one thing for me? For all of us? See Forde now and again. He loves you very much. Just talk to him, explain how you feel, even if it doesn't make sense. Don't shut him out, not now. This is his child too.'

Melanie nodded. 'I know that,' she said, through the tightness in her throat. 'And—and I'm seeing him tonight.'

'Good.' Isabelle's voice became brisk. 'Now, drink your coffee and have another piece of cake. Two, if you wish. You have to keep your strength up and you're eating for two, remember.'

Making a great effort, Melanie responded to the lightening of the conversation. 'The health experts would take you to task for that thinking these days.'

'No doubt, but I've never yet listened to what the experts say, and I'm not about to start now.' Isabelle chuckled. 'I'm an irksome old lady, I know.'

Melanie smiled, her voice soft. 'You're a lovely old lady,' she said, with a tenderness that brought moisture to Isabelle's eyes.

Melanie had two more pieces of cake and they talked about the progress of the garden and the weather and other such non-intrusive subjects before she left the house and went outside to break the news to James, whereupon Isabelle immediately picked up the telephone and called Forde.

James was busy working on the large informal pond Isabelle had requested in a low-lying area of the garden, his artfully random arrangement of large stones enhancing the soft outlines and sinuous curves of the water feature. Knowing how passionate Isabelle was about wildlife, Melanie had suggested the margins of the pool be masked by soft, naturalistic planting, which extended into the shallows to provide safe shelter for fish fry, amphibians, and bathing or drinking birds.

He looked up as she approached, his gaze taking in her red-rimmed eyes and pink nose, and his face was openly apprehensive as he stood up.

'I'm fine, don't worry,' Melanie said before he could speak. 'But there's something I've got to tell you because I won't be lifting or carrying anything heavy for a while. I'm having a baby.'

James took a step backwards as though she was going to deliver on the spot. 'What?' he all but screeched.

Melanie laughed; she couldn't help it.

Smiling sheepishly, James said, 'Forde?'

She nodded. 'Of course. Who else?'

'So you're back together?'

'Not exactly.' But a reasonable assumption, she supposed.

'Right.'

Not for the first time Melanie blessed the fact that James was the sort of easy-going soul who accepted people for exactly what they were. She was going to have enough explaining to do to various folk over the next months, but with James no explanation was necessary. 'The baby will be born early May, which isn't the best time, I know. We usually get busy then after the winter.'

'No sweat.' James grinned at her. 'We'll manage.'

'I've been thinking for a while of getting someone else on board, perhaps over the next weeks would be a good idea so we're ready for the spring?' And then, in case he thought he was being usurped, she added, 'They could be your assistant.'

He nodded. 'Whatever you think.'

She smiled, and they began to get on with some work, but Melanie's mind was buzzing. James had said 'whatever you think,' but that was the thing—she didn't know what she thought about anything any more. Except that she loved this baby with every fibre of her being. She hadn't known of its existence this time yesterday, but now it was the centre of her universe.

For the rest of the day she worked automatically, her mind a seething cauldron of hope and doubts and fears, but as she drove home from Isabelle's in a deep November twilight she felt she knew what she had to do. Maybe she had known it from the moment Dr Chisholm had told her she was carrying Forde's child. She just hadn't been able to bear acknowledging it.

It was dark by the time she parked the truck and walked wearily into the cottage. Once inside, she went through the routine of a working day—outdoor clothes and boots left in the kitchen, upstairs to strip off and then a hot bath. It was close to seven o'clock when she emerged from the bathroom, pink and warm after a long soak, and once in the bedroom she knew she just had to lie down for a few minutes before she began to get ready to go out with Forde. She was so tired she felt drugged.

Promising herself she would simply shut her eyes for a little while and relax her aching muscles, she snuggled under the duvet, and was asleep as her head touched the pillow.

CHAPTER EIGHT

FORDE knew he had a fight on his hands. He would have known that without his mother's phone call earlier in the day, but when she'd repeated her conversation with Melanie it had confirmed everything Janet had spoken about.

He frowned to himself as he drove the miles to Melanie's cottage. Damn it, he didn't understand her. He loved her, more than life itself, but this consuming need to punish herself—and indirectly him—for something that neither of them had been able to prevent was something outside his comprehension. And this idea of hers that she brought misfortune on those she cared about was sheer garbage. His mother was convinced the idea had taken root even before they'd married due to Melanie's past, and the miscarriage had given credence to something that would have faded away in time, shrivelled into nothing when it hadn't been given sustenance. But the accident had happened.

He gripped the steering wheel, his face grim. And the seed of this nonsense had been watered and fed by her depression that had followed.

He realised he was so tense his body was as tight as piano wire and forced himself to consciously relax, expelling a deep breath as he stepped on the brake. He'd been driving far too fast, way over the speed limit.

What the hell was he going to do? How could he convince her that life without her was an empty void, devoid of any real joy or satisfaction? In her crazy, mixed-up mind she thought she was protecting him in some way by cutting the threads that bound them. In reality she was killing him, inch by inch. And now there was the baby, a product of their love. Because it *had* been love that had given it life; this child had been created by passion and desire certainly—he only had to look at her to become rock hard—but love had been the foundation of their relationship from their first date. *Before* their first date. He had been born waiting for Melanie to appear in his life and he had recognised she was his other half early on. It really had been as simple as that.

A fox skittered across the road a little way ahead of him, a flash of red and bushy tail in the headlights. It was a timely reminder he was still going too fast and he checked his speed accordingly. He'd driven the car too hard too often lately—yet another indication that his normal self-control wasn't as sharp as it could be. The trouble was, thoughts of Melanie were always at the forefront of his mind, thoughts that triggered a whole gamut of emotion and tied him up in knots. His mother had told him she was worried Melanie would crack up completely if something didn't give soon and it had been on the tip of his tongue to say her son was in the same boat.

He smiled grimly to himself. He hadn't, of course. His mother was concerned enough as it was. And it would have been a trite remark anyway. He had no intention of going to pieces. He was going to get his wife back come hell or high water, and the news about the baby only meant it would be sooner rather than later. He was done with the softly-softly approach and pretending to play along with the divorce. When she had first left him he'd told her she would divorce him over his dead body and that still held.

Forde glanced at the huge bunch of pink rosebuds and baby's breath on the passenger seat at the side of him, next to the bottle of sparkling wine—non-alcoholic of course. Melanie had been obsessional regarding eating and drinking all the right things when she'd been pregnant before.

His brooding gaze softened. She'd pored over all the baby books she had bought, drunk gallons of milk, and the first time she had felt flutterings in her belly that were definitely tiny limbs thrashing about had been beside herself with joy. She would make a wonderful mother; he knew that. Her experiences as a child had made her determined their child would know nothing but love and security. He would remind her of that tonight if she persisted in this ridiculous notion of continuing with the separation.

He began to mentally list all the arguments and counter arguments he would put to Melanie to support his cause for the rest of the journey, playing devil's advocate some of the time until he was absolutely sure she couldn't put anything to him he hadn't thought about.

When he parked in the little car park belonging to the row of cottages he was feeling positive. She loved him and he loved her, that was the most important thing to remember, that and the miracle that their night of love in the summer had made a little person, a composite of them both. She couldn't dispute that. Come the spring there was going to be clear evidence of it. A baby boy or girl, a living, breathing reality.

He felt such a surge of love for Melanie and his unborn child that it took his breath away. He'd been wrong when he'd thought she partly blamed him for Matthew's death; he realised that now after talking to Janet and his mother. Melanie had condemned herself utterly. Maybe he should have refused to let her withdraw from him in those early days after the miscarriage? The doctors had told him to give her time, that it was natural for some women to detach themselves from what had happened for a while, nature's way of assisting the mind to deal with something too devastating to take in all in one go.

But it hadn't been like that with Melanie. Why had he listened to anyone when all his instincts had been telling him to *make* her let him in? He hadn't known if he was on foot or horseback, that was the trouble. They had still been wrapped up in the rosy glow of finding each other and getting married, then the thrill of finding out she was pregnant—life had been perfect, scarily so with hindsight. And then, in the space of a heartbeat, their world had fragmented. He could still remember her face when he'd got to the hospital and found her in labour…

He shook his head to dispel the image that had haunted him ever since.

Getting out of the car, he looked towards the cottages. If he had his way she would be returning home with him tonight. Janet had told him not to take no for an answer when he'd told her everything earlier that day, which was all very well, but this *was* Melanie they were talking about. A corner of his mouth twisted wryly. She might look as though a puff of wind could blow her away, but his wife was one tough cookie when she had the bit between her teeth about something or other.

An owl hooted somewhere close by, otherwise the night was still and quiet, unlike his churning mind. He took a deep breath and composed himself, feeling like a soldier preparing himself for battle. Which wasn't too far from the truth, he thought sardonically. And Melanie was one hell of a formidable opponent…

At Melanie's front door, he took another deep breath but didn't pause as he rang the doorbell. He had expected some lights to be on downstairs but the place seemed to be in darkness. He frowned, waiting a few moments before ringing again. Nothing. He glanced at his watch. A couple of minutes to eight. Surely she wouldn't have gone out to avoid him? But no, Melanie wouldn't do that, he told himself in the next moment, ashamed the thought had come into his mind. Whatever else, Melanie wasn't a coward, neither did she break her word. She had said she would be here so what was wrong?

Concerned now, he threw caution to the wind and banged on the door consistently with all his might. The cottages either side of Melanie were in blackness, but there was a light on in one a couple of doors down. He'd go there in a minute if he had to. Her truck had been in the car park—he'd parked right next to it—so she couldn't have gone far. Unless she was lying injured inside…

He knew a moment of gut-wrenching relief when the door creaked open. Melanie stood there in the robe she'd worn that night in August, her eyes heavy-lidded with sleep and her blonde hair tousled. 'Forde?' Her voice was husky, slow. 'What time is it? I only meant to have a rest for a few minutes.'

'Eight o'clock.' He had a job to speak. From being worried to death about her, he now found himself wanting to ravish her to heaven and back in her deliciously dishevelled state.

He gave her the flowers before bending to pick up the bottle he'd put down in order to batter the door, his body so hard with desire it was painful to walk when she said, 'Come in, and thank you for the flowers. Rosebuds and baby's breath, my favourite.'

'I know.' He smiled and received a small smile in return as she turned away. He followed her into the house. Unlike the previous time he was here she didn't suggest he sit in the sitting room like a guest, but led the way to the kitchen.

'I'm sorry, I'm not ready,' she said flusteredly, stating the obvious as she rummaged about for a vase in one of the cupboards. 'It'll take me a few minutes. Can I get you something to drink while you wait? Coffee, juice, a glass of wine?'

'A coffee would be great.' He didn't really want one; he just didn't want her to fly off upstairs immediately. On impulse, he said, 'We don't have to go out for a meal tonight if you're tired. I can order something in. Chinese, Indian, Thai? Whatever you fancy.'

He could see her mind working as she looked at him. Going out for a meal would be less intimate, less cosy, but the thought of not having to dress up and make the effort to go out was clearly tempting. He waited without saying anything. She fiddled with the flowers as the rich smell of coffee began to fill the room, but he still didn't speak.

'There's a Chinese in the next village,' she volunteered after a few moments. 'The leaflet's under the biscuit tin there.' She pointed to a tin close to where he'd sat himself on one of the two kitchen stools tucked under the tiny breakfast bar. 'Perhaps you could order while I get dressed.'

'You don't have to on my account.'

Her whole demeanour changed and he could have kicked himself. 'Joke,' he said lightly, although it hadn't altogether been. 'What would you like?'

'Anything, I don't mind.' She clearly couldn't wait to escape. 'Help yourself to coffee. I won't be long,' she added as she turned away.

He sat for a moment after she had gone and then stirred himself to pour a mug of coffee. Melanie looked exhausted and no wonder—she'd been living on her nerves for well over twelve months now. She was like a cat on a hot tin roof most of the time. A soft, warm, blonde cat with big wary eyes and the sweetest face, but a cat that was nonetheless quite liable to show its claws if the occasion warranted it.

Forde reached for the menu under the biscuit tin and glanced through it. He was absolutely starving, he decided, and quite able to do justice to double helpings. After a little deliberation he thought one of the set dinners would be a good idea to give Melanie plenty of choice. He picked up the telephone and ordered one that was allegedly for three people comprising of sweet and sour chicken Cantonese style; king prawn, mushrooms and green peppers in spicy black bean sauce; shrimp egg Foo Young, chicken in orange sauce; beef with ginger and spring onion; dry special fried rice and prawn crackers.

Walking through to the dining room, he found the table was relatively clear, just a file or two piled in one corner. Placing these on the floor, he dug and delved until he found cutlery, place mats, napkins and glasses. Then he returned to the kitchen and poured himself another coffee.

Ridiculously he found he was nervous, his stomach full of butterflies as it had been on their first date. It had been the evening after they had met at their mutual friend's wedding; he hadn't been able to wait for more than twenty-four hours to see her again. He had wined and dined her in a plush restaurant, playing up to the image of wealthy, successful tycoon while being inwardly terrified the whole time she wouldn't want to see him again. She had invited him in for a coffee when he had dropped her back to her bedsit—just a coffee, she'd emphasised.

They had talked for three hours.

He smiled to himself, remembering how it had been. He had never talked to a woman like that before in the whole of his life but with Melanie it had seemed right, natural to keep nothing back. And she had been the same. Or he'd thought she had.

Restlessly, he walked over to the back door and opened it, stepping into the tiny garden. The night was chilly but not overly cold, and from the light of the house he saw the small space had been trimmed and manicured for the winter. The heady scent of the roses was gone but a softer perfume was in the air and he saw several shrubs in large pots were flowering.

He wasn't aware of Melanie behind him until she said, 'I still like splashes of colour in the winter. That's a Viburnum bodnantense in the corner. Pretty, isn't it, with those clusters of dark pink flowers? And the Oregon grape is about as robust as you can get and I love the way its foliage turns red in winter. I've planted several in Isabelle's garden.'

He glanced down at her as she moved to stand with him. She had dressed in a soft white woolly jumper and jeans, and her pale blonde hair was pulled into a shining ponytail. She wore no make-up and she looked about sixteen, he thought shakily, swamped with a love so fierce it took a moment before he could say, 'Is that where the scent is coming from?'

'Oh, you mean the winter honeysuckle.' She pointed to a shrub close to the wall of the house. 'It's called Winter Beauty and it flowers right through the winter into the spring. Beautiful, isn't it?'

'Yes,' he said, not taking his eyes from her face. 'Very beautiful.'

She looked up at him and he saw a tremor go through her. 'You're cold.' He took her arm and turned her into the warmth of the house. She felt fragile under his fingers, as though if he pressed too hard she'd break. Warning himself to go carefully, he kept his voice light when he said, 'There's plenty of coffee left. Shall I pour you a cup?'

She shook her head. 'I'd love one but I'm limited to one or two cups of tea or coffee a day now. Caffeine, you know.'

It brought back memories of what had seemed like an endless list of dos and don'ts when she'd been pregnant before, and not for the first time he reflected that there were women who ate and drank what they liked, smoked, even took drugs, and went on to have healthy babies, whereas Melanie... Not that he agreed with such a selfish approach, of course, but Melanie had done everything right first time round. It seemed the height of unfairness she'd lost Matthew the way she had. Quietly, Forde said, 'Juice, then? Or shall we open that bottle of fizzy grape juice I brought? Non-alcoholic, by the way.'

She had walked into the kitchen so that the breakfast bar was between them, and everything about her suggested she wasn't about to lower her guard in any way. Her body language was confirmed when she said, 'Forde, I agreed to see you tonight but I don't want you to think it means anything other than I recognise we must talk. This baby is as much yours as mine. I know that.'

It was something. Not much, but better than having to persuade her to face that very fact.

'The thing is,' she began hesitantly, only to pause when he lifted his hand palm up.

'We're not talking about "the thing" or anything else until we've eaten.' He was going to have to fight to get through to her and he was quite prepared for that, but he was damned if he was going to do it on an empty stomach. 'The food should be here any minute, OK?'

As though on cue the doorbell rang.

Within a minute or two the table was groaning under an array of fragrant, steaming foil dishes and a positive banquet was spread out in front of them.

Far from picking at her food, as Forde had feared, Melanie ate like a hungry cat, delicately but with an intensity that meant she more than did justice to the meal. There were only a few morsels left by the time they were both replete, and as Melanie leant back in her chair she sighed blissfully. 'That was delicious. I didn't realise I was so hungry.'

He grinned. 'Eating for two, sweetheart.'

A shadow passed over her face. 'Forde—'

'Or maybe three. It could be twins. There are twins on my father's side, remember, so who knows?'

Her eyes wide with something like alarm in them, Melanie said weakly, 'I'm going for a scan this week. I'll let you know if there's two.'

'Twins would be great,' he said, tongue in cheek. 'Double the joy.'

'And double the feeding, changing nappies—' She stopped suddenly, as though she had been reminded of something. 'Forde, we have to talk. Now.'

'OK.' He smiled as though his heart hadn't gone into spasm at the look on her face. Whatever she was going to say, he knew he wouldn't like it. 'Let's go into the sitting room with our drinks, shall we?'

She had relaxed when they were eating, even allowing herself to laugh a few times at the stories he'd purposely told against himself, but now she was as stiff as a board as he followed her into the other room. She chose to curl up on one of the sofas in a way that meant he was forced to take the other one.

'So?' He found he was done with prevaricating. 'What do you want to say, Nell?'

He watched her take a deep breath and it caused him to tense still more.

'I—I can't keep this baby when it's born. If—if you want to I think you should take it.'

Whatever he'd prepared himself for, it wasn't this. He knew his mouth had fallen open, and shut it with a little snap, trying desperately to hang onto reality. 'What did you say?'

'It would be better if it was brought up by one of its natural parents,' Melanie said woodenly. 'And you have your mother and a whole host of relations. It—it would have roots, a sense of belonging, and you're wealthy enough to hire the best nanny, and there's Janet too—'

'What are you talking about?' Only the sure knowledge this wasn't really what she wanted enabled Forde to keep his temper. 'The best nanny in the world is no compensation for a child's mother, a mother who would love it beyond imagination in your case. You were born to be a mother, Nell. You know that as well as I do.'

'No,' she said in a stony voice. 'I can't keep it.'

Struggling for calmness, he said, 'Why not? Explain. You owe me that, not to mention our unborn child. Have you considered how our son or daughter is going to feel when it finds out its mother wanted nothing to do with it after it was born?'

She shut her eyes for an infinitesimal moment. 'That's not fair.'

'The hell it isn't. Face facts, woman.'

I am facing facts.

The loss of control was so sudden he jumped visibly as she sprang to her feet.

'If I keep it, if I'm its mother, something will happen. Like it did with Matthew. Or to you. Something will happen to stop us being a family and it will be because of me. Don't you understand that yet? It's because I love it I have to stay out of its life.'

He stared at her. She was standing with her hands clenched into fists at her sides, her body as straight as a board, and he could see she believed every word. Softly, he said, 'And that's why you walked out on me, on our marriage.' It was a statement, not a question. But he had to make her hear herself, acknowledge the enormity of what she had confessed. 'Because you've told yourself this lie so often you believe it.'

It was dawning on him just how much he had failed her. He should have insisted she went for counselling after Matthew's death, forced her to confront the gremlins, but he had been so frightened of causing her more pain. Of losing her. Ironic.

'It's not a lie.' She drew in a shuddering breath.

'Oh, yes, it is.' He stood up and crossed the space between them, taking her stiff, unyielding body into his arms. 'Life doesn't come in neat, sanitised packages, Nell. People die in accidents, of diseases, of old age, in—in miscarriages and stillbirths and a whole host of other medical issues. It isn't nice and it isn't fair but it happens. You weren't to blame for Matthew's death. I don't know why it happened and I have to confess I've shouted and railed at God ever since because of it, but I *do* know you weren't to blame. You've got to get that into your head.'

'I can't.' She pulled away, stepping back from him. 'And I've got to protect this baby, Forde. If you take it and I stay out of your lives it will be all right.'

Her white face and haunted eyes warned Forde that he had pushed her to the limit of her endurance. His mind now working rapidly, he kept his voice steady and low. 'It goes without saying I'll take our baby, Nell. But I think you owe it one thing. I want you to go and talk over how you feel with someone who is completely unbiased and who has experience in the type of grief you're feeling. Will you do that for it? And me?'

She'd taken another step backwards. 'A doctor, you mean? You think I'm crazy?'

'Not in a million years.' He wouldn't let her retreat further, covering the distance between them in one stride and taking her cold hands in his. 'But I know someone, a friend, who's trained in this type of counselling. She offered to talk to you months ago in a professional role, just you and her and everything confidential between the two of you, OK? You'd like Miriam, Nell. I promise.'

She extracted her hands from his. 'I don't know.'

'Then trust me to know. Will you do that? And what have you got to lose? I love you, Nell. I'll always love you. If you won't do this for yourself, do it for me.'

He saw the confusion in her eyes and, acting on instinct, he reached out and touched her cheek. Her skin was soft like raw silk and as warm as liquid honey. Leaning closer, he bent his head and kissed her, a gentle, undemanding kiss, before drawing her against him.

They stood together in the quiet room, Forde nuzzling the top of her head and Melanie resting against his chest without speaking. Her hair smelt of the apple shampoo she favoured and there was the faintest scent of vanilla from her perfume. Why two such fairly innocuous fragrances should make his blood pulse with desire he didn't know, but then Melanie had always had that effect on him. He wanted her so badly he ached with it, but he steeled himself against betraying it, knowing at this moment she wanted nothing more than to be held and comforted.

After a minute or two, he murmured, 'I'll ring Miriam tomorrow and ask her to see you. She's a busy lady but we go way back and I know she'll find time.'

Melanie was quiet for a moment, then her voice came faintly muffled from his chest. 'Way back? What does that mean?'

He caught the tinge of jealousy she was trying to conceal and almost smiled. 'She's the mother of a close friend, grandmother of six and has been happily married for forty years.' Miriam was also much sought after and at the top of her field professionally, but he wasn't about to mention that.

'Forde, it won't change anything. You know that, don't you?' She raised swimming eyes to his. 'You have to face the inevitable. I have.'

'Go and see her, that's all I'm asking,' he said softly. He kissed her again, and in spite of telling himself to go carefully it deepened into something more than comfort. A restless urgency surfaced and he knew she felt it too by the way she clung to him in a hungry response that took the last of his control. His hands roamed over her body, touching her with sensual, intimate caresses, and then he scooped her up in his arms as he murmured against her lips, 'I want you. Tonight. But if you want me to leave now, I'll go.'

Her answer was to kiss him with a desire that was

unmistakable, and with a small growl Forde carried her up the stairs to the bedroom. He laid her on the bed and in frantic haste and without speaking they tore off their clothes and then he lay down beside her, cupping her face in his palms and kissing her deeply and passionately.

She had always been a lover who gave as much as she got and now her hands and mouth explored him as hungrily as his did her, twisting and turning with him as they moaned their pleasure. Her breasts felt fuller in his hands and as he took one rosy nipple in his mouth she arched with a little cry.

'They—they're more sensitive now,' she gasped against what he was doing to her, and as his mouth returned to hers he swept his tongue inside and then pulled back and bit her bottom lip gently.

'You're so beautiful, my love,' he murmured shakily. 'I don't think I can wait much longer.'

'Then don't.'

She was wet and warm for him when he entered her. She hooked her legs round him and raised her hips and they moved together in perfect unison towards a release that had them both calling out as they tipped over the edge into white pleasure. Then he circled her in his arms, one thigh lying over hers as she opened drugged eyes. 'You don't know how many cold showers I've taken in the middle of the night recently,' he murmured wryly.

She half smiled, but he could see she was thinking again. 'Forde, we shouldn't have—'

'Yes, we should.' He brushed back a strand of hair

from her face. 'I wanted you and you wanted me. It was that simple. Don't try to complicate it.'

'But it doesn't—'

'Change anything,' he finished for her. 'Yes, I know. Don't worry. Go to sleep.' He pulled the duvet over them.

Her expression was one of total confusion and remorse. 'It's not fair to you,' she whispered.

'Nell, believe me, I can live with this sort of unfairness,' he said drily.

She smiled again but a proper smile this time and he grinned back at her. 'Go to sleep,' he said again, kissing the tip of her nose and then her mouth. 'Everything's OK.'

She was asleep within moments, snuggled close to him, but Forde lay and watched her for a long, long time. *Everything's OK.* What a stupid thing to say, he thought ruefully. His wife had told him she was going to hand over their baby to him at birth and then disappear out of their lives, and he'd said everything was OK. But he had no intention of letting her do that, not for a second, so maybe everything was, if not OK, then clearer than it had been for a good while.

With a feather-light touch he reached out his fingers and ran them across her belly. It might be his imagination but already he thought he could feel a slight swell. His child was alive in there, tiny now but each day gaining strength.

Tears pricked at the backs of his eyes. It had been a long, hard road since they'd lost Matthew, and they still weren't at the end of it yet, not by a long chalk, but against all the odds a miracle had happened and

Melanie was pregnant. That one night of loving had produced this baby and no matter what he had to do to achieve it, they were going to be a family. If he had to kidnap Melanie and take her and their baby to some remote place in the back of beyond until she accepted that, he'd do it.

She stirred in her sleep, murmuring his name before breathing steadily and quietly once more.

It was a tiny thing, but it cheered him. She was his. End of story, he thought fiercely. And promptly fell asleep.

CHAPTER NINE

MELANIE woke first the next morning, aware she was wonderfully warm and cosy and sleepy. Then her eyes snapped open. *Forde.* He was curled into her back, one male arm resting possessively across her stomach.

Very, very carefully she eased his arm off her and then turned to face him. He was fast asleep, the duvet down to his waist revealing his wide, muscled shoulders and the black curly body hair covering his chest. She drank him in for some moments and then slid silently out of bed. She didn't intend to sneak away like the time before, she wouldn't do that to him again, but neither did she want to pretend they were like any other couple waking up together.

Gathering her clothes in her arms, she padded through to the bathroom, locking the door behind her. When she emerged, fully clothed and coiffured, she glanced through the open bedroom door. Forde was sitting up in bed, his hands behind his head, and her heart raced like a runaway horse. He looked like every woman's fantasy of what she'd like to find in her Christmas stocking.

'Hi, sweetheart,' he said lazily. 'All finished in there?'

She nodded jerkily. And then found she couldn't tear

her eyes away as he flung back the duvet and stood up. She had seen him naked many times but she didn't think she would ever grow tired of looking at him. The flagrant maleness was intoxicating and he moved as beautifully as one of the big cats, his muscles sleek and honed and not an ounce of fat on his hard frame. He had almost reached her before she pulled herself together, but as she went to disappear down the stairs he turned her round with his hand on her arm. His kiss was firm and sweet but he didn't prolong the embrace, although as he turned away and strolled into the bathroom Melanie noticed a certain part of his anatomy was betraying his desire for her in the age-old way.

Heat slammed into her cheeks as she scurried downstairs, but then the faint feeling of sickness that would gather steam throughout the day before dispersing round seven or eight o'clock in the evening made itself felt. It was the one thing about pregnancy she truly hated, she told herself, forcing down a couple of dry biscuits once she reached the kitchen. Before she had become pregnant with Matthew she had always imagined morning sickness was just that—you woke up, you vomited, and then you got on with the rest of the day as right as rain. Instead this horrible nausea and the overall feeling of being unwell dogged her all day, but if this baby followed the same pattern as Matthew it would only be another two or three weeks before she felt better.

Melanie plugged in the coffee machine and then stood with her hands on her stomach, the wonder that a little life was growing inside her engulfing all her worries and fears and doubts for a few moments. 'You'll be told about your brother, little one, as soon as you're old enough to understand,' she whispered. 'He was our first child and greatly loved, but that doesn't mean you won't be loved too, for who and what you are.'

Would this baby understand that she had to leave it for its own good, though? Could any child take that on board? It might hate her. But would that matter so much if it was safe and protected and having a good life? The turmoil came in again on a great flood of anguish. She *was* doing the right thing, wasn't she? Yes, yes, she was. She couldn't doubt herself. And there must be no more nights like last night. This separation had to stand. And that meant she mustn't see Forde any more, because if he was there, in front of her, then all her resolve went out of the window. She wasn't strong enough where he was concerned.

'What's wrong?' said Forde sharply from behind her.

Melanie swung round, her hands springing away from her belly. 'Nothing, nothing's wrong.'

'You were standing there like that and for a minute I thought you were in pain,' he said thickly, his eyes searching her face as though he still wasn't quite sure if she was telling him the truth.

'I'm fine.' She took a deep breath. She had never voluntarily mentioned Matthew or what had happened, Forde had always been the one to broach the subject and more often than not then she had refused to discuss it, knowing she would break down if she did, but now she said quietly, 'I was thinking of Matthew, that's all. I—I don't want him forgotten. I want this baby to know it had a brother.'

'Of course.' His voice was soft but with a note in it that made her want to cry. 'That's taken as read, Nell.'

'Forde, if I agree to go and see Miriam, to talk to her, I want—' she took a deep breath '—I want you to promise you won't come here again. That's the deal. I mean it.'

She saw him take a physical step backwards as though she had slapped him across the face.

'We can't keep—' She shook her head. There was no kind way to say it. 'I don't want you here. It complicates everything and it will just make the final parting all the harder. I can cope on my own.'

'And if I can't? Cope, that is?' he said grimly. 'What then? Or is this all about you to the exclusion of anything else?'

Now she felt as though *he* had slapped *her*.

'You're carrying my child,' he said with deliberate control. 'That gives me certain rights, surely? You can't shut me out as though I don't exist.'

'I'm not trying to shut you out, not from the baby.'

'Oh, I see.' He raised dark brows. 'So I promise to stay away for the next nine months—'

'Six. I'm already three months pregnant.'

'Six months,' he continued as though she hadn't interrupted, 'and then what? I get a phone call saying the baby's born and I can come and pick it up? Is that what you've got planned?'

She stared at him. He had a right to be angry but now she was angry too. 'I didn't *have* to tell you I was pregnant,' she said stiffly. 'Not so early on anyway.'

'As I recall, it was me turning up at the doctor's that forced you to reveal it. Right? Whether you would have told me if you'd had time to think about it, I'm not so sure.'

Probably because he had touched on something she had been questioning herself about for the last twenty-four hours, Melanie was incensed. 'I'm not discussing this further, but I'd like you to remember that this is *my* house and I have a perfect right to say who comes over the threshold.' She glared at him, hands on hips and her eyes flashing.

'If you weren't pregnant I'd try shaking some sense into you,' he ground out between clenched teeth.

She knew he didn't mean it. Forde would never touch a woman in anger. Nevertheless her small chin rose a notch. 'You could try,' she said bitingly, 'but don't forget what I do for a living. I'm stronger than I look.'

'Actually, I've never doubted how strong you are,' he said tersely. 'It's your best and your worst attribute. It got you through the first twenty-five years of your life until you met me but now it's in danger of ruining the rest of your life. You need to let me in, Nell. You don't have to fight alone. Don't you realise that's what marriage is all about? I'm in your corner, for better or worse, richer or poorer, in sickness and health. I love you. *You.* The kind of love that will last for ever. I'm not going to give up on you whatever you say or do so get that through your head.'

'And you get through your head that I can't be what you want me to be. I'm not good for you, Forde. I'm not good for anyone.'

'You are the best thing that ever happened to me,' he said from the heart. 'The very best. Now you can try to tell yourself different if you like, but I know what I feel.'

She stared at him. 'I can't do this,' she said flatly, the

tone carrying more weight than any show of emotion. 'I want you to go, Forde. Now. I mean it.'

She did. He could see it in every fibre of her being. But he had one last thing to say. 'Even before the accident, you were expecting the bubble to burst, Nell. It became a self-fulfilling prophecy and you are the only one who can change that. I don't think I can do or say any more but I hope you have the courage to dig deep and face what you need to face, for the sake of our child as much as us.'

Her chin was up and her voice was tight and thin when she said, 'Have you finished?'

He gave her one last long look and then walked into the dining room, where his jacket was still hanging over the back of a chair, shrugging it on and leaving the house without another word.

Melanie heard the front door slam behind him but she didn't move for a full minute simply because she couldn't. She felt sick and ill and wretchedly unhappy, but she told herself she'd done what had to be done.

After a while she poured herself a coffee because if ever she had needed one it was now, walking into the sitting room and sinking down on one of the sofas. She sat for some time. It had started to rain outside, big drops splattering against the window, and she shivered. The weather was changing at last. Winter was round the corner.

It was the following evening when her phone rang just as she was finishing dinner. She hadn't felt like a meal, but had forced herself to cook a cheese omelette after she'd had her bath and changed into her pyjamas, con-

scious that she had to eat healthily now. To that end she'd
had a glass of milk with the omelette and finished with
an apple crumble and custard. Shop-bought but tasty
nonetheless.

Her heart thudded as she picked up the phone but
it wasn't Forde. Instead a woman's voice said, 'Can I
speak to Mrs Masterson, please?'

'Speaking.' This had to be the woman Forde had
mentioned.

'This is Miriam Cotton. Forde asked me to give you
a ring.'

'Oh, yes.' Melanie suddenly felt ridiculously nervous. She didn't want to go and see a stranger and talk
about her innermost feelings, but she had made a bargain with Forde that he'd leave her alone if she did so.
'I—I need to make an appointment, Mrs Cotton. I'm
sure you're very busy so I quite understand it might not
be for a while.'

It was another minute or two before she put down
the phone and her head was spinning. She was going to
see Miriam Cotton after work the next day. She didn't
doubt that Forde had pulled strings to make it happen;
'strike while the iron was hot' was his style.

She sat and brooded for a good hour, looking at the
address and telephone number Miriam had given her
and wondering whether to call her back and cancel the
appointment. It would mean she would have to take a
change of clothes to work and get ready before she left
Forde's mother's house, but that wasn't really the issue.

She was frightened. Scared stiff.

As the thought hit she realised her hands were
clenched into fists in her lap and she concentrated on

relaxing her fingers slowly. Forde had said she would have to find the courage to dig deep. Why should she put herself through that? What if it did no good? What if it made her feel even worse?

Panic rose, hot and strong, and then she remembered something else Forde had said, something she'd tried to put out of her mind, but which had only been relegated to the subconscious, waiting to jump out the minute she let it. He'd said she'd been expecting the bubble of their marriage to burst all along, that it had become a self-fulfilling prophecy and she was the only one who could change that. It had made her so mad she could have cheerfully strangled him, and she'd told herself at the time that was because it was untrue and terribly unfair.

She shut her eyes tightly. But it wasn't.

Opening her eyes, she stood up. She was exhausted; she couldn't think of this any more. She was going to bed and in the morning she would decide what she was going to do. But even as she thought it she knew her decision had already been made. Because something else Forde had said had cut deep. She had to do this for the sake of the baby. She had to *try*. It might be a lot of pain and anguish for nothing, and in digging up the past she might open a can of worms that was best left closed, but if she didn't try she would never know, would she?

She didn't even bother to brush her teeth before getting into bed, so physically and emotionally tired her limbs felt like dead weights, but in the split second before she fell asleep she acknowledged it wasn't just for the baby she was going to see Miriam tomorrow. It was for Forde too.

* * *

Miriam Cotton wasn't at all what Melanie had expected. For one thing her consulting room was part of her home, a cosy, friendly extension to the original Edwardian terrace overlooking the narrow walled garden consisting of a neat lawn and flowerbeds with an enormous cherry tree in the centre of it. And Miriam herself was something of a revelation, her thick white hair trimmed into an urchin cut with vivid red highlights and her slim figure clothed in jeans and a loose blue shirt. She had a wide smile, big blue eyes and lines where you would expect lines for someone of her age on her clear complexion. Altogether she gave the impression of someone who was at peace with herself. Melanie liked her immediately.

Once sitting in a plump armchair next to the glowing fire—artificial, Miriam informed her cheerfully, but the most realistic Melanie had ever seen—and with no consulting couch, which she had been preparing herself for all day and dreading, Melanie began to relax a little. There was something about Forde's friend's mother that inspired trust.

Miriam smiled at her from the other armchair. 'Before we go any further I must make one thing perfectly clear. Anything we talk about, anything you tell me is strictly between the two of us. Forde is a dear man but he will not be party to anything which is said in this room, not unless you wish to confide in him, of course. You have my absolute word on that.'

'Thank you.' Melanie nodded and relaxed a little more. She didn't want to have any secrets from Forde, it wasn't that, but knowing she still retained some control was nonetheless reassuring. It made her feel safe.

'Forde tells me you're expecting another baby?' Miriam said quietly.

Melanie nodded again. She was glad Miriam had said 'another' and not pretended Matthew hadn't been born. 'Yes, in the spring.' She hesitated. 'I suppose that's the main reason— No.' She paused, shaking her head. 'That's not right. It's *one* of the reasons I'm here. I guess falling for another baby has brought everything to a head.'

'Everything?' Miriam said even more quietly.

Melanie looked into the gentle face opposite her. There were family photographs covering one wall of the room and she had noticed one little girl was in a wheelchair. This woman knew about trouble and heartache, she thought, biting her lower lip. She would have known that even without the photographs. It was in Miriam's eyes. 'Shall—shall I start at the beginning?' she asked. 'My childhood, I mean.'

'That would be good,' Miriam said softly. 'And take your time. You can come to see me here as often as you like, every evening if you wish, until you feel ready to stop. Forde has been a wonderful friend to my son and you take priority right now. All right?'

Melanie left the house at seven o'clock feeling like a wet rag. She, who prided herself on not wearing her heart on her sleeve, had wept and wailed through the last two hours in a manner that horrified her now she thought about it.

She climbed into the pickup, which she'd parked a few metres from Miriam's front door. It looked somewhat incongruous in the line of mostly expensive cars the well-to-do street held, but Melanie didn't notice.

She took several deep breaths before she started the engine. She was far from convinced all this was a good idea, she told herself grimly. She felt worse, much worse if anything, after all the emotion of the last hours. Admittedly Miriam had seemed to guess how she was feeling and had assured her it was the same for everyone initially. She had to persevere to come out of the other end of the dark tunnel, according to Miriam. But what if she got stuck in the tunnel? What then?

She drew out of the parking space into the road, a deep weariness making her limbs feel heavy.

Then she straightened her back and lifted her chin. She had promised Forde and she would keep her end of the bargain. She would come back tomorrow and all the other tomorrows until this thing was done.

Melanie drove home slowly, aware she was totally exhausted and needed to be ultra careful. Once at the cottage she fixed herself a quick meal before falling into bed. She was asleep as soon as her head touched the pillow.

That evening was to set the pattern for the next few weeks, but the morning after her first visit to Miriam she attended the local hospital for her first scan. It was a bittersweet day. She remembered how she and Forde had come together for Matthew's first scan, excited and thrilled as they had waited to see the baby on the monitor, and slightly apprehensive in case everything wasn't as it should be.

This time she sat alone in the waiting area, which was smaller than the one in the hospital in London—her own choice, she reminded herself as she watched the couple in front of her come out of the room where the scan took place wrapped in each other's arms and smiling.

Once she was lying on the bed it was more of a repeat of the time before. The lady taking the scan was smiling; all was well, heartbeat strong, baby developing as it should be and no concerns.

She left the hospital clutching two pictures of the child in her womb and with tears of relief and thankfulness streaming down her face.

Once she was sitting in the truck in the hospital car park she took a few minutes to compose herself before phoning Forde on his mobile. He answered immediately. 'Nell? What's wrong?'

'Nothing's wrong. I've been to the hospital for the first scan and everything's fine with the baby. I just wanted you to know. I've a picture for you. I'll leave it with Isabelle.'

It was a moment before he spoke and his voice was gruff. 'Thank God. And I mean that, thank God. They can't tell if it's a boy or a girl at this stage, can they?'

'No. That's at twenty weeks. Do you want to know?' They hadn't found out with Matthew.

'I don't know. Do you?'

'I'm not sure. I'll ring you near the time and discuss it then. I have to go to work now. Goodbye, Forde.'

His voice was husky when he said, 'Goodbye, Nell.'

It took her another ten minutes to dry her eyes and compose herself again before she could start the truck and drive out of the hospital confines, but by the time she got to Isabelle's house she was in command of herself.

Isabelle insisted on giving her a hot drink before she

joined James in the garden, and her mother-in-law was entranced with the picture of her future grandchild. 'Do you mind if I take a copy of it for myself before I pass this on to Forde tonight?' Isabelle asked as they finished their hot chocolate and custard creams at the kitchen table. 'He's calling in later for dinner. I don't suppose you'd like to stay too?'

Melanie shook her head. 'I'm going to see Miriam again.' She had thought it only right to tell her mother-in-law what she was doing yesterday and now she was glad she had. It was the perfect excuse and had the added bonus of being the truth.

'Is it being nosy if I ask you how it went?' Isabelle said gently.

'Of course not.' Melanie shrugged. 'But I can't give you much of an answer because I'm not sure myself. It was…traumatic, I suppose.'

'But helpful?'

Melanie shrugged again. 'I don't know, Isabelle. I guess time will tell.' She drank the last of her hot chocolate and stood up. 'I'd better go and help James with the planting.'

Once outside, she lifted her face to the silver-grey sky. Helpful. How could anything so painful be helpful? She wasn't looking forward to the next weeks.

November turned into December amid biting white frosts and brilliantly cold days, but she and James managed to complete the work at Isabelle's by the end of the first week of December.

And Forde kept his word. He didn't come to the cottage and he didn't call her. In fact he could have fallen off the edge of the world and she'd be none the wiser, Melanie thought to herself irritably more than once, before taking herself to task for her inconsistency.

Pride had forbidden her to mention him to Isabelle while she had still been working at her mother-in-law's house. It seemed the height of hypocrisy to do so anyway after she had left him and was still refusing to go back. What could she say? Was he well? Was he happy? And after that time when Isabelle had asked her to stay for dinner on the day of the scan, her mother-in-law had talked about everything under the sun except Forde. Which wasn't like Isabelle and led Melanie to suspect her mother-in-law was obeying orders from her son.

She could be wrong, of course, maybe she was being paranoid, but, whatever, she couldn't complain.

But she missed him. Terribly. It had been bad enough when she had first left him in the early part of the year, but then she had been reconciled to the fact her marriage was over. She had thrown herself into making her business work and finding herself a home, and, although that hadn't compensated for not having him around, it had occupied her mind some of the time. Furnishing the cottage, turning her tiny courtyard garden into a small oasis, making sure any professional work she did was done to the best of her ability and drumming up business had all played its part in dulling her mind against the pain.

But now…

Since he had muscled his way into her life again that night in August he'd reopened a door she was powerless to shut. He'd penetrated her mind—and her body, she thought wryly, her hand going to the swell of her belly.

And in spite of herself she wanted to see him, the more so as the sessions with Miriam progressed.

She was finding herself in a strange place emotionally as her deepest fears and anxieties stemming from her troubled childhood and even more troubled teens were unearthed. She had to come to terms with the truth that she'd buried the fact she'd always felt worthless and unloved behind the capable, controlled façade she presented to the world. And as time had gone on something had begun to happen to the solid ball of pain and fear and sorrow lodged in her heart. It had begun to slowly disintegrate, and, though the process wasn't without its own anguish and grief, it was cleansing.

Gradually, very gradually she was beginning to accept the concept that her confusion and despair as a child had coloured her view of herself. She hadn't been responsible for her parents' death or that of her grandmother, or her friend's tragic accident either. None of that had been her fault.

The miscarriage was harder to come to terms with, her grief still frighteningly raw. It helped more than she could ever express that Miriam had pushed aside her professional status and cried with her on those sessions, revealing to Melanie that she'd lost a baby herself at six months and had blamed herself for a long time afterwards.

'It's what we do as women,' Miriam had said wryly as she'd dried her eyes after one particularly harrowing meeting. 'Take the blame, punish ourselves, try to make sense of what is an unexplainable tragedy. But you weren't to blame. You would have given your life for Matthew as I would have given mine for my baby.'

'Forde said that once, that I'd have given my life for Matthew's if I could,' Melanie had said thoughtfully.

'He's right.' Miriam had patted her arm gently. 'And he loves you very much. Lots of women go a whole lifetime without being loved like Forde loves you. You can trust him—you know that, don't you?'

But could she trust herself? She wanted to. More than anything she longed to put the past behind her and believe she could be a good wife and mother and a rational and optimistic human being, but how did she know if she had the strength of mind to do that or would she fall back into the old fears and anxieties that would cripple her and ultimately those she loved?

Melanie was thinking about the conversation with Miriam on the day before Christmas Eve. She was curled up on one of the sofas in her sitting room, which she'd pulled close to the glowing fire, watching an old Christmassy film on TV but without paying it any real attention. She had finished work until after the New Year; the ground had been as hard as iron for weeks and heavy snow was forecast within the next twenty-four hours.

She and James had finished the job they'd gone on to once Isabelle's garden was completed and James had disappeared off to Scotland to spend Christmas with his parents and a whole host of relations, although she suspected it was more the allure of the Hogmanay party his parents always held on New Year's Eve that he didn't want to miss. He had invited her to go with him, telling her his parents' house was always packed full over the festive season and one more would make no difference, but she'd declined the offer. A couple of her friends had invited her for Christmas lunch, and both Isabelle and Miriam had made noises in that direction, but she had politely said no to everyone.

She had forbidden the one person she wanted to spend Christmas with from coming anywhere near her, and although part of her wanted to call Forde and just hear his voice, another part—a stronger part—didn't feel ready for what that might entail. She had bought him a Christmas card and then decided not to send it because for the life of her she couldn't find the right words to say. She knew she would have to phone him after Christmas about the next scan; it was only two weeks away now.

She rested her hand on the mound of her stomach and in response felt a fluttering that made her smile. That had happened several times in the last week and it never failed to thrill her. Her baby, living, growing, moving inside her, a little person who would have its own mind and personality. She had felt this baby move much earlier than she had Matthew but her friends who had children had assured her it was like that with the second. And with each experience of feeling those tiny arms and legs stretching and kicking she had wondered how ever she'd be able to hand their child over to Forde and walk away. It would kill her, she thought, shutting her eyes tightly. But would it be the best thing for her baby? She didn't know any more. She had been so sure before she'd started seeing Miriam, but now, the more she understood herself and what had led her to think that way, the more she'd dared to hope. Hope that maybe, just maybe, the depression that had kicked in after the miscarriage and that had been fed by the insecurities of her past had fooled her into thinking that way.

'You're not a Jonah, Melanie.' Miriam had said that at their last session as they were saying goodbye. 'You are like everyone else. Some people sail through life without encountering any problems, others seem to have loads from day one, but it's all due to chance, unfair though that is. I can't say the rest of your life is going to be a bowl of cherries, no one can, but I *can* say you have a choice right now. You can either look at the negatives and convince yourself it's all doom and gloom, or you can take life by the throat and kick it into submission. Know what I mean?'

'Like Cassie and Sarah?' she'd answered. Sarah was the little girl in a wheelchair in the photograph. She was beautiful, with curly brown hair and huge, limpid green eyes, but she had been born with spina bifida and other medical complications. Cassie, her mother, was devoted to her and in the summer Cassie had been diagnosed with multiple sclerosis, but according to Miriam her daughter was determined to fight her illness every inch of the way. Sarah, young as she was, had the same spirit, her proud grandmother said, and was a joy to be with. Miriam had admitted to Melanie she'd cried bitter tears over them both but would never dream of letting her daughter or granddaughter know because neither of them 'did' self-pity.

'My Cassie must have had her down times over Sarah and now this multiple sclerosis has reared its head, but, apart from in the early days with Sarah just after she was born, I've never seen Cassie anything but positive.'

Miriam had looked at her, her eyes soft. 'You can be like that, Melanie. I know it.'

A log fell further into the glowing ash, sending a shower of sparks up the chimney. It roused Melanie from her thoughts and she glanced at the dwindling stack of logs and empty coal scuttle. She must go and bring more logs in and fill the scuttle before it got dark, she thought, rising to her feet reluctantly. James had helped her build a lean-to in her small paved front garden in the summer for her supply of logs and sacks of coal. She hadn't wanted to lose any space in her tiny private courtyard at the back of the property, and as the front of the properties only overlooked a local farmer's hay barns there was no one to object. Nevertheless, they had taken care to give the lean-to a quaint, rustic look in keeping with the cottages and as one side was enclosed by her neighbour's high wooden fence it kept her fuel relatively dry and protected.

When she opened the front door an icy blast of air hit her and the sky looked grey and low although it was only three in the afternoon. She filled the scuttle to the weight she was happy to carry now she was pregnant and took it inside, before going back for some logs. She took an armful in and then went back for some more, and it was only then she noticed a slight movement close to the fence behind the stack of wood.

Petrified it was a rat—one or two of the neighbours had mentioned seeing the odd rat or two, courtesy of the farmer's barns, no doubt—Melanie hurried back inside the house, her heart pounding like a drum. As soon as she had closed the door she knew she had to go back and make sure what it was, though. What if a bird had somehow got trapped or some other creature was hurt? Situated as the cottages were in a small hamlet surrounded by countryside, it could be anything sheltering there.

Wishing with all her heart she hadn't gone out for the logs and coal and were still sitting watching TV in front of the fire, she put on a coat before opening the door again. The temperature seemed to have dropped another few degrees in just a minute or two. There was no doubt excited children all over the country were going to get their wish of a white Christmas, she thought, treading carefully to where she'd seen the movement. She bent down, her muscles poised to spring away if a beady-eyed rodent jumped out at her.

But it wasn't a rat that stared back at her. Squeezed into the tiniest space possible, a small tabby cat crouched shivering in its makeshift shelter, all huge amber eyes and trembling fur.

'Why, hello,' Melanie whispered softly, putting out her hand only for the cat to shrink back as far as it could. 'Hey, I'm not going to hurt you. Don't be frightened. Come on, puss.'

After several minutes of murmuring sweet nothings, by which time she was shaking with cold as much as the cat, Melanie realised she was getting nowhere. She could also see the cat was all bone under its fur but with a distended stomach, which either meant it was pregnant or had some kind of growth. Praying it was the former because she was already consumed with pity for the poor little mite, she stood up and went to fetch some cooked roast chicken from the kitchen, hoping to tempt it with food where gentle encouragement had failed.

The cat was clearly starving, but not starving enough to leave its sanctuary, roast chicken or no roast chicken.

'I can't leave you out here. Please, please come out,' Melanie begged, close to tears. It was getting darker by the minute and the wind was cutting through her like a knife, but the thought of abandoning the cat to its fate just wasn't an option. And if she started to move the pile of logs it was sheltering behind they might fall and crush the little thing. She had tried reaching a hand to it but was a couple of inches short of being able to grab it.

'Nell? What the hell are you doing out here and who are you talking to?' said Forde's voice behind her.

She swung round and there he was. Whether it was because she was frozen or had moved too quickly or was faint with relief that he was here to help her, she didn't know, but the next thing she knew there was a rushing in her ears and from her crouched position beside the cat she slid onto her bottom, struggling with all her might not to pass out as the darkness moved from the sky into her head and became overwhelming.

CHAPTER TEN

IN THE end Melanie didn't lose consciousness. She was aware of Forde kneeling beside her and holding her against him as he told her to take deep breaths and stay still—not that she could have done anything else. She was also aware of the wonderful smell and feel of him—big, solid, breathtakingly reassuring. It was when he tried to lift her into his arms, saying, 'I'm taking you indoors,' that she found her voice.

'No. No, you can't. There's a cat, Forde. It's in trouble,' she muttered weakly.

'A cat?' The note of incredulity in his voice would have been comical under other circumstances. 'What are you talking about? You're frozen, woman. I'm taking you in.'

'*No.*' Her voice was stronger now and she pushed his arms away when he tried to gather her up. 'There *is* a cat, behind the wood there, and it's ill or pregnant or both. Look, see for yourself.' She allowed him to help her to her feet but wouldn't budge an inch, saying again, 'Look, there. And I can't reach it and it's terrified, Forde. We can't leave it out here in this weather—'

'All right, all right.' Thoroughly exasperated but less panicked now she was on her feet and seemingly OK,

Forde peered into the shadows where she was pointing. At first he thought she must be imagining things and then he saw it—a little scrap of nothing crouched behind the logs. 'Yes, I see it. Are you sure it won't just come out and go home once we leave it alone?'

Her voice held all the controlled patience women drew on when the male of the species said something outrageously stupid. 'Quite sure, Forde. And I don't think it has a home to go to. Whatever's happened to it, it isn't good. The thing's absolutely scared stiff of humans, can't you see? And it's starving.'

Forde narrowed his eyes as he tried to see in what was rapidly becoming pitch blackness. 'It looks plump enough to me,' he said eventually. 'In fact quite rotund.'

'That's its belly. The rest of it is skeletal, for goodness' sake. We have to do something.'

'Right.' In a way he was grateful to the cat. He'd come here tonight because he'd heard the weather was going to get atrocious and it was the excuse he'd been looking for to see her for weeks. While she'd gone to see Miriam as promised he hadn't wanted to do anything to rock the boat, and her demands had been very explicit—no contact. But, he had reasoned to himself on the drive from London, she could hardly object to him calling to see if she was well stocked up with provisions and ready for the blizzard that had been forecast for some days. He'd bought half of his local delicatessen just in case, as well as a few other luxuries he could blame on the festive season. He'd been hoping she would be mellow enough to ask him in for a drink, but he hadn't expected to be welcomed with open arms like this—even if it was due to a homeless moggy. But beggars couldn't be choosers.

'What are you going to do?' she said. 'We have to help it.'

He glanced at her. She was literally wringing her hands. Feeling that chances like this didn't come that often, he gestured towards the cottage. 'Go and open the door and get ready to close it again once I get the thing in the house.'

'But you won't *reach* it,' she almost wailed.

'I'll reach it.' If there was a God, he'd reach it. Once she was in position in the doorway to the cottage, he reached into the narrow void between the fence and the logs. He heard the cat hiss and spit before he felt its claws but somehow he got it by the scruff of the neck and hauled it out so he could get a firm hold. He realised immediately Melanie was right, the poor thing was emaciated apart from its swollen stomach, which, if he was right, was full of kittens.

He had grown up with cats and a couple of dogs and now he held the animal against the thick wool of his coat talking soothingly to it and trying not to swear as it used its claws again. But it hadn't bit him. Which, in the circumstances, was something. Especially as it was frightened to death.

Melanie was all fluster once they had got it into the house and shut the door but he still held onto the cat, which had become quieter. 'Nell, warm a little milk in a saucer, and we'll need some food.' He sat down on one of the breakfast bar stools, holding the cat gently but firmly. 'Have you got a cardboard box we could use as a bed for it?'

She shook her head as she slopped milk into a saucer and then began to chop some chicken up. 'I can fetch a blanket if you like? I've several in the airing cupboard.'

'Anything.' The cat had calmed right down but was still shaking. He loosed one of his hands enough to begin stroking it and to his surprise it didn't squirm or try to escape, but lay on his lap as though it was spent. Which it probably was, he thought pityingly. How long it had been fending for itself was anyone's guess, but it hadn't done very well by the look of it. He could imagine it had been a pet that had got pregnant and—with Christmas coming up and all the expense—had become expendable to its delightful owners.

Melanie brought the saucer of milk over and held it in front of the cat as it lay on his lap. It took seconds to finish the lot. Her voice thick with tears, she said, 'The poor thing, Forde. How could someone dump a pretty little cat like this?'

So she had come to the same conclusion as him. 'Beyond me, but I'd like five minutes alone with them,' he said grimly. 'Try the chicken now. I don't want to put it down yet in case it bolts and we frighten it trying to catch it again.'

The chicken went the same way as the milk. Opening his coat, he slipped the cat against the warmth of his cashmere jumper and half closed the edges of the coat around it, making a kind of cocoon. 'It needs to warm up,' he said to Melanie, 'and holding it like this is emphasising we don't mean it any harm. That's more important than anything right now.'

'Shall I get some more milk and chicken?' she asked, putting out a tentative hand and gently stroking the little striped head. The cat tensed for a moment and then relaxed again. It was clearly exhausted.

'No, we don't want to give it too much too quickly and make it sick if it's been without food for a while. Leave it for an hour or two and then we'll try again.'

She nodded, her hand dropping away. Then she looked him straight in the eyes and said honestly, 'I've never been so glad to see anyone in my life. I didn't know what to do.'

Anyone. Not him specifically. But again, better than nothing. He grinned. 'I left my white steed in the car park but it's good to know I can still warm a fair maiden's heart. Talking of which, there's various bits and pieces in the car I need to fetch in a while.'

'Bits and pieces?'

'I wanted to make sure you were stocked up with provisions in view of the snow that's coming.' Considering how well he'd done with the moggy he thought he could push his luck. 'And I was hoping we could perhaps share a meal?' he added with a casualness that didn't quite come off. 'Before I go back?'

Melanie's big brown eyes surveyed him solemnly. 'That would be lovely,' she said simply.

The cat chose that moment to begin purring and Forde knew exactly how it felt. To hide the surge of elation he'd felt at her words, he smiled, saying, 'Listen to that. This is a nice cat. In spite of what's happened to it it's still prepared to trust us.'

'I'll make us a coffee. It's decaf now, I'm afraid.'

'Decaf's fine.' Mud mixed with water would have been fine right at that moment.

He drank the coffee with the cat still nestled against

him, now fast asleep. They talked of inconsequential things, both carefully feeling their way. Outside the wind grew stronger, howling like a banshee and rattling the windows.

After a while Melanie fetched a blanket from her little airing cupboard and they made a bed for the cat in her plastic laundry basket. They fed it more milk and chicken before Forde gently extracted it from his coat and laid it in the basket, whereupon it went straight to sleep again. Melanie had placed the basket next to the radiator in the kitchen and it was as warm as toast.

'It's still a very young cat,' said Forde as they stood looking down at the little scrap, 'but those are definitely kittens in there and if I'm not much mistaken she's due pretty soon.'

'How soon?' Melanie showed her alarm. She liked animals but she had never had much to do with any while growing up. As for the mechanics of a cat giving birth...

'Hard to tell. Could be hours, could be days.'

'But time enough to get her to a vet?'

'That might freak her out.' Forde was thinking. 'How far is your nearest vet?'

Melanie stared at him blankly. 'I've absolutely no idea.'

'OK. Look in the telephone directory while I get the stuff in from the car and find a local vet. It's—' he glanced at his watch '—getting on for five o'clock but they should still be working. I'll give them a ring and ask if someone can come and make a house call.'

'Would they do that if they don't know us?' Melanie asked doubtfully. 'It's not as if we're clients, is it?'

'We won't know that till we ask.'

Without thinking about it she reached up and looped her arms round his neck, kissing him hard and then stepping back a pace before he could respond.

He stared at her, clearly taken aback. 'What was that for?'

'For caring.'

'About the moggy?'

'No, not just the cat,' she said softly.

Something told him not to push it at this stage. 'I'll get the food in. You find that number.'

When he called the veterinary surgery, which was situated some fifteen miles away in the nearest small market town, the receptionist was less than helpful, although she did eventually let him speak to one of the vets after Forde wouldn't take no for an answer. As luck would have it, the woman was young, newly qualified and enthusiastic, added to which Forde used his considerable charm along with offering to pay the call-out fee with his credit card over the telephone and any further costs with cash before she left the cottage.

But Melanie, listening to Forde's end of the exchange, was quite convinced it was the charm that had swung it when the vet said she would be with them within the hour.

Once she began to unpack the bags Forde had brought in she could hardly believe the amount of food he'd bought. A whole cooked ham, a small turkey, a tray of delicious looking canapés, a mulled-cranberry-and-apple-chutney-topped pork pie, cheese of all descriptions, jars of preserves, a Santa-topped Christmas cake and a box of chocolate cup cakes, mince pies, vegetables, nuts, fruit, and still the list went on.

'Forde, this would feed a family of four for a week,' she said weakly when the last bag was empty. 'There's only me. Whatever possessed you?'

'I must have known you'd have a visitor.' He smiled at her over the heaped breakfast bar as she began to stuff what she could in her fridge.

'A visitor?' She glanced at him, colour in her cheeks. He nodded towards the sleeping cat.

'Oh, yes, of course, but she's hardly going to eat much,' she said flusteredly. For a minute she'd thought... But no, he wouldn't invite himself to stay, not after the rules she'd made. If she wanted him to spend Christmas with her she would have to ask him. But did she want that? Or, more precisely, did she want what that would mean in the days after Christmas and beyond? Because one thing was for sure: she couldn't play fast and loose with his heart any more. She had to be sure. And she wasn't; she wasn't sure. Was she?

'You'd be surprised. She's going to have kittens to feed and she's got lost time to make up for.'

And as though on cue the cat woke up, stretching as she opened big amber eyes and then stood up amid the folds of the blanket. When Forde lifted her out of the laundry basket she didn't struggle but gave a small miaow. Melanie quickly warmed more milk and cut more chicken, and this time Forde set the little animal on its feet to eat. She cleared both saucers, stretched again and then walked over to her makeshift bed and jumped in, settling herself down by kneading the blanket how she wanted it. Then she looked at them.

Melanie knelt down beside her, stroking the brindled fur beneath which she could feel every bone. 'She's so beautiful,' she murmured softly, 'and so brave. She must have been desperate, knowing her babies are going to be born and she had no shelter, no food. It's a wonder she's survived this long.'

A steady, rhythmic vibration began under her fingers as the little cat began to purr; it made her want to cry. How could anyone treat this friendly little creature so cruelly? To throw her out in the winter when they must have known her chances of survival and those of the kittens was poor?

'But now she's found you,' Forde said quietly. 'And she knows she can trust you to look after her.'

Flooded by emotions as turbulent as the weather outside, Melanie looked up at him. She felt as though she were standing at the brink of something profound. 'Do you think I should keep her?'

He didn't prevaricate or throw the ball back in her court. 'Yes, I do. She needs someone to love her unconditionally.'

Melanie blinked back tears. 'But she's so fragile and thin. I can't see her surviving giving birth, Forde. And what of the kittens? If their mother's been starving, what shape will they be in when they're born?'

'Take it a moment by moment, hour by hour. She might surprise you. I think she's a tougher little cookie than she looks. Don't give up on her yet.'

'I'm not about to give up on her,' said Melanie, a trifle indignantly. 'That's the last thing I would do.'

'Good.' He smiled. 'In that case she has a fighting chance.'

The ringing of the doorbell ended further conversation. The vet turned out to be a big, buxom woman with rosy cheeks and large hands, but she was gentleness itself with her small patient. The cat submitted to her ministrations with surprising docility and when she had finished examining her, the vet shook her head. 'I'd be surprised if she's more than a year or so old. She's little more than a kitten herself. That's not good for a number of reasons. She might find it difficult giving birth and in her state she hasn't got any physical strength to fall back on. Being so malnourished I don't know if she would be able to produce a good quality of milk for the kittens, should she or them survive the birth. But—' she looked at them both '—she's a dear little cat, isn't she?'

'What can you do to help in the short term?' Forde asked quietly. 'We want to give her every chance.'

'The main thing she needs is rest and food and food and rest. Have you got a litter tray so she doesn't need to go outside? It's important to keep her warm.'

Forde shook his head. 'But I can get one.'

'Not at this time of night. Follow me back to the surgery and I'll give you one of ours, along with a food made specially for pregnant females and feeding mothers. I'll give her a vitamin injection now and once she's a little stronger she'll need various vaccinations for cat flu and other diseases. I don't want to tax her system by doing that now, and as long as you keep her confined to the house for the time being she won't come into contact with other felines who might be carrying diseases. I think she's due very soon, although it's difficult to tell in a case like this. If she does begin and you're worried for any reason, call me. I'll give you my mobile number.'

She smiled. 'Having done that we can almost guarantee she'll start as I sit down for my Christmas lunch.'

'That's very good of you,' said Melanie.

'This is an exceptional case,' the young woman said quietly. 'I hate to think what she's been through in the last weeks. Now, let her eat and drink little and often in the next twenty-four hours and try to get as much down her as she wants. But I have to warn you—' again she glanced at them both '—the odds are stacked against her giving birth to live kittens. I can give you vitamin drops to put in her food but I'm afraid it might well be too little too late.'

Melanie nodded. 'Nevertheless, we want to try.'

'Good. Fuss her, talk to her and give her plenty of TLC. You won't read that in any veterinary journal but in my opinion it works wonders with animals that have been ill treated. They understand far more than we give them credit for.'

The vet gave them a few more instructions and then she and Forde left, leaving Melanie with Tabitha, as she had decided to call the pretty little animal. She found she was on tenterhooks all the time Forde was gone. Forde had carried the basket into the sitting room for her before he departed, setting it on the thick rug in front of the fire, and after a little more food Tabitha had gone soundly asleep. Melanie tried to watch TV but her whole attention was fixed on the sleeping feline.

The vet had run through the signs to look for when the cat started labour and what to expect, and Melanie found herself praying the whole time nothing would happen before Forde got back. He'd know what to do; he always did.

The relief she felt when she heard him call to her when he let himself in with the key she'd given him was overwhelming. She flew out into the hall, her words tumbling over themselves as she said, 'Did you get everything? Should we try and give her some of the special food right now? Where should we put the litter tray? Do you think she'll let us know when she needs to use it?' She stopped to draw breath.

Forde regarded her with amused eyes. 'Yes, yes, litter tray by the basket and maybe.'

He looked big and dark and impossibly attractive in her tiny hall, and sexy. Incredibly sexy. Before she knew what she was saying, she blurted, 'Will you stay here tonight, in case something happens?'

He smiled a sweet smile. 'I didn't intend to leave you by yourself, Nell. Now, we'll get our patient organised with some more food and then we'll eat ourselves, OK? Ham and eggs, something quick and easy. Have you got a spare duvet I can use tonight and perhaps a pillow for the sofa?'

'You'll never sleep on my sofas.' His long frame was double their length. 'I can stay down here with her.'

'You need your sleep.' He glanced at the swell of her stomach under the soft Angora sweater-dress she was wearing. 'And I'll be fine. Now, let's see how she likes this food compared to the chicken.'

The food smelt quite disgusting when they opened the tin, the odour of fish overpowering, but Tabitha finished a saucerful without seemingly pausing for breath.

'Cat caviar,' commented Forde drily. 'It should be too, considering the price. Remind me to come out of property developing and into cat food.'

Melanie smiled. It was scarily good having him here. And not just because of Tabitha.

They ate their own meal at the dining-room table. Melanie was glad she'd cleared it of paperwork a few days before and put a festive centrepiece of holly with bright red berries in pride of place. That, along with her small, fragrant Christmas tree decorated with baubles and tinsel in the sitting room and the cards dotted about, gave the impression she'd made some effort. In truth, she'd never felt less like celebrating Christmas. Or it had been that way until she had heard Forde's voice.

Melanie had insisted on having Tabitha's basket where they could see her while they ate, and after they'd finished the meal she carried their decaf coffee and the chocolate cup cakes Forde had bought through to the sitting room, while Forde brought Tabitha. The little cat looked out serenely from the basket as Forde set it in front of the fire again, apparently quite happy with all the coming and going.

The cup cakes were heavenly. Melanie ate three, one after another, and then looked at Forde aghast. 'I'm going to be as big as a house before this baby's born. Now the sickness has gone all I think about is food. I no sooner eat breakfast than I'm thinking about lunch and then dinner, and Christmas doesn't help with all the extra temptations of cake and plum pudding and chocolate.'

'Nell, you could never look anything but gorgeous to me.' He lifted her small chin, licking a smear of chocolate icing from the corner of her mouth before kissing her as though no one else in the world existed. Her lips, as soft and warm as mulled wine, moved against his and she kissed him back, her hands sliding up to his shoulders and tangling in his hair.

He caught the moan that fluttered in her throat with his breath, his kiss deepening still more and his tongue beginning an insistent probing that brought every nerve in her body to singing life. Before she knew what he was doing he had moved and lifted her so she was sitting on his lap. Now his mouth moved from her lips to trail a burning path to her throat and down into the V of her cleavage.

Melanie gasped and he lifted her head to look into her flushed face. 'I want you,' he murmured softly, 'all the time. At my desk when I'm working, in the car, at home when I'm eating a meal or taking a shower. There's not a minute of a day when I'm not thinking about you. You're in my blood, do you know that? For life. A sweet addiction that's impossible to fight.'

'Do you want to fight it?' she asked faintly, his silvery eyes mesmerising.

His mouth twisted in a bittersweet smile. 'There have been times when I've thought the pain would be easier if I did, but, no, I don't.'

This time she kissed him and his body throbbed with the contact. His hands ran over her breasts, the soft wool beneath his fingers moulding to the rounded globes and her nipples hard and engorged. She didn't object when he tugged her dress upwards, helping him by lifting her arms as he pulled it over her head. Her lacy bra showed her breasts were fuller and her cleavage deeper, the firm mound of her belly making his breath catch in his throat. Her body was changing, to accommodate his son or daughter. The surge of possessive love expanded his chest and made it difficult to breathe.

'Forde?'

'You're so beautiful, Nell,' he whispered, his eyes brilliant with unshed tears. 'So beautiful.'

They undressed each other slowly and completely, touching and tasting as they did so until they were both naked and trembling with desire. Then she climbed on top of him on the sofa where they were lying, sitting astride him as she lowered herself onto the proud rod of his erection.

Her body was warm, unbelievably soft and welcoming as it accepted him, and as she began to move he struggled to keep control so she was fulfilled along with him. He could see the pleasure in her face and it was almost more erotic than he could bear, his body shaking as his muscles clenched against the release it was aching for.

He felt her climax and went with her, their sanity shattering into pure sensation and then reforming in the aftermath of drugged passion. It was a few moments after she had snuggled against him before either of them could speak. 'Wow,' murmured Forde huskily. 'Tell me this isn't a dream and I'm going to wake up in a minute back at the house.'

'It's real.' She shivered as she spoke and he reached for the throw hanging over the back of the sofa, wrapping it round them as she settled her head on his chest. Within moments she was fast asleep, just the odd spit and crackle from the fire disturbing the pine-scented stillness. He glanced at the basket. The cat was sleeping too amid the folds of the blanket, its small striped body barely moving with each breath.

I owe you, Forde told it silently. *And now you've got me this far I'm not leaving.*

The room was all dancing shadows, the flickering flames of the fire and the lights on Melanie's Christmas tree creating a soothing, womblike feeling. Outside the wind continued to moan and howl, and now sleet was hurling itself against the windows with a ferocity that made the room even warmer and cosier in comparison to the storm outside.

Holding Melanie close, he shut his eyes.

CHAPTER ELEVEN

A DISTANT vibration brought Melanie out of a satisfying dream. She opened sleepy eyes to find she was lying with her cheek on Forde's hairy chest and with her body snuggled into his side like a little animal burying itself into the source of its comfort, his heartbeat still echoing in her head. She didn't let herself think for a few moments, relishing the feel and smell of him and the fact that he was here, with her. The baby moved, the flutterings the strongest yet, as though it knew its father was close.

And then she smiled to herself at such fanciful imaginings.

She raised her head carefully to look at Tabitha, aware she and Forde must have slept for an hour or more, but the cat was still sound asleep. The vet had said the best medicine for her was food and rest; if only they could make sure she had a few days of both before she delivered her kittens they might all make it, along with their mother. *Please, please, God, let this be a happy ending,* she prayed silently. *I want a happy ending for once. She's only a little cat—don't take her before her life has really begun. And the kittens, let them live to*

*grow and play and feel the sun on their fur in the sum-
mer. Please.*

Forde had said Tabitha knew she could trust them to
look after her, that she needed someone to love her unconditionally. She knew now why his words had struck
such a chord in her. It was how Forde was with her; from
the day they had met he had put her needs before his,
in the bedroom and out of it, and his love had been un-
limited and without reservation.

She drew in a shuddering breath, her mind clearer
than it had been for months.

After Matthew had died her guilt and remorse
had turned her mind and heart inwards. She'd been
so wrapped up in her own culpability and self-
condemnation, so convinced she was a jinx and that
Forde would be better off without her, that she hadn't
considered she might be wrong. She'd been too self-
centred. Wrapped up in her own grief, she hadn't taken
on board he was suffering too, not really, not as she
should have. She had learnt a lot about herself over the
last weeks with Miriam, and some of it had been hard
to take.

But Forde didn't see her as she saw herself. He
loved her. Utterly. Absolutely. As he'd told her to love
Tabitha—unconditionally. When she had left him he
had told her he would never let her go, that she could
divorce him, flee to the other side of the world, refuse
to see or talk to him, but he would never give up trying to make her see sense and come back to him. It had
panicked her then, terrified her even. But now…

She raised her head and stared at his sleeping face.
Now she was humbly and eternally grateful. Her

hand went to the swell of her belly wherein their child lay. And she could never walk away from her baby and its father. How could she have considered such a possibility even for a moment? But deep inside she'd always known she wouldn't have the strength to give her baby up. That had been what had *really* frightened her once she'd known she was pregnant, because then she had still believed she was a curse on those she loved.

And now? a little voice outside herself asked insistently. What did she believe now? Because if she went back to Forde it had to be with all her body, soul and spirit. She'd asked for a happy ending for Tabitha but she had to believe in one for herself. Believe she could trust Forde implicitly, give him that little part of herself she had always kept back. Could she do that?

She heard a scratching sound and raised her head again. Tabitha was awake and turning round and round in the basket and Melanie could have sworn there was a faintly worried expression on the cat's delicate face. Tabitha gave a little cry that was more of a yowl than a miaow, and then jumped out of the basket and disappeared behind the other sofa.

Oh, no. Melanie sat bolt upright and in so doing woke Forde, who mumbled dazedly, 'What the... Nell?'

'I think Tabitha's going to have her kittens.' Even to herself her voice sounded thick with fear. 'It's too soon, Forde. I wanted her to have some days of good food and rest. What are we going to do?'

Forde sat up, swinging his feet onto the carpet and raking back his hair. 'Where is she?' he asked, eyeing the empty basket.

'Behind the other sofa. The vet said she might hide.'

He stood up naked as the day he was born and walked across the room, peering over the back of the sofa. Damn it, Nell was right. The cat was behaving exactly as the vet had warned it might. They had all been hoping they could have a few days of feeding her up but it looked as if time had run out.

He turned, gathering up Melanie's scattered clothes along with his own. 'We can do very little now except keep an eye on her. The rest is up to Tabitha. I'll move the basket behind the sofa if that's where she wants to be. Get dressed and go and make us a hot drink. This could take a while.'

'It's too soon,' Melanie said again, her old fears and doubts resurfacing in a flood.

Forde reached out a hand and stroked her cheek for a moment. 'Stop panicking. Tabitha will pick up on it. Animals are incredibly sensitive that way. Bring some warm milk and food in for her when you get our drinks, OK? Now get dressed, there's a good girl.'

Once in the kitchen Melanie realised the icy sleet had turned into snow while she and Forde had been sleeping and already it was a couple of inches thick. The swirling flakes were fat and feathery and the sky was laden. If the storm continued in its present form she doubted if the vet would be able to get through to them if they needed her.

She stood for a moment, eyes wide and her top lip clamped in her teeth before telling herself to get on with what she had to do. Tabitha would be all right. Anything else wasn't an option. And the kittens would be fine too. They had to be.

Tabitha drank the milk they slid in to her in her hiding place but wouldn't touch the food, and as the yowls increased in volume Melanie had to force herself to sit still and not pace the room. Forde went out to fetch more logs and coal at one point and when he returned, Melanie said simply, 'I know,' in answer to the look on his face regarding the weather.

Forde had resorted to lying on the floor and peering under the sofa by the time the first kitten was born some three hours later. Tabitha had ignored the basket at the side of her but she dealt expertly with the tiny thing, biting off the birth sac and beginning to lick it all over with her abrasive tongue. When Forde saw it squirm he experienced a profound relief, more for Melanie than the cat.

Another kitten was born fairly quickly, and as they watched Tabitha begin the same procedure with this one as she had with the first Melanie whispered, 'Look at that, Forde. She's going to be a brilliant mother. And the kittens are alive and well.'

He looked at her where she lay at the side of him on the carpet. He'd been about to warn her that it was early days yet, that a hundred and one things could go wrong. There were more kittens to be born and they might not be as lucky as the first two, and Tabitha herself might be too exhausted to survive much more of this. But then he looked into her deep brown eyes and something in them checked his words. Instead he put his hand on hers.

There followed a wait that seemed endless to Melanie and Forde. They hardly dared move from their vigil but then a third kitten made its appearance and once again Tabitha went into action. This time, though, once the kitten was cleaned up to its mother's satisfaction, Tabitha picked up the tiny creature and jumped into the laundry basket where she deposited the squirming little scrap before fetching the other two, one by one, to the place she deemed as safe. She then made short work of the food and fresh milk Forde had slid under the sofa next to the basket and joined her kittens after using the litter tray.

'Do you think that's it? There were just the three?' Melanie found she had a crick in her neck and was utterly exhausted. She was also more elated than words could have described.

'Looks like it.' Forde was trying not to reveal how relieved he was that things had gone so well. Tabitha seemed to have taken the whole process in her stride despite her poor state of health and the kittens had wriggled to their mother's teats like homing pigeons. He also blessed the fact that Mother Nature had seen fit to give the little cat just three kittens to cope with. They stood a far better chance than if it had been a large litter. They hadn't been able to see clearly what the kittens looked like, their view had been restricted, but the fact that the little animals were sleek and damp from their mother's ministrations meant they really didn't look like cats at all.

'What do we do now?' Melanie sat up and stretched her aching neck. 'I don't like the thought of leaving her alone.'

'Looks like Tabitha's ready for a well-earned rest.' Forde stood up and pulled her to her feet. 'You get off to bed and I'll sleep with one eye open down here.'

Melanie looked at her husband. This had to come from her. She knew that. 'Or you could carry the basket upstairs and put it near the radiator in the bedroom so we could be on hand if she needs us? We could take some milk and food up with us and put it near the basket in case she's hungry in the night.'

Forde looked at her, a look with a deep searching question colouring it.

'I—I don't want to sleep alone for one more night,' she whispered. 'I was wrong about so many things, Forde. I knew that deep down, I guess, but seeing Miriam allowed everything to be brought into the light of day, all the doubts and fears. I—I want us to be together, not just for Christmas but for the rest of our lives and—'

She didn't get any further before she was lifted right off her feet and into his arms. He kissed her as if there were no tomorrow and she kissed him back in the same way, clinging to him so tightly he could hardly breathe.

Setting her down after a long minute, he drew her over to the sofa and then sat her on his lap. 'Are you sure?' he said softly. 'That all the doubts and fears are gone, I mean?'

He deserved the truth. She touched his face with the side of her palm. 'I want to be,' she said honestly. 'And I know myself so much better now, but I guess to some extent I'm still a work in progress. I was so scared tonight, with Tabitha.'

'Nell, so was I. That's natural.' He kissed her hard on her lips. 'It goes hand in hand with love, the worry and the fear that you'll lose the beloved. It's the other side of the coin, I suppose. But the best side makes it worth coping with the flip side—know what I mean?' He kissed her again. 'And most of the time the best side is uppermost. You had a rough start to life and you developed a defence mechanism to keep people at arm's length so you couldn't be hurt and you couldn't hurt them. I understand that. And then I came along and everything changed. If things had been different with Matthew you would still have had to face the fact, sooner or later, that you needed to unearth some of the issues you'd buried way deep inside. But it would have happened slowly, more naturally.'

'But the miscarriage did happen. Matthew died.' It still hurt as much as ever to stay it and she wondered if that would ever change. But the nature of the grief had changed subtly over the last weeks. It was still as intense but more bearable because the crucifying guilt had gone. She could mourn her perfect, exquisite little boy without feeling she had to punish herself every second of every day.

'Yes, he died.' There was a wealth of emotion in Forde's voice. 'And there will always be regrets, especially because with an accident of that nature there are so many ifs and buts in hindsight. You aren't the only one who blamed yourself. I knew you weren't too good that day. I could have stayed home with you. What does work matter compared to you and our son? And Janet had her own self-reproaches too. She wished she'd stayed with you while you ate and then brought the tray down, but none of us *knew*.'

Melanie nodded. How many times had she longed to turn back the clock until the morning of the accident so she could have done things differently? Too many to count. She had relived every minute of that fateful morning until she'd thought she was losing her mind. It had to stop. Once and for all, it had to stop. She had to be strong for this baby and for Forde, and for Matthew too. He had a right to be remembered with passionate love and devotion, and, yes, with a certain amount of pain too, but the memory of her precious baby son had been in danger of being marred and destroyed by her corrosive guilt.

'He was so beautiful,' she whispered through her tears.

'And so tiny.' Forde's voice was husky. 'He weighed nothing at all in my arms.'

She rested her forehead against his as their tears mingled, but for the first time since Matthew had died they were healing tears. After a long time when they just held each other close, she said softly, 'I love you. I have always loved you and I always will. I want you to know that. You are the other part of me, the better part.'

'Never that.' He kissed her fiercely. 'You are perfect in every way to me, never forget that. And I will never hurt you, Nell. I might get it wrong at times, I might even drive you crazy now and again but I will never hurt you. We will have our children—' he rested his hand on her stomach for a moment '—and grandchildren too, God willing, and grow old together. How does that sound?'

'Pretty good.' She smiled dreamily at him but then her stomach spoilt the moment by rumbling so loudly that Forde chuckled. 'I can't help it,' she protested. 'I haven't eaten for hours and I'm hungry again.'

'How about if you go and get ready for bed and I'll bring us up some supper?' Forde suggested. 'And tomorrow we have a lazy morning. Breakfast in bed, maybe even lunch in bed.'

'You missed out elevenses.'

'That too.' He grinned at her, feeling slightly light-headed that the last nightmarish months were over. He had come here this afternoon with no expectations beyond that they might share a meal together before he drove home. He'd hoped, of course. Hoped that Melanie seeing Miriam might have made a difference, that with the baby coming she would see it had two parents who loved each other and shouldn't be apart, but he hadn't known how long it would take before she conquered her gremlins. But it *was* Christmas after all, a time of miracles...

They ate a hodgepodge of a supper, which Forde brought up on a tray for them to share after he'd installed Tabitha and her kittens by the bedroom radiator in the basket. Wedges of bread from a crusty loaf, slices of fragrant ham, some of the canapés and cheeses he'd bought and slivers of the pork pie, and a couple of enormous pieces of Christmas cake. Curled up close to him in her bed with the snow falling thickly outside and Tabitha fast asleep in the basket, her kittens snuggled into their mother's warm fur, Melanie thought it was the best meal she had ever had.

Afterwards, sated and replete, they made love again, slowly and sensually, the earlier urgency gone. She went to sleep lying in his arms as he held her close to his heart, feeling she wanted this night to last for ever. In a few hours her life had changed beyond recognition, and she had felt closer to Forde as they had made love than she had ever done in the past. Maybe it was because they had come through the fiery trial and were the stronger for it, she thought drowsily, or perhaps for the first time she had met him as an equal partner in her mind and emotions and had kept nothing back. Her guard was lowered and her defences were down, and because of that she could set aside every inhibition.

She opened her eyes one last time to check on Tabitha and the kittens, smiling as she saw three tiny shapes busy feeding. Now the kittens' fur was dry it had fluffed up and they actually looked like baby cats. One appeared to have lighter colouring than the other two but as the room was dimly lit it was hard to see them in the half-light. But all three seemed to be doing well, although, of course, it was early days.

They had to live, she told herself, shutting her eyes and nestling into Forde's body warmth. Tabitha had been remarkable and so brave. After all she'd gone through the little cat had to have the satisfaction of rearing her babies.

She already knew she was going to keep Tabitha and all three kittens. Their house in Kingston upon Thames had a large garden just perfect for four cats; she could already picture the kittens playing and chasing each other across the lawns and shrubbery and climbing the trees. And in the summer all four could lie in the sun together or find a cool place in the shade. Tabitha would never know what it was to be hungry again, she vowed as she drifted off to sleep. Or unloved and unwanted. Not while she had breath in her body.

Melanie awoke on Christmas Eve morning to being kissed deeply and passionately. She opened heavy-lidded eyes to a room full of white light and Forde, clad in nothing but her kitchen apron, smiling at her.

'Your breakfast tray, ma'am.' He indicated a tray holding a full English breakfast, toast and preserves and a glass of orange juice on the bedside table. 'Is there anything else madam would like?'

She would never have dreamt in a million years that a fairly ordinary plastic apron could turn into something so erotic. Remembering the events of the evening before, she raised herself onto her elbow. 'Tabitha?'

'Fed and happy and downstairs by the kitchen radiator again with her three offspring, who are all doing extremely well. I had a nasty moment when I first woke up because the basket was empty, but once I'd found her and the kittens in the bottom of your wardrobe snuggled in a jumper and put them back in the basket, she seemed quite happy to accept that's where they all had to stay.'

'In that case there *is* something else I want.' The apron was swathed around Forde's hips and the way his chest hair arrowed to his navel entranced her. He had never looked more sexy. She opened her arms, winding them round his neck when he bent down to her again and pulling him down beside her on the bed. 'I love you,' she murmured before kissing him hungrily. 'So much.'

'Words don't even begin to say what I feel for you.' He moved back slightly, taking her face between his hands as he stared into the velvet-brown of her eyes. 'You do know I'm never going to let you go again? Whatever happens in the future, whatever it holds, we walk it side by side. Mountaintop or valley, good times and bad, I'm not budging, OK?'

'OK.' She kissed him again.

'And after Christmas I'm taking you home. No argument,' he said softly.

'Me and Tabitha and her brood.' Melanie punctuated each word with a kiss. 'They're ours now. I always wanted pets one day. I just didn't expect to have
four in one go.'

'We're keeping them all?'

'Of course. Tabitha deserves that.'

'And me?' Forde murmured huskily, enfolding her
against him so she could feel every inch of his hard
arousal. 'What do I deserve?'

'Everything,' she whispered throatily.

'Well, in that case…'

He kissed her until she was pulsing with desire,
bringing her to fever-pitch time and time again as he
stroked and pleasured her, caressing her until she was
trembling in his arms.

How had she managed to exist these last long, lonely
months without him? she thought wildly. But that was
all she had done: exist. This was life; being close to
Forde, feeling him, loving him. And it wasn't all about
sex, mind-blowing though that was. It was his tenderness, his care towards her, the patience and love he'd
shown ever since they'd met. Even when Matthew was
taken from them he hadn't blamed her for one moment;
putting his own feelings of grief and sorrow aside to
comfort her and be strong. She loved him so much…

She met him kiss for kiss, caress for caress, and when
he finally eased her thighs apart she was shameless in
her need of him inside her. They moved together as she
grasped him tight and close, the sheer exquisite physical pleasure taking them both to new heights. They
climaxed together in perfect unity, wave after wave of

sweet, hot gratification causing them to cry out their release.

They lay wrapped in each other's arms as they drifted back to reality, the remnants of pleasure taking some time to disperse.

Forde smiled as he traced her mouth with the tip of his finger. 'Breakfast is cold,' he murmured, kissing the tip of her small nose.

'It'll still taste good.' Anything would taste good right now. And then, as she felt the baby inside her move more vigorously than it had before, she caught his hand and placed it on her belly. 'Can you feel that?'

His face lit up. 'I think so. It's just the slightest ripple but, yes, I can feel it.'

'Our child, Forde.' And as she said it she realised the fear had gone…

CHAPTER TWELVE

IT STARTED to snow again just before lunch, but Forde had cleared a path to the logs and coal and they were as snug as bugs in rugs in the cottage. They spent most of the day curled up in front of the fire watching TV in each other's arms, eating the provisions Forde had brought and observing Tabitha with her kittens. The little cat was eating like a horse, seemingly intent on making up for lost time, and all three kittens seemed remarkably strong considering the state their mother had been in shortly before they were born.

Mid-afternoon when the snow had stopped and the sky had turned mother-of-pearl with streams of pure silver, they were surprised to hear a knock at the door. The vet stood there, her sturdy legs encased in green wellingtons and thick trousers and her padded jacket making her appear twice as big.

'I've just paid a visit to a farm not far from here so I thought I'd look in,' she said cheerfully, as though she weren't standing in half a foot of snow. 'How's the patient?'

Melanie made her a hot drink while she examined Tabitha and the kittens, announcing mother and babies to be in remarkably good health considering the odds that had been stacked against them. 'The little ginger one is a tom,' she told them, giving the kitten back to Tabitha, who began to give it a thorough clean. 'And the two black-and-white ones are females. As she seems to be getting on with being a good mother we'll leave well alone at the moment. Certainly the kittens' bellies are full and they don't appear unduly hungry or distressed.'

She downed her coffee as though she had a tin throat and left, remarking as she stepped out into the cold afternoon, 'All's well that ends well, I'm pleased to say.'

Forde held Melanie's hand very tight. 'Yes,' he said quietly. 'All's well that ends well. Merry Christmas.'

They awoke disgracefully late on Christmas Day, having gone to bed early but not to sleep. They had been both playful and intense in their lovemaking, one as eager as the other for the night not to end, until, in the early hours of the morning just before it got light, they'd gone to sleep with their arms round each other.

The morning was sparkling bright and clear, the sky icy-blue crystal and the scene outside the cottage a winter wonderland. In the far distance they could hear the faint sound of church bells ringing, and the world seemed reborn in its mantle of pure white.

Forde got up and went downstairs to check on Tabitha and make some coffee, which he brought back to bed after putting the turkey on, causing Melanie to feel deliciously lazy. Her languorous air was abruptly shattered when she saw the small but beautifully wrapped gift next to her coffee and toast, though. She shot up in bed, her voice a wail. 'Forde, I haven't got you anything. You shouldn't have.'

'Yes, I should.' He smiled at her, amused at the very feminine response. 'Besides, I had a slight advantage over you, didn't I? I knew I was coming here. I was going to leave this somewhere for you to find after I had gone,' he added softly. 'I wasn't expecting you to throw yourself on my bosom and beg for my help, nice though that was, I hasten to add.'

'What is it?'

He joined her in bed, handing the little box to her. 'See for yourself, but first—' he took her in his arms and kissed her very thoroughly '—happy Christmas, my darling.'

She undid the ribbon and pulled off the paper before lifting the lid off the box, gasping as she saw the exquisite brooch it held. The two tiny lovebirds were fashioned from precious stones forming a circle with their wings and their minute beaks were touching in a kiss. It was the most beautiful thing she had ever seen. 'Forde.' She raised shining eyes to his. 'It's so perfect. Wherever did you find it?'

'I had it specially commissioned.' He put his arm round her, kissing the tip of her nose. 'It says what I want to say every day of my life to you.'

The stones were shooting off different colours in the shaft of sunlight slanting in from the window, making the birds appear alive, and as the baby in her womb kicked suddenly Melanie had a moment of pure joy. They were going to be all right, she thought with a deep thankfulness. They had weathered the storm and come out the other side. She could believe it.

It was a perfect Christmas Day. Forde prepared the dinner while they listened to carols and Christmas songs courtesy of Melanie's CD player. He wouldn't let her lift a finger, expertly dishing up the food once it was cooked, and flaming the plum pudding with brandy and making her squeal with surprise.

Tabitha tucked into her portion of turkey and stuffing with gusto, and when Forde put down a saucerful of cream for the little cat it was clear she couldn't believe her luck. She seemed to have settled with the kittens and hadn't moved her little family again. Melanie hoped it was because Tabitha knew she was safe and secure now.

After lunch, with Tabitha and the kittens fast asleep in their basket in front of the fire in the sitting room, Melanie and Forde built a snowman in her tiny courtyard as the sun began to set in a white sky, sending rivers of red and gold and violet across the heavens. The air was bitingly cold and crisp and somewhere close a blackbird was singing its heart out, the pure notes hanging on the cold air.

For a moment Melanie knew a piercing pain that Matthew wasn't with them. He would have probably begun to toddle by now, she thought, lifting her face to the sunset. He would have loved the snow.

'You're thinking of him. I can always tell.'

She hadn't been aware that Forde was watching her, but now he enfolded her into his arms, holding her tight, as she murmured, 'I would have loved to tell him that we love him, that we'll always love him no matter how many other children we have. That he'll for ever be our precious little boy, our firstborn.'

'You'll be able to tell him that one day and give him all the cuddles and kisses you want, my love.'

'Do you believe that?' She pulled away slightly to look into his dark face. '*Really* believe it?'

'Yes, I do.' His eyes glinted down at her in the half-light. 'But for now we're here on earth and we have to get on with our lives and care for and love other children we're given. We are going to become a family when this child is born, Nell, and although the grief of losing Matthew will never fade you will learn to live with it and stop feeling guilty that you can still experience happiness and pleasure.'

'How do you know I feel like that sometimes?' she asked him, her eyes wide with surprise.

'Because I felt the same at first,' said Forde softly. 'I think all parents must in the aftermath of losing a baby or child. It's not only a terrible thing, but it's unnatural too, the wrong order in life. A parent should never outlive its child.'

She leant into him, needing his strength and understanding. 'It *will* be all right this time, won't it?' she said very quietly. 'I couldn't bear—'

'None of that.' He lifted her chin with one finger, gazing deep into her eyes. 'We are going to have a beautiful son or daughter, Nell. I promise you. Look at Tabitha and have faith, OK?'

She smiled shakily. 'People would think it was stupid to believe because one little cat made it against all the odds, it's a sign for us.'

'I don't give a damn what people think.' He pulled her more firmly into him. 'And this is Christmas, don't forget. A time for miracles and for wishes to come true. Who would have thought a few days ago we would be standing here like this, Nell? But we are. We're together again and stronger than ever before. And talking of miracles—' he touched her belly '—one night of love and this child came into being. Now, I know we would still have been together in the long run because I would never have accepted anything else, but this baby was a catalyst for you in many ways.'

His voice was so full of the relentless determination and assurance she'd come to associate with the man she loved that Melanie smiled again. 'So you're saying we're part of a Christmas miracle?'

'Dead right, we are.' He grinned, looking up into the sky. 'Look at that. It's specially for us, you know. A true modern-art spectacular.'

Melanie giggled. 'You're crazy—you know that, don't you?'

'For you? Guilty as charged.' He turned her to look at their snowman, who was definitely something of a cross-dresser, having one of Melanie's scarves tied round his neck—a pink, fluffy number with tiny sequins sewn into it—and one of her summer straw hats complete with ribbons and tiny daisies. 'Is he finished?'

'Just about.'

'Then I suggest we go inside and warm up.'

'In front of the fire with a mug of hot chocolate?'

'Possibly.' He eyed her sexily. 'Not quite what I had in mind, though. I was thinking of something more… cosy.'

'More cosy than hot chocolate?' she murmured, pretending ignorance.

'As in one hundred per cent.'

'Oh, well, in that case…'

'And remember.' He took her cold face in his hands,

suddenly serious. 'I love you and you love me. Anything else—*anything*—comes second to that.'

Melanie nodded. She wanted to believe that. She *needed* to. And perhaps that was what this was all about: a step of faith. She linked her arms round his neck. 'I love Christmas.'

He kissed her forehead, dislodging her bright scarlet pom-pom hat in the process. 'Best time of the year,' he said huskily. 'The very best.'

CHAPTER THIRTEEN

MELANIE was remembering the magic of Christmas as Forde drove her to the hospital in the last week of May.

The weather couldn't have been more different. For weeks the country had been enjoying warm, sunny days more typical of the Mediterranean, and James and the assistant she had hired to help him had been rushed off their feet with work. Business was booming and already her small company had a reputation for excellent reliability and first-class results, which boded well for the future. But Melanie wasn't thinking of James or the company as Forde's Aston Martin ate up the miles to the hospital; she was lost in the enchantment of those days when she and Forde had been enclosed in their own isolated world, along with Tabitha and the kittens, of course.

The kittens had grown swiftly into little cats developing distinct personalities of their own. They had named the two little females Holly and Ivy, and the larger boy Noel, and it was a good thing Tabitha was something of a strict mother because the three could be quite a handful. But Melanie loved them passionately and because love begot love, they loved her back, even if it was in the somewhat superior feline version of that emotion.

Her favourite was Tabitha though. The little tabby was devoted to Melanie in the same way a dog would be, following her about the house and liking nothing more than to lie at her feet or on her lap whenever she could. She kept her troublesome threesome under control by a swift tap of the paw now and again and the odd warning growl when they stepped out of line, but on the whole it was a happy household.

It was Tabitha who was at the forefront of Melanie's mind as she said, 'You made sure the cats were all in before we left?'

'Absolutely.' Forde's voice was indulgent. She had asked him the same question twice before. 'And the TV's off and the back door's locked. OK?'

Melanie smiled at him. She had been in labour for some hours but the contractions had followed no particular pattern and there had been no urgency about them. Then, with a suddenness that had surprised her and panicked Forde, they'd increased dramatically in intensity with considerably less time between them.

Her overnight bag had been packed for weeks and left in the same place, at the foot of their bed, but somehow Forde had been unable to find it until she had lent a hand. She glanced now at the speedometer, her voice deliberately casual when she said, 'We're doing fifty in a thirty zone, Forde.'

'I know.' His voice was a little strained.

'There's plenty of time.' But even as she spoke a new contraction gripped her, her muscles tightening until it was nigh on unbearable before loosening again.

'OK?' Forde hadn't slowed one iota and the glance

he shot at her was desperate. 'I told you we should have left hours ago, Nell.'

'It's fine.' She was able to smile again. 'Three of the mothers from the antenatal classes were sent home again due to false alarms and I'd just die if that was me. I wanted to make sure.'

Forde groaned. 'Would having the baby in the car convince you?' And then realising that wasn't the most tactful of remarks, he added quickly, 'Not that we wouldn't cope with that, of course, if it happened, but I'd prefer you to be in hospital.'

She would too, actually. And she was beginning to think she might have left it a little late—not that she'd admit that to Forde. Not the way he was driving.

Melanie focused her thoughts on the baby, willing herself to be calm and composed. They had decided they didn't want to know the sex of their child at the twenty-week scan at the beginning of the year. It didn't matter. The only thing that was important was that the baby was healthy after all.

They arrived at the hospital in a violet twilight that was balmy and scented with summer, but for once Melanie was oblivious to the beauty of the flowering bushes surrounding the car park as another contraction held her stomach in a vice. She held onto Forde at the side of the car as it gathered steam and then began to pant like an animal, her nails digging into his flesh.

'I'll go and get a wheelchair,' he said, glancing round with a hunted expression on his face as though one were going to pop into his vision any moment. 'Sit back in the car.'

She held onto him with all her strength until the contraction was over and then said firmly, 'I am most certainly not using a wheelchair, Forde Masterson. They're four minutes apart so we can get to Reception before the next one and then I can wait a while before we go to the maternity unit.'

He looked at her with huge admiration. Since she had returned home with him after they had spent Christmas in the cottage, she had taken everything in her stride. He had to admit he had been like a cat on a hot tin roof the past couple of weeks waiting for the baby to come, but Melanie had been what he could only call serene. They had decorated the nursery in pale lemon and cream eight weeks ago and everything was ready for the new arrival. They just needed the baby now. His stomach jumped with excitement mixed with concern for Melanie. He hadn't expected her to be in such pain, although perhaps he should have.

They didn't make Reception before the next contraction had her clinging onto him. Now fear was added to the mix. He had visions of the baby being born in the car park and delivering it himself. He should have made her come to the hospital earlier, he told himself desperately as Melanie's fingers fastened on his wrists like steel bands. But she was so damn stubborn. And wonderful and beautiful and amazing.

After what seemed an eternity her grip lessened, although he could see beads of perspiration on her brow. 'Wow.' She smiled shakily. 'Do you remember what they told us in the classes if the baby comes unexpectedly?'

'Don't,' he said weakly.

He half carried her the rest of the way and once they stepped through the massive glass doors into Reception the hospital machine took over with an efficiency Forde was thankful for. In no time they'd been whisked along to the maternity unit and placed in a delivery room. For a moment he remembered the last time they had been in the unit and his guts twisted, but when he looked at Melanie she was concentrating on following the midwife's instructions. He stared at her face, at her total look of concentration and the courage she was displaying, and his world swung back onto its axis.

'You're doing fine, sweetheart,' he murmured, wishing he could share the pain. 'Not long now.'

In fact the contractions continued at three-minute intervals for the next two hours, which seemed a lifetime to Forde, although the hospital staff didn't seem unduly concerned.

Melanie was getting tired, even dozing between one contraction and the next in the couple of minutes' respite, but she still held onto his hand with the strength of a dozen women and every so often would smile and tell him everything was all right. He felt helpless, badgering the midwife once or twice until that good lady sent him a look like a dagger.

Then, suddenly, a little while after midnight, everything speeded up. Melanie began pushing and another midwife joined them, the two women stationed either side of Melanie's bent legs while he sat by the bed holding her hand. He wouldn't have thought she had enough strength left for what was required but as ever she proved him wrong, pushing with all her might when the midwives told her to push and panting like an animal again when they told her to stop.

Twenty minutes later their son was born and he was

a whopper, according to the midwife who immediately placed him in Melanie's arms. Forde knew if he lived to be a hundred he would never forget the expression on Melanie's face as she gazed into the little screwed-up face. And the baby looked back with bright blue-grey eyes as if he knew his mother already. 'Hello, you,' she whispered softly, the tears running down her face as she kissed his velvety brow. 'I'm your mummy, my precious darling. And this is your daddy.' She turned to Forde with a radiant smile to see his cheeks were wet too.

'He's so beautiful.' Forde kissed her tenderly before offering his finger to his son, who immediately grasped it with surprising strength, making them both laugh. 'And look at all that black hair.'

'He's going to be as handsome as his father,' said one of the midwives, beaming at them both and their transparent wonder at the little person they had created. 'My, he's a bonny lad and no mistake. Over ten pounds, I'll be bound.'

In actual fact, Luke Forde Masterson weighed in at ten pounds nine ounces—something, Melanie said in an aside and with great feeling, that didn't surprise her.

The midwives bustled off, promising to return in a few minutes with a cup of tea for them both. Melanie sat cradling her son with Forde perched on the bed at her side, his arm round her shoulders.

'How do you feel?' he said very softly as she stroked one tiny cheek with the tip of her finger.

She didn't try to prevaricate. 'Wonderful,' she said equally softly, 'and a tiny bit sad, but that's only natural, I suppose. It doesn't mean I love Luke any the less, just that I wish things had been different with Matthew.'

He nodded, his arm tightening for a moment.

'Isn't he beautiful, Forde? And he already looks like you,' she went on. 'He's got your nose. Can you see it?'

Forde looked at his son. He *was* beautiful, certainly the most beautiful child in the whole of England, but he simply looked like a baby, he thought, wondering how women could say these things and genuinely see what most men couldn't. He smiled. 'I'd prefer him to look like you.'

'Oh, no.' She shook her head. 'Our daughters will look like me and our sons like you.'

After what she had just been through he found it amazing she could talk of having more children just at that moment. He kissed her hard on the lips. 'I love you, Mrs Masterson.'

'And I love you, Mr Masterson. Always.'

EPILOGUE

MELANIE and Forde went on to have the family they had dreamed of. Eighteen months after Luke was born, twin girls—Amy Melanie and Sophie Isabelle—made their appearance. True to Melanie's prediction the girls were the very image of their lovely mother. And two years after that another boy, John William—William had been Forde's father's name—made their family complete.

They had left the house in Kingston upon Thames just after the twins were born, moving to a huge old Elizabethan mansion in the country, which had acres of land attached to it along with magnificent gardens that would delight any child. It even came with a fine tree house built in one of the giant oak trees a little distance from the house, and this was nearly as big as Melanie's little cottage. She hadn't been able to bear to sell the cottage, not with all the memories it held of the wonderful Christmas when she and Forde had come together again, and now James had taken up residence there. With Melanie's growing family he had taken a larger part in the running of the firm, which had continued to go from strength to strength. James had three full-time employees and two part-time under his direction, along with a middle-aged lady who had taken on most of the paperwork involved with the company.

Tabitha and her little family had been joined by two rescue dogs—the cats ruling the roost with iron paws—and as time went on the children had a couple of small ponies so they could learn to ride, and an aged donkey—again a rescue animal—that Melanie wanted to end its days in comfort with others of its kind for company.

It was a happy household, but when John started school Melanie felt it was time to put an idea to Forde that had been in the back of her mind for a long time. Isabelle had been living with them for the past few years, having become too frail to continue in her own home, but sadly had died in the spring, peacefully though and in her own bed.

Melanie and Forde were sitting by the swimming pool Forde had had built shortly after they had moved to the house. They were watching the children and some of the children's friends playing in the water before Forde organised a barbecue for lunch. It was a beautiful summer's day at the beginning of June, the sky high and cornflower-blue without a cloud to be seen, and the scents from the garden intoxicating.

Melanie took a deep breath and turned to Forde, who was lying on the sunlounger next to hers clad only in his swimming shorts. As always when she looked at him, her pulse quickened. His body was as taut and lean as it had ever been and he oozed sex appeal, which was all the more potent for his unawareness of his devastating attractiveness. She deposited a long kiss on his sexy, uneven mouth before settling back on her own lounger. 'I need to talk to you.'

He smiled, his silver-blue eyes crinkling. 'You don't need to make an appointment, sweetheart. We are married, remember?'

Oh, yes, she remembered all right. The heavenly nights of bliss in their huge bed were a constant reminder.

'This is serious, Forde. I want us to start long-term fostering, taking in the sort of troubled child I was, the sort no one else is really keen to have.'

Forde sat up straighter.

'Now John's started school and your mother's gone, I feel it's the right time. When I was nursing Isabelle I felt she needed all my attention and a peaceful life at her age, but now that's not a consideration any more.'

Forde looked at his wife. He never tired of looking at her. He thought she got younger with every passing year, the joy of family life turning her into a female Peter Pan. 'Are you sure about this?' he asked quietly. 'It would mean huge changes and it won't be easy some of the time. The children would have to make some adjustments too.'

Melanie nodded. He hadn't said no outright. 'I know that. This isn't a whim, believe me. As for our children, you know I love them beyond words and they will always come first. But...' She paused, finding the right words. 'They have no idea of the unhappiness some children live with every day of their lives, and I'm glad they don't know that for themselves, of course I am, but sharing their home—and us—with such children will make our four better human beings in the long run. They are privileged, Forde, so privileged, and I'm grateful for that, but I don't want them to grow up without understanding everyone's not as fortunate as they are.

I—I remember how it was for me as a child and I want to give something back. I want to help such little ones, give them a chance to feel wanted and loved. This is such a big house with wonderful grounds and we have four spare guest rooms we rarely use.'

Forde frowned. 'What about the sheer mechanics of caring for more children, giving them adequate time and attention? I can be around more but not all the time and I don't want you worked into the ground, Nell. It was hard work with my mother towards the end when she got very poorly and, although this will be different, you'll need help.'

'I know that.' She was trying very hard to keep the excitement out of her voice but nevertheless it sneaked in. 'And part of what makes me feel this is the time to do it is that I spoke to Janet the other day. You know we meet for lunch a couple of times a year?'

Forde nodded. It had been too far for Janet to travel when they had moved house, besides which Melanie had been keen to take over the role of full-time mother and housewife, which was why she had given most of the running of the business into James's capable hands. But she hadn't lost contact with their old housekeeper, meeting her occasionally and sending huge hampers to the house every Christmas.

'Well, her husband died last year as you know, and two of her children are married now and have left home. The girl that's left is the one with learning difficulties but she's great at cooking and cleaning like her mother. It's a rented house and I know Janet would love to come here as housekeeper and cook with her daughter helping her. Between the three of us we could run the house fine, and having Janet and her daughter here would free me up to take care of our children and any we foster, with Janet available as a back-up in any emergency. It would work, Forde. I know it would. But you have to want it too, I know that.'

'Where would Janet and her daughter live? In the granny annexe we built for Mother?'

'Would you mind that?'

'Of course not.' He ran a hand through his hair as he did when he was anxious or thoughtful. 'But I'd have to look into this more fully. *We* would have to look into it more fully.'

'Absolutely.'

'There'll be checks and red tape and who knows what. It'll mean opening up every area of our life to strangers before we could get a go-ahead.'

'I know that too but it would be worth it. I'd like to try, Forde. If nothing else I'd like us to try. If it doesn't happen—' she shrugged '—so be it.'

A slow smile spread over his rugged features. 'Nell, I know you well enough by now to know you don't mean a word of that. This is important to you, isn't it?'

'It is but unless you're completely happy we won't go ahead about even finding out the ins and outs.'

He leaned towards her, touching her cheek with his hand. 'If it's important to you it's important to me—you know that.'

When he looked at her like that all she wanted to do was fling herself into his arms and ravish him. She contented herself with cupping his face in her palms and kissing him deeply and passionately. 'So I can go ahead and make some enquiries?'

Lifting her left hand to his lips, Forde pressed a gentle kiss on the finger that held her wedding and engagement rings. 'We'll do it together at every stage, OK?'

'OK,' Melanie whispered, wanting him, loving him.

Social Services welcomed them with open arms. As Forde had forecast the red tape stretched for ever, however, but by Christmas they had all the necessary pieces of paper in place and their initial two children, a boy and a girl who weren't related but had spent some time together in short-term care, had arrived to spend the Christmas holiday with them to see how they all got on.

The children's case histories were dire and there was no doubt they regarded all adults with deep distrust and, in the boy's case, a great deal of pent-up anger, but from the moment Melanie saw their small, wary faces she loved them. They came to the house a couple of days before Christmas and on Christmas Eve Melanie sat on the boy's bed and told him a story of a little girl who had been in care and who felt abandoned and alone. He listened with hostile eyes until the moment she told him she had been that little girl, and then it was clear she had taken him aback.

It was the breakthrough she had prayed for. From being surly and suspicious he began to ask her question after question and in so doing some of his own traumatic history came out quite naturally. The rest of the children were fast asleep, waiting for Santa to fill their stockings, and Melanie spent two hours talking to him before he settled down to sleep.

When she joined Forde downstairs, he reached out a hand to her, drawing her towards the French windows and opening them so the crisp, biting air caressed their faces. A few desultory snowflakes were beginning to fall on the sparkling ground, which was white with frost, and the trees surrounding the house looked breathtakingly beautiful in their mantle of white. 'A fresh new world,' he murmured softly, drawing her tight into his side. 'And that's what I want for these children, Nell. I crept up and listened at the bedroom door while you were talking to him and I know you're going to transform his life.'

'We both are,' she said softly, emotion making her voice husky.

'But you most of all.' He smiled, kissing her hard. 'We're going to have more Christmas miracles, Nell, and our family is going to grow in a way I hadn't thought of but which is perfect. Because of you, my love. All because of you. What did I ever do to deserve you?'

'That's what I think every time I look at you,' she whispered. 'You didn't let me go when I walked away. You came after me. You will never know what that meant.'

'We won't let these little ones go either.' He looked up into the pearly gray sky from which more and more snowflakes were falling. 'This is going to be another wonderful Christmas, my darling.'

And it was.

* * * * *

THE NIGHT THAT
STARTED IT ALL

BY
ANNA CLEARY

THE NIGHT THAT
STARTED IT ALL

by

MANDY BAGGOT

As a child, **Anna Cleary** loved reading so much that during the midnight hours she was forced to read with a torch under the bedcovers, to lull the suspicions of her sleep-obsessed parents. From an early age she dreamed of writing her own books. She saw herself in a stone cottage by the sea, wearing a velvet smoking jacket and sipping sherry, like Somerset Maugham.

In real life she became a schoolteacher, and her greatest pleasure was teaching children to write beautiful stories.

A little while ago she and one of her friends made a pact each to write the first chapter of a romance novel in their holidays. From writing her very first line Anna was hooked, and she gave up teaching to become a full-time writer. She now lives in Queensland, with a deeply sensitive and intelligent cat. She prefers champagne to sherry, and loves music, books, four-legged people, trees, movies and restaurants.

For lovely Amy Andrews,
a brilliant and versatile author and a wonderful friend.

CHAPTER ONE

SINCE the break with Manon, his long-time lover, Luc Valentin mostly resisted seduction. Sex risked ever more desire, and desire was a downhill slope to entanglement in a web of female complications. Before a man knew it he could be sucked into an emotional shredder.

So when Luc strolled into D'Avion Sydney and the pretty faces at the front desk lit up like New Year's Eve, their smiles were wasted on the air.

'Luc Valentin,' he said, handing over his card. 'I'm here to see Rémy Chénier.'

The first beguiling face froze. 'Luc—*Valentin*? *The* Luc Valentin? Of…'

'Paris. Head Office. That is correct.' Luc smiled. Rarely had his appearance at one of the company offices sparked such a dramatic effect. 'Rémy, *mademoiselle*?'

The woman's eyes darted sideways towards her fellows. It seemed a strange paralysis had overcome them. 'Er…Rémy isn't here. I'm sorry, Mr Valentin, we haven't seen him for days. He isn't answering his messages. We don't know where he is. We don't know anything. Do we?' she appealed to the others. She consulted her mobile, then scribbled an address. 'You might try here. I'm sure if he's in Mr Chénier will be deligh—over*joyed* to see you.'

Luc doubted it. Since his plan was to encourage his cousin

to explain the shortfall in the company accounts then wring his unscrupulous neck, joy was likely to be limited.

There would be a woman involved, Luc guessed, driving across the Harbour Bridge under an impossibly blue sky. With Rémy there was always a woman, though in Luc's thirty-six years never the same one twice.

The address was for a sleek apartment complex on Sydney's northern shore. Luc pressed the buzzer twice before it connected. Then for several tense seconds all he heard was the rustle of white noise.

Prickles arose on his neck.

At last, *enfin*, a voice. It sounded muffled, more than a little croaky, as if its owner had a terrible cold. Or had been weeping.

'Who is it?'

Luc bent to speak into the intercom, which hadn't been designed to accommodate tall guys with long bones. 'Luc Valentin. I am wishing to speak with Rémy Chénier.'

'Oh.' Through the woman's husky fog he could detect a certain relief. 'Are you from his office?'

'You could say I'm from D'Avion, certainly.'

'Well, he's not here. Praise the Lord.' The last was muttered.

Luc drew his brows together. 'But this is his apartment, yes?' The place looked like the sort of residence Rémy would choose. All gloss and sharp edges.

'Used to be. Not that he ever seemed to know it,' she added in an undertone. 'Anyway, he's gone. Don't know where, don' care. Nothin' to do with me. I'm outta here.'

Luc's eye fell on a small pile of carefully stacked possessions inside the glass entrance, among them cooking pots and a frilled and very feminine umbrella.

'Excuse me, *mademoiselle*. Can you tell me when was the last time you saw him?'

'Months ago. Yesterday.'

'*Yesterday*? So he is in Sydney still?'

'I—I hope not. Maybe. I don't *know*. Look... Look

monsieur…' Luc noticed a slightly mocking inflection in the 'monsieur' '…I'm very busy. I can't keep—'

He jumped in quickly before she cut him off. 'Please, miss. Just one more thing. Has he taken his clothes?'

'Mmm…' There was a pregnant pause. 'Let's just say his clothes took a tumble.'

Luc hesitated, picturing the scene those words conjured. He had an overwhelming desire to see the face that went with the foggy voice. 'Are you Rémy's girlfriend, by some chance? Or—perhaps—the maid?'

There was a long, loaded silence. Then she said, 'Yeah. The maid.'

'*Pardonnez-moi*, miss, but will you allow me to come upstairs and speak with you face to face? There are some ques—'

The intercom disconnected. He waited for the door to unlock. When it didn't he pressed again. Finally after one long, persistent ring, she came back on. 'Look, get lost, will you? You can't come up.'

'But I only wish to—'

'*No.* You *can't.*' There was alarm in her tone. 'Go away or I'll call the police.'

Luc straightened up, frowning. What after all would he expect? Rémy had never been known to leave friends in his wake. Though if she was the maid, why would she be weeping?

She must have a cold.

He noticed a box jammed against the glass. Through its half-open lid he saw it was packed with shoes, some of them a little scruffy. Though certainly feminine in shape and size, these were not the shoes of a femme fatale.

He slid behind the wheel of his hire car, wondering what had happened to his powers of persuasion. In the past he'd have had that door open in a second and the maid eating out of his hand. Of course, in the past he hadn't learned what he knew now.

The gentle sex were deceptive. The *gentle* sex were capable of eviscerating a guy and throwing his entrails to the wolves.

From behind a curtain at an upstairs window Shari Lacey watched the car drive away. Whoever he was, he'd had quite a nice voice. Deep, serious and quiet. Charming even, if she hadn't been over French accents. *So* over them.

She shuddered.

In the next thirty-six hours Luc ran through everything at the D'Avion office with a fine-toothed comb. Every file, every Post-It note. Tested Rémy's team until the PA was sobbing and the execs a whiter shade of grey. He sacked the finance officer on the spot. The guy should have known.

Significant sums had vanished from the accounts, neatly siphoned away, while nothing he uncovered gave Luc a clue as to his cousin's likely whereabouts. With the directors' meeting in Paris looming, Luc felt his time was running out. With grim clarity he saw the moment was close when he must let the law loose on his cousin.

A chill slithered down his spine. Another family scandal. They'd dredge it all up again. His embarrassment. The public ignominy. "The Director, His Mistress, Their Dog and Her Lover" splashed all over the world again in lurid, shaming letters.

He stared grimly through the office window at Sydney Harbour, a treacherous smiling blue in the midday sun. One way or another he had to find the *canaille*. Hunt him down and force him to make reparation.

There was one final resort, of course. Luc sighed. He should have known it would come to this.

The family connection.

Emilie, Rémy's twin, was married to an Australian now, but as far as Luc knew she and Rémy had always been close. Despite not having seen her for a few years, Luc thought of Emi with affection. Though she shared Rémy's gingery curls and blue eyes, she was as different from her twin as a warm, happy wren from a vulture.

Trouble was, like all the women in his family she wanted to know too much.

Eyeliner in hand, Shari leaned closer to the mirror. Dark blue along right lower lid, continue without breaking across bridge, now ease onto left lower lid.

She winced. *Careful.* While the swelling had subsided, her bruise was still tender. Her badge. The perfect parting gift, really, for a mouse. It brightened up her face. It seemed she could never have compared to all those exciting women Rémy had known in France. *And* she was too demanding. Suspicious. Difficult. Too clever for her own good. Too emotional— Well, that one was certainly true. Too mouthy. Too jealous. Too unforgiving. *Frigide.* A frump. Needy. Victorian…

His complaints had mounted over time. No wonder the poor guy had forced to seek so much feminine consolation far and wide.

She knew in her mind the trick was not to believe the things he'd said, but to ridicule them. Though in her *heart*…

He'd stopped being sweet some time back, but this recent encounter had been…a shock. Nothing she'd ever anticipated. Though she needed to remind herself it could have been far worse. For a while there she'd thought he might actually force her into sex.

Hot shame swept through her again. To think something like this could happen to her. The irony of it, when her girlfriends had so envied her for her sexy Frenchman. At one time. Before they noticed his roving eye. However tactful they tried to be around her, Shari knew they'd seen it.

But if any of them found out it had come to this squalid end—the ones she had left, that was—what would they think of her? Would they assume he'd been violent all along? Would they think she'd *tolerated* it?

She wished she wouldn't keep thinking of all those battered wives she'd seen on television shows over the years. All those sad women, too beaten down to defend themselves, believing they deserved their punishment, making excuses for their abusers. Forgiving them, walking the domestic tightrope fearful of saying the wrong thing.

She started breathing fast, getting too emotional again. It was no use getting worked up again. She wasn't those women. She hadn't been too entangled in the relationship to see she had to extricate herself. She'd acted swiftly and decisively, give or take a couple of cruel tweaks of her hair. A twist of her ear. A nipple. Shari Lacey would not be, could never be, downtrodden.

From now on it was all good. She was in her lovely old Paddington again, with every pretty street teeming with the sort of inspirations a children's author needed. She had everything to sing about.

Still, it was amazing how a man's fist had only needed to be slammed in her face the one time to leave her as jumpy as a kitten. Thank heavens she'd already dealt with the estate agents and fixed up the details of her move before Fist Day, or she wasn't sure how she'd have coped.

But she was a rational person. She was safe now. She would get over it. The important thing was to fight fear. Not to turn into an emotional cripple, cringing at the sound of every male voice. She could still enjoy men and indulge in a little flirty chit-chat.

Maybe.

Rémy was *not* typical. Her head knew this. Once again, though, it was her heart that was the trouble.

In fact it was a good thing, a needful thing, that Neil was insisting she come to his party. There'd be loads of men there, all quite as civilised as her lovely brother. It could be her testing ground. From this moment on, serenity was her cloak and her shield.

When her hand grew steady again, she lined both lids with

the darker shade, painted a band of purple shadow beneath her eyes and on the upper lids, then switched to the turquoise brush inside the corners, across the bridge and all the way to her brows.

Standing back to examine her handiwork, she felt a surge of relief. Not only was the bruise undetectable, the stripe across her eyes looked quite atmospheric. It was dramatic, maybe a little over the top, but it suited her. Somehow it made her irises glow a vivid sea-green.

If she hadn't been kicking herself over what a fool she'd been, how needy she must have been to fall for such a cliché, she'd have laughed to think of how poor old Neil and Emilie would freak when she turned up looking like Daryl Hannah in *Bladerunner*.

Though Emilie was no fool. She *had* grown up with Rémy.

That set Shari worrying again, so as an added decoy she drew a frog on her right cheekbone.

Now what to wear to Neil's fortieth? If a woman was forced to go to a party wearing a stripe, it might be best to look gorgeous. A little shopping might be called for. Her smile broke through. With her camouflage in place, the frump could go out.

She'd cried her last tear over the man who couldn't love. Cried and cried till she was empty.

It was time to get back on the horse.

CHAPTER TWO

Luc was made to feel abundantly welcome in Emilie and Neil's pretty harbourside home. Luc, and at least a hundred of their friends. The place was crowded, its family atmosphere so warm it was palpable.

Too warm. A reminder of all that had departed from his world.

And, *quelle surprise*, Emilie was pregnant.

It seemed to Luc everyone was. Everywhere he looked from Paris to Saigon to Sydney women were swollen, their husbands strutting about like smug cockerels. The epidemic had spread across the equator.

He doubted he'd have noticed if he hadn't looked, really looked that day, at the *boulanger* in the Rue Montorgeuil strolling with his pregnant wife, a brawny tender arm around her waist. The guy had been so proud, so cock-a-hoop, so in love with life and the world, Luc had carried the image home with him.

Worst mistake in history.

Apparently, when lovers ran out of things to say to each other, the last remedy to propose was marriage. Manon's response to the suggestion of a child had been as swift as it was ferocious.

'What has happened to you, darling? Do you suddenly want to tie me in chains? I am not the brood mare type. If you want *that*, find another woman.' Her smile hadn't diminished the anger in her lovely eyes.

Once he'd recovered from the shock, he'd realised the enormity of what he'd suggested. The fact that some women did agree to sacrificing their freedom and autonomy to reproduce was nothing short of a miracle.

Inclining his head, he accepted another canapé, wondering how long he would have to wait here in this hothouse of domestic fecundity before Rémy put in an appearance. He was beginning to have his doubts it would even happen. Could his cousin have got wind of his arrival? He'd hardly known himself until the last minute, when he was due to leave Saigon and thought of his pleasant Paris apartment waiting for him.

That empty wasteland. Traces of Manon in every corner.

Otherwise he doubted he would ever have dreamed of travelling so far. But from Saigon a few extra hours' hop to Sydney had had its appeal. Deal with the Rémy problem, enjoy a few days of sunshine, blue seas and skies. Postpone work, Paris, his life. What was not to enjoy?

He should have realised. Wherever he went in the world, *he* was there.

At least Emi hadn't changed. Like the sweetheart she was, every so often she darted back to the corner he was lurking in to ensure he wasn't neglected.

Smiling, she offered him wine, her blue eyes so reminiscent of her twin's. Or would have been if Rémy's had ever possessed any kindness, humanity or the tiniest hint of the existence of a soul.

'So tell me, Luc…is it true? Manon is pregnant?'

A familiar pincer clenched Luc's entrails, though he maintained his smile. 'How would I know? I don't keep up.'

Emilie flushed. '*Pardon, mon cousin.* I don't mean to intrude. I was just so surprised when Tante Marise mentioned it. I wouldn't have thought… Manon never seemed the—the type to want babies.'

No, Luc acknowledged behind his poker face. She hadn't been the type when she was with him. But there were only so many forms of betrayal a man cared to discuss.

He steered Emilie away from the blood-soaked arena of his personal life and onto the subject of burning interest to Head Office.

'Do you see Rémy often?'

Emilie shook her head. '*Mais non*. Not so often since he was engaged.' She smiled fondly. 'He is in love at last. I think he has no need of his sister any more.'

Her hopeful gaze invited Luc to think the best of her beloved brother. Fat chance. The notion of Rémy in love with anyone but himself was about as easy to gulp down as this over-oaked blend.

'Maybe he has gone to the outback to see a client,' Emi said eagerly. 'You know he needs to fly to the clients sometimes.'

Luc frowned. 'Without informing his staff?'

Emilie coloured and cast a glance at her husband, who'd just joined them. 'Well, Rémy's always been—private.'

'Secretive,' Neil put in.

'*Neil*. Don't say *secretive*.' Emilie gave her husband a spousely shove. 'I'm sure he's done nothing wrong. He may just have forgotten to leave a message.'

Reading Neil's suddenly bland face, Luc had the impression Neil didn't share his wife's confidence in her charming brother.

Shari took a moment to nerve herself before pressing Neil and Emilie's bell. She'd stopped wearing the ring weeks ago, of course, but if anyone asked her about it, if they even mentioned Rémy's name, she still wasn't sure how far she could trust herself not to turn into a complete wuss and burst into tears.

Too emotional. Just too emotional.

Emilie opened the door.

'*Enfin*, Shari, after all this time…' She stopped short, looking Shari up and down. 'My God. Is it really you? You look…

incroyable.' Emilie kissed her on both cheeks and dragged her inside. 'I adore it. So sexy and *mystérieuse.*' Emilie thought she was speaking in English, but it often came out sounding like French.

With gratifying awe she examined Shari's transformation. The stripe across her eyes was intriguing enough, Shari supposed, but it was her chiffon dress and new five inch platforms that really had Em reeling.

'Oh-h-h,' the darling woman enthused. 'I am *green.* How can you walk in them? But what have you done to your eyes?' Shari's heart suffered a momentary paralysis, but Emilie continued exclaiming. '*Pretty*, so pretty. Is that frog a tattoo, really?'

Shari eased back out of the direct light. 'You know me. Always faking it.'

Emilie giggled. '*No*, don't say so. Now, where's Rémy?' She peered out into the dark street.

Shari tightened her grip on the strap of her shoulder purse. 'Rémy isn't coming.'

'Not?' Emilie looked nonplussed. 'Oh, but…quick, phone him. Tell him he has to. Our cousin is here to see him and he's looking so stern everyone is terrified.'

Shari looked steadily at her. 'No, Em. I can't.'

Emilie blinked bemusedly at her, and Shari was about to drop the bombshell when more guests piled in through the gate and hailed the hostess.

Shari seized her escape.

'Catch you later.' She smiled, and walked through to the party like a woman riding a storm.

It was a while since she'd visited. As things had deteriorated on the engagement front, she'd chosen to avoid the perceptive gazes of her brother and Em. Little changes had taken place in their home since the last time she'd dropped by to hang and read to their little girls.

Tonight the rooms were crowded, people spilling from the

living rooms to the pool terrace. A small army of hired staff
was flitting about, distributing hors d'oeuvres like largesse
to the poor.

Heading for a quiet corner, Shari felt conscious of eyes
turning to follow her. For a scary moment she feared her stripe
wasn't holding up, until a likely lad stepped in her path and
told her she looked hot.

Hot? Oh, that glorious word. Pleasure flowed into the dry
gulch where her self-esteem had once bubbled like the tran-
quil waters of an aquifer. Her spine stiffened all by itself. She
loved the sweet-talking hound.

Standing way taller on her new platforms, she blew him a
kiss. 'Too hot for you, sweetie,' she tossed over her shoulder
as she swished by.

There now, that wasn't too hard, was it?

She greeted a few faces she recognised, flashed a wave here,
a smile there, just as though everything in her little corner of
the world was hunky-dory. She hoped no one inquired about
her so-called fiancé. She should never have promised to allow
Rémy time to break the news to Em in his own way. She might
have known he'd never drum up the courage.

Face it, she'd known all along she should have told Neil and
Em herself. Weeks ago, she saw now, instead of feeling she
had to avoid them all this time. How much could she tell Emilie about her beloved Rémy, though? It was clear she couldn't
reveal anything tonight, with her sister-in-law under pressure.

And she'd have to be careful how much she told Neil. She'd
long sensed he didn't like Rémy. He'd always been so protective of her, heaven knew what he might do if he knew about
this last thing. And how might that impact on Emilie?

She spotted Neil then, standing in a group with a tall, dark-
eyed, sardonic-looking guy who was scanning the room, looking gloomy and detached.

Luc noticed his host waving at someone and suppressed
a yawn. These Australians were so open. So forward. So re-

lentlessly friendly and lively. To a jet-lagged Frenchman, a houseful of them was overwhelming. He listened, nodded, made meaningless conversation with strangers and mentally gritted his teeth.

These days, an hour in any roomful of couples was an eternity.

He watched a couple's unconscious linking as they chatted with other people. Hands brushing. Hips. Under duress he could admit to himself he missed those touches. The tiny automatic intimacies a man had with his lover.

At least he lived cleaner now. No promises, no lies. And no pain. It was honest, at least.

As though in ridicule of this absurd reflection a pang of yearning sliced through him. If only he could grow *used* to this life with no alleviating softness in it. No excitement. No warm body to open to him in the deep reaches of the night. What he needed was a…

Through a chink in the crowd his eye was snagged on a flash of colour. He looked. And looked again. He caught a fleeting glimpse of a face, and for a minute the breath was punched from his lungs.

The crowd moved, and now only her soft blonde hair was visible to him. He waited, not breathing, until she angled his way again. Ah. An intriguing sensation thrilled through him. It was her eyes. They were fascinating. So deep and alluring and mysterious. Eyes to haunt a man.

He felt his blood quicken.

The crowd parted again and he was able to take in the whole of her. She'd have fitted in well in any nightclub, but in this assembly she looked almost theatrical. Fragile, with her long legs in the high heels, the soft chiffon dress slipping off one shoulder, neat little shoulder purse knocking against her hip.

Mesmerised, he couldn't drag his gaze away.

Shari smiled as a waiter proffered a tray. She helped herself to a shot of vodka, downed it, then replaced the empty glass and took another to be going on with. She was casting about for a friendly face when she noticed the dark-eyed guy still watching her, his brows lowered and intent.

What the…? Had she broken the vodka laws?

His eyes had a strangely hypnotic quality. A girl had to ask herself if it was really the vodka that was so capturing his attention.

She attempted to crush his impudence with a haughty glare, but he didn't even flinch. Shaken by a momentary pang of insecurity, she hastily drowned it with another gulp of the potato elixir.

For goodness' sake, she was at risk here of tipsiness, not a good thing in platforms. If the guy didn't look away soon she'd be unable to lie on the floor without holding on.

Luc was aware other women were probably present. Pretty women with breasts and soft hair. Women with an air of mystery. Blondes. Legs, long and lovely, shimmering with every slight movement.

He just hadn't until this moment burned to touch one particular one.

Shari eyed her vodka guiltily. Although why should she? She was free, single and twenty-eight, and it was a party. She called the waiter back and rescued another glass from the tray. Turning then to face her examiner, she held them up and waved them at him, then took a sip from each.

His frown intensified. He shook his head at her a little, and she felt her blood stir thrillingly. At the same time a nervous shiver slithered down her spine. This guy was inviting a connection. The question was—what kind?

Shari flicked a glance about to see who else he might be with. He must belong to someone. In that swish dark suit and black silk shirt only a madwoman would have let him out on his own.

But no. At this actual moment, he only seemed to be with Neil.

His dark eyes swept her, bold, sensual while at the same time mildly censorious. Was he disapproving of the vodka, or what? If it had been Rémy he'd have been pouring the stuff down her throat to make her more compliant.

This vodka was a highly underrated substance. She could feel a warm glow coming on. Amazing how it could boost the confidence. Despite the fabled ice packing her mouse veins, she was pretty sure if she passed by that guy she could scorch him with her body heat.

In a roomful of people, why not give it a shot?

Enough of all this shillying and shallying, surely it was time to hug the birthday boy. With a deep breath, and assuming her most glamorous and mysterious expression, she summoned her inner Amazon and swished across to Neil, where she planted some lipstick on his cheek.

'Happy birthday, bro,' she said huskily.

Dear old Neil looked appreciatively at her. 'Didn't I see you in the movies?' He gave her a brotherly hug, then peered into her face. She had to steel herself not to flinch away for fear of him spotting the reason for her disguise. 'That's not a tattoo there, is it?' He wrinkled his brow. 'What do you think, Luc? Do we want our women branded with frogs?'

But the guy's dark velvet gaze had travelled well beyond her frog. He was drinking her all in, razing her to the parquet. True, tonight her curves were exceptionally appealing, but anyone would have thought this was the first time he'd ever laid eyes on a woman.

Though she seriously doubted it. Not with his bones.

Her chiffon top slid off one shoulder and she saw his eyes flicker to the bare section. Against all the odds, a shivery little tingle shot down her spine.

The guy queried Neil without taking his eyes from her. '*Qui est-elle?*'

'My sister,' Neil said, his arm around her. 'This is Shari. Shari, meet Luc. Em's and Rémy's cousin.'

'Oh.' An unpleasant sensation rose in the back of Shari's throat and she took an involuntary backwards step. The door guy. He hadn't mentioned being related.

The guy's eyes—*Luc's*—sharpened, while Neil goggled at her in surprise.

Recovering her party manners with an effort, Shari pulled herself together.

'De*light*ed,' she lied through her teeth. Lucky she was holding the two shot glasses and wasn't required to touch Rémy's cousin. Just her luck though, Neil chose that moment to exercise what he considered his brotherly prerogative, and snatched the glasses from her.

'Thanks for these,' he said, and swilled the contents one after another.

Trapped. There was no preventing the Frenchman from taking her hand.

'Shari,' he said. '*Enchanté, bien sûr.*' He leaned forward and brushed each of her cheeks with his lips.

Oh, damn. Her skin cells shivered and burned, though they'd been inoculated against the male members of this family.

Not that this guy resembled the Chéniers, with their reddish hair and blue eyes. Where Rémy was impulsive, surface cute and brutal, this cousin seemed more measured. Graver. Seasoned. Harsher face, experienced eyes. Dark compelling eyes, with golden gleams that reached into her and made her insides tremble.

'Do you live nearby?'

Ah, the voice. The deep, dark timbre was even more affecting without the intercom, that tinge of velvet accent around the edges.

Clearly he didn't recognise hers. She guessed she must have sounded different over an intercom with a busted eye and a swollen nose.

'Paddington, across the harbour. And you?'

'Paris. Across the world.'

She cast him a wry glance beneath her lashes, and he smiled and shrugged. The tiny, instantaneous communication lit the sort of spark in her blood a recently disengaged woman probably should have had the taste to ignore.

In a perfect world.

No wedding ring marred the tanned smoothness of his hands. A faint chime in her memory struggled to retrieve something of a story she'd once heard over coffee with Emilie. Something about a Parisian cousin, possibly a Luc—or did she say a duke?—and a woman. Some sort of scandal.

If he was the one, she didn't care to imagine too closely what had happened with the woman. His part in it.

'I see stripes are in this season.' He continued to hold her in his gaze. 'Do you always binge on vodka?'

'Unless coke's on offer.'

Beside her, Neil choked on the bruschetta he was wolfing. 'Steady on, girl. Luc'll get the wrong impression.'

She'd forgotten Neil. Smiling, she patted the brotherly shoulder. Neil needn't have worried. Luc was receiving her loud and clear, all right. For one thing, he seemed drawn by her rose carmine lipstick. She was in a likewise hypnotically drawn situation. The more she looked, the more she liked. Her eyes could scarcely unglue themselves.

He didn't seem at all fazed by her coke pun either. Instead, he smiled too, as if he understood she was kidding but it was a secret shared only by them.

'You don't look like a Chénier.' Heavens, was that her voice? Suddenly she was as throaty as a swan.

'I'm not a Chénier,' he said at once, a tad firmly. 'I'm a Valentin.'

That was all to the good. She tried not to betray herself by staring, but his mouth was so intensely stirring she couldn't resist drinking in the lines. Stern, yet so appealingly sensuous. A mouth for intoxicating midnight kisses. The trouble was, a woman could never be sure how a man would turn out beyond midnight.

'Forgive me if I mention it...' He moved a smidgin closer and she caught her breath in the proximity. 'You seem a little tense. Don't you enjoy parties?'

In need of fortification, she snagged a champagne flute from a passing waiter and let her roséd lips form a charming smile. 'I adore them. Don't you?'

'No.'

'Ah. Then I guess that's why you smoulder. I was beginning to think you were a misogynist.' Like his cousin.

She'd once read a novel in which a Frenchman whose honour was being challenged assumed a very Gallic expression. Perhaps that described the expression crossing Luc's handsome face at that very instant.

She could sense Neil's ripple of shock. It gave her a charge of pure enjoyment.

Luc's dark lashes flickered half the way down. 'I like women. Especially provocative ones.'

'How about dull, mousy, dreary ones?'

He cocked a brow at her, then, amused, glanced about. 'I don't see any here.'

'They could be in disguise.'

His dark eyes lit. 'But what dull, mousy, dreary people would ever think of wearing a disguise? Only very exciting, sexy, playful women do that.'

Her spirit lifted with a warm buzz. At last a man was divining her true nature. She *was* exciting, sexy and playful, given the proper inspirational framework. She felt his glance touch her throat and breasts, and the glow intensified. Imagining his smooth fingers tracing that same pathway, she might have begun to emit a few sparks.

She noticed Neil shift restlessly at her side, then mumble something and drift away.

Alone in a crowded room with a sophisticated Frenchman,

another sophisticated Frenchman, Shari felt her feet edge to the precipice. A whisper of suspense tantalised the fine down on her nape. This *might* have been just a bit of aimless flirting, but something in his eyes, something intentional behind his glance, made the breath catch in her throat.

All men weren't like Rémy. Of course they weren't.

The Frenchman gazed meditatively across the room, then back at her. 'What are you trying to drown with all that alcohol?'

'Tears, of course. My broken heart.'

'There are better ways.'

Meeting that dark sensual gaze, she had no doubt of it. The battered old muscle in her chest gave a warning lurch. *Keep it light, Shari.*

She felt his gaze sear her legs and, smiling, inclined her head to follow his glance. 'Oh. Have I snagged a stocking?'

'Not that I can see. Your legs look very smooth.' His mouth was grave. 'Quite tantalising.'

His fingers were long. Imagining how they would feel curved around her thighs triggered an arousing rush of warmth to a highly sensitive region. Ridiculous, she remonstrated with herself. Inappropriate. Here she was, raw on the subject of men, *bruised*, and he was a total stranger. And so close to family. Family connections were such a mistake.

She supposed she was succumbing to flattery. The sad truth was Rémy's endless series of nubile nymphs had messed with her confidence. Her view of herself had altered. While she'd laughed in his face at some of his insults, always delivered with that mocking amusement, a few had penetrated her heart like slivers of glass.

With a momentary pang of panic it struck her she wasn't really ready to get back on the horse. But her rational self intervened. How would she know unless she tried a little canter?

As though alive to the odds she was weighing, Luc's dark eyes met hers, sensual, knowing. 'Are you with someone?'

Her heart skittered several beats. 'No. Are you?'

'No. It's hot in here, do you find? Will we walk outside in the cool air?' Smiling, he took the champagne from her and placed it on a side table. The flash of his white teeth was only outdone by the dazzle in his dark eyes.

She felt a warning pang reverberate through her vitals and mingle with the desirous little pulse awakened there. The guy was smooth. But what would the old Shari have done, just supposing a Frenchman had ever been this suave?

Oh, that was right. The old Shari would have fallen into his hands like a ripe and trusting plum. But having finally achieved exciting, sexy and playful status, was she to just throw it all away?

With dinner about to be served, people were swarming inside. Only a scant few were left out there on the pool terrace. But what was the guy likely to do? Black her eye? Could she allow herself to remain socially paralysed for the rest of her life?

While she was still wrestling with the possibilities, Emilie came fluttering by. 'Oh, Shari. Good, good, you're looking after Luc. *Luc, pardonne-moi, mon cher.* I so want to find out all the family gossip. But as you see, now I am a little *occupée*…Shari can show you…' One of the staff came to murmur something in her ear, and with more profuse apologies Emilie flitted away to deal with her domestic crisis.

That sealed it. Stepping out into the balmy night air, Shari knew she was doing her sisterly duty. Luc was her responsibility. Looking after him was her given work.

He glanced down at her. 'Do you love that moment when you feel suspended on the edge of something?' His dark eyes shimmered with a light that made her insides frizzle and fry.

'On the edge—of what?' The night seemed to gather around her and listen.

'Something—exciting. Perhaps unforgettable.' His eyes caressed her face with a seductive awareness. 'You're not nervous, are you?'

'Yes.' She gazed at him. 'At this moment, I'm quite nervous.' He looked taken aback, and she hastened to stutter, 'A—a-are you in Sydney long?'

He made a negative gesture. 'Tomorrow I must fly out. I really came tonight in pursuit of my cousin. There are things I need to discuss with him on behalf of D'Avion. But for once in his life Rémy has done something—great.'

'What's that?'

He smiled to himself, then shot her a glance. 'Failed to show.'

Hear hear, she could have cried above her thundering heart. It was reassuring to know he saw through Rémy. Maybe he was one of her kind, after all.

They reached the end of the pool terrace and paused. Beyond, pale garden lights reflected the moonlight and illuminated the pathway that snaked down through the shrubbery to the boathouse. Beyond, lights glimmered from craft moored in the bay.

She noticed Luc's glance stray towards the path.

With a surge of adrenaline she knew wickedness beckoned down that shadowy track. Or—maybe just friendliness. A respectful cousinly chat. She was no longer engaged. Why should every move be such a struggle?

Though this *might* be the moment she should let slip her knowledge on the subject of Rémy. Tell Luc his charming cousin was bound to be in LA by now. No doubt with a woman along, maybe even the twenty-year-old he'd recently taken up with. That was if he'd been able to find his missing passport, after turning over the apartment *and* her in his fruitless, vindictive search.

It was all so ugly. The old revulsion threatened, and she turned impatiently away from all things Rémy. Tonight she needed to wipe him from her mind.

'Are you very important in D'Avion?' she said conversation-
ally, just as if she hadn't noticed their feet were on the path.

The air was heavy with the sweet sultry fragrance of night
jasmine. The back of Luc's hand touched hers and her skin
cells shivered in welcome.

They turned the corner and were out of sight of the house.
Excitement infected her veins with a languor, as if her very
limbs had joined the conspiracy.

'Very,' he said gravely, though his eyes smiled. 'And you?
Are you in the theatre, by some chance?' She shook her head,
and he considered her, his lashes heavy and sensual, his eyes
appreciative. 'Let me guess.' He touched her nape, drew a caressing finger down to the edge of her top. Magic radiated
through her skin and into her bloodstream. 'Something cre-
ative. You give the impression of not always being bound by
the ordinary rules. Would that be true?'

Her heart lurched. It was such a line, but all at once it
seemed quite possibly true. Especially now she was in disguise.

'Oh, well.' She hated to exaggerate her minuscule claims. 'I
guess I'm an artist of sorts.' She flashed him a brilliant smile.
Gouache, crayons and cuddly possums didn't go with five-inch
heels and red toenails, but they had their excitements.

'So you paint?'

She barely hesitated before she nodded. 'Partly.'

'What does that mean?'

'Well, I write stories for children. And paint—you know,
the illustrations. I'm not that good yet, but I have actually had
a book published. It's a picture story book about a cat.'

She pulled herself up, not wanting to babble on about herself and bore the man to tears, but he was gazing intently at
her as if genuinely interested.

He drew in a breath. '*Tiens*. Shari, that's very impressive.'
He spoke so warmly she couldn't doubt his sincerity. 'You are
a genuine author.'

Inwardly, she absolutely glowed. 'Oh, in a very small way.'

He took her hand and pulled her to face him. It had been so long since a man had touched her in that special way. She trembled inside her bones with a nervous yearning. What if she froze and couldn't summon the necessary fire? What if she embarrassed herself and shied away at the crucial moment like a scared animal?

She felt her mouth dry to an uncomfortable clumsiness.

'You are modest.' He said rather hoarsely, 'I think you are not what I expected.'

She said breathlessly, 'What did you expect?' Compelled to moisten her lips, she saw a hot flare in his eyes.

He kissed her then, a firm, purposeful sexy pressure that shot a delicious flame through her blood and made her entire being tremble with longing.

Ready to swoon, she moved against his hard body, opening up to the full sexy onslaught, but he pulled back and released her. He gazed at her, his eyes unreadable, then traced the outline of her face with his finger. He pressed her lower lip with his thumb and her insides melted in the blaze.

'You taste *douce*.' His voice was a little gravelly.

Douce. *Douce*? Was that all? To her parched senses he tasted like man and sex and long, hot nights.

With her adrenaline pumping like crazy, they resumed walking until they reached the end of the path where the boathouse gazed out over the water, its windows blank and enigmatic. As they stepped onto the boardwalk near the landing stage, the moonlight contoured the Frenchman's face with hard lines and angles. She caught the desire glowing in his velvet eyes, and felt confused.

Having seduced her thus far, was he having second thoughts?

'What sort of things inspire you to write?' he said.

'Oh, well.' She made an expansive motion with her hand. 'All sorts. Owls. The moon.' His mouth was so achingly close. Her lips, her entire being hungered to be touched, stroked, enjoyed, caressed, pampered, kissed, *loved*...

Would he touch her again, or was that *it*?

'Owls?' He sounded surprised.

'Oh, owls are really very magical, ethereal beings. Have you…have you ever read—*Rebecca*?'

He frowned in thought. 'What is that? Is it to do with owls?'

'No, no.' She laughed heartily. 'It's…I guess it's a romance. A—mystery. A bit of a thriller. Rebecca has the family boathouse furnished like a private apartment. Her secret love nest where she can meet her illicit lover.'

He lifted his hands. 'I don't think I know it. *Romances, enfin…*' He made an amused, negative shrug.

What an idiot she was. Of course men didn't read romances. Just as well, or they'd know too much.

His eyes glinting, he cast a smiling glance at Neil and Em's boathouse. 'What do you think? Would this one—have furniture?'

All the fine hairs stood up on her spine and shivered in suspenseful, gleeful exultation. She hesitated a breathless instant, then spread her hands. 'Well, we could always see. I know where they keep the key.'

He looked keenly at her. Said offhandedly, like a guy who didn't care one way or the other, 'Are you sure?'

The thing was, though, his voice had deepened in timbre just that betraying bit.

She gazed fleetingly into his eyes, not needing to read beyond that hot, lustful gleam. He cared all right. He wanted her, and she felt propelled by a wicked, reckless desire to mount that untamed stallion and do something wild.

'Sure I'm sure.' Her breath came faster.

She slipped her hand under the iron tile between the pylon and the floor where she'd seen Neil hide the key a dozen times.

Bingo. It was there.

Her hands shook so badly as she fitted it into the lock, she had to hunch to prevent Luc from seeing.

Once inside, she was assailed with the boat smell of paint

and varnish and salty, fishy weekends. Neil's cruiser floated silently in the lower room, a ghostly presence in the silent dark. A flight of steps led to the upper loft where supplies were stored.

Shards of moonlight illuminated the walls. Shari indicated the way, stumbling once on the stairs. Luc took her arm to steady her.

She didn't speak, just turned her breathless gaze to him. Even in the dim light his eyes were burning. Her blood ran hot in her breasts, fanned fire between her legs.

They finished the climb to the loft. She was trembling again, in the grip of something more elemental now than mere nerves. She faced him, aflame.

He pulled her to him. This kiss was a rough and hungry collision, his tongue in her mouth, possessive, lustful, his hands in her hair, moulding her shoulders, unfastening her bra. She dragged at his shirt and fumbled to release the buttons, avid to feel his naked skin beneath her palms.

With the mingled scents of aftershave, wine and man rising giddily in her head, she thrilled as he stroked her breasts. Then his mouth closed over her nipple and the blaze in her blood roared. She sobbed in deep quivering breaths as he slipped his hand inside her pants, caressing, stroking her engorged sex until she swooned with ecstasy.

Then he slid a finger inside her and massaged, sending waves of erotic pleasure thrilling through her burning flesh. She rocked against his hand, maddened, desperate.

'Oh,' she groaned, clinging to his shoulders. 'Yes, yes, yes.'

To her intense disappointment his hand paused. She felt his hot breath on her neck.

'I don't have any protection with me,' he said hoarsely. 'Do you have anything?'

'What? *What*?' She could hardly believe her ears, but the exigency of the moment must have jerked her memory, because she dredged up an image of a thin emergency package in the deepest reach of her purse.

Maybe fate or the devil were on her side, for, scrabbling among the debris, her fingers located the precious article. She held up the battered package.

'Here,' she breathed in triumph.

She saw his eyes as he snatched it from her. Their focused, hungry gleam incited such an intense and burning heat in her, such an inferno of responsive lust, she could barely wait for him to sheathe himself.

Swiftly it was done.

She clung to him and locked her legs around his waist. Then he thrust his virile length inside her again and again, filling her up, stroking the inner walls of her yearning, burning flesh. It was good, so, thrillingly, shudderingly good.

As she felt his fabulous hardness inside her her passion escalated out of control and she zoomed to an extreme and explosive climax. Her first during the actual act. Fantastically, *his* tumultuous spill happened almost at the same time, groans of release shuddering through his big frame while pleasure rayed through her bloodstream like light.

He held her close to his beating heart, crushing her damp breasts, his hot breath fanning her ear. She felt shattered, and bathed in jubilation. She needed to pinch herself. So *this* was what all the shouting was about.

Of course she couldn't rely on it happening every time. It might even have been a fluke, brought on by the forbidden aspects of the scene.

Even so, it was such a precious moment. For a wild minute she adored Luc Valentin. Felt pretty sure she would adore him *and* this boathouse for the rest of her life.

'We should go back,' she breathed into his ear at last. 'We don't want to be missed.'

He held her away from him, his dark gaze urgent, compelling. 'Come with me to the hotel. We'll have a little supper and enjoy each other properly. You will come?' He gazed at her, then kissed her. '*Bien sûr* you will.'

Excited, relieved, she hardly knew what she said. '*Oh*. Well…who can resist a little supper? I'll have to say goodnight to Neil and Em, though, you know. Otherwise they'll wonder…'

His mouth was grave, though his eyes gleamed. 'No, we don't want them to wonder.'

CHAPTER THREE

SHARI slipped from the downstairs bathroom, anticipation bubbling in her veins. Luc was across the hall, waiting. Like her, he was spruced again, as immaculate as if their stolen encounter had never happened.

She started towards him just as Emilie emerged from the dining room. They both halted, Luc backing into a convenient doorway before he was noticed.

'Oh, *chérie*,' Emilie exclaimed. 'I've been wanting to ask you. What's happening with Rémy? Where is he?'

Shari hesitated and glanced past her to see if Luc had heard. Her heart lurched when she saw his expression. He was staring at her, his eyes sharply alert.

'Well, he...I—I—I don't know for certain.' In a low voice Shari added, 'He's gone away, I think. I'll tell you about it tomorrow, I promise.'

But Emilie wasn't to be fobbed off. 'You don't *know*? Come on, Shari, something is going on. We haven't seen either of you for months. He's your *fiancé*. You should know. What game is he playing with you, *chérie*?'

As she felt the blistering intensity of Luc's concentrated gaze on her face Shari's guilty cheeks burned. 'Tomorrow, Em. I'll tell you everything. I promise.'

Emilie looked as if she was about to insist, but some other people burst into the hall, laughing, from the dining room, and she compressed her lips. She threw up her hands and exclaimed in a lowered voice, 'It's always something with him. When will he ever—? *D'accord*, Shari. Tomorrow. Don't forget. I won't sleep until I know.' She hurried away to her guests.

Luc waited until they were alone, then bore down upon Shari, his eyes glittering danger. She felt an involuntary pang of alarm.

Resisting an impulse to back against the wall, she stood her ground. 'I know what you must be thinking,' she said in a hurried murmur. 'It's not how it looks. I can explain.'

'Of course you can.' His voice was smooth as silk and laced with sarcasm. 'You are engaged to my cousin.' His eyes were hard and accusatory. 'That was you in his apartment.'

'Shh,' she whispered, glancing towards the nearby dining room. 'Yes, yes, it was me, but *no*, I'm not his fiancée. Not any more. The engagement, such as it was, has been broken for weeks. Months.'

'Then how is it Emilie doesn't know? Your sister-in-law?' He looked incredulous.

'Well…I—put off telling them. Rémy's her brother, Neil's *my* brother…' She spread her hands. 'Em has had difficulties with her pregnancy and… She's so attached to Rémy, and any bad news is bad for her blood pressure. Rémy talked me into keeping quiet because he wanted to break the news himself.' She grimaced. 'He's probably dead scared of some of the things I might tell them.'

'What things?' His dark eyes were stern.

She glanced at him, then darted a glance towards the living room. 'This isn't a good place to talk. I'll explain more when we're alone.' She slipped her hand into her purse and grabbed her mobile. 'Do you have your own wheels, or shall I phone for a cab?'

'A moment.' He raked her with his eyes, then turned sharply away from her as if the very sight were deadly. He crooked an elbow over his eyes, shading them from some dangerous glow she emitted. His voice sounded as if it were being wrenched

from the centre of the earth. 'This—*break-up*. Just how recent is it?'

'I *said*. I *told* you…' Her voice faltered a little. She could see
where he might be headed with this. 'Not that recent.'

'*How* recent?'

She started to feel annoyed at his tendency to fire questions
like bullets. 'Well, officially I gave the ring back a couple of
months ago. Though by then it was well and truly on the rocks.'

'"*Officially*".' He made mock quotation marks with his fingers. There was a definite snap in his voice that riled her. 'What
does that mean?'

She glared at him. 'Look,' she whispered fiercely, 'not that
it's anyone's *business*, but he and I imploded almost at the start,
only like a fool I kept on…'

He swung about to impale her with his gaze. 'Forget the
excuses. Give me a straight answer. When was the last time
you were together?'

Her blood pressure rose. 'Does that matter?'

'It may not to some guys, but I have a strong distaste for
screwing women who are still hot from my cousin's bed.'

She flushed. 'I'm not *hot from his bed*.' Her chest heaving
with indignation, she added sweetly, 'Though until a minute
ago you could have said I was hot from your arms.'

For an instant his eyes flared, then he concealed them behind his dark lashes. 'When was the last time you saw him?'

'Wednesday, okay?'

'This week?' His frown intensified, though his glance
strayed to her mouth.

'Yes. He was looking for his passport. He accused me of
holding onto it after I threw his things out of the apartment. As
if I would. He said he had to go to LA on the firm's business.'

A tinge of contempt touched his face. '*Vraiment*. So…did
you give him the passport?'

'I told you. I didn't have it.'

His dark eyes flickered over her, searching, suspicious. It

was pretty clear he didn't believe a word she said. The hackles rose on her neck. She was so *over* being insulted by the men in this family.

'So,' he said with maddening silkiness. 'You sleep with a man on Wednesday, then you sleep with his cousin on Saturday.'

She hissed in a long, simmering breath. 'Only if his cousin's very, very lucky.'

The raw anger in her voice finally penetrated Luc's brain. She wasn't taking his perfectly natural concerns well. As he scanned her face his certainties suffered a jolt. There was a sparkle in her eyes that gave him pause.

Her luscious mouth was firmly compressed, when only minutes ago those lips had been so soft and yielding, so tinglingly responsive.

She turned away from him.

With quicksilver rapidity a dozen arguments flashed through his mind. From her point of view she might have been telling the truth. She was a woman, after all. What woman ever understood the dictates of honour between men? Particularly men of the same family?

The night's original agenda scintillated in his mind's eye. Perhaps he was being harsh. Overly fastidious. If she was no longer *officially* engaged…

And he'd be gone from Australia tomorrow. They'd be ships in the night, et cetera. Passing on the stormy seas of his bed at the Seasons. Plunging and plunging in the sweet, fresh sheets, her naked beauty his to enjoy to the full. Totally naked, and by lamplight…

Gazing at her sweet profile, he felt a renewed urgent stir in his loins. It would be too cruel to have to sacrifice this now. Rémy would never have to know.

At that admittedly seedy reflection shame started to seep through him. What was he doing? He'd come to relieve Rémy of his job, not his woman. For all he knew they'd had a mere lovers' tiff and she'd be back in his bed in a few days.

Avoiding looking at her for fear of succumbing to temptation and throwing honour out of the window, he chilled his tone. 'Let's be adult about this. I think we have to acknowledge that our recent—interlude—was an error of judgement.'

She turned coolly on her heel and stalked away in the direction of the front door.

'*Shari.*' Galvanised to action, he caught up with her in a couple of strides.

A mere beat ahead of him, she was first to grab the door knob. As he reached over her blonde head to take it from her he heard a small startled sound issue from her throat and just for an instant he noted a curious rigidity in her. He touched her shoulder and she started, then spun around, alarm in her eyes.

'*Pardonne-moi.*' He drew back in concern. 'I didn't mean to scare you.'

'You *don't* scare me. And you'd better believe that.'

Bemused by the tense glitter in her eyes, he tried to placate her. 'You're upset. Shari, please.' He gestured imploringly. 'Be reasonable. Maybe you're angry with Rémy. Try to understand, I cannot allow myself to be exploited as a weapon of revenge in some—dispute between lovers.'

'*Exploited,*' she echoed, her voice low and trembling. '*Revenge.*' She closed her eyes. 'Oh, why didn't I see? You're just like him.'

'How am I like him?' he retorted, stung.

Her eyes sparkled fiercely. 'Everything you're saying, every word is—is—accusing me of *cheating*. You're calling me a-a-a slut.'

His blood pressure made a surprising leap, but he cooled that purely visceral response. 'No,' he said coolly. 'I am far too polite.'

She wrenched the door open and walked quickly down the path.

After a second, driven by some impulse, he strode in pursuit. He'd almost caught up to where she stood outside on the pavement, when without warning she dashed forward and hailed a passing taxi.

The car drew into the kerb and she scrambled in. As it moved into the road she turned to cast him a last icy, burning look through the window.

He felt stunned. *Nom de Dieu.* What sort of guy did she think she was dealing with? With fire flaring in his veins, he raced for his hire car.

Attempting to keep her cab in sight among the many, he wove in and out of the traffic—absurdly heavy for a country of this size—rationalising his impulse. At least if he talked to her again he could explain his position more fully. Surely it was important to leave their encounter on a positive note.

They were practically family, weren't they? She'd be grateful, as he would be. After all, it had been a fantastic few minutes they'd shared. Fantastic.

Her silky softness still seemed to be in his senses, her voice, her very *essence*… His hands tightened on the wheel. If he was honest, he wasn't ready yet to call it quits with her.

They left the Harbour Bridge behind, wound a way through the neon city and plunged into a maze of narrow one-way streets lined with terraces. Having lost the taxi a couple of times, he *thought* he still had the same one in view, and was heartened when he saw the name Paddington on a shop front.

Wasn't that where she'd said she lived?

Just his luck, he was trapped on the wrong side of a red light. By the time he started again, the cab was out of sight.

He cursed long and colourfully. Taking the direction he calculated his quarry must have taken, he crossed a couple of intersections before he reached one where he caught a fleeting glimpse of someone alighting from a stationary cab. The distance was too far for him to be certain it was Shari, but it was a chance. His only chance.

Curbing his impatience, he recircuited the block and waited for the lights again, drumming his fingers on the wheel in his urgency to backtrack.

By the time he reached the terrace he'd estimated was the one, the cab was well and truly gone, the street quiet.

Breathing fast, her heart still thumping painfully, Shari paused in the delicate task of stripping her face bare. She would not accept the verdict. She wasn't guilty of anything.

She'd done nothing to feel ashamed of. She didn't care what Luc Valentin thought of her. She'd allowed him to enjoy her body purely out of generosity.

She took some deep calming breaths to slow herself down, then, when her hand was steadier, gingerly dabbed the paint from the bruise, revealing it in all its violent glory.

Was it her imagination it looked worse? She cleaned her teeth, then changed into her flowery old oversized tee shirt and slipped into bed. Lying there in the dark, she rolled the events of the evening around in her mind.

It was *his* problem if he couldn't appreciate an honest human exchange without labelling a woman. And the insulting way he'd refused to believe a word she'd said. What was that all about?

She was startled from her reflections by noise from outside. Her heart thudded until she remembered tonight was the neighbourhood's bin collection night. Hers was crammed full to overflowing with trash left by the previous tenants.

She should get up and take out the bin. She should.

From his park across the street Luc scrutinised the row of houses in the terrace. He suspected 217 could be the one, for a light had recently gone out in its upper front window. Now the entire house was in darkness, as was its neighbour.

What if he was mistaken? He began to see how ridiculous his mad chase was. He couldn't knock on every door in the terrace. And how likely was Shari to open the door to him anyway? She'd probably accuse him of stalking her.

Le bon Dieu, he *was* stalking. Whatever it was about her that had got under his skin was compelling him to linger there even now, when he knew he'd lost any opportunity he might have had if only he'd been able to keep the cab closer.

It wasn't as if he could throw pebbles at her window. The chances were he might terrify some poor little old lady to death.

He was about to cut his losses and call it a night when he heard a familiar rumbling, then at 221 an old guy came into view hauling a wheelie bin. He trundled it through his gate and parked it next to some others lined up under a streetlight.

A minute or two later one after another all the lights came on at 219.

Luc waited, watching, then his heart leaped. Another bin was being wheeled from the gate of 219, this time by a woman.

A *blonde* woman.

He got out of the car and strode swiftly across the street.

She'd changed from her party clothes into some long, flowing robe-like garment, but as he drew nearer he saw it was Shari. Admittedly, his heart was beating a tad too fast for a cool guy in charge of the situation.

She angled the bin into line with its neighbours just as he caught up with her.

'Shari.'

She jumped, and with a strangled cry started back through her gate.

Realising the enormity of having suddenly seemed to appear out of the dark, he was filled with contrition. 'Shari.' He only just restrained himself from grabbing her. 'Forgive me for startling you. I—I only want to talk. I just want to explain…'

'Luc.' Her voice was stunned, incredulous. 'Do you have any *idea*…? What—what are you even *doing* here?'

He noticed her draw the lapels of her garment close and

fold her arms across her breasts. It affected him with a burning desire to hold her to him, kiss her hair.

'Shari,' he said thickly, advancing on her. 'Shari…'

The light fell full on her face then, and he narrowed his eyes for a closer look. With a gut-wrenching shock he saw it wasn't a shadow darkening the area surrounding her right eye.

She turned sharply away, covering the bruise with her hand, and started striding for the house. 'Leave me alone.'

After a second of stunned paralysis, comprehension flooded through him and he was aware of a sharp twist in his chest. Her whimsical make-up had had a purpose, after all. He bounded after her onto her little verandah with the blind intention of pinning her down and making her talk to him, but she reached her door first.

Before she could close it, he rammed his knee against it. 'What happened? Who did that to you? Was it him? Rémy?'

'Of *course* not. What do you think, that as well as being a slut I'm a…a…? I had an accident, all right?' She was flushed and trembling, so achingly vulnerable in her fierce pride he felt something inside him give.

Accident, *vraiment*. He couldn't believe that. At the fragile pretence he felt so torn with tenderness and remorse, he hardly knew what he was saying, only that his voice grew hoarse. 'Shari, *chérie*. Don't be so…I didn't mean to imply… This—this is *not* how we should say *au'voir*.'

In the verandah light her naked face was strained, her eyes dark with emotion. 'We are strangers. We will never meet again. Move away from the door, please.'

She closed it in his face.

CHAPTER FOUR

BUT the world as Shari knew it jolted off its axis. It was Rémy she never saw again.

Soon after dawn one morning in the autumn, Neil came hammering on her door with the shattering news. Rémy had been driving too fast on a foggy Colorado mountain road, misjudged a corner, and skidded over a cliff.

The shock was so immense, Shari was overcome with nausea and had to run to the bathroom to throw up. The details were sketchy, but it was clear Rémy hadn't been alone in the car.

What a surprise.

In the hours that followed, once Shari had begun to assimilate the news, she wished she could cry. At least poor Emilie had that release. Em was so distraught, so overcome with grief, Neil was beside himself with anxiety for her health and that of their soon-to-be-born twins.

The best Shari could do was to change into her old track pants and run for miles, thanking heaven Luc Valentin wasn't there to see her in her running clothes. Her emotions were a mess, not improved by an even more than usually massive dose of PMT.

She tried not to speculate about what Luc would be thinking about Rémy's loss, and concentrated on feeling sad. Of course she must be, deep down. She must be torn with sadness, though the main feeling she was aware of was her sympathy for Em.

Overcome as she was, as they *all* were, she refused to delude herself about Rémy.

His death didn't change the cruel things he'd done. Some of the wounds he'd inflicted had had a bitter afterlife.

All right, maybe her plunge into adventure with Luc had been a bit soon after the end of the engagement, but officially— *technically*—despite the things Luc had said to her, she had done nothing wrong. Impulsive maybe, to share pleasure with a man who couldn't appreciate a woman's generosity in the best spirit, but not wrong.

She'd stick to that even as Luc Valentin tied her to the stake and applied the flaming torch.

No. If she did feel any guilt, the real reason, the one she could never admit to Em, was that, where Rémy was concerned, the worst she could feel was this terrible, awful hollowness. On the other hand, where Luc was concerned, she felt—

Raw.

The shock shook some Parisian quarters as well. In his executive office high above the Place de l'Ellipse, Luc Valentin was riveted to the police report, his pulse quickening by the second.

The loss of a young life was a tragedy, of course, though his cousin hadn't exactly endeared himself to many of his relatives. Luc guessed poor Emilie would be the one who suffered most. The only surprise was that it had been an accident. Despite Rémy's oily ability to slip out of tight situations, the chances had always been that eventually someone would murder him.

Someone like himself.

He'd considered it a few times after his tumultuous encounter in Sydney.

All at once finding his office suffocating, he took the lift down to the ground.

He strode block after block, seeing nothing of the busy pavements as the vision that haunted his nights invaded his being.

Shari Lacey, powerful, vivid, as searing as a flame. Shari, her emerald eyes glowing with the sincerity of her denials. Shari…

Her very name was a sigh that plucked at his heartstrings. No, he mused wryly, wrenched them. If only Australia hadn't been so far away. If he could talk to her. Hear her voice…

In the midnight hours he'd once or twice considered taking a month's vacation and taking the long flight back. Just to— catch up. See if she needed protecting.

Those last bitter moments at her house stayed with him. *We are strangers* still rang in his ears. In English the words sounded even harsher than they did in French. That cold click of her locking her door, locking him *out*, had reverberated through him with a chill familiarity.

He grimaced at himself. Suddenly women were rejecting him on both sides of the world. Why? He'd never been a guy to pursue an unwilling woman. *Vraiment*, until Manon's sudden betrayal he doubted he'd ever before experienced one. All his life, he'd taken for granted his ease at acquiring any woman he desired.

But first Manon, and now Shari… Somewhere on the journey, he'd lost his way.

Maybe he should have stayed in Australia and persevered. If it hadn't been for that crucial directors' meeting he might have stayed and… What?

Remonstrated with her? Sweet-talked her? Tried to make her *forget* Rémy? But how could he have? What man would dream of trying to impose his will on a woman who was already wearing the evidence of brute masculine force?

His fists, his entire being clenched whenever he thought of it. If he ever came across the *canaille* who'd done that to her…

He felt certain it had been Rémy. No wonder she'd been weeping when he'd gone to the apartment in search of him. How could such a woman have been sucked in by the guy?

He threw up his hands in bafflement.

Was that why Shari had insisted her wound had been an accident? She was still in love with her fiancé, *ex*-fiancé, whatever he'd been?

One thing was certain, whatever her status that night, she wasn't engaged now.

Nom de Dieu. This impulse to contact a woman on the other side of the world, make some sort of approach, remind her he was alive, was ludicrous.

His feet slowed at the place where the red-curtained windows of a bar spilled an inviting glow into the grey afternoon.

Signalling the bartender for cognac, he took a table by the window. A couple of women came in and sat down. One of them had fair hair, not unlike Shari's.

He drew the accident report from his pocket and re-examined it. Had they told Shari about the other woman in the car? Maybe she was in despair, grieving for the *coquin*.

He took out his mobile, calculated the time in Australia, then with a gesture of impatience slid the phone back into his pocket.

A blonde woman at the other table turned his way.

He dropped his glance, conscious of disappointment. There wasn't the slightest resemblance.

Jolted from sleep, Shari dragged her eyelids apart as her phone vibrated with maddening persistence. She stretched out her hand for the bedside table.

'Hello,' she croaked.

'Shari. *Ça va?*'

The masculine voice slammed Shari with a sickening shock. Her heart froze.

'*Rémy?*'

There was a nightmare instant of suspense, then the voice, contrite, apologetic, said, 'Shari, *c'est moi*. Luc. I'm sorry if I'm disturbing you.'

'Sorry? You're *sorry?*' The relief, the warm, weakening relief flooded through her like a sob and gave her back her speech. 'Do you *know* what time it is? Phoning in the middle of the night and speaking French... Are you trying to *terrify* me? And d-d-did you think I would want to speak to you ever again in my life? How did you get this number, anyway?'

'From Neil.' His voice dried. 'Forgive me. I see this was a mistake.'

'*Another* mis—' she started to say, but Luc Valentin, the man who felt disdain for her, the man who knew her shame, disconnected before she could finish.

She lay awake until dawn, staring into the dark, alternately regretting her anger, then burning with it all over again. If only he hadn't surprised her that night without her make-up. If only he'd left her some shred of dignity, she might not have had to feel so angry with him. She might have been able to hear his voice without all this agony.

It seemed her agony was never-ending. The excruciating reports of the efforts to reclaim Rémy went on for days before he was recovered. Messages flew thick and fast between Sydney and Paris. Luc's name came up so often in Neil's conversation, Shari wanted to cover her ears.

It was hard enough trying to squash down her memories of the party night. Shari didn't *care* if Neil thought Luc was a great guy. But she couldn't say so. She just had to grin and bear it all. And of course, poor Emilie needed to reminisce and talk about Rémy and her other family members. The least Shari could do for her grieving sister-in-law was to listen.

Emilie produced some photos of a visit she and Neil had made to France as newly-weds, before Rémy emigrated. One in particular smote Shari's eye. It was of a foursome, leaning against a ramshackle fence in some rural setting. Rémy and Emi were linking arms with Luc and a spectacular-looking brunette with cheekbones and long, straight, shampoo-model's hair.

'See, Shari? Here's Luc and Manon. This was the day we visited Tante Laraine's farm. Do you remember, Neil? How happy we all were?' Her eyes filled with tears.

'Oh, Em.' Shari put her arms around her and stroked Em's hair. Naturally, anyone in tears always brought hers on as well.

When they'd all mopped up, Shari glanced again at the picture, once or twice. Manon was beautiful, no doubt about it. Some would say she and Luc looked good together. *Right* together, both being so tall and good-looking. Though Shari was not one of those people. How people looked was hardly the point.

She tried to persuade herself Luc didn't appear all that happy in the picture. He wasn't exactly grinning like the others, just smiling a little at Manon in that amused sort of way that made his eyes warm.

It scraped her heart. She turned away from it. Family photos had never interested her, anyway.

As it happened, she knew enough about Manon, since naturally, after the Luc debacle, she'd come across a few things on the Internet about Manon and her sensational affair with Jackson Kerr. Not that she was all that interested in Kerr and Manon at Cannes, or Kerr and Manon in LA. There'd been a million articles about Kerr's discarded actress wife, with the usual wild gossip over the trashing of the marriage.

The tabloids had been pumped with it all when the affair was fresh, though now after all this time it had gone off the boil.

Luc hardly came in for a mention, except she saw his name mentioned in a couple of French newspaper articles about business. Who cared, anyway?

She buried herself in work. Anything to blot out reality.

She was involved in mapping out paintings one morning for her owl story when a magnificent bouquet of flowers was delivered to her door. Wow. It must have been ruinously expensive. Carrying the fragrant mass in to join her accumulating hothouse, she opened the card.

And felt a rapid pounding in her temples.

To Shari. Sincere condolences for your tragic loss from my heart. Luc Valentin.

She sat at her kitchen table, staring at the card, smarting. What did he mean by it? He knew enough about Rémy. He'd seen her bruise. Was he using this occasion to needle her?

Meantime, Neil continued to pour information into her unwilling ears. While Rémy had recently made his home in Australia, he'd still kept his French citizenship. His true heart had always been in Paris, according to the family. He must be transported there and buried in the family tomb.

'Emilie's devastated that she can't go, Shari,' Neil's voice issued down the phone. 'Not with the twins so close.'

'Oh, *of course.* I know. It's such a shame.' Shari felt so sad for poor Emilie, and helpless. 'Poor Em. It's a horrible tragedy. But what can she do?'

'She thinks someone must go in her place.' Neil's voice faltered a little. 'We er...we know you'll want to be there, Shari. So we're—counting on you.'

Shari blenched to the soles of her feet. *'What*?'

The image of Luc Valentin, backed by a phalanx of hostile aunts, turned her hoarse. 'Neil, *no.* Rémy and I didn't even part as *friends.* Far from it. He wouldn't— *They* wouldn't want me there. I don't even know Paris. I—I—I...*Neil.* You know I can't afford it.'

'Don't worry, lovie,' Neil said with surprising gentleness for a brother who was usually fairly brisk. 'We'll buy your ticket. We insist. It's the least we can do for you.'

'But... *Please,* Neil, tell Em I'd love to represent her, but I can't. You of all people know I'm no good with funerals. And I'm too... Lately I've just been so tired. And I haven't a thing to wear. Anyway, I hardly know a word of French. Neil, Neil— I couldn't bear that long flight.'

There was a long silence. Then Neil's voice came through again. Serious this time. Kindly. 'Sis... Listen to yourself. You *need* to do this. Em and I have seen how down you've been these past weeks. You're not yourself.'

'What do you mean?' Though she knew as soon as she said it she'd probably been tetchy and miserable. How could she have been anything else? Rémy had *died*, for goodness' sake. She'd never been able to handle death.

As well, she'd been shamed by a man she'd offered herself to, she was struggling to create a book, and if all that weren't bad enough her PMT crisis had gone on for so long her boobs were exploding out of her bras.

'Emilie and I have talked it over. You're in denial, we think.'

'Neil.' She laughed hollowly. 'Don't be silly.'

Typical of her brother to come up with some pop psychology. If only it were possible to explain to a man without him immediately leaping onto the bandwagon of sexist propaganda about hormones affecting women's intelligence.

The truth was, stress had always given her menstrual problems, right back to her high-school days. Crushes, exams, falling in passionate love with her English teacher... The pangs of adolescence had thrown her querulous body clock out of whack every time.

She knew from experience that once her period started she'd feel better in every way and be able to cope properly and be a decent, loving support to her sister-in-law.

'Come on, Shar. The truth is you've been grieving over Rémy and the engagement a long, long time. We think you need to make this pilgrimage to properly close this episode in your life.'

Oh, *right*. Where did they get their psychiatric expertise from? Doctor Phil?

A few retorts jostled on her tongue, but most of them would only add fuel to Neil's assertion that she wasn't being herself. Her mousy, frumpy, slutty, hormonal self.

'We absolutely *insist* on sending you first class,' Neil persisted, enthusiastic since it didn't have to be him. 'See? You can sleep all the way. It'll be a rest. And don't worry about Paris. The family will look after you. Look how well you got on with Luc.'

Visions of the boathouse, their hot, panting urgency, Luc's hard length filling her up, making her cry out, making her *wild*, making her yearn *every night since*, sent Shari's knees weak. 'No,' she said faintly. 'You're wrong about that. We detested each other.'

'Are you sure? It hardly seems like a week since you were here fluttering your lashes at him.'

Shari wanted to shout *Stop*. If only he knew what he was saying. Every word was a spike in her heart. Considering that Luc Valentin was the only person now living who knew the shame of her battered woman status...

Considering she'd actually had *sex* with him...

Considering he thought her the lowest, most pathetic creature he'd ever laid his aristocratic eyes on...

And how recently she'd snarled at him on the phone like a wild animal.

She shuddered to the core. She could never face him again.

'Come on, Shar. *Please*. If not for yourself, do it for Emilie. Em wants to ask you herself, but she's afraid you'll think she's imposing on your generous nature.'

Right. Fine. The Big One. The Emilie card.

Emilie was fragile, Neil reminded her. The twins could be distressed. Any further disturbance could bring on a premature birth situation. They could *lose the twins*. They could lose Emilie.

Shari's conscience twinged. She loved Em as much as she loved Neil. With sinking resignation it dawned on her she didn't have a chance of wriggling out of it unless she wanted to feel shame and self-reproach for all time.

Succumbing to the intense and excruciating pressure by painful degrees over days, she accepted that this was what family members did for each other. For once in her life she must put aside her personal fears and phobias and do something for someone else. Regardless of what Luc Valentin thought, she did have courage *and* self-respect, and she could behave honourably, and like an adult.

She could go there and meet him on his home turf with cool composure.

Though she did lay down some stipulations. She would only go briefly. And she would arrange it all herself. She wanted no interference.

There would be no advance warnings given. She made Neil solemnly promise on his honour as a brother and a stockbroker. No jolly welcoming committee at the airport. No feather bed tucked under the charming rafters of Tante Laraine's rustic roof.

Emilie was shocked and wounded at this—Tante Laraine was her mother's beloved cousin, *and* the mother of Luc—but Shari insisted. She would rather stay in a hotel.

She would rather stay in a drain.

All right, she could admit to herself she was scared. Call her a coward, but everyone knew the French loathed strangers. Especially if they couldn't speak the language creditably. Rémy had always found her attempts to use her high school French hilarious.

Naturally, the last thing she wanted was to stay in a household where her name was a byword. One of her deepest fears was that Luc would have informed his entire family about the whore of Babylon Rémy had engaged himself to. It wasn't as if she'd be able to defend herself there by telling them the truth about their golden boy.

Boys.

And as if everything else weren't enough, the truth was, as Neil very well knew, she'd been severely traumatised by funerals ever since her mother's. If Neil hadn't been there to put his arms around her quivering ten-year-old self in the bad days and nights that had followed she'd probably have had to be sectioned.

Dragging herself to the task, she booked a room in a hotel near the Louvre. At least it didn't sound too bad. There was something solid about an Hôtel du Louvre. If her nerve failed her when it came time to attend the ceremony, she could always sneak to the museum and hide among the Egyptian antiquities.

The flight she booked was transferable, just in case anything came up where she was required to stay longer. If Luc Valentin got over his disgust at the way she'd spoken to him on the phone, he might feel forced to take her to dinner, or something. She should probably accept, for the family's sake, although she'd be reserved, even rather chilling.

She took steps to ensure she had something decent to wear to the ceremony. Luc might have a low opinion of her morals and her self-regard, but she would give him no opportunity to sneer at her clothes. Rémy had often declared that a Frenchmen could only ever feel distaste for the woman who was careless of projecting her beauty.

It had never been any use explaining to him how easy it was for an author/artist to forget to change out of her pyjamas for twenty-four hours when in the grip of her muse. Even Emilie had wrinkled her nose when she found out her guilty secret. Shari doubted Luc would be any different.

Just as well she wouldn't be there long enough to get found out. She would establish a lasting impression of herself there as a woman of faultless grace and dignity.

Taking Emilie's advice, Shari stuffed the corners of her suitcase with scarves. A woman could get away with much in Paris, Em promised, so long as she wore a scarf. Along with the scarves Shari included a massive pack of tampons. When her period finally, blessedly, did eventuate, it was bound to be Niagara Falls.

The moment arrived when, braced for every kind of horror, she boarded the flight.

By the time she disembarked at Charles de Gaulle mid-evening twenty-five hours later, among other things she was feeling rather wan. An hour before landing, a minor bout of turbulence had made her lose her dinner. Fear, no doubt, combined with motion sickness.

She cleaned herself up as best she could, scrubbed her teeth and sponged her neck, but her hair was lank, her clothes wrinkled and her breasts felt tender and vulnerable.

At least no unwelcome man loomed up in Arrivals to witness her failure to project her beauty at the airport. One thing she never wanted to give Luc Valentin the chance to see was Shari Lacey in transit. He'd seen more than enough.

Soon she was in a taxi being whisked incognito through the streets of the City of Light.

Though it was officially spring, Luc's home turf must have been suffering a cold snap. A drizzly rain obscured its fabled beauty and chilled Shari to her soul. When she alighted from the cab, her teeth chattered.

She glanced around her, pursing her lips. So this was Paris.

Drawing her thin trench coat around her, she regarded the hotel with grim misgiving. Its façade was imposing, in keeping with the surrounding palaces on the grand boulevards.

But a smiling porter strolled out to take her bag and usher her through the revolving doors, and inside, thank the Lord, the lobby was warm, the people surprisingly welcoming.

Feeling empty after her mishap during the flight, Shari planned to order a snack from the restaurant. But once settled in her airy room with its long, graceful drapes at the windows, all she had energy for was the hot shower she'd craved the last five thousand miles. Then, clean, warm and comforted, she slipped between the sheets.

CHAPTER FIVE

SHARI woke to the pale grey light of a Paris dawn. Straight away the horrors of the day ahead sprang into her mind and her stomach swam in total rejection.

Naturally. There wasn't a lot to look forward to.

Rémy, in his c—*situation*. Luc Valentin on his home turf. Remembering his last view of her. Judging her. Looking the way he looked in her dreams. So damned sexy.

She dressed with gentle movements so as not to antagonise her insides. It struck her that every garment she donned was doubly appropriate. Funereal, for mourning, and sinful, sultry and black for her wicked, whorish nature.

Emilie had lent her a beautiful, elegant silk suit from her pre-pregnant days. Shari had to suck in her breath to close the skirt zip, but at least the cinched-in waist flattered her curves, especially her breasts in the new lacy C-cup she'd bought to accommodate the recent rise in volume.

With sheer black stockings and high heels, she judged the overall effect satisfactorily black, and possibly more elegant than she'd ever achieved to date. Now for the hat.

She'd managed to prevail on Em for a loan of her wide black organza Melbourne Cup number with the luxuriant velvet rose adorning its brim. Shari loved the gorgeous thing. All it lacked was a veil.

Positioning it carefully over the simple chignon she'd managed to achieve, she had the wistful sense it still made something of a disguise. None of her friends would have recognised her. Perhaps Luc wouldn't.

Though she'd smoothed on some make-up, her strain shone through. Staring at herself in the mirror, she understood breakfast wasn't even a remote possibility. Lucky for her the barfridge offered a convenient bottle of the blessed black fizz, among other things. She crammed it into her shoulder bag for later. Just in case.

All too soon the dreaded moment came. With a dry mouth, Shari took the lift down and asked the concierge to find her a taxi. The guy obliged by strolling out to the kerb and summoning one with a piercing whistle. Normally that would have delighted an Aussie girl from Paddo. Not today.

Shivering, she climbed into the taxi like a serving wench into a tumbril. Neil and Emilie had provided her with all the details she needed. Rémy, her former lover, fiancé and abuser, was to be buried at Père Lachaise.

With her feet pressing an imaginary brake through the floor, Shari was carried inexorably through the cemetery gates. The car followed a winding street through a city of stone. At the very end loomed a domed chapel.

Her heart lurched. Gathered in front was a small congregation of mourners, all garbed in black. But superimposed on her vision of all of them was Luc. He was standing a little apart from the others looking grim and inaccessible. Her stomach clenched itself nastily.

It was the crunch of her tyres on gravel that dragged Luc from his reverie.

He turned and narrowed his gaze against the grey glare, attempting to make out the taxi's occupant. The graceful curve of cheek and neck he glimpsed beneath the hat brim looked youthful and extremely feminine. Surely…

No, it couldn't be Manon. She wouldn't have the gall to come *here,* flaunting her condition.

Shari got out, not sure she could trust her legs to suppor

her. As the taxi drove away she stood on the stone apron before the chapel, an alien in a foreign land. All eyes turned to stare at her.

Shari *felt* the instant Luc recognised her. A tremor jolted through his tall frame that communicated itself to her at a deeply visceral level. For whole seconds he stared at her, the curious intensity blazing in his dark eyes paralysing her where she stood.

He started towards her.

Shari's heart accelerated, far too fast. It was the first time she'd seen him in daylight. How could she have forgotten how—how he was? He looked powerful and autocratic, the expression of his strong, lean face grave and intent. As he neared she tried not to focus on the stirring lines of his mouth. Oh, Lord. This was hardly the time to be reminded of how it felt to be kissed by that mouth, but as he approached her insides roared into a mad, uncontrollable rush.

'Shari.' He searched her face, then bent formally to kiss each of her cheeks.

She'd mentally prepared herself for this. She'd promised herself she wouldn't allow him to touch her, kiss her, even brush her cheek with his roughened jaw, let alone touch her with his gorgeous lips. But when it came to the crunch…

'*Bonjour*,' she breathed, barely able to stand on her marshmallow knees. She felt the backs of her eyes prick and was possessed by a despicable longing to cling to his lapels.

Though gentle, his dark velvet voice seared her nerves like a bow drawn across the strings of a cello. 'I am sorry for your loss.'

'Oh. Oh, yes. Thanks. I know. It's dreadful, isn't it? Same—same to you, of course.'

Amber glowed in the depths of his dark eyes as they searched hers. With chagrin she supposed he was looking for traces of the bruise.

'You must be desolated,' he said.

Was he serious? Was this more mockery?

He continued. 'I did not expect... When did you arrive? Why did you not say? Who are you with? Where are you sleeping?'

Beneath her silken finery her breasts all at once felt indescribably tender. Some of the insulting assumptions he'd made during their previous encounter flooded back with raw immediacy, and she found herself breathing rather fast.

'Perhaps you mean with whom.'

His eyes glinted. '*Comment?*' He tilted up one thick black brow. '*Vraiment*, it's coming back to me. How you are.'

How she *was,* though, seemed to wholly concentrate his attention, because he devoured her from head to toe, raking her ensemble with a wolflike, smouldering curiosity that eliminated the rest of the world from her awareness. At the same time, the smoothness of his deep voice was having its old hypnotic effect. She might have been walking with him through the shrubbery on a summer's night.

'You are very pale. Your *lips* are pale.' He examined them with an intense interest. 'And you are thinner.' His gaze swept over her, lingering a second longer than was necessary below her throat. 'Though not too thin, fortunately.'

Scandalously, her overly sensitive breasts swelled to push the boundaries even of this new bra, and she began to feel almost aroused.

Inappropriate. *Thoroughly* inappropriate.

All these conflicting sensations were making her giddy, but somehow she stayed upright and said things. Some things, at least.

As if in a dream she inclined her head. 'I'm sure you mean that as a compliment, though I have no idea what you expected. It's only been a couple of weeks.'

She realised she'd made a gross tactical blunder when the ghost of a smile touched his mouth and she caught a glimpse of his white, even teeth. 'Five weeks and three days, to be exact.'

'I wouldn't know,' she said crushingly. 'I haven't been counting.'

She had the disconcerting feeling that the slight twitch at the corner of his mouth signalled satisfaction. But what did he have to be satisfied about? Why did he think she'd come here? For him?

He gestured then to the fascinated onlookers, in particular to a couple of elderly women who were circling to view her narrowly.

'*Maman, Tante Marise, c'est Shari,*' he said. '*La fiancée de Rémy.*'

'*Ex*-fiancée,' Shari corrected hurriedly, but her words were lost in the babble as family members closed in around her and subjected her to a gamut of curiosity. Only thing was, their questions, arguments and observations were all for each other, not for her.

Not that she'd have understood them anyway. Their French was so rapid and idiomatic she could scarcely pick up a word.

Except for the term *fiancée*. That was being bandied about quite furiously.

The next thing she knew someone patted her, though stiffly. Then someone else murmured something to her about Rémy and gave her a kindly nod. More people spoke to her, some with increasing warmth until everyone, including a hearty uncle with a face not unlike a truffle, seemed to be hugging her, kissing her and calling her *ma pauvre* and *ma puce*.

CHAPTER SIX

SHARI had visualised herself sitting in the rear of the chapel, alone, concealed perhaps by a marble pillar, a remote, mysterious, but essentially inconspicuous ghost. That wasn't how it went.

For one thing the ghost space was heavily occupied. Once inside that chapel, the passing of a life cut short was uppermost, whether or not Luc Valentin was present, overwhelmingly attractive and closely scrutinising her every move. As for being inconspicuous, the aunts had hustled Shari into the second front pew, across the aisle from Luc.

She'd always been far too emotional in stressful situations, and Rémy was all too powerfully present for comfort. And when Luc rose to deliver a brief eulogy, mainly in French, and a couple of people on her side of the aisle snivelled, Shari couldn't help shedding a couple of polite tears in sympathy.

The trouble was her tears took on a life of their own. It was so ridiculous. Once started they wouldn't stop. She cried so much about Rémy's stupid, selfish conceit, the agony he'd caused her and the humiliating things she'd let him get away with, that she filled up bunches and bunches of tissues. Though she tried to keep it as quiet as possible, her sobs probably sounded pretty heartbroken, when she wasn't *at all*. Face it, she wasn't all that sad.

But Rémy's family assumed she was. Those nearby patted and consoled her. Aunts, cousins, even the uncle shuffled seats to get near her and murmur comforting things until she gave in, laid her head on the truffle's shoulder and cried all down his suit.

Luc kept halting his speech to glower at her with a brow as dark as thunder. She could hardly blame him. When the worst of the embarrassing paroxysm had passed, he lowered his austere gaze to his text and continued on in English with a rather biting courtesy.

Shari supposed she should appreciate the consideration, although she doubted Rémy *was* the finest flower of the French nation, cut down in his prime by a heartless fate. She knew damned well what Luc meant to imply by that. A heartless *whore*.

And when he said a man was known by the quality of those who'd loved him, and went on to describe Rémy as a man who'd been possessed of earthly treasure and looked directly at her, she glared incredulously back through her tears. Oh, come *on*.

The man was a hypocrite. If she hadn't been so weepy and trembly from stress and the lack of a breakfast, she might have jumped up and said a few very gracious, dignified though at the same time rather terse things.

But the emotional toll of the past few weeks chose that critical moment to suspend her freedom of choice. Once again, just when she wanted to be at her sophisticated best, she was overcome by a wave of nausea.

Without time even to fumble for a dry tissue, she sprang up and rushed for the entrance, stumbled outside into the chill air and retched into a flower pot.

Nothing much came up. How could it? Nothing had gone down.

Sweating and gasping, as the last wrenching spasm subsided, she noticed a pair of masculine, highly polished leather shoes standing nearby. It occurred to her, even in her woeful state, they looked as if they'd been handmade by some Italian master.

'Are you better?' Luc's concerned voice broke through her humiliation and distress. 'Can you stand?'

'Of course,' she gasped. 'I'm fine.' She straightened up, grateful to feel his strong hand under her tottery elbow, and blotted her upper lip and forehead with a tissue. Foraging in her bag for another, she came across the bottle of cola. God bless the Hôtel du Louvre. Unscrewing the cap, she took a swig and turned aside to discreetly rinse her mouth. 'Excellent,' she panted, applying a tissue to her lips. 'I'm just a little empty. I haven't had any breakfast.'

'*Elle n'a pas pris de petit déjeuner!*' an excited voice relayed from close at hand.

'*Comment! Pas de petit déjeuner?*'

Until that ripple of concern about her non-breakfast electrified the crowd, Shari hadn't really noticed people streaming from the chapel and regrouping. Some had positioned themselves quite near to her and Luc, and were scrutinising her every move.

From under her chic *chapeau*, Tante Laraine in particular was watching her with an expression Shari couldn't quite interpret. Well, how would she? It was a very French expression. Though encountering the woman's disconcertingly shrewd gaze a second time, Shari corrected that analysis. A very *womanly* expression.

She wished she could melt through the stonework. Didn't these people understand a woman's need to retch in private? Several of them seemed anxious to remedy her plight, talking rapidly about taking her somewhere and plying her with food and blankets. Judging by the offers and counter-offers one relative tossed to another, and all with cool determined smiles, she gathered there was some sort of a polite contest under way.

Tante Marise for one was warmly insistent that Shari should go home with her and try a little *bouillon* and an egg.

Luc frowned at that and shook his head, instantly quashing the idea. The uncle bounded forward with an offer, but at a cool steel glance from Luc the words died on the old boy's lips and he retreated.

Then Tante Laraine intervened. Shari thought she could detect her resemblance to her son. While austerely gracious, this Laraine exuded a certain authority. Shari gathered the matriarch was strongly in favour of whisking her *chez Laraine* and feeding her some energising *chocolat.*

Luc, however, seemed even less keen on his mother having first shot at Shari. '*Non,*' he said ruthlessly. '*Pas du chocolat.*' He murmured something to hold them all at bay, then put his arm around Shari and held her close against his lean, powerful body.

'Come. You are shivering. We need to get you out of here.'

'Oh, but…' she quavered, regretting the *chocolat.* Even the *bouillon.* Now that her nausea had passed she really was quite cavernously empty. The egg would have been heaven. And if it had come with some hot buttered toast… 'I—I—I haven't properly expressed my condolences.'

He gave her a sardonic glance. 'I believe you have made your feelings perfectly clear. *Parfaitement.*'

It was glaringly apparent from his tone that the French despised a show of excess emotion. Shari cursed herself for her weakness. On top of everything else he thought was wrong with her, she had to keep giving into this crass emotionalism. It just had to stop.

Unexpectedly, a ray of watery sun pierced the grey world and lit the amber depths of his dark eyes, their glow sizzling through her bloodstream.

Luc steered her across to the first of several long, sleek limos that had silently drawn up in the last few minutes, and she went without resistance. Waving the driver back to the wheel, he opened the rear door for her himself and urged her inside. Shari sank into the warmth, grateful for the comfort.

She waited until he'd given his instructions to the driver and was settled at the other end of the wide seat before impressing him with her serene dignity.

'I'm sorry,' she said stiffly. 'I don't usually make such a spectacle of myself. I don't know what got into me. I feel— *mortified* to have embarrassed everyone.'

'No need to apologise.' A tinge of amusement momentarily relieved the saturnine severity of his expression. 'They loved it. They'll talk about it for months.'

She flushed. Though she kept her voice low, it still sounded fraught and emotional. She couldn't seem to control that. 'Heaven only knows what they think of me. I'm surprised they were so kind.'

His voice, on the contrary, was silky smooth. 'Why wouldn't they be kind? It is clear you are the very model of a grieving *fiancée.*'

She drew in a breath. Her voice grew all throaty and she was dangerously close to another bout of the waterworks. 'You know very well—I told you—I'm *not* a fiancée. Rémy and I broke up. I didn't even like him in the end. I despised him. Why must you taunt me? Are you always so cold and judgemental towards women?'

He flushed darkly. A muscle moved in his lean cheek. 'I don't believe so. That is not how I feel when I think of you. Far from it. But I'm naturally—surprised. You despised him, yet you have made this very long journey to say goodbye to him. And now to show such—*emotion.*'

'Well, but it was all so overwhelming, I just… Wouldn't *you* feel sad to say goodbye to someone you once loved?' She turned to look at him.

Through the smudged mascara her aquamarine gaze pierced Luc. An unpleasant knowledge solidified in his brain and skewered him straight through his gut. It hadn't mattered whether or not she'd liked the bastard. She'd loved him.

He said tightly, 'I can't imagine being sad about someone

who—violated the rules of civility. But I believe there are women who love certain men—whatever they do.'

A flicker of pain disturbed the cool green sea of her irises. She made a small, defensive gesture that sent a pang through Luc. The moment they'd shared at her front door flooded back to him with sharp immediacy. What an insensitive fool he was to bring that up now. He was handling this so badly. *Dieu*, was he jealous of a dead man?

'I doubt they do,' she said quietly. 'I think that's a myth.' The pride and earnestness in her voice touched him in some susceptible spot. 'Women fall in love then out of it, but some remain trapped by circumstances. That has never applied to me. It *could* never.' He watched her slim hands twist. The hat brim prevented him from seeing more than a section of cheek, an exquisite curve of chin.

His blood stirred with a sharp and bittersweet desire. He closed his eyes. She was here now, overwhelmingly present. Not a dream, not a fantasy. Whether he wanted it or not, yearning had him in its grip.

He sought for something to say to soften his former harshness. '*Très bon*. Men too can find themselves trapped. Passion is a dangerous thing. It can—drag you in.' She lanced him with her clear green gaze and he caught his breath. 'Not recommended for ones' health.'

'No,' she agreed, lowering her lashes. 'If only it were possible to consider your health at the time, no one would ever take the risk.' She hesitated. 'I—I…I'm sorry about the night you phoned. I know you meant to be kind.'

'I woke you from your sleep?' She nodded. He studied her face. 'You were angry.'

'Yes, well… It was a difficult time. I'm sorry.'

'Don't apologise. I phoned because I longed to hear your voice.'

Shari looked sharply at him, her heart revving up. His eyes

were scorching hot and were having quite a dizzying effect. Could he really talk as if nothing had happened?

This was no time for desire an hour after she'd farewelled Rémy. And hadn't Luc made it clear what he thought of her? Did he assume she was ready to ride that thorny road with him again? Had he *forgotten* what had happened after their boathouse tryst?

She started unsteadily, 'I don't know why you think I came all this way, Luc…'

'Then tell me. Why did you?' His dark eyes were compelling, alert, and at the same time so searingly sensual.

'For Emilie, of course. To—honour her loss. Pay our family's respects. And to—to acknowledge the love I once had for Rémy. Naturally.'

His gaze flickered over her, searching, intent. Then he lifted his shoulders in a gentle gesture. 'I always wonder when someone gives many reasons for doing something *grande* if they only really have the one. The one they wish to conceal from themselves.'

Her heart made a maniacal skitter. What? Did he think it had to do with him? Did the guy think one little encounter had affected her that deeply?

'And what do you suppose it to be?' She smiled in mocking disbelief. 'The one I need to conceal?'

His dark gaze was mercilessly direct. '*Bien sûr*, you came to see me.'

She gasped. Before she could deny it he curled his fingers under her chin and took her mouth in a fierce, highly sexual kiss. After the initial paralysed instant, her body sprang into tingling life. An erotic charge electrified her blood, her nerve fibres, her tender intimate tissues, as if this and this alone were her *raison d'être*.

Who said she couldn't communicate adequately in French? It was clear now all she'd ever needed was the inspiration. Luc

Valentin's hand merely had to caress her kneecap and slide up under her skirt and she burst into flame.

All right, she was bad. Bad in every way, but he felt *so good*. The delicious sinful pleasure of him thrilled through her and inflamed her every wanton molecule.

Sadly, just when she was ready to crawl onto his lap and express her appreciation more fulsomely for them both, he broke away. Drawing back, he studied her, his dark eyes beneath their thick black brows smouldering and amused.

'Good. Some colour in your cheeks.'

She felt herself flush. She supposed those cool, insolent words were intended to convey his macho self-possession. But to the sensitive ears of the guilt-ridden woman, the slightly thickened texture of his voice was a welcome giveaway. Luc Valentin was affected by her. Strongly affected.

'That was hardly appropriate,' she said breathlessly, patting down her suit and adjusting her hat. '*Now*. Of *all times*. Aren't you ashamed?'

'No. I would say—triumphant.'

Too shocked for words, she stared speechlessly at him, and he laughed and kissed her *again*. She was struggling for more words to express her discomfort at this bold exploitation of her weakened state, when the limo noticeably slowed.

Paris in all its glory had been flowing by—cafés, bridges, palaces, La Seine—and she'd barely had a chance to take in a thing. Now here they were at the city's throbbing heart. Even as she looked they drew up before a palace with ivory awnings over its several entrances.

'Where is this? Where are you taking me?' Straining, she narrowed her eyes to read the inscription on the nearest.

'To breakfast.'

A single word, emblazoned in a flowing script, adorned the graceful awning.

Ritz.

CHAPTER SEVEN

THE Ritz was the perfect antidote to an ordeal. The beauty, the food, the luscious notes of a string ensemble wafting on the air... Even the silk-festooned windows in their own lavish way declared the hotel's sincere desire to swaddle the emotionally gouged woman in loving and soul-restoring luxury.

There was a placard in the reception area announcing that the hotel was soon to close its doors for a major renovation and refurbishment. Shari prayed fervently they wouldn't change a thing.

The bathroom alone was an oasis of tranquillity, though she nearly freaked when she saw herself in the mirrors. Her face was blotchy, the tip of her nose red from all the bawling, and her mascara reminiscent of a bad Hallowe'en hangover. She looked a fright. How could Luc have wanted to kiss her?

She repaired the damage with the emergency kit at the bottom of her bag. Then, refreshed and reconstituted, she floated to join him in the restaurant. After all the emotion, she'd arrived on a tremulous smiley plateau where everything looked hazily beautiful. Especially the dark-eyed man drinking coffee and texting someone on his mobile.

Kill that thought. After all she'd gone through over him, was she to just fall into his arms? Was it always to be the same old thing? Shari Lacey, unable to resist a handsome Frenchman? Another one she knew little about and would be insane to trust?

He glanced up as she approached and his eyes shimmered,

inciting an excited clench in her insides. Then, just to mess with her defences, he rose and pulled out a chair for her.

She sat down, that car kiss still tingling through her nerve sockets. Somehow she would have to take a stand. Lay her position on the line before events rocketed out of control. Before she did.

He resumed his chair, his long lanky posture so relaxed and unbothered by anything he'd done to her in that limo it was a damned disgrace.

She steeled herself not to be affected, weakened or seduced.

'It's very good of you to bring me here, Luc. Very generous, but...' His brows twitched up. 'I—I—I think I should make it clear to you that anything of a-a sexual nature that may have happened between us in Sydney was a one-off. We agreed then it was a mistake, and... Well, so much has happened, and... As far as I'm concerned the whole thing should be wiped from our minds.'

He nodded along with her words as she spoke, though she noticed a certain tension infuse his gorgeous limbs. Then he lifted one quizzical brow. 'Ah. You think I should forget about meeting you at Emilie's?'

'I do. We should both forget it.'

'So then...' His black lashes flicked tauntingly downwards. A silky note entered his voice. 'You wish me to forget Emilie's garden?'

She eyed him carefully. What in particular might he be remembering about the garden? The last thing she needed to be reminded of was how easily she'd succumbed to that dark stroll into the shrubbery. 'I'm—surprised you even remember the garden.'

His eyes gleamed in reminiscence. 'Are you? But it was so pleasant, *d'accord*? In the dark, with all the fragrances and the moonlight.' His long fingers toyed idly with his spoon. The same fingers that had recently toyed with parts of her.

'You must remember the moonlight.' Her nerve jumped. 'The harbour lights.'

'Where are we going with this?' Although she knew where he was headed with it, all right.

He leaned forward, a lazy smile playing on his sexy mouth. 'I think you know where. Where else but to the boathouse? You're not expecting me to forget the *boathouse*, *chérie*, *n'est-ce pas*?'

'Well, I've forgotten it. As far as I'm concerned, nothing about it was very memorable.'

He threw back his head and laughed. He looked so handsome, with amusement illuminating his face and the light dancing in his eyes, a wave of hot and bitter frustration swept her. He had no right to be so attractive and to mock her. *He* was the one who'd found the magic moments shameful and made her feel like a disgrace to womanhood.

Luckily the waiter arrived just then, or she might have snatched up the coffee pot and whacked Luc over the head with it.

Controlling her annoyance, she turned her full attention to the menu, consulting earnestly with the waiter, feeling Luc's lazy glance scorch her face, throat and hands.

Everything enshrined on the list sounded delicious, but in the end she confined herself to ordering a spoonful of gentle, soothing yoghurt, along with some strawberries claimed to have been washed in morning dew. To follow she requested the buttery scrambled eggs, waiving both the caviar garnish and the champagne to wash them down.

Well, she had to show some respect for her stomach. It felt fine now, but who knew when it might rear up again in revolt?

While she enjoyed her yoghurt, Luc reflected on the effect their encounter had left on him. He still thought of it. No wonder he'd followed her home like a madman. *Nom de Dieu,* was only flesh and blood. Would he ever forget holding her in his arms in that dark, sea-salty place? Her throaty little cries as he buried himself in her moist heat?

As he watched her soft lips close over a strawberry his blood stirred unbearably.

His underclothes tightened and he had to exert careful control over his voice. 'How—long do you plan to stay?'

'A couple of days. Tomorrow I thought I might visit the *Musée D'Orsay*. I fly home the day after that.'

Every sinew in his body tensed in utter rejection of that ludicrous plan. But outwardly he controlled the reaction. 'But how will you see Paris?'

'Well, I—I haven't come for a sightseeing tour, have I?'

She raised her glass to her lips. As she swallowed he noticed the muscles contract in her satin throat. Without warning a rush of hot turgid blood raced to his groin. He forced himself to shift his agonised gaze to the wall, the window, the orchid in its vase. Everywhere, anywhere until he could trust his voice.

'That's—a very brief visit. Surely…you can transfer your flight to a future date?'

She shot him a glance. 'I'm not sure why I would do that.' He waited for the next flash of green, his breath on hold. 'I suppose…if I had a *reason*…'

He could think of a damned good one, but not one that was sayable. Surely she could feel the pulse as strongly as he? Why did things have to be so complicated with women?

'A reason to stay in Paris,' he mused aloud. 'Not many people in the world would find that a challenge.'

The sensual note in his voice registered in Shari's hearing. With his lashes at half mast she was reminded of a devious, smouldering wolf. Why should she find that so scarily thrilling? The dangerous little tongue of flame threatening to undo her licked deep.

Her scrambled eggs were set before her, moist, speckled with parsely, and accompanied by pale golden toast. The eggs melted on her tongue, while the hot chocolate might well have been the most divine ever to pass human lips.

Unusually for her, however, she didn't manage to clean up every last scrap. It was hard to concentrate her attention on even food when such a man was distracting her.

When the waiter returned to clear her dishes, she noticed Luc listening to her flowery praise of the chef, a smile lurking in his eyes.

'You were very kind,' he observed after the man had gone.

'Artists ought to be appreciated.'

'Artists like you?'

'Now who's being kind?'

He met her gaze, smiling in return, making her helpless heart somersault. 'I believe I have seen your book.'

She widened her eyes. 'Here? Honestly? *Here*?'

'*Oui*. In a bookshop. I happened to wander in and—there it was. I thought it was—' every nerve in her body held its breath in trembling hope '—so—beautiful.'

Oh, the relief. Her fearful heart glowed so fiercely she could have danced, sung and cried all at the same time. It didn't matter if he was sincere. Just that he was being kind. Just for that moment she loved him. Loved Luc Valentin with all her heart.

'Thanks.' Her smile burst through. 'It's always lovely not to be crushed.'

He grinned, then his face grew rather grave and he cleared his throat. '*Alors,* Shari, I do wish to express how...I—I—regret the way it ended in Sydney.'

'I'm glad you brought it up,' she said tensely, thinking of all those sleepless nights of futile yearning, knowing he thought so badly of her. The injustice of the things he said. Her mortification when he caught her at her most naked. Her anger and misery, and... *Oh, God.* Maddening, unsatisfiable desire. 'I—I don't think you know how those things you said—*hurt* me. I...'

He blinked, then concealed his eyes behind his lashes. He said stiffly, 'Perhaps you took it all too much to heart.'

She sat back and smiled coolly. 'Which part?' She could feel herself start to tremble. 'The part where you didn't believe me? Where you accused me of being a dishonourable slag? Or the bit when you followed me home like a stalker?' She kept on smiling, though her heart was suddenly working like a piston.

A tinge of colour darkened his bronzed cheek. 'Perhaps it seemed that way. But you must see that at the *time…*'

'*No.*' She disciplined herself to keep her voice low. 'At the *time*, Luc, I was not a liar. If I committed any crime it was a crime against myself. My own code of behaviour—and—and—*safety* in offering the pleasure of my body to a man I didn't know and couldn't trust.'

'Trust?' He spoke so sharply she jumped. '*Vraiment*, this was a matter of honour. I was afraid you—might still be involved with *my cousin*.'

Startled by his vehemence, she compressed her lips, but, unable to hold in *some* defence of herself, she burst into a fierce whisper. 'If I *had* been do you think I'd have betrayed him? Are you still thinking of me like that? As a—a *whore*? Oh, it's too much. Too much.' She threw down her napkin and rose to her feet, emotion rising faster in her than high tide at Bondi.

'Shari, no, no, I don't think that. Please.' He sprang up and took her arms, his eyes earnest and intent. 'I have never *said* that. I thought you were a very passionate and beautiful woman in the midst of a—a complex situation. I could see we needed to discuss it and—analyse it like rational adults. Why do you think I followed you home?'

'Oh, *why*? Obvious. You thought you could sweet-talk your way into my bed. And is that why you've brought me here to the Ritz? You're hoping to try your luck *again*?'

He looked shocked. His handsome face assumed such a gravely wounded expression she wondered if she'd been unjust.

'That is a—disappointing suggestion.'

It was a suggestion that had only just surfaced in her mind, but once it did, it took root.

He was shaking his head in austere denial of the charge when her glance fell on his mouth. Paradoxically, against all reason and logic, in total betrayal of herself and the sisterhood of women, she was seized with an irresistible impulse to ravage that stirring mouth, to tease those sternly compressed lips apart with her tongue and drink in every last masculine drop of Luc Valentin.

At the same time her nipples, the tender vibrant tissues between her legs tingled and flamed with a violent, feminine yearning impossible to repress.

As though he were divining her lustful state a piercing gleam lit Luc's eyes. He lifted his brows. A subtle change came over his demeanour. 'Shh, shh, *chérie*.' His voice became silky smooth. 'It has been a stressful morning. Sit down again for a minute. Come, now.'

She glanced about. Naturally, there were a few interested parties straining to catch every word—a couple of princes, several duchesses with their beaux and a sheikh—though none of them seemed to be goggling with as much curiosity as they would have if this scene had been taking place in a Sydney restaurant.

In a fever of confusion, she resumed her place. How could she desire someone who'd caused her such distress? How could she want to bite his bronzed neck, drink his blood and eat him alive?

He leaned forward, his lean face stern, his eyes searing her with an urgent intent. 'We need to talk. Settle this somewhere private, where we can be alone.' Suddenly he was radiating energy, like a ship's captain taking charge of a serious aquatic catastrophe. He grasped her hand and squeezed. 'Give me two minutes—I'll arrange a quiet corner.' He stood up. 'Will you be OK here? *Oui*? Now, don't leave.'

He gave her a firm look to hold her there, then strode away.

Shari closed her eyes. What was wrong with her? She'd been angry with him for so long, now as soon as she met him

again, she felt— Oh, face it. Thrilled to be with him. Everything he said—even the bits that outraged her—every small
nuance was etching itself on her heart.

He was devastating her again. The last time a Frenchman
made her feel this way... Look what happened! She should
have walked out. Summoned a taxi and flown back to the
Hôtel du Louvre. Taken off her hat, crawled into bed and eased
her mad and insatiable desires as best she could in the time-
honoured way.

But his electrifying squeeze was still burning her hand. And
she needed to hear what he had to say. Maybe he would apologise so sincerely she could honourably forgive him.

Forgive him and...

Anyway, it would be a shame to take off the hat before it
was absolutely necessary.

To evade more vulgar curiosity, she swanned to the bathroom and, armed with her toothkit from the plane, managed
to give her teeth a good minty scrub.

She emerged in time to see Luc return from the direction
of the reception area. He walked with such confident masculine authority, such athletic energy in his long limbs, she felt
a flame of longing sear deep inside her.

He caught sight of her and changed course, strolling across
to smoothly, possessively take her arm. 'Come.'

Slipping her bag onto her shoulder, she savoured the erotic
graze of his suit fabric on her skin. 'Have you—found a place
where we can talk?'

'No problem.' His dark gaze dwelled smoulderingly on her
face. 'They assure me it will be very, very quiet.'

He ushered her into a lift and pressed the button for the
fifth floor.

'Have you...?' She turned to gaze at him. 'Have you ever
read *The Pursuit of Love*?'

He glanced keenly at her, eyes gleaming. '*The Pursuit of...*?'

She tried not to show it, but she was breathing so fast her

breasts were rising and falling like twin peaks during a major quake. '*Love*. The heroine finds herself stranded at the Gare du Nord without any money. This Frenchman strolls by...'

His eyes sharpened. 'A Frenchman?'

'Yes. A tall, very sexy, very wicked duke. He persuades her to go home with him and he...'

He lifted his brows. '*Oui*? What does he do?'

'Oh. Well, er...' She stared at his mouth and said breathlessly, 'I may need to revisit that part of the story to remind myself.'

His eyes burned. The air crackled with a tension that singed her very nerve endings.

The doors slid open and he guided her along a hushed corridor until they came to a door numbered 514. He slipped the card into the lock.

The door opened to a light, elegant foyer.

Shari blinked. 'But—this is a room.'

He shrugged. '*Bien sûr*.'

She walked in, tingling with a primitive anticipation. The room was spacious, with beautiful panelled walls and moulded ceilings at least four metres high. The carpet under her feet felt as deep and soft as a cloud. The further in she walked, the more there was to steal her breath.

A fine antique tapestry. Paintings, sparingly placed. Silken panels in shades of carmine and duck-egg blue, reflecting the gorgeous colours in the Persian rugs. Then there were the double windows with their long sensuous drapes, the moulded fireplace and heartbreakingly exquisite Louis Quinze furnishings.

What was most significant to her eye, though, and zinged through her like an ocean wave, was beckoning through an open door. A magnificent king-sized bed, arrayed with plump, inviting pillows set atop a charming counterpane.

'Oh,' she said faintly. 'It's a suite.'

'As private as we could wish for, surely.' He strolled across to the windows and gazed down into the street. She noted a sudden tension in the set of his wide shoulders. A suspenseful tension that communicated itself to her and electrified the very room.

He turned to her, and her lungs seized. Beneath his heavy brows his dark eyes shimmered with a molten, lascivious intent.

He said softly, 'Would you care to take off your hat?'

She tingled all over. Her heart was thundering. Her feet started to move, and as he strode swiftly across to her she practically flung herself at his hard body. She threw her arms around his neck and met his fierce, thirsty impassioned kisses with reckless disregard for any moral or overruling principle.

Her hat landed on the sofa, and while she tore at his shirt and unbuckled his belt to open his trousers he dropped her suit on the rug, unclipped her bra and stripped her bare.

The lithe beauty of his lean, muscular body, never seen, only felt, was as thrilling as her most fevered imaginings.

She gasped as his powerful erection rose in proud and gorgeous majesty. But her questing hands barely had time to stroke, squeeze and relish the prime virile beauty before he fell upon her nakedness like a hungry beast.

He kissed her breasts, licked her engorged nipples, blazed a trail of greedy kisses down to her navel and below.

Then he dropped to his knees. Embracing her thighs, he ravaged her curls with his mouth, then pushed her to the sofa. She trembled with sheer excitement. Parting her thighs, he paused a moment to feast his eyes, then, while she whimpered for blissful joy, bent his dark head between her legs and licked the tickly velvet. Tingles of erotic pleasure radiated through her in dark liquid waves.

When he took her clit between his gorgeous lips and sucked—heaven on earth—her panting moans turned to sobs of pure ecstasy.

With an actual blossoming orgasm, she cried out in disbelief when he drew away, leaving her hanging on an edge. 'Don't stop *now*. Please, please, keep...'

But, ignoring her complaints, he stood up to draw a small package from his jacket pocket. Swiftly he sheathed himself, then, taking her hands, pulled her off the sofa and into his arms. In the stumbling rush to the bedroom, she hooked her arms around his neck, her legs around his hips.

There was a thrilling urgency to his haste. Devouring her mouth with what could only be called passionate savagery, he plunged inside her even before she hit the mattress.

Once on it, she gave herself up to the heavenly friction. And he was a master. He filled her so full her body exploded with light with his every sinuous movement. Rocking her into an urgent pulsing rhythm, he ignited rivers of magic in her flesh. Fireworks infused her every capillary.

And just like the first time, the fierce and hungry fervour in his eyes and the athletic synchronicity of their bodies rocketed her passion to an explosive and fantastic climax.

Long after her wild, appreciative cries subsided, she floated, eyes closed for seconds, minutes, maybe even hours on a cloud of blissful contemplation.

Vindicated. Vindicated as a woman.

When her heartbeat was back to near normal Luc lay on his back, lashes half the way down to reveal only slits of eyes, like a slumberous lion after a killing.

She smiled. 'That was fantastic.'

'Likewise,' he said gravely. 'You are *formidable*. So passionate.'

'Thanks.' She blushed. Her heart glowed at the recognition. Positively beamed through her chest wall. 'And you know, it felt *amazing*. It's rare for me to ever feel so—hot. It was truly liberating. It must have been the reaction to all the stress.'

'I'm so happy the stress worked for you,' he said smoothly, his eyes glinting.

She guessed Frenchwomen, being so mysterious and so-phisticated, didn't confess their feelings after sex.

'Well, there was that other time too, of course. My first ac-tual...' She screeched to a halt in the bare nick of time.

His lifted an eyebrow. 'Your first...?'

'Boathouse. I recall feeling pretty well piping hot there.'

Heavens, time to shut the heck up. She'd brushed pretty close to giving away her fatal flaw. Knowing she was back in the orgasmic hot zone though, so to speak, was fantastically motivating. After her rocky start this morning, she could hardly believe she'd achieved this marvellous and formidable feeling of heavenly freedom and pleasantness.

After a moment he said, 'But you must have known many other occasions when you felt so piping hot, having been en-gaged?'

'Oh, sure. Of course, of course.' She gave her hand an airy wave. 'Although...' She hesitated, and added with a self-conscious flutter, 'Well... The conditions can't always be per-fect, can they?'

'They can't?'

'Well, I don't know how a man feels, but I guess a woman needs to feel—admired.'

He drew his brows in a frown. 'But Rémy admired you, *d'accord*? He asked you to marry him.'

'Not marry, exactly. Just—to get engaged. Marriage was to be in the distant future. He wanted to establish D'Avion in Australia properly first.'

He laughed softly. '*Tiens.*'

'I think what he really meant was he wanted to romance every woman in Sydney first.' She laughed sadly, though it was a rueful sadness now, not the broken-hearted one it had once been. Rueful, she supposed, for her part in everything that had gone wrong. Sad, because Rémy, having hurt so many people, would now never even have the chance to redeem himself.

Luc leaned over and kissed her. 'He was a fool. He didn't know what he had.'

'You're not wrong.' She smiled.

He took her in his arms and kissed her again, more deeply this time. Quite emotionally in fact. It was really very stirring and beautiful. And the graze of his chest hair against her breasts was so erotic, she felt as if she was in the most perfect location on the planet.

When the kiss ended they drew apart, then laughed a little embarrassedly at their intensity. 'Who'd have thought we'd have ended up here?' she said, grinning.

'Not me. When I saw you this morning I thought I was hallucinating.'

'*I* thought I was going to faint.'

'I have that effect,' he said modestly, laughing when she gave him a playful punch. He stacked the pillows up behind his head. 'But I can't understand why you agreed to be engaged to *him*? What was it about him?'

'Dunno. I was a fool. Naive, I s'pose. He seemed—charming. Exciting. Romantic.'

'*Romantic*?' His face expressed Gallic disbelief.

She hardly wanted to admit she was a Georgette-Heyer-style Regency heroine with deep-held fantasies about marrying a sexy earl. Not that Rémy was in any way an earl, though he'd *claimed* to have one in his family.

'Well, he *was* my first Frenchman. All my girlfriends thought he was really, really hot. I felt so lucky…I was sort of swept along, I guess. For a while.' She compressed her lips. 'I s'pose in fairness he was too. And Em was so thrilled. I *think* she was relieved he'd finally decided to settle down.' She grimaced. 'The irony of that. He was about as settled down as Casanova. I've sure learnt my lesson. Settling down is highly overrated.'

'Be careful who you settle down *with* next time.'

She squeezed his pleasingly hard bicep. 'Haven't you been listening, *monsieur*? There won't *be* a next time.'

'How can you say so? There'll be some good solid guy searching the world for you even now.'

She felt a sharp pang. He wasn't thinking of himself in that regard, then. She said rather tartly, 'Tsk, tsk. Poor him. He can wash his own socks and cook his own dinners. From now on I intend to be a woman of affairs, living for the good times.'

Luc appraised her face. She was smiling, but there were shadows in her eyes. As on that night in Paddington, that impulse seized him. That desire to drive away those shadows and wipe the darkness from her life.

He'd have laughed at himself if it hadn't been for a flash of his return to his hotel that night. Blindly negotiating the city streets, scored with longing and regret. Guilt. One of the most rugged journeys of his life.

At the time he'd burned to snatch her out of harm's way. But, of course, the cold light of morning had reminded him of his reasons to board the plane, Rémy's theft from the company being foremost.

He frowned. 'Was it—so bad?'

She glanced quickly at him. 'Not at first. But—gradually. As the gloss wore off. I think you've guessed...' She dropped her eyes. 'He wasn't always—very nice.'

'He was—violent?'

There was a tiny tremor at the corner of her mouth, and he felt something inside him tighten.

'Not with his fists, no, except that one time at the end when he was desperate to find his passport. He was just cruel—in little careless ways. Things he said. About me, about Neil. Sometimes he'd touch me, pull my hair in a joke, though always a little bit too hard. Not like a person who loved you.'

Luc lay frowning, his pulse beating hard with the increase in his blood pressure. His fists had bunched involuntarily. It was a good thing Rémy was where he was now, or he'd have felt this fierce need to go after him and teach him something about civility and decency. Not that more violence would ever be the answer.

He glanced at her downcast face. 'I had heard—Rémy's papa wasn't very kind. There were rumours in the family...'

'I know. Emilie mentioned it once. But I never expected—*that*.'

'Of course not.'

Perhaps unlucky Rémy had been poorly conditioned as a child, but... Luc burned to think of a man treating *any* woman this way. To enjoy hurting Shari... How could the guy have? Examining the fragile lines of her face, he guessed there was more she could have told. Far more.

Caution sounded a warning note in his brain. Perhaps it was better he didn't know those things. His rational mind told him the more a man learned about a woman, the more he saw into her, the deeper he sank into the emotional quicksand. Already his responses to her were out of all proportion. Way out. Just one morning with her and he was dangerously close to relaxing his guard completely.

Had he forgotten where it could all end?

Shari felt a tension in the lengthening silence. Maybe she'd said too much. She could almost hear his brain analysing the evidence, weighing it all up.

'Anyway, enough about my little case,' she said lightly. 'Everyone's break-up is painful, is it not? *C'est la vie*, hey, *monsieur*?' With a rueful smile she reached up and rubbed her knuckle over his cheek. 'Haven't we all loved and lost?'

His expression lightened almost at once. 'You are right. My last lover preferred a famous movie star to *me*. Can you imagine?' He made a comical face, and she joined him in a laugh.

As the room grew silent again she wondered if there was a certain brooding flavour to the atmosphere. 'She must be insane,' she murmured.

He grimaced, then his face lightened to a smile. 'I thought of you every day, after we parted.'

'About the bruise?'

He frowned. 'Not that. About you. How beautiful you are. How—original.' She hardly believed it. Even so, her mouse heart thrilled to its little rodent core. 'Every hour...of every day.'

'And I thought of *you* every day. I wanted to murder you. I wanted to make you *sorry*. I wanted to put my hands around your strong, beautiful neck and...'

A flame lit his dark eyes. 'Come here.' He reached for her. He whispered the words against her mouth. 'I was sorry. I *am* sorry. Now I want you to forget—*everything*.'

This time his passion was darker, more fervent, more tender. A fierce and ardent light glowed in his eyes as he rocked her, filled her and pleasured her until she was blazing with light and higher than the moon.

And she did forget. She forgot everything in existence except the world of his arms, his passionate mouth, his beautiful, hard, thrusting body, the fierce heat in his eyes.

While Paris ticked over outside and the day drew on, their lips grew raw with kissing, their bodies sated. With exhaustion in view, Luc dragged up the sheet to cover them. Shari lay face to face with him, languorous eyes to eyes.

Gently, he pushed her hair from her face. 'Two days is too short. You should stay longer.'

'What for?' She traced the outline of his mouth with her finger.

'For this.'

Her heart skipped a heavy beat. What was this? This mad, uncontrollable need to hold him to her and never let him go. When had she ever known this intense mutual tenderness and passion? She wanted to run outside and shout it to the world. Luc Valentin wanted her. He was asking her to stay in Paris. In his apartment.

She said carefully, 'I only have my hotel room for the three nights. They mightn't be able to let me keep it longer.' She held her breath.

'*Bien sûr*, stay here.'

'*Here*?' A pang of disappointment, so intense it was scary, cut through her. She dragged up an empty laugh while inwardly she cringed. 'Oh, I don't think so.'

Oh, how she'd misinterpreted.

'I can't tempt you? A week at the Ritz? You can do your sightseeing while I'm at work, then in the evenings… More sightseeing.' He lifted his brows suggestively.

She concealed her gaze from him. 'You can tempt me to some more of those scrambled eggs. I'm hungry enough to eat everything in this room.' What a *fool* she must be. What a needy, susceptible fool. A few sweet words and she was ready to believe anything.

Imagine if she did stay the week. In no time she'd be dreaming of a future. Deluding herself, listening for clues of his intentions. Laying herself open to disappointment.

Hello, heartbreak, her old BFF.

She showered with him while waiting for the food, then, wrapped in a peach towelling bathrobe, shared the feast Luc had ordered.

'I'll have to put some clothes on soon,' he said, sighing. 'We'll need more protection if I am to keep you happy. Mustn't risk anything going wrong.'

She stared down at her scramble. A paralysing thought surfaced in her mind. Perhaps it had always been there, just below her consciousness. Since the boathouse. Since the PMT that hadn't eventuated into anything. The nausea on the plane. No, there'd been more even before that.

With too much to think about—Luc, Rémy, Emilie, the twins, booking her journey, the dread and excitement at seeing Luc again—she'd allowed her body no room in her thoughts. Too frightening to acknowledge, too catastrophic, the vague and extreme possibility crystallised in her brain with ruthless digital clarity.

'No,' she said hollowly. 'It would be awful if anything went wrong.'

Her heart plunged in freefall.

CHAPTER EIGHT

LUC was on the move early, needing to attend to his office. Shari stayed in bed, waving away any suggestion of breakfast. 'I want to sleep a little more,' she said weakly from her pillow, knowing what would happen if she tried to sit up.

'Are you sure? Not even some *chocolat*?'

She only just repressed a shudder.

'Ah…if you are still wishing to visit the d'Orsay, I could collect you here at eleven.'

'Oh, right. The d'Orsay.' Though at that exact moment, pictures were not the first thing on her mind. 'Oh, so you—want to come too?'

His eyes veiled and he said carelessly, 'Unless you prefer to be alone when you look at pictures.'

She hated to hurt his feelings. 'No, no, not at all. I'd love you to come.' She should be able to fix herself up before then, one way or another. 'How about I meet you there? I'll enjoy finding my own way.'

He looked more closely at her, his brows drawing together. 'Are you feeling quite well?'

'Oh, heck yeah. Just tired. What would you expect?' She conjured up a grin.

'*Très bon*.' Smiling, he wrote down his mobile number for her, dropped a kiss on her forehead and left.

The second the door closed behind him, Shari dragged herself up and lunged for the bathroom. There was another ghastly attack, though she seemed to deal with it more briskly this time. Maybe she'd even get used to it. Panting, she screwed up her face. How fun to be a woman. The likely diagnosis loomed with a hopeless inevitability.

After showering and washing her hair, she felt slightly more human, if no braver. She dressed and took the lift down to the lobby.

The concierge directed her to a nearby pharmacy. Outside, in cruel mockery of her situation, the sun was daring to shine weakly, the sky having the crass insensitivity to glow with a pale, hopeful blue.

With a pregnancy testing kit burning a hole in her bag, Shari hurried back to the hotel and requested a taxi. Her own room at the Louvre felt more the place to face the moment of truth.

An hour later she sat on the smooth coverlet of her bed, hot and cold by turns. An initial bout of sheer panic and desperation had given way to something like bleak acceptance, though her brain was in a jumble. Did she *want* to be pregnant? Without a relationship to depend on?

Of course not. She couldn't do it. She was in no position to. Her mother had been left to raise her on her own, and look how hard their life had been. Never two cents to scrape together. Shoes that wore through the soles before they were replaced. Her mother working two jobs. If Neil hadn't been there as a support she didn't know how they'd have held together.

She supposed she'd always assumed she would have a child some day, but not until she had the man. Never, never without the man. She just didn't have that sort of courage and she was hardly in any financial position, with her career still in its shaky infancy.

One book published, and a tiny little advance for the next?

Another attack of panic gripped her as her conscience chimed in to taunt her. Too late, Shari. A child has started now. *Your...*

She broke out in a sweat. She needed to think. Focus on immediate practicalities. Like how to inform Luc.

Oh, God.

Whether to inform him.

A man who invited a woman to stay for a week—*in a hotel*—wasn't contemplating an ongoing relationship. She doubted if even his offer of the Ritz would stand once she told him. Everything would be over. He'd get rid of her fast.

Nothing like the prospect of a responsibility to cool a man's ardour.

Although… Although… Try to think straight, Shari. Luc was a man of the world. He would be sophisticated about it. Suggest the logical solution. Surely that would be for the best.

If only she hadn't been so ignorant about France. Knowing Rémy and Emilie had given her some insights, but Rémy was hardly likely to have been typical of Frenchmen.

Surely the French were very religious, *Notre Dame de Paris* and all that. If she told Luc, maybe he would insist she go through with it.

And what? Leave her stuck with a child and send her money every month?

The alternative was no less confronting. Her thoughts skittered towards movie images of the clinic waiting room and shied away again.

If only she had a friend she could talk to, right here, right now—Neil. If only she had her brother. He was on her side, no matter what, and at least in Australia she knew the rules. With such huge scary decisions to make, a strange country was not the place to be.

She considered phoning Em, but what was the point? She knew what Em would say. Anyway, Australia would be asleep now.

Whatever, she'd better be on that plane tomorrow.

Luc arrived at the Musée d'Orsay a few minutes before the appointed time. He strolled about before the entrance, enjoying the brisk air, avoiding tour groups and keeping his eye on the taxis that drew up to disgorge visitors.

He felt no concern about taking another day away from the office. *Zut*, he might even take a few more.

He glanced at his watch. A minute or two past the hour. Then some extra-sensory instinct alerted him and he glanced up. That dizzying swoosh as the breath caught in his lungs. She was on foot, strolling from the direction of the Pont Royal that crossed the river from the Tuileries.

She looked as casual and unFrench as any of the tourists queuing up for entry to the museum, wearing a trench over jeans and sneakers. Scarf carelessly knotted around her neck, her blonde hair rippling free. When she drew near a smile touched her mouth, fleetingly, then she grew serious again.

He narrowed his eyes. How pale she seemed.

When he kissed her, her cheeks felt cold against his lips. He slipped his hands inside her trench and drew her close, inhaling the sweet fragrance that enveloped her from head to toe. Desire quickened his blood. His mouth watered with the yearning to kiss her properly.

'Are you tired from walking? Or did I wear you out?'

Drawing back after a few blood-stirring seconds, her heart still thumping, Shari met his warmly sensual gaze. Like her, he'd changed clothes. He was clean-shaven and sexy in dark trousers and a black polo-neck with a dark brown leather jacket.

That electric current was tugging her, making her want him. Astonishing she could still feel that way when her tender places were in need of some respite from the action. And with *this*… How could she even *want* to feel like this now?

Madly though, like an addict, she did.

'It wasn't that far. I love to walk.' She showed him the map given her by the concierge at the Hôtel du Louvre. 'See? I wanted to see as much as I could before I fly away.' And maybe the exercise would do her good.

'But you aren't flying yet. You're staying a week. Two weeks.'

Two now? She lowered her gaze. 'We'll see.'

See how keen he would be when he knew. When she told him what was growing inside her and taking over her body, her life, the *world*. How would he handle such news? That moment in Sydney when he'd heard Rémy spoken of as her fiancé flashed into her mind. His reaction had been severe enough then, but that had been nothing like *this*.

Would she blame her? A bolt of pure panic made her hands and armpits moisten, and for a second she nearly reeled. Oh, God in heaven, she should get a grip. Luc wasn't the violent type. After yesterday and last night, how could she even think of comparing him with Rémy?

Examining her face, Luc felt the slightest twinge of anxiety. Surely she wasn't still thinking of boarding that flight? A petite woman shouldn't undertake such a harrowing journey again so soon. She still hadn't recovered from the first. Why else would she be so pale?

For the next two hours Shari wandered through the gallery in a turmoil of unreality. Staring blindly at work after exquisite work, she was unable to think of anything except—*it*. It was a mere embryo now, she supposed. Not much more than a few tiny little cells. With a face, already? How long would it take eyes, nose and lips to develop?

She wished she could dash somewhere private to look it up on the Internet. Maybe when she got back to the hotel. Find out the developmental stages. Despite everything, she was curious to at least see what it looked like.

She felt Luc send her a couple of searching glances, and realised she'd hardly said a word. She needed to clean up her act. This was no way for a grown woman to take charge of what was, after all, a perfectly normal though terrifying situation.

'What do you think?' he said, paused before a *Starry Night Over the Rhone*.

She tried to focus. The painting shimmered before her gaze, ablaze with passion and aspiration, hope and the purest joy in simple things. How could such a treasure have been created by someone in a far worse life predicament than she could ever contemplate?

Oh, she was such a coward. Tears swam into her eyes. 'It's— a dream. Magic. The *vibrancy* of it. You imagine you know about something, but when you're up close to it, in real life, and it's connected to *you* your entire perception changes. You suddenly realise fate has you in its sights, and you're helpless against nature. You're nothing. You thought you had power to control your life but...' Suddenly sensing his keen scrutiny, she stemmed the wild flow with a lurch of dismay.

What on earth had she been babbling?

'That's how *I* feel,' he exclaimed. 'It's as if Vincent knew exactly what was in my heart when he painted this picture. I am so pleased you feel the power of it too. But not surprised,' he added warmly. 'Not at all surprised.'

He put his arm around her and hugged her to him as if she was a precious thing. She smiled, relieved, so pleased to still be in accord with him, but underneath her glow her anxiety only intensified. He was warm *now*, so admiring, appreciative of her charms. Liking her. How would he feel when she told him? Would she see a swift and deadly turnaround?

Just imagining him turning cold and distant made her heart pang with dread.

'Are you feeling very well?' He was looking closely at her.

'Sure. Fine. Do you—do you visit here often?'

He continued to scrutinise her. 'Not so often now. Though I know it well, of course. If I'm in Paris at the weekends I like to visit the smaller galleries—ones out of the usual way of the tourists.'

'I'm a tourist,' she reminded him.

But she was thinking how little she knew of him. This tiny little minuscule face was unfurling, maybe resembling *his*...

She squashed that hysterical thought. Ridiculous when she knew zilch about the whole development thing, and anyway she had no idea what she was planning to do about it.

'What do you do at weekends when you aren't in Paris?'

He lifted his shoulders. 'Different things. My family have a little farm in the country. I visit there sometimes.'

'A farm? Is that where your mother lives?'

He smiled. 'Sometimes she goes there. Sometimes the Alps, or the beach, especially when Paris is too hot. But in winter she prefers her apartment.'

'And your father?'

'He lives in Venice.'

'Why Venice?'

He lifted quizzical brows at her. 'His lover lives there.'

She flushed. 'Forgive me for asking so many questions.' How crass she must have sounded. 'I feel as if you know everything about me and I know so little about you.'

He looked amused. 'Ask what you like.'

He looked relaxed enough, but all at once she felt shy. She knew she was bound to make a mess of framing the right questions. What were they, even? Where to start? There should be a manual available for the woman who was knocked up in a one-night stand.

She hesitated. 'Well, do you…? You mentioned your ex-fiancée. Manon—is it? Emilie told me a little bit about her.'

She sensed a sudden stillness in him. Then he said smoothly, 'She was not my *fiancée*.' He gave an insouciant shrug. 'We—had a looser arrangement than that.'

'Oh?'

She paused before a painting of a village church. Heavenly blue and the most glorious, joyous yellow she'd ever imagined possible. Honestly, all this beauty was playing so excruciatingly on her emotions, her eyes kept pricking. It was probably one of the symptoms. As if she needed any more.

She glanced at him. 'What of now? As of this moment. Do you have someone?'

Though he was amused, his eyes glinted. 'As of this moment I am here with you.'

She moistened her lips. 'Were you and she together—a long time? You and Manon?'

'Some years. Six. Seven.' His lashes swept down.

'Oh. That is a long time.' She felt surprised. She hadn't realised the relationship had been quite so—established. For a loose arrangement it seemed long. Whatever 'loose' meant.

A man who'd been in a seven-year relationship didn't seem like a man who fooled around, at any rate. She glanced speculatively at him. Would he have...?

Frowning, she moved on to the next picture. Pretended to examine it. 'I saw a picture of her. She's very beautiful. Emilie said she's renowned for her elegance and *chic*.'

'Did she?' His lip made a sardonic curl. 'I must thank Emilie for informing you so well. No doubt she told you about the dog.'

She glanced at him in surprise. 'No. She never mentioned a dog.'

'*Tiens*. I am grateful.'

Though if there was a dog, it was sounding far more domestic than she had imagined from her understanding of loose arrangements.

'Did you...?' She drew a breath. 'Did you never think of marrying her?'

His eyes veiled, then slid away. Suddenly he leaned forward to study a scene where some fully clothed men were picnicking by a stream with a naked woman. 'Do you not admire the artist's use of the light here? If I could only achieve this effect I believe I might be content for all time.'

Shari took a moment to digest the stunning snub. Maybe she should have expected it. Clearly, the intimacy of the bed did not translate to the museum. There were lines she must not cross.

Why, oh, why had she even *asked* him? It wasn't as if she

expected him to marry *her*. But that was what he would assume when she broke the news. He'd think she was looking to
trap him in playing happy families.

Breaking into a sweat, she edged away from him.

Face it, it was clear he was still pretty raw about losing the
beautiful woman. Well, it was only natural. Any guy's ego was
bound to feel trashed if his girlfriend ran off with a movie idol.

Especially if the guy was still madly in love with her.

'Why are you wrinkling up your face and looking as if you
tasted a lemon?' She started. Luc slipped his arms around her
and kissed her ear. 'Is Renoir such a disappointment?'

She flashed him a rueful smile. 'Never. How could he be?
To be honest I—I was feeling guilty. I think I've intruded, asking you things you don't care to discuss. I guess you're thinking those things some French people say about Australians.'

'What do they say?'

'Oh, you know. We're too open. Too—forward.'

He laughed easily. 'Who says that? Come, we will eat
déjeuner. My mother wants to meet you properly. The family
will be there.'

Shari's heart sank. 'Lovely.'

There was no sign of the limo. Luc ushered her to a neat
little Merc parked in a nearby street. As soon as they were in
the car, he pulled her into his arms and kissed her, a steamy,
highly explorational clinch that sucked all the breath from
her lungs and shut down her brain entirely. Responding to the
sexual cue, her wanton body was instantly aroused, then disappointed when he drew back.

With a husky laugh, he murmured, 'Not here, *ma chérie*.
Soon, soon.'

Soon? How likely was that, once he heard the news? But
after the outcome of her recent tactful inquiry, it felt impossible
to break it just then. She'd have to wait until he'd forgotten it.

She hoped the lunch wouldn't take long. What if it went on
for ever and she lost the chance to be private with him? Though,

was it best to be completely private with him? For this sort of news, maybe it would be as well to have witnesses. A public place would be preferable, perhaps a café.

'You're too quiet,' he observed on the way, paused for some lights. 'What's going on inside that head?'

She met his slanting glance. 'I was just—wondering about your dog.'

'*Comment*?'

'You know. You mentioned a dog.'

He said sharply, 'There is no dog.' Then, flushing a little, he broke into a reluctant laugh. 'Manon—my ex-girlfriend—had a passion to acquire a Russian wolfhound. The Borzoi. You know the one? We discussed it and—decided it would not be practical. I preferred something else.' His hands lifted from the wheel in agitation. 'After the—split, someone in the press heard about it, suggesting that our partnership ended because I would not allow Manon to have the pet she craved. You can imagine, in *France*…I was crucified in the tabloids. You see?' He smiled ruefully.

'Oh.' She swallowed. 'Yes, yes. I see.'

Staring out at the Seine, she kept her hands tightly clasped in her lap. She could see all right.

'What was it you preferred?' she said.

A muscle flickered in his lean cheek. The corner of his mouth made an infinitesimal downward curl that was really quite heartbreakingly attractive. 'Something smaller.'

Tante Laraine lived in the seventh *arrondissement*. Luc pressed a button in what looked like an ordinary wall in the street, and a panel slid open to reveal a security plaque. He dialled in a code and a door opened. Inside, to Shari's surprise, was a beautifully manicured garden with a fountain. A gravelled path led to the side entrance of a gracious old building with the distinctive Parisian mansard roof and dormer windows.

Several children were darting here and there among the

shrubbery, playing a game that required sudden shrieks and bursts of laughter. A couple of them called to Luc, and he waved back.

As she approached the entrance Shari's nerve began to fail. The people inside all thought she was Rémy's fiancée, and here she was, fresh from Luc's bed, pregnant with Luc's child and planning to…what? How could she possibly carry off such a dilemma?

'Luc.' She started to breathe faster than a woman approaching the finish line in the London marathon. 'Do you mind if we don't go here?'

His brows lifted in surprise. '*Pardon?*'

'Could we just go to a café or…' She tried to swallow but she was all out of saliva.

His eyes narrowed on her face. '*Que veux-tu…?*'

'There's something I might have to tell you.'

Some people burst through the doors then, exclaiming when they saw her and Luc. Amidst all the embraces and introductions, her moment was lost, though on the way up in the lift with the others Luc kept looking searchingly at her. He whispered, 'Are you feeling well? Is everything fine?'

'Yep. Fine,' she lied through her lying teeth.

Laraine's apartment was on the top floor below what Shari imagined would be a garret for starving artists and bohemians. When she was ushered inside, though, it seemed possible Laraine kept an army of maids and footmen up there.

The ceilings were extraordinarily high and ornate. As for the furnishings…Shari doubted if the precious pieces had been created any later than the eighteenth century.

Several other family members were present, some Shari recognised from the funeral. Tante Marise. Oncle Georges, whose eyes lit up when he saw her. A couple of younger cousins, Anne-Sophie and Sophie-Louise, with spouses. She'd never remember which Sophie was which. Though warmly welcomed and kissed by all, Shari suddenly felt burningly aware of her casual attire.

A scarf could only go so far to catapult an ordinary Aussie girl into Parisian society. If only she'd done something with her hair. The Sophies looked chic, even in jeans.

Luc glanced at her often, a slight frown in his eyes that made her heart quake. Trust her to choose the exact right moment. She'd alerted him to trouble, and she could see he was speculating.

Contrary to things she'd read, the family seemed happy to converse in English on her behalf, except when they forgot. Luc poured her a sherry and handed her the glass. Feeling his mother's quick glance flick between them, Shari accepted it, taking care not to touch him.

Laraine suspected, Shari saw suddenly. Though how much? Was the Ritz etched into their body language? Or did Laraine have X-ray vision?

Even imagining the impossibility made Shari a tiny bit giddy. With the family all believing she was Rémy's woman, how must it look?

As she allowed her restless glance to wander her nerve jumped. On a side table where some family photos were displayed, the lovely couple blazed out at her. Luc in evening dress, Manon in a beautiful bare-shouldered gown, her hair up, on this occasion honey-blonde. Another of them in relaxed weekend mode with several of the present company. Clearly, Manon had been part of the family.

Excruciatingly out of her comfort zone, Shari answered questions about her journey, Sydney, Emilie and her children, the new twins about to be born, smiling, smiling. Babies, mothers, newborns—all were popular here, apparently.

Shari gazed at her sherry. Would it look suspicious if she didn't drink it? In a limbo of indecision, she held the glass in her hand, untouched.

Not that any of those pregnancy rules would have to apply

to her, necessarily. After all, if she didn't stay pregnant... Why was it so hard to control one's breathing and slow it down?

There was a bit of discussion about Rémy, then the conversation moved on to other things. People appealed to Luc often for his opinion, and when he replied he was always pleasant, measured, amused. Occasionally though he seemed not to hear them. He kept staring at the floor, or at Shari. Then he looked grave and so darkly handsome she felt the twist in her heart that signalled trouble ahead.

As if she didn't have enough.

At a point where the conversation grew loud and lively Luc strolled over to her and murmured, 'What did you want to talk about?'

'Nothing, nothing. Shh.' She smiled as if everything were as normal as gramma pie while on the inside she was imagining herself growing huge, going to hospital all by herself and coming home to her flat in Paddington, with a... Well, not quite by herself.

The meal was an exquisitely prepared torture.

At first there was foie gras on slivers of toast on her plate. In her strangely disconnected state she couldn't help wondering how many poor geese had died to produce it. Lucky there was some lettuce she could chew on, a few curls of celery.

Sensing Luc's gaze, she was tempted to let their eyes tangle for an instant. His compelled her, questioning, uncertain, and she skittered hers away.

Oh, God. Had he guessed?

'You have made a journey *très, très, vraiment* long, Shari,' Laraine said. 'A pity the occasion is so melancholy.'

The family showed their concern for the grieving fiancée with a series of questions, punctuated by discussions about the food and family concerns Shari wasn't privy to, interrupting themselves and each other so rapidly she found it barely possible to get in a word.

'*Oui, les pois, s'il te plait*. How long were you and Rémy engaged, Shari?'

'Not long. You see—'

'Try some of this, Sophie-Louise. So, Shari...had you planned your wedding soon?'

'No. Well, actually—'

'You are not enjoying your wine, *ma chérie*?' That was Tante Marise, worrying she wasn't partaking of enough sustenance.

Not to be outdone in the hospitality stakes, Laraine quickly asserted her authority. '*Vite, Gilbert, apportes ce Sancerre*. Shari, you have had a terrible ordeal. You must eat to recover your vitality. You will find this chablis is very fine.' She beamed.

It looked beautiful, pale and chill in its crystal glass. Without a doubt, all the food was of the finest, though Shari could barely do more than taste. A rabbit that had scampered across meadows fragrant with thyme before it was murdered. Artichokes dressed in a manner a duke from the Perigord had only recently demanded on his deathbed.

If she didn't drink the wine, would she give offence? Maybe just a sip, though even a sip could damage something very small and fragile. What if she drank it and the poor little face shrivelled up in agony?

Her insides clenched. She put her glass down.

'While you are here you must visit the village where Rémy and Emi grew up,' someone offered.

'I am certain Luc would be happy to take you there and show you everything,' Tante Laraine said warmly. '*Tiens!* I say, we must all go together and picnic in the woods.'

'*Bien sûr*, Shari,' Tante Marise added kindly. 'Rémy would have liked to see you there.'

She guessed they weren't intending to torture her, but with her world now dominated by an embryo—*Luc's*—this constant harking back to Rémy was an agony.

When she wasn't moving her food around the plate or being addressed by someone, Shari rested her gaze on a burnished antique sideboard with lovely pieces of delicately painted china. An exquisite vase holding jonquils, a Chinese bowl, a fragile urn painted with birds and flowers.

Once she disciplined herself to look at Luc firmly, like a normal, non-pregnant person. His eyes locked with hers, alert, guarded, and her heart turned over.

It was during the cheese she lost her cool. Tante Marise said, 'Poor Shari, you must feel you have lost your whole world *Tsk-tsk-tsk-tsk-tsk.*'

Shari shook her head, ready to deny the charge and explain about Rémy, when Laraine exchanged a meaningful glance with all the others and leaned tenderly towards her.

'Forgive us, Shari. This is a delicate subject, *ma chérie,* but it must be dealt with. We have spoken with Emilie and do not believe Rémy has left any instructions. Are you aware of his thoughts? We must decide how to dispose of his ashes. It is good you are here in France and you are able to participate.'

Appalled, Shari said, 'Oh, look. No, no, please.' She glanced about at their enquiring, sympathetic faces and cast an agonised look at Luc. Then she rose to her feet, the better to breathe.

'Please, you know, you're all being so kind, but I—I really must explain.' She saw Luc's dark brows draw into an alarmed frown, but she carried on regardless. 'The truth is, that while I *was* engaged to Rémy for a while, it was not a—a very happy thing. Our engagement ended several months before he—before the accident.'

A heavy stillness descended on the room. She could hear pigeons cooing on a distant steeple.

'I haven't wanted to mislead you. And truly, I don't want to hurt anyone. I know you all loved him, he was part of your family, but in fact to *me* Rémy wasn't always the most gentle person. He could lose his temper and be really quite—' Just at that moment, her eye fell on the painted urn resting innocently on the bureau.

A horrifying realisation shocked through her. She grasped at her throat. Unable somehow to manage breathing, she felt herself grow unbearably hot, then without warning whirled forward into a bottomless black hole.

Through a misty haze she heard Luc's shocked voice, distant chairs scraping, a babble of consternation. She opened her eyes again immediately, or so it seemed to her. Well, perhaps some time had passed, because she was now horizontal and in another room, her head on a feather soft pillow, a feather-soft blanket tucked around her.

Luc's mother was sitting at her side patting her knee while Luc was standing over her, looking anxious. They didn't notice she was awake because they were deeply involved in an intense, murmured conversation.

Shari couldn't follow it because they were speaking in rapid French. Not all of it, anyway. There was *one* word she picked up. She knew it rather well from years of experience with Emilie.

Enceinte.

She knew the meaning of that, all right. It meant pregnant; with child; having conceived; in the family way; up the duff; in the pudding club; fat. It was Laraine who uttered the fateful word, and when she did Shari saw Luc's face change.

CHAPTER NINE

A STRAINED silence persisted all the way from Tante Laraine's to the Luxembourg Gardens. Luc had hustled Shari so fast out of the family lunch she was breathless. But not nervous. She had no reason to be scared. He was a civilised, non-violent guy, she was an adult woman capable of making her own decisions and defending herself, so this silence wasn't playing on her nerves.

Much.

It was just that, in a small car, when they were physically in such close proximity, she could hear his very breathing. In. Out. In. Out. Or maybe that was the jackhammer in her heart.

Anyway, he parked and took her for a charming stroll through the afternoon shadows, under trees, past grassy banks to a beautiful old rhimey fountain. Most of the people had left or were on their way home. The clowns, a juggler in his harlequin costume. Lovers holding hands. A kid playing with a hoop. Mothers pushing their babies.

Shari wouldn't have minded a few of them hanging around, just in case, but she guessed it was time for them all to repair to their kitchens and prepare the family *cassoulet*.

She concentrated on small things along the way. Water lilies floating on the pond. Jonquils nodding along the garden path, closing their faces now as the shadows lengthened.

They paused by the fountain. Luc faced her. She made her mind go empty, the way she always had when she suspected Rémy was about to strike.

'Do you have something to tell me?' He took her arms in a gentle grasp that might as well have been of steel. There was no escaping this moment of truth.

'Yes.' Not breathing, she met his compelling gaze. 'It's true. I only found out for sure myself this morning. I'm—*we're*—pregnant.'

She braced.

He scrutinised her face for what felt like for ever. Worlds of calculation glinted in his eyes while he evaluated the available data. In a romance novel he would have said *Then we must get married. No question about it.*

'And you are certain?'

That expression on his face. The tinge of doubt. She remembered it well from the night in Sydney. That occasion when he'd asked her how recently she'd seen Rémy. How recently she'd been hot from his cousin's bed.

'Pretty certain,' she said tonelessly. 'I took a pregnancy test this morning. It came up positive. It was what I—expected.'

He didn't lash out, just sat down with her on a nearby bench. But she could see he was in shock. He was blinking fast and there was a pallor under his olive tan, a grave set to his mouth.

'I know what you are wondering,' she said suddenly. 'You're wondering if the child is yours. You're thinking I might be—exploiting this opportunity to foist Rémy's child onto you, and…' Her voice choked up. Tears came into her eyes and she turned her face away.

He took her hand and held it tight. 'Please. I have to ask the question. Is it mine?'

'Yes. *Yours.* Rémy and I hadn't been—together in that way for a long time.'

He searched her face, frowning. Then, dragging his fingers through his hair, he got up and started to pace. 'This—needs serious thought.' He walked, halted, walked again, like a man iven by terrible conflicts. After a few minutes he paused before her. 'What do you want to do? Whatever you choose, will help you.'

Her heart trembled. 'I don't know. I'm still coming to term with it.'

She crossed her fingers. This was the point where the her would take her in his arms and tell her it was the most beauti ful news he'd ever received.

He was silent for a moment. '*Bien sûr*, this is not the idea way for a—a child to be conceived.'

'No.'

'You live in Sydney. I live here. We are separated by a grea distance…'

She closed her eyes. He was a man, she was a woman. Dif ferent planets of origin. He hardly needed words to describ the status quo. The separation factors. His hands did the talk ing for him. Crushed her wayward little hope and put it bac in its box.

'You have a career. You are an independent person. Natu rally, you value your autonomy.'

'Well, yes…'

He added carefully, 'In France, of course, there are option I'm not sure how the law exists in Australia…'

She lowered her eyes. 'There are options.'

'Here…I believe it can be as simple as taking a pill.'

She nodded.

He stared at her a while, his eyes glittering, his face tense 'This is not something—either of us would have planned.'

'No.'

'This—this changes lives. I would not have afflicted yo with this problem.'

'Of course not.'

He lowered his lashes, frowning and breathing rather har 'So…' A grim tension tautened his lean face. 'Perhaps the obvi ous thing to do then would be to—take action. *N'est-ce pas?* His gaze scoured her face, questioning, searching.

The sun went out, or maybe a cloud doused the world. Her limbs suddenly felt chilled. Shivering, she pulled her trench closer. 'Do you mind if I go back to my hotel now? I'm feeling very tired all at once.'

'Of course, of course.' He helped her up, so courteously, so concerned for her comfort, she had the feeling he'd have carried her to the car if she'd requested it.

The drive to the Hôtel du Louvre was even more tense, if possible, than the drive to the Luxembourg Gardens. But it was a different sort of silence. More like Hiroshima, in those minutes after the bomb.

Before all the agony set in.

When they drew up at the hotel, he paused before turning off the ignition, frowning at the hotel entrance. 'Will you be okay here?'

'Of course. It's a lovely hotel. It's very comfortable.'

His frown deepened. 'I—I've never heard anything *against* it. I'm sure it's of a reasonable standard. Clean.'

She nodded.

'And safe? You feel safe here?'

'Yep. Safe.'

'The staff. They are respectful?'

'Very.'

'And the facilities are—*très bon*?'

He was so concerned that despite her internal suffocation she nearly laughed. '*Mais oui. Très, très bon.*'

He got out and strode around to open the door for her, then ushered her in through the revolving door.

He glanced around the small lobby, then faced her, the lines of his face even more taut. When he spoke his words sounded suddenly jerky. 'So—so what will you do now? Will you sleep?'

'Hope so.'

His eyes strayed in the direction of the restaurant, which to her eyes looked warm and charming, with its banquettes bright with red regency stripes. 'What about your dinner? Do you feel you can eat in this place? You hardly ate a bite at lunch.'

'Oh, yes, yes, I did.' She hoped her appetite problems hadn't wounded his feelings. 'The lunch was delicious. Your mother's a wonderful cook. Anyway, I'll—I might have something sent up later.'

He took both of her hands. 'Are you sure this is what you want? To be here now?'

'Where else? I'm not really in the mood for the Ritz.'

He turned sharply away, but not before she saw the flush darken his cheekbones.

She said earnestly, 'Look, you don't need to worry. I just need to think on my own for a bit. I'm sure we both do.'

He kissed her cheeks, then walked to the door, hesitated then strode back and kissed her on the lips. 'I'll call you later. *D'accord*?'

'Fine.' She nodded. Smiled brightly. 'Thanks.'

Luc drove towards his apartment but not there directly, because he unbelievably took a wrong turn in the streets he'd known since childhood and was forced to backtrack.

Upstairs, he poured whiskey and stood at his window, gazing out over the rooftops, thinking. No, attempting to grasp onto a thought and hold it still.

Of all the women on earth for him to have accidentally impregnated... To think he'd been condemning his cousin's abuse of her, when now he himself had caused her—this.

He hunched as hot shame rocked through him. Shame on Luc Valentin. Shame, shame, shame.

The ironies weren't lost on him.

His ex-lover choosing to have a baby with another man. His new lover—would she even agree to being called that?—reluctantly pregnant with his child.

If it was his.

He tried to think through all the things she'd ever told him about Rémy and the break-up. The time in the boathouse, that moment of exultation when she'd produced the battered package from her purse.

He knew what some guys would think. Had she really just taken the test today? Was it possible she'd come to Paris to snare him, knowing all along she was pregnant? With his cousin's child?

For money?

The image of her face, her gentle womanly dignity when he'd questioned her in the Gardens resurfaced. Shamed him afresh. *Scathed* him. *Mon Dieu*, what was he doing? Attempting to escape responsibility?

Needing to escape himself, he locked the apartment behind him, took the creaking old lift down and plunged into the streets.

The lights were glittering all over the city as the evening deepened. Luc strode along in the brisk air, hunched into his jacket, hands in pockets, attempting to clear his mind.

He was a rational guy. In charge of his life. It wasn't such a big thing, after all. People dealt with these little surprises all the time. All the time.

He'd been with Manon when he'd dreamed of them having the child. That time was gone now, destroyed, but he'd learned from it. The male of the species didn't have the right to impose his children on an unwilling female. He could see the justice of that. How some guys still managed to get away with it was a mystery.

An unbidden image of him and Shari with a child flashed through his head, and he banished it. Even if she wanted that, it would never work. Somehow, over the years, disillusionment had accumulated on his heart like so much snow.

Anyway, she'd made it clear she'd never again chance the domestic partnership model. He could well imagine her expression if he suggested anything as archaic as marriage. For all her gentleness and fragility, she could be as sharp as a knife.

She'd laugh in his face. And after her experience with Rémy, who could blame her?

No. In this case the rational decision was the only one. He'd support her through it, every step of the way.

Hopefully what she had to go through wouldn't be too painful. His gut clenched.

The restaurants were filling, people strolling to their entertainments. Tourists, students. He recognised a few of the locals from his neighbourhood. All at once he saw the guy from the *boulangerie*. He was with his wife, laughing with her as they crossed the street.

Luc could see the bulge of something the guy was transporting carefully inside his down jacket, wine bottles perhaps. When they drew nearer and the guy sharpened in focus, Luc saw with a searing pang that the zipper had been pulled down a little to allow a small curly head to peep out.

He turned his face away.

Shari had a good cry in the bath, then got out. Carefully. Her disappointment was cruel, but not a sensible option. Oh, how she hated that word. For a while there she'd imagined she'd glimpsed something more than desire in Luc's dark gaze, more than the amused affection that naturally existed between lovers who'd enjoyed some pleasant intimacy between the sheets.

Maybe if they lived in the same country she'd have a chance with him. But there was no use wanting someone who viewed her as a temporary diversion.

Realising that despite everything she really felt quite genuinely hungry, as if she could actually eat, she dressed in her other jeans and soft blue sweater, adding a pale cream scarf in case, and went down to the restaurant.

The *potage du jour* turned out to be a nourishing vegetable soup. Combined with crusty bread, it was food fit for angels, always supposing angels could eat. Afterwards, feeling fortified enough for anything, she asked the desk manager for an Internet key.

* * *

Luc followed the clerk's directions up to the mezzanine. Through the open office door he saw Shari seated at a desk, her blonde head bent in study of a screen. She was so deeply immersed he knocked twice before she heard him. *'Ça va?'*

She started, glancing up. 'Oh. I thought you were meaning to phone.'

'I needed to see you. Face to face.'

He saw her eyes light up as she searched his face for...what?

Seeing her in the flesh, he ached to touch her, hold her, but he could hardly muscle her out of her chair. Not in her condition.

He stood a little way from her, held back by an invisible line. 'Did you sleep?'

'I tried, but my brain kept going round.'

'Thinking about—*it*?' He grimaced.

She looked wary. 'What else?'

A flicker at the edge of his vision caused him to glance at the computer screen. There was an image of this large glowing ball. A sunburst, or something.

'Tomorrow,' he said firmly. 'We'll see a doctor. Have it confirmed. Take any steps that need to be taken.'

She moistened her lips. 'I'm not sure I'm ready to see a doctor.'

He felt a bolt of surprise. 'But...we must ensure you're safe. I've heard it said that these things are better attended to sooner rather than later.' He noticed a tension in her posture, though she spoke quite casually, her eyes lowered.

'The steps, you mean?'

'Alors, the—the medical support, the—everything.'

He had the sudden sensation his words weren't getting through.

She swivelled her chair a little so she was angled away from him. Her back was straight, her hands clenched on the desk. 'Luc—I'm going home tomorrow.'

The news shocked through him like a blow. Resistance

burned inside his chest. *Mon Dieu*, this… This was surely a reproach, a lack of confidence in his response as a concerned, honourable guy.

'*Mais*, Shari, *chérie*…' He made to grasp her arm, then restrained himself when he saw her start back. It wasn't quite a flinch, but close, and it shocked him. He remembered a couple of other times he'd noticed her brace herself as if expecting physical force, and the dismayed thought occurred to him that she didn't trust *him*, either. Even after they'd been together. After the things they'd said. Things she'd shared with him about Rémy.

It wasn't easy with all this churning inside ramping up his blood pressure, but he made a stern effort to moderate his tone, slow himself down. Not to sound so—forceful.

He said with difficulty, 'I thought we agreed you would stay longer.'

'Things were different then. Anyway, I didn't really agree. I was just—considering it. I don't think we'd enjoy a week at the Ritz now, somehow.'

Even as she made the comment he could see the resolution firming in her face. That pretty chin could be quite determined. But he had to accept the justice of her words, *bien sûr*. In this context the Ritz suggestion sounded ludicrous. But the prospect of her leaving immediately with everything unresolved was—wrong.

The screen caught his eye again and he saw it wasn't a ball, not really. It was a woman's anatomy. Or one part of it, greatly enlarged.

He summoned the most persuasive smile he was capable of at that moment. '*Nom de Dieu*, Shari, I'm not implying that we should just—carry on regardless. But you must agree, something like this requires careful—reflection. And time. Time to make a reasoned decision.'

'Oh?' She glanced up. 'I thought you'd already decided.'

He spread his hands. '*Zut alors*, we've both decided, *n'est-*

ce pas? Remember what we said in the gardens? We agreed, yes? And we are—aren't we?—on the same page with this?'

There was something in her eyes then that made his heart lose the beat, then speed up like a fury.

He hastened to add, 'W-well, as far as one *can* decide at first instinct. We need first to examine all the medical issues. I'm thinking here of your health.'

She lifted her shoulders. 'My health's fine. Anyway, they have the best possible health care in Australia. There's nothing here that I can't have there.'

He said sharply, 'You won't have *me* there.'

His change of tone made her blink. He noticed her stiffen and hold herself so rigidly, anyone would have thought she'd been expecting a blow.

His heart thudded. What did she think? He was like Rémy? After last night? Breathing harshly, he swung away from her towards the door. '*D'accord*, you want to leave. *Très bon*. You must do as you wish. What time is your flight?'

'Noon. I need to be there by ten-thirty.'

'I'll pick you up an hour before.'

'Oh, look. No need to put yourself out. I can take a taxi.'

'*Shari*. Of course I will drive you there.' Shocked, wounded, he stared at her, struggling to interpret the meaning of all this—rejection. Didn't women say they *wanted* guys to support them in this sort of emergency?

She looked so fragile. One of those small, blonde, fragile women one saw at every market. No, he thought at once. Correction. One of those small, blonde, fragile *pregnant* women.

He hesitated for fear of scaring her again. But he couldn't just accept this—dismissal. He needed to remind her of who he was. How they'd been.

He strode back and pulled her up out of the chair, crushed her to him and kissed her. Not a mere milk-and-water kiss like the earlier one in the downstairs lobby, either. This was one of the true ones. Fierce, like his inexpressible heart, and passionate, his hands on her breasts, her gorgeous bottom, the curves that had given him such exquisite pleasure and even now were making him so hard he could have her here and now on this desk.

And he was vindicated. After a stunned second she melted against him and joined him in the torrent of fire, clinging to him with all the fervour and passion he felt himself.

Blessed victory in his hands at last, he broke the kiss. 'Let's go to your room,' he said thickly. 'You don't want to be alone tonight.'

He could see his desire reflected in her eyes, but she dropped her lashes and turned her face away. 'No, look. It's probably best if I *am* alone.'

'*Chérie.*' *Dieu*, his voice was a groan. What was she doing to him? 'I can't—I can't imagine how you will sleep thinking of all these things. You need me to hold you. How else am I to persuade you not to fly away tomorrow?'

She made a grimace. 'That's just the trouble. No. No, honestly.' Evading his hands she backed away, opening a good two metre distance between them. 'I won't be able to think straight if you're here. I owe it to—to myself, to have this night alone. Please, Luc. You have to understand. I *know* Australia. I'll feel more comfortable there, whatever I have to go through. So please...for my sake and for— Well, for *my* sake.'

She virtually *shoved* him through the door. The failed guy, eliminated. The partner in crime, repudiated. The unwanted mate, condemned to a night of sheer and utter hell.

She smiled ruefully, but he saw that in fact she was as inflexible as steel. 'Goodnight.'

Something—*everything* about her seemed different, although maybe it was himself, seeing her through different eyes.

CHAPTER TEN

SHARI had ordered tea and toast to wake up with, and was relieved the early bite made some difference to how she felt. It couldn't have been very beneficial to have been operating on near empty for so much of yesterday. No wonder she'd collapsed at *chez Laraine* and created all that drama.

When she was packed and organised, she rang for her suitcase to be taken down, then waited in the breakfast room where she could watch the street, her trench folded on the banquette beside her. It was still far too early to expect Luc.

From where she sat she could see the waiter across at the Café Palais Royale arranging chairs under his red awning, while next door the patron was sweeping his section of pavement.

Even with her nerves stretched taut as bowstrings she could enjoy the scene, though it was a pleasure tinged with regret. If only she'd had more time to soak up the beauty.

Half her mind was already set on home. Neil had emailed her through the night to announce the safe arrival of the twins. In her rocky state those first photos had been almost too confronting. She supposed drearily if she didn't miscarry it would be comforting to have him and Emilie close at hand to advise her. It wasn't as if she'd be completely alone.

There was a constant ebb and flow of taxis in the square outside, and she had a cowardly impulse to run out and hail one. It wouldn't be fair, but it might spare her some grief. After last night she suspected Luc wasn't altogether satisfied with the prospect of her slipping from his grasp.

Although, maybe now he'd had time to think, he would accept her escape as an easy solution for himself as well. Whatever choice she made, he could go on with his life undisturbed.

She was just considering a tactful way to point this out to him when he walked in, ninety minutes ahead of the appointed time. Her heart lurched. The instant she saw his face she knew this would be no easy departure. It flashed through her mind he must have had an inkling he needed to be quick.

He stood gazing silently down at her, then bent to brush her cheeks with his lips.

He was unshaven, deep lines around his mouth and eyes suggesting he'd experienced a rugged night.

'May I?'

'Of course.' She flushed, ashamed he'd felt he had to ask.

He swung around to signal the waiter. '*Café, s'il vous plaît.*' Then he turned back to her. Scanned her face. She could sense him assessing her mood. 'Shari…'

She braced herself, her heart knocking in her chest.

His dark eyes were arresting in their gravity. 'I can't let you go like this.'

Her nerve plunged. 'But—'

He took her hands and it was as if an electric charge pulsated through her. 'Now I've had time to think, I can guess why you want to run away. I believe I didn't listen to you well enough. Somehow I—didn't hear what you were wanting. *C'est vrai?*'

She looked warily at him. 'Well….you seem—*seemed*—very certain of the way to go.'

'I'm not certain of *anything.*' The words were as raw as if they'd been wrenched from his soul.

'But yesterday you were so keen to—abort at once.'

He flushed deeply. 'Yesterday… *Alors*, I will admit, I felt the need to act.' He opened his hands in appeal. 'Try to understand. My first reaction was to think that for you this is a terrible blow. You are a free, lovely woman—how could I have done this to you? I wanted to deal with it. Spare you as much anxiety as possible.'

He sounded so sincere, she had to believe him.

'I see.' She sat back against the banquette, surveying him. 'I guess I thought you were horrified. Well, naturally, who wouldn't be? Your worst nightmare realised. Me a—a virtual stranger, at the same time embarrassingly connected to your family, and...'

'*Mais non*. How can any of that matter? But I can't deny I do feel—responsible.'

'I know. I do know that.'

Though, to be honest, she hadn't really given his feelings much consideration. She'd assumed he'd made up his mind at once to rid himself of the problem asap. It hadn't really occurred to her he might actually feel perturbed about having potentially changed her life irrevocably.

If she could believe that, it would be a bit of a revelation.

She glanced covertly at him. Apart from Neil, who was a human being, the salt of the earth and the kindliest pushover in the world, the men she'd known hadn't shown much concern for the woman or the child. Obviously they all hadn't been as selfish as Rémy—he'd been in a class of his own—but take her father, for instance. He was no Sir Lancelot. He'd run out on his family *and* on the child support.

Unless he was angling for an Oscar, Luc seemed genuinely distressed. His eyes held a sort of endearing shell-shocked confusion. She slid her hand into his and curled it around his fingers. 'Look, it wasn't just you who made it happen, was it? It was also me. Every step of the way. I wanted to be with you that night. I wanted to experience—you.'

A flame lit his eyes and smouldered there so fiercely she felt scorched. 'And I *you*.'

His glance was so flagrantly sexual at that moment she almost expected him to leap across the table and grab her in full view of the early-morning breakfasters of the Brasserie du Louvre. And, crazed as she was, she'd have let him.

Thoroughly inappropriate.

'And I was the one who produced the faulty you-know-what.'

He winced. 'Don't remind me.'

The waiter set down a coffee pot and cups. Luc slipped the guy a note, then poured the milky coffee.

'So.' He straightened his shoulders and captured her gaze, his eyes serious and compelling. 'I think we must tell each other the truth. What are you thinking, really?'

Aha. Here it came again. The moment of truth.

There were some details too dangerous to share with a man whose first instinct was to pull the chain. Tiny developing eyelids and heartbeats were not likely to sway a guy who was a big player on the Bourse, as Neil had informed her when he was trying to convince her of Luc's importance as a hard-hitting businessman.

She tiptoed as cautiously as a lark upon a leaf.

'Well, er…like you…at first I was so panicked all I could think of were ways of escape. But now…' She strove to keep her face cool and expressionless. She'd learned from Rémy that betraying her schmaltzy interior was a mistake. Squeeze her and she'd squish, and hadn't he just loved to watch that happen? 'The more I—consider, the more I realise I'm not ready to do anything—irrevocable. There's time to decide. A few more weeks, I believe.'

He nodded, slowly and gravely. '*Oui*. I too would like a few more weeks.'

'Really?' She felt a stab of surprise. Why? What was in it for him? Was he having some sort of brainstorm? She tried to read his eyes. 'After all, it is a huge decision.'

He nodded. '*Vraiment* it is huge. So huge we should make it together. Agreed?'

A warning gong tolled deep within her. Togetherness was all very well if they wanted the same thing. But if they didn't...

He watched her face. She could feel the clock ticking for her answer.

'Well...' She reached for her cup. Her hand shook a little and she withdrew it, though not before he'd noticed, to her chagrin. 'Certainly we need a clear picture of where each other stands.'

His eyes glinted, then he frowned down at his coffee. When he looked up he spoke quietly, his tone measured. 'I'm hoping you will agree to stay in France while we consider.'

'What, *here*?' She cast an involuntary look around. 'Oh, no, no. Sorry, I'm not able to manage that. Anyway, I'd prefer to be at home coping with this than in a hotel in a strange country.'

'You misunderstand.' A flush darkened his bristly cheek. 'Not here, *chérie*. With *me*. In my apartment.'

'Oh.'

The apartment, no less.

A sunbeam dangled itself enticingly in the direction of her heart, with hope dancing up and down it in sparkly stars.

She rejected the treacherous thing outright. She'd been sucked in by that sunbeam before. *Big* time. Stars, spangles, the works. This time the risks were far too great. It wasn't just her dreams she had to worry about being flushed down the toilet.

'And you won't be coping alone,' he added, smiling. But she sensed determination behind those eyes. And in the set of his handsome jaw she read assurance. Authority. The man asserting his rights. 'You will have me,' he declared softly.

'Of course.' She beamed him a smile, though her insides were twanging with warnings of caution. 'And I appreciate the offer, I truly do, but I'm probably better to be independent and in charge of my own space, you know?' A wry twitch of his lips only added more momentum to her misgivings. 'I told you. I learned the hard way I'm not cut out for togetherness and the domestic life.'

Maybe he had the misguided belief he was an equal partner in this enterprise, but it wasn't all happening to him, was it? He wasn't incubating little developing networks of nerves and synapses. Arms. Legs.

'Anyway,' she added hastily, 'I haven't brought enough clothes with me for a longer stay, and…I have a book contract I have to fulfil. I need to work. I really do.'

'You can work at my place.' He spread his hands, smiling, insistent. 'Why can't you? And don't worry a thing about your clothes. I'll take care of all that for you. I'm good with clothes.'

This was no recommendation. Rémy had been good with clothes. Good at telling her when she'd got it wrong.

He made a rueful gesture. 'Don't look so mistrustful.' He took her hand and held it between both of his, his dark gaze grave. 'Shari… Please understand. I'm not Rémy. Listen to me. I promise—on my honour I would never do anything to cause you harm.'

His eyes shone with a light that threatened to pierce her total serenity.

With her wobbly heart trembling in its niche all of a sudden, she felt a severe need to loosen her scarf. 'Well, *quel* relief.' She moistened her lips. 'That's…very nice.'

Glancing at her watch, she saw there was still plenty of time, but she wouldn't have minded bolting for the airport right at that very instant. She made to gather her trench. 'Actually, Luc, I don't want to be rude and rush things, but…'

He leaned forward, holding her captive in his dark gaze. 'You're not listening to me, Shari. I'm begging you to stay. I want to support you.'

'Oh, heavens.' Her pulse raced faster than Black Caviar at the Melbourne Cup. Was this the guy in the romance, or was she reading too much into a few words again? 'Why would you want to do that? I can support myself. And I've got Neil. I told you—I'm probably not meant for togetherness.'

'You know why.' His eyes glowed with a serious intensity.

'I want you. I don't want you to disappear to the other side of the world and lose you.'

Oh. Oh, God and the whole set of heavenly virgins. He *looked* so gorgeous, with his dark eyes so intent and sincere...

Like the crazy fool it was, her susceptible heart drank the words in like honey. It faltered in its resolve. Admit it. She was thrilled. All those romantic novels she'd brainwashed herself with from an early age wouldn't be suppressed. In less than an instant she was floating into the realm of candlelit dinners, cuddles by firelight, strolls hand in hand along the banks of the Seine, night after night after glorious night of bliss...

With her lashes fluttering out of control, she said breathlessly, trying not to fixate on his sexy mouth, 'But—you see...I have to be certain. I can't risk...' Like the fool she was, tears chose that moment to swim into her eyes. 'You must understand, I won't be hustled into anything.'

'I do understand. I understand exactly.' He kissed her hand and held it to his chest. 'Feel this? I promise on my heart I won't hustle you into anything you don't enjoy to do.'

She could feel the big muscle pumping under her palm, communicating disgracefully with her clitoris. She was so burningly conscious of the vibrant flesh and sinew beneath his shirt she had to yank her hand back before she did something scandalous.

The temptation to throw herself into his arms and kiss him rapturously down onto the banquette was extreme. But she held back, her bloodstream a torrent of yearning while her last resistance dithered. She'd never so much needed to be rational.

Honestly, maybe she'd be foolish to leave now. Why close off all her options? If he'd truly had a change of heart, this could be for the best, couldn't it? Maybe he would fall in love with her and she'd be the love of his life. Maybe they'd have several children. Two girls and two boys. They'd all go to the Sorbonne and become philosophers, artists and doctors with Médecins Sans Frontières.

'I see. Well. Well, then…' She made herself sound businesslike. Let him know she was in charge of her life and her uterus. 'Perhaps I could consider a—a brief trial. Only a trial, mind. No promises. How about say…a weekend?'

After all, what could he make her do against her will in a weekend?

'A week at least,' he insisted, dark eyes gleaming. 'I will use some vacation time and we can take this chance to—know each other.' That gleam grew so unmistakably sensual she thought she could guess what sort of knowledge he had in mind.

While she knew she mustn't allow herself to be seduced into a maelstrom of mindless passion, her highly susceptible pheromones all thrilled in anticipation.

She said, a little breathlessly, 'But—we need to be practical about this. Are you sure you have enough room? Once I get started on my work, I do tend to spread out a little.'

He threw his head back and laughed, his eyes alight with amusement. 'Don't worry. I can accommodate you no matter how far you spread.'

Well, that was heartening. So was the kiss he locked her in as soon as they were in the car. Well, at any rate it started out as fiery, but then he cooled it to a more tender, controlled sort of kiss, which was all the more arousing because she was so aware of his restraint. By the end she was bursting out of her bra, and aflame between her thighs.

If such a modest kiss could affect her so wildly, surely her decision to stay a while couldn't be all wrong?

On the way to his place, though, she was naturally besieged by second thoughts. How warm would he continue to be when her inner frump broke out? How long could she fake this *soigné* sophistication? Before she knew it she'd be forgetting to wear a scarf and clumping around in Ugg boots.

But he seemed so genuinely chuffed, grinning, chatting, his eyes shining as he pointed out various landmarks to her, she didn't have the heart to pull out right then. And when he opened the door of an apartment on the sixth and topmost floor of a centuries-old building in the *deuxième arrondissement*, and she walked in and saw Paris spreading below through tall windows at every turn, it was a heady moment.

Not quite real, actually.

Luc Valentin wanted her. As she gazed about, blinking at the silk curtains, the ornate mirrors, the rich oriental rugs vying for supremacy on the gleaming wooden floor, the elegant velvet sofas, an actual chandelier in the sitting room, those words kept spinning around and around in her head.

Even with a bun in the oven he wanted her. Could he have noticed how pregnant women *looked* a few months in? Had he realised she wouldn't remain her svelte and lissom self for long?

Maybe he wasn't expecting her to stay pregnant. Her fears all came flooding back, highlighted in red.

'*Bienvenue*,' he said, holding her shoulders, then kissing her lips as she stood in a luxury-induced trance. For such a rich and sophisticated man, he seemed a trifle awkward. 'Please— be as if you are at home.'

'Thank you.' The decor here could put the Ritz to shame. She had a shameful wish it had been a tiny bit more humble. Imposing bureaus and credenzas, while admirable, could be quite lowering. As could walls of peach-coloured silk and a thousand metres of yellow curtains.

But who was she to criticise? She felt strangely tongue-tied, as if the Tardis had set her down in a distant universe.

As his victory glow calmed a little Luc looked closely at her. She stood apparently rooted midway between the sitting room and the entrance, gazing about. He felt a pang of uncertainty. Somehow here she seemed smaller and more vulnerable, as if she'd shrunk back into herself.

'Are you feeling well?' he said. 'Can I offer you something? Coffee?' With a leap of inspiration he came up with his furthest reach of hospitality to date. 'Tea?'

Not that he could guarantee there would be any.

'Not just now, thanks.'

He felt a strong and manly urge to seal his triumphant possession of her on the nearest available surface, but he sensed the timing would be wrong. And with her condition, he might have to check first about the safety issue.

He made a mental note to conduct some research at the earliest opportunity.

'Perhaps you would like to—unpack?'

She cast him a hesitant glance. He had the sinking feeling she was about to refuse, but she only said, 'Your apartment is very nice. Are all of these family heirlooms?'

'Somebody's, perhaps. Not my family's.'

'Oh. I—I was reminded a bit of your mother's. I thought she might have…' she waved her hand '…you know, contributed when you moved out of home.'

Amusement at the thought of Maman parting with her precious things to accommodate Manon's ambitions made Luc smile. Then he saw Shari flush and felt an instant rush of remorse. What a clumsy idiot, embarrassing her when she was clearly feeling shy.

'Nothing like that,' he hastened to assure her. He flicked a glance about at the place. It was so long since he'd really looked at it, he'd forgotten how appalled he was initially by all the yellow. A man could get used to anything. But could a woman? An *Australian* woman?

'My ex-girlfriend is—er *was* a—a… What do you call—a professional designer. This was how she—liked things.'

Nom de Dieu. Horror gripped him by the balls. Had he really brought up Manon in the first minute? *Zut,* why was it that with Shari Lacey he was as inept as an adolescent?

'Come,' he said hurriedly. 'I'll show you everything.' He reached for her suitcase.

Feeling gauche, Shari followed. Now she could see the hand of a designer everywhere she looked. The matching armchairs by the fireplace. Those two chairs she glimpsed facing each other across that small perfect table in the kitchen. All the yellows blending, complementing each other.

Maybe it was her imagination, but the sum effect was of more than mere luxury. It was also somehow—intimate. As if two minds entwined as one occupied this retreat from the world.

She followed him along a silk-lined hall to some double doors.

'*La chambre à coucher.*' He opened them with an offhand gesture.

Shari drew in a breath. Wow. What a chamber. Spacious, panelled in more peach silk, it was a decorator's dream, rich with fabrics and plushness.

At Luc's urging she ventured in a few steps, and felt an immediate sense of having intruded. Naturally, she supposed, the space had a deeply personal ambience. She let her gaze dwell on the three sets of windows with long silk lemon curtains tied back with sashes. She could see charming little balconies outside.

She tried not to stare at the most dominant piece in the room, but it screamed at her. Wherever she looked, Luc and Manon's bed bore down upon her with its handsome bedhead, the matching lamps on either side. Their pillows. Their sumptuous counterpane.

Feeling Luc's narrow appraisal, Shari turned away, wondering if it was striking him how awkwardly she fitted here in his private space. *Their* space.

Directly facing the bed and above the fireplace was a modern erotic painting of lovers locked in the primal embrace. Following her gaze, Luc started, blinking at it, then stepped forward and snatched it down. Sliding it to the floor, he turned it to the wall.

He gave a jerky, dismissive wave. 'A poor choice. I've always been meaning to dispose of it.'

He turned away to open another set of doors that led into

a smaller chamber of lamps and mirrors, with large wardrobe cupboards lining one wall, a sumptuous chaise longue and a pretty bathroom beyond.

'*Le boudoir.*' He placed her suitcase inside. 'For—the woman. I have my own dressing room next door, as you see.'

Shari's gaze settled on the woman's dressing table. It was delicate-looking, with wavy lines, a beautiful winged mirror and a matching chair covered in rose and lemon patterned silk. Some highly polished perfume bottles sparkled before the mirror, while a tortoiseshell hairbrush still lay in wait for its rightful owner. Shari could almost see the chic and elegant woman seated there, completing her *toilette*.

Luc hastily strode forward and swept the surface bare, dropping the items into a silk-covered waste bin. 'The maid should have attended to this. I'm extremely sorry.' He looked so stern Shari hoped the maid wouldn't have to face him soon. He opened a closet door, then with a muttered curse closed it again quickly before she could see inside.

The air prickled with discomfort. Shari hardly knew what to say. 'It's all—gorgeous.' She gestured around at the exquisite room. 'My suitcase is ruining the effect.'

He closed his eyes. 'Not at all. Your suitcase is the only reality in a—a ridiculous fantasy. She—Manon—liked to feel like a courtesan of the First Empire.' He gave a terse laugh, then backed out of there rather quickly. 'And ah…as you see… all—all of our balconies are very small, I regret to say.' He gave a swift smile. 'Not like in Australia.'

'Nothing is like in Australia.'

He stared at her for a strained second, then said tensely, 'There is another bedroom you might prefer until we prepare this one properly. Come and see.'

He slipped his arm around her and kissed her ear. Pulled her against him and buried his face in her hair. 'Ah…the scent of you. Shari…' he breathed. 'Relax. Don't be upset by small things. Don't worry. I will…' He kissed her and she felt the vibrancy of his hard body pressed against hers, but she disentangled herself.

It didn't feel right kissing him in there.

The guest room was charming, though not in the same class of opulence. While there was no boudoir attached, Shari thought the capacious armoire more than sufficient for her belongings. As well there was a chest of drawers and a small bathroom.

'This'll be fine,' she said, smiling. 'I'm probably not the courtesan type.'

With a flush darkening his tan, he took her arms. 'Shari,' he said stiffly. 'Please accept my apologies. I should have thought before I— I don't spend any time here now, so I never look at the rooms. I can't imagine why I haven't thought of changing things. It's purely an oversight.'

'It's okay, really. It's not as if you had any advance warning. I'm fine. Don't worry.'

'It won't be so terrible in here for an hour or two, *n'est-ce pas*? I believe the bed is soft. Would you like to unpack?' He stared hungrily from her to the bed. 'Or—to rest?' His eyes grew searingly wolfish.

'I wouldn't mind going for a walk, actually.' She definitely needed a breather. Time out to reflect. 'Stretch my legs.'

He looked worried, but then he shrugged. *'D'accord.'*

It was a relief to be out in the air. Shari sensed Luc feeling more relaxed too. Conversation was easier without the ghostly presence of his ex. And there was so much to see around her, every boulevard and every narrow alluring lane, she tried not to dwell on the glimpse she might or might not have caught into the inner guy.

Did a man keep his old lover's belongings intact simply because he forgot to remove them? Or because he couldn't bear to part with them?

Or was the maid entirely to blame? Could she have been a Mrs Danvers, by any chance?

Anyway, this wasn't a Gothic novel and she was probably reading too much into a small thing. And it was pleasant strolling with a gorgeous guy who took her hand from time to time and seemed to regard her as a fragile vessel.

It was an impression she was eager not to correct before she'd at least had a good wallow in it. Just supposing she stayed the whole week. It was comforting to remember she still had options.

Although she'd managed by the skin of her teeth to postpone her flight home for another week, the day of departure could be changed again, depending on available seats. Nothing was set in concrete.

It wasn't as if she were dreaming of moving in. But a week's holiday with him could be very acceptable. *Could* be. Though he wasn't just talking a week, was he? Underneath it all, she sensed he wasn't kidding about wanting her to stay longer.

She chewed her lip.

Even if he was still in love with Manon, what difference did it make? Did a woman need to be loved by the father of her child? She could still have a good time with him, couldn't she?

Anyway, what was she angsting over? The elegant woman was long gone.

Surely.

She gave Luc's bicep a friendly squeeze through the cashmere. Finding it so satisfyingly hard she couldn't even make a dent, she grinned. 'How I love a hard man. What do you do in the evenings, monsieur?'

He shrugged. 'Until this moment I—work, or I attend dinner meetings, *soirées*. *D'Avion* is quite important to the French economy, so sometimes I'm invited to attend receptions with people in the government. Concerts, the opera, the cinema… What does anyone do?'

She had visions of him in evening dress, whirling around the sophisticated Parisian social scene. No doubt since he didn't have Manon to accompany him he'd found other women to escort. Maybe he held a different beauty in his arms every night of the week.

Though not in his apartment, clearly.

'Don't you ever feel like a night in?'

'I think I might feel like one tonight.' Though he spoke gravely, his eyes gleamed and she felt a tingle of excitement. It could be all right. If she gave it a chance.

At least he was patient to walk with. He didn't seem to mind or try to chivvy her along when she stopped to gaze into shop windows. Even when she ventured inside for a closer look he hung around outside, talking on his mobile. Probably chatting to government ministers or giving instructions to people in his office. Or maybe he was warning his girlfriends not to expect him for a night or two.

After a few fascinating blocks they turned into the Rue Montorgueil, which was a market crowded with shoppers patronising the dozens of cafés and patisseries, food and wine shops.

Charmed to her socks, she forgot all her misgivings and oohed and ahhed like a tourist. The rue was a Monet come to life.

'Do you cook?' he enquired, pausing by a cheese emporium.

'Not in France. Do you?'

He laughed at her quick response. 'I don't have to. I have a hundred restaurants on my doorstep. But for you I'll turn the leaf.'

He purchased several varieties of cheese, some sausage slices, a crusty loaf and fruit, olives and some salad vegetables from a market stall brimming with fresh produce. Then, apparently exhausted by such heavy domestic activity, he suggested lunch, steering her towards a café with red geraniums spilling from planters on its window ledges.

Relieved not to be returning to the apartment straight away, Shari sank down gratefully at the table the waiter had directed them to, while Luc piled his purchases on an empty chair. So much had happened in the last twenty-four hours she felt close to a reality overload.

She gave her order, then listened while Luc discussed his choice with the waiter. When the guy bustled away, Luc excused himself and drew out his phone.

'Are they needing you at your office?'

'Not at all. I'm conducting some research.'

After a while she said gingerly, 'Did... Was Manon a good cook?'

He kept his eyes lowered to the phone. 'She could barely cook an egg.'

It was pretty clear what he'd seen in the Parisian paragon. 'Did you and she dine out every night?'

He frowned. 'Most nights. Though our work commitments often meant not with each other.'

'When did you ever talk?'

He said drily, 'There was nothing to talk about.'

She studied him covertly. His face was as close to expressionless as a frowning man could achieve.

'I can see your point about keeping a large dog in your beautiful apartment.' She filled her water glass and took a sip.

He looked up sharply then, his eyes so cool she nearly jumped back in her chair. 'Have you noticed we have had nearly two full days now without rain?'

'Sorry.' She winced. 'Too forward?'

He took up his phone to deal with an incoming text. 'There are so many other things worth discussing.'

The waiter arrived with their meals. Shari welcomed the diversion. She felt a bit shaken, actually. She certainly hadn't intended to strike any major nerves.

She murmured to the waiter, 'Could you please bring my salad now?'

The waiter's brows elevated. 'Now? Both? At the one time?'

'*Oui, s'il vous plaît.*'

He threw up his hands, then hurried away to comply, shaking his head at her unfathomable foreignness.

Shari contemplated her *croque Mediterranéen*, conscious of a jagged sensation. Though Luc continued courteous, there was something forbidding in his expression. She accepted it was her own fault. She'd pushed the boundaries and now he'd vanished behind a steel barrier.

All at once she felt adrift in an arctic sea. The Luc who had begged her to stay and kissed her in the car had become a stranger. She'd never been good at coping with angry people. If he didn't smile soon she didn't know what to do. 'Look, I—I apologise if I intruded. I know it can take a long time to forget.'

He looked up at her, his dark eyes glinting and alert. 'That depends on what there is to forget.'

'Of course, of course. Sorry. What do I know?'

She tasted her salad. Oh, *God*. Divine. The dressing was to die for. Exactly what she'd anticipated.

It was just as Rémy had declared. Every French person expected—*demanded*— their salad be dressed with just such a superb vinaigrette. She'd never managed to get it exactly right for him. What was she doing here? How could she possibly contemplate a whole week with another Frenchman? What did she know of Luc anyway? He dined with people in the government. He attended soirées. He was in love with a beautiful woman she could never compete with.

Glancing about her, she had the panicked realisation she'd never make it here. She just didn't fit. In his apartment. In his life. She started as Luc's voice cut through her musings.

'You're not losing your nerve?'

She glanced up guiltily. Was she so transparent? But what was there to say? She should have boarded that plane and be headed for the Antipodes right now.

His dark eyes searched hers, questioning, bemused. 'Seriously, Shari... Because of a few bottles?'

'No, no. It's—a matter of common sense. Of—of—self-preservation.'

He stared at her, shaking his head, then, leaning forward, said earnestly, 'It's a matter of trust, *chérie*. And of courage. The risk is no greater for you than it is for me.'

'But yes it *is*. You are safe and secure in your country, your culture, while *I* am…'

He grabbed her knife hand to stop its flailing. 'Do you think I haven't considered all of this? But what do *I* know of *you*? I've known you five minutes and you have a child inside you—my child, so you *say*—and unless I'm a perfect saint of a guy you are threatening to run away with it either to abort it without my knowledge or let it be born without me.'

Some of those words sliced her like knives. All her hopeful instincts, fragile as they'd been, shrivelled. She laid down her knife and fork, breathing hard, and met his blazing eyes.

'Yep. That's about the size of it.'

She got up and walked out. Once in the street, she ran.

CHAPTER ELEVEN

IT WAS as well Luc's strides were longer than Shari's because she could run amazingly fast for a pregnant person.

When had a woman been more difficult to pin down? It was absurd how hard this—this *conquest* was proving. An unwelcome flash of déjà vu rocked through him just then and nearly stopped him in his tracks.

Zut, it was his recurring nightmare. The last time he tried to pin down a woman she'd left him. Abandoned her home and her world.

Surely this wasn't the same though. It was in no way the same.

Dodging people and traffic, he cursed himself fiercely for the fiasco of the day. Everything had gone wrong. He'd *known* Shari was in a volatile frame of mind. Of course she was, in her condition. Why hadn't he noticed the state of the apartment? This was no way to bring a woman home.

But why couldn't women understand that forcing a man into this ridiculous pursuit procedure only roused him to more lust? The more he ran, the more his blood seethed in his veins with a single red-hot intent.

As if he hadn't done enough to her already, he was conscious of a primitive need to catch her and take her down. On the pavement. On the street. Or at least rush her to his bed and plunge himself into her until she surrendered herself to him in screaming ecstasy.

At the same time he felt constrained by an opposing instinct to handle her as if she were made of the most delicate porcelain. The woman had him tied up in knots.

His heart muscle was working overtime by the time he caught up with her. When he saw how her eyes hardened to see him, his gut clenched. The impulse to grab her and kiss her, plunge his tongue into her mouth until her knees buckled was overwhelming, but he restricted himself to gently touching her arm.

'Shari. Please, will you calm down?'

She slowed her pace to a very fast walk, her face set against him.

'What are you doing? Where are you running?' He knew his voice sounded too harsh, courtesy of his pounding blood pressure. '*Should* you be running?'

'I'm going back...'

'*Mais pourquoi? Bien sûr, je suis un bâtard, Shari, mais j'ai...*' In the stress of the moment he didn't hear everything she'd said, then realised it was the apartment she was returning to. For the moment, anyway.

'...my things.'

'But why?' He'd just launched into an emphatic and just defence of his behaviour when a series of shouts that had been in the corner of his ear all along finally captured his attention. Turning, he recognised Louis, the waiter from the café, jogging along behind him with the shopping bags.

With emotion running higher than the Eiffel, he was hardly in the mood to smile, but there might have something comical in the scene. The red-faced guy puffing to catch up with them acted as a circuit breaker. He was obliged to stop and was relieved to see that at least Shari paused too, looking on with a polite smile while he showered Louis with thanks and euros.

With passions under tighter controls, they resumed walking, Luc racking his brains for something he could say to minimise the damage and manoeuvre events into a situation he could control.

'Perhaps I need to explain,' he said, as calmly as he was able with his adrenaline ready to burst the levees. 'What I said in the café was not intended the way it may have sounded. I didn't mean you to think I don't accept your word.'

'No?' She cast him the sort of glance usually reserved for snakes.

He felt stirred to defend himself. '*Chérie*. What I said burst from my heart in the heat of the moment.'

'Exactly.'

'*Mais non*. You misunderstand. I was trying to demonstrate how we must trust each other.' He waved the salad bag. '*Vraiment*, we are in similar boats, you and I.'

'You think?' She gave a hollow laugh. 'I doubt if you'd like the view from this canoe, *monsieur*.'

Anyone would have thought he was a selfish animal, without a vestige of humanity. But since they were approaching his building, he restrained his impassioned defence.

'*Mademoiselle*,' he said with restrained dignity, 'we are nearly there. Let us not argue before *Madame la concierge*.'

She froze him with a glance.

It was challenging to know whether she was so complicated because she was a woman or because she was an Australian. Or was it purely the result of her being pregnant? Of course, he had to remember she was used to being with a violent psychopath.

She needed to learn there were guys in the world who knew the meaning of civility, even if they occasionally overlooked a few minor details in the matter of their surroundings.

He turned away from her to greet the concierge. '*Madame. Comment ça va?*'

He listened with greater attention than usual to the latest about the old woman's grandson, her daughter-in-law, and her arthritic cousin in Nantes. Only when the *vieille* was threatening to open up her concerns about her entire extended family did he deal with the issue of addressing the boxes he'd instructed the maid to leave with her. As well, he provided Madame with enough euros to cover the cost of postage, along with a generous contribution towards her retirement fund.

After that burst of friendly conversation, the journey up to the apartment was tense, as if one false word could detonate an explosion. He kept to his side of the lift, Shari to hers.

Shari held herself taut, resisting the current of sexual electricity rampant in the confined space.

Every so often his hot angry glance flickered over her, causing her to burn with indignation. While she'd at last intuited that he wasn't likely to slam her with his fist, it was pretty clear there were other desires percolating through his handsome head.

As if.

Did men ever think of anything else but sex?

He looked as sulky as a boy, but what right did *he* have to be upset? It was as clear as a bell what she had to do.

In the apartment, while he shoved his purchases into the fridge willy nilly, she said politely, 'Would you mind if I used a laptop?'

'*Certainement.*' He crammed the door shut on the foodstuffs. Then with the most elaborate courtesy he showed her into his office and switched on his computer. He leaned down to type in a password. 'If you are wishing to send an email…'

'I'm booking a flight.'

His handsome face stiffened. 'I see. Then in that case…'

He hit the Internet connection and stood back, with a flourish of his hand indicating she should use his office chair.

She sat down and clicked to the site. She could feel his hand on the chair, his fingers brushing against her hair. 'Are you intending to watch over my shoulder?'

He said evenly, 'I'm not watching. I am remaining here to offer my moral support.'

'Just a bit late,' she murmured.

She regretted saying that, actually. Glancing up, she caught an accidental glimpse of his reflection in a mirror that hung outside in the hall.

He'd moved back to glower against the filing cabinet, his arms folded across his chest, dark eyes smouldering, his brow like a storm cloud. Every line of his lean body looked furious. But what did *he* have to feel so raw about? She was the one In Trouble.

Considering he didn't want to be burdened with another man's offspring, he was taking her decision to leave hard. She supposed it must be a macho thing. The caveman wanted to feel in control of the cavewoman, regardless of whose embryo she was incubating.

She typed in her credentials, then scrolled through the flight times.

Disappointingly, all remaining flights for the day had been filled. Conscious of Luc's acute gaze trained on the screen, she tried for tomorrow's with the same result. Incredulously she tried the following day's flights, and the day's after.

No good. She realised despairingly that, unless she wanted to sacrifice the ticket Neil had purchased for her and try another airline, she was stuck for the whole week.

She even tried other airlines, knowing she'd never really waste Neil's generous gift. Then, to underline her terrible luck, the website she was struggling with froze.

Only just resisting smashing something and bursting into tears, she stood up abruptly and turned towards the door. 'This is a waste of time. I'll go back to the Louvre instead.'

'Why?' he said sharply. 'Because I stated what is true between us? *Ecoute.*' He grabbed her and turned her to face him. His dark eyes were cool and stern. 'I'm not a perfect guy, Shari, but I am attempting to be—to *do* what is the right thing. I understand you were upset today with the perfumes, the apartment, but—most of that is fixed now. I was tactless to say what I said in the café, perhaps, but what do you expect?' He flung up his hands. '*Zut*, we are from opposite ends of the earth. And, yes, yes, I know. *You* are a woman, *I* am an idiot. I will offend you—you will offend *me*, perhaps—many, many times, but... *Nom de Dieu*. This talking with you is like walking on eggs.'

She hissed in a breath through her teeth. Her overstressed heart smarted. But while strongly in need of sinking down in a heap and weeping the hot, bitter tears of the chastised damsel, somehow she managed to resist caving in to that final humiliation.

'In case it has escaped your notice,' she said stiffly, the merest tremor in her voice, 'there are some things that do upset the average woman.'

'I've heard. And I'm guilty of all of them.' He flung up his hands, his sexy lips crushing each other in their vehemence.

'No.' She made a desperate bid to gather her serenity about her. 'Maybe you're right. I may have been a bit tense today. Maybe I've been unfair, but at least *try* to extend the limits of your male imagination. I have something—some*one* growing in here.' Raking his lithe, angular, non-pregnant form with her eyes, she clutched her stomach region. 'It's hard to be charming and elegant when little eyes and ears are suddenly developing inside you. How do you think you'd cope with it, *monsieur*?'

His eyes glinted. 'I think I can imagine it. I have seen *Alien*, the movie. But surely the ears don't start to develop for another week or two?'

'What?' Jolted, she ignored his silky Gallic sarcasm to stare bemusedly at him. 'Where'd you get that?'

A rather diffident expression crossed his face. Then his sensuous mouth relaxed and he looked less angry. Less sulky. His dark lashes flicked down as if he was suddenly feeling confident. Smug, even.

He lifted his shoulders with elegant nonchalance.

'Last night, naturally, I was—working. As a pure accident or some strange prompting of fate I happened to stumble across a website that illuminated the—what do you say?—prenatal stages. It seems it is a long process, this development of the senses.' While she goggled, his hands made an earnest demonstration of her abdomen growing to the size of a football field. '*En fait*, while some hearing will certainly be possible soon, I believe the entire auditory channels aren't properly established until some time well after the baby's birth. Eighteen months or so. It is still a very sensitive time in a child's brain.'

'Oh.' She mouthed the word, actually. For though she parted her lips, no sound would come out.

Shock, of course. She'd imagined he'd used both the b word and the ch word, when even in her deepest womanly recesses she hadn't permitted *herself* to think those frightening terms.

He placed his hand gently over her womb. 'We'll have to be very careful.'

As she stared down at that lean, tanned hand a sexual lightning bolt sizzled along her veins. Her mildly emotional state intensified a thousandfold, only it was with a more positive emotion, a more *physical* emotion, if such a thing could exist.

It certainly existed right then. Her devastated heart opened to him, while the rest of her being hotted up like crazy.

'*Well*. I had no idea you…I'm surprised,' she breathed. 'I didn't *expect* you to… Well, to be interested.'

'I am interested.'

'I thought you were deeply horrified by—the situation.'

'I am thirty-six years old, Shari. An unexpected child—could be a beautiful gift.'

Oh, God. Her thrilled heart shook like an alder. 'Well, you know…I'm so sorry about everything.' Her eyes misted and her voice choked a little. 'I know I've been too difficult. And too emotional. And I am a terrible frump.'

'No, you haven't. And you are not.' His deep voice thickened. His hands travelled up her arms to her shoulders, where it was a short and entirely natural distance to her breasts. 'I've behaved like *un imbécile*. Here you are feeling strange and unnatural and I have to behave like a… You're—an angel. You're perfect. So beautiful, so feminine. I want to…'

What he wanted to do he never quite had the chance to say, because even as her heart thrilled with more incredulous trembly emotion he started to kiss her face and eyes and throat. But he did murmur, 'I don't want us to be angry, *chérie*,' and a lot of passionate and tender-sounding things in French—at the same time as sliding his hands under her top and unfastening her bra.

His lips found hers. She was so glad she hadn't fled home with her tail between her legs. A man who could kiss like this deserved every chance to prove himself. While his tongue touched the insides of her mouth with fire and ignited her blood, he held her breasts in his hands and gently pinched her wildly responsive nipples.

She made no attempt to resist the sexual maelstrom. With desire blazing in every corner of her being she burned like a beacon, pushing up his black sweater the better to explore his gorgeous chest and rouse him to the same flaming lust consuming her.

She didn't even have to try. The heat of his satin skin seared her palms, while one lick of his nipples had a dynamite effect. The rigid length straining against his jeans testified to that.

He stopped her hands from travelling too far, though still kissing her, he slipped *his* hand down inside her jeans. At the first delicious stroke of his fingers through the fabric of her pants she was moist, urgent to take him inside.

She clung to him, wrapping her legs around him as he carried her. Somehow they divested themselves of their clothes without completely separating for more than a second here, a moment there.

He pushed her onto the bed with his powerful body, and she surrendered, locking her ankles around him. His magnificent penis, hot, hard and virile, teased the yearning entrance of her sex deliciously.

Thrilling, she held her breath.

His dark eyes burned fiercely into hers. 'Are you certain we should? Will it be too rough? Am I too *grand*?'

She held back a laugh. 'Never too *grand*, monsieur. And I'm hoping for some rough.'

His eyes gleamed, then he thrust inside her with devastating conviction. The fantastic friction turbo-charged her excitement to such a violent pitch of ecstatic passion, she exploded into climax faster than was decent.

It was a long afternoon. After a time, though time was hazy, she pushed Luc onto his back and said, smiling, 'Now then, lover. I'll try not to be too rough.'

Straddling his narrow hips with sinful intent, she slid onto him and rode him until his dark impassioned eyes lost focus and the world dissolved in bliss.

CHAPTER TWELVE

IN THE heat of the moment, Shari hadn't paid a great deal of attention to the *chambre à coucher* to which she was being transported. But there came a time when her eyes opened wide.

The room was still a yellow fantasia, but the empty space above the fireplace was now occupied by an exquisite rococo painting of some gentlemen with ladies—fully clothed—in voluminous dresses, lounging under the spreading boughs of a tree.

She studied it thoughtfully. She felt pretty sure she'd seen it somewhere before. It was too far away for her to take a squiz at the artist's name, but she thought she'd wait until she was alone before investigating.

An expedition to the boudoir revealed that all evidence of any female occupation prior to her own had been obliterated. *Her* perfume bottle now graced the dressing table, and her clothes, meagre as they were, were hanging in the wardrobe. Her shampoo bottles imbued the bathroom with a personality she could feel at home with.

Returning to Luc's arms, she snuggled against his chest. His bristly jaw brushed her forehead. 'I love that picture.'

'Mmm.' His voice was a contented growl. 'Me too.'

She spun a whorl of chest hair around her finger. 'Since you've got a maid to leap to your every command, I'm thinking now I might stay the whole week.'

He sighed. 'Suppose I hire a *chef*? Then you will stay even longer.' When she failed to reply, he gazed down at her. 'Be my lover...'

Well. This came pretty close to sounding like a commitment, of sorts. Her heart shivered with joyful doubt and excitement. 'You do know I'm about to get really enormous?'

'Every man in Paris will envy me.'

She wrinkled her nose. 'Are you sure? Wait till I tell Neil.' Then meeting his amused, tender gaze, she said, 'This isn't just because I'm pregnant and you've been harbouring some weird sicko fantasy about pregnant women?'

He laughed heartily, then tenderly tweaked her hair. 'It's because you are you.' His eyes grew serious. 'Beautiful, unique you.'

He kissed her then, with such passionate ardour she believed him. Believed every word.

And knew she was in love. All at once Paris was heaven. The sun came out, the trees glowed greenly and the flowers in the gardens all opened their beauteous faces. She strolled along the banks of the Seine with her lover, argued with him, teased and drank coffee with him in cafés on the Left Bank. She visited Notre Dame de Paris with him and was awed.

She prevailed on him to take her to all the tourist hangouts, and he obliged without protest, regaling her with a dizzying lunch at the top of the Eiffel Tower, hours and hours of pictures in galleries all over Paris, and dinners in restaurants where the waiters could run up steep flights of stairs balancing steaming trays aloft on one hand.

It was too early to share her news with the world, so she was cagey even with Emilie and Neil. 'I've decided to stay on for a week or two,' she told them in her email. 'Luc has come to my rescue and he's letting me stay at his place for some of the time.'

At his place. Not *with* him. She hoped they got the distinction, though, red-eyed and sleepless from attending to the latest set of twins all night through, they were hardly likely to notice anything.

She included a few pics of Disneyland, some of them strolling in Montmartre, and one rare one she just couldn't resist of Luc laughing while getting drenched in a downpour of rain.

When the possibilities of varying her limited wardrobe reached saturation point, Luc took her to a boutique in the Rue Cambon, near the Ritz, that blessed venue, and some others in the Rue du Faubourg St Honoré. She tried on dozens of things, and he wanted to buy her most of them, but she accepted one lovely pale green dress to wear for daytime occasions and two for evening—one a simple, stunning black, the other a pale silvery cream.

She would never have been able to afford them herself, though she kept a tally of the cost so she could pay him back when her first truly massive royalty cheque arrived, just supposing one ever did. And she allowed the generous guy to give her some pearls and matching earrings as an outright gift.

She insisted on buying herself the shoes though, and, with the weather warming, trawled the Galleries Lafayette for some cooler things for casual wear. She couldn't imagine how large she might be in a few months' time, but there was the rest of spring and a certain amount of summer to live through first.

In her third week in Paris she was booked for her first prenatal visit. A private clinic had been recommended to Luc by a friend in the medical profession. It was the finest in Paris, the friend had assured Luc; reputed to be the most cutting edge in Europe.

The clinic was in the sixteenth *arrondissement*, across the river from Tante Laraine's, though not far as the crow flew. In fact, after their big appointment, as Luc casually informed Shari over his breakfast croissant, his mother had suggested they join her for lunch.

'Oh, have you *told* her?' Shari said quickly.

'Only that you're still in Paris,' he said soothingly, the shimmer in his eyes informing her he was perfectly alive to her alarm on the mother front.

The consultation alone was enough for Shari to worry about, without mothers—and *such* mothers—thrown in.

She put her anxieties aside and focused all her energies on preparing her questions for the doctor. Luc seemed as eager and excited as she was herself, an energy in his stride and a gleam in his eyes that melted her heart whenever he glanced at her.

Finally they were ushered into the consulting room and spent an arduous and exciting hour with the obstetrician, who was a pleasant and efficient Frenchwoman.

There was an endless list of questions for each of them to answer in regard to their family health histories, forms to fill out and government stuff to take care of.

Her official status in France was one of the items at issue.

'My visa is good for another two months,' Shari explained. 'It will have to be extended, of course.' She glanced at Luc. 'Will that be a problem, do you think?'

He looked thoughtful, then shrugged. 'Somehow we will deal with it.'

Then it was time for her examination. Luc didn't appear to enjoy the pelvic part. Not that he was able to see much from where he was standing, wearing an expression of extreme pain.

His face lightened with relief when the doctor finally peeled off her gloves and pronounced her healthy, and, as far as she could ascertain, *l'enfant* progessing normally.

L'enfant. Shari's heart skipped a beat.

And that was just the beginning. By the time the doctor had informed them of the sort of changes to expect along the way, the routine tests and ultrasounds Shari would undergo and her dietary requirements, her head was spinning.

'We will book your ultrasound for twelve weeks. Then we can measure your baby, check for certain of the possible abnormalities, the heart, et cetera. If we have any concerns at that point there's a remote possibility we might schedule you for an amniocentesis test.'

'I've read about that.' Shari couldn't help wincing. 'Is that where they insert a needle into your womb?'

For Luc's benefit, the doctor explained the procedure and its purposes fully.

'It is not routine these days to take this test. Only if there are particular concerns, and of course even then it is your own choice whether or not you have it,' the doctor continued. She produced a booklet that described the whole thing in detail.

Luc looked worried. 'But it sounds... How safe could it be?' He glanced from Shari to the doctor.

'*Bien sûr*, any intervention carries a risk, *monsieur*,' the doctor replied. She indicated the booklet with all the different tests profiled. 'The risk is there, but it is quite small. The statistics are tabled in here. I advise you to study everything carefully.' While encouraging, her cool professional smile revealed no clue of her own feelings on any matter.

Out in the street, floating, dancing, pirouetting the few blocks to where they'd left the car, while Luc was absorbed in some deep Gallic thinking, Shari was infected with an Australian need to babble.

'It's beginning to feel very real.' She fanned herself with pamphlets. 'I'm actually creating a new person. I'm turning into a mother before your very eyes. *Me.* Who would've thought?'

Luc roused himself from his reverie and slipped his arm around her. 'It isn't so impossible to imagine.'

'You think? Have you imagined it? What about you? Do you see yourself as a papa?'

He shrugged nonchalantly, straightened his shoulders and flexed a thousand or so muscles, but his gorgeous eyes glowed. 'Maybe.'

'I can imagine it. You'll be stern and thoughtful and *très très vraiment* strict.'

He grinned at her mimicry. '*Me— Zut*, I am thinking of that ultrasound. It will be—amazing.'

'I know,' she breathed. 'To hear the little heartbeat.'

He grabbed her hand. 'Come. I'm not ready to be with other people. Let's go where we can talk.'

The Ritz wasn't to hand, but luckily there was a patisserie on the next corner, Le Brioche d'Or. As they approached the crowded café Shari heard some jazz being played within. As if her heart wasn't high enough.

All the aromas made her mouth water. Though ravenous after her scant breakfast, she was mindful of the upcoming lunch. It would be a serious social solecism not to eat at Laraine's on this occasion. So she confined herself to selecting only tea and a miniature *tarte aux pommes* from the pastry counter. Luc ordered coffee.

Sliding into a booth in the upper room at a window overlooking the street, Shari spread out the information pamphlets and selected one, only raising her head when the food was delivered.

The tea was weak and watery, but these days that was how she liked it. She cut the pastry into two pieces and shoved one across to Luc. While perusing a screed about suggested dietary modifications for pregnancy, she bit into her scrumptious flaky pastry. Luckily there was nothing on the forbidden list about butter, apple a squidgin on the tart side, or rich heavenly custard.

The entire *tarte* was the sheerest bliss. She felt so sorry for all the people in the world who weren't in Paris with Luc. She eyed his untouched piece.

'Are you sure you want that?'

Without looking up the gorgeous man passed it back to her.

'Thank you. This one's in French only,' she murmured, applying her paper napkin to the corner of her mouth. 'Though I can manage most of it. You know, if I'm going to have this baby here I'll have to enrol in some French lessons.'

Luc glanced up from the booklet he'd been perusing. 'If? What is this *if*?'

'Oh.' Jolted, she met his sharp gaze. 'Well… It's just a figure of speech. I've booked into the clinic now so—I guess
I'm—having the baby here.' She grinned reassuringly. 'If I
can fix my visa.'

He glanced away from her. When he looked back again his
eyes were veiled. 'And you're content—with that?'

'You mean—am I content with *tu*?' She smiled at his searching gaze. 'I am. I'm quite content.'

He returned to his reading. Glancing at him a couple of
times, she noticed his brows edging closer and closer together.
Was it something she'd said?

The next time he spoke, he sounded his usual calm self.
'Why were you thinking about this amnio needle test? Are
you concerned there might be something wrong?'

'Oh, no.' She sighed, then pressed her lips together. 'I don't
even want to think about anything like that.' She hesitated,
then blurted something that had been nagging at the edge of
her mind. 'The thing is, apart from checking for abnormalities, the test can also determine the baby's DNA.'

'So?'

She gazed at him. 'Maybe we should have it. Just to—settle
any tiny little doubts you might have.'

His eyes glinted. 'I don't have any doubts.'

She could feel her pulse beating a little too fast, but she disciplined her voice to stay serene and reasonable.

'Still, the question has been raised between us, and I—I—
well, just for my own peace of mind—need to know that if I'm
staying here with you, if we are together in this, you have no
reason to doubt me.'

With a rueful expression, he reached across the table and
grabbed her hand. '*Chérie*, I don't doubt you. I don't doubt
you at all.'

She covered their clasped hands with her free one. 'That's
lovely of you to say, Luc, but I'm thinking ahead to when this
baby is born. What if he or she doesn't immediately resem-

le you? Or what if I can see the resemblance, but you can't? Don't you see? I'm quite an affectionate person. By that time I'll have spent nearly a year of my life with you, and I could probably end up being really quite—attached to you by then. If that happened and you doubted me, I wouldn't be able to bear it. The ending would be bad. *Big* time.'

He concealed his lowered gaze behind his dark lashes, frowning deeply. The moment stretched and stretched until her nerves nearly snapped.

Finally he said, 'If you think it will bring you peace of mind…' He threw out his hands. *'D'accord.'*

D'accord? Just like that?

Like a sandbagged zombie, she poured more milk into her tea and made it even weaker. If coffee wasn't recommended, tea probably shouldn't be either. And if a man agreed to having a DNA test to verify his paternity without a fuss, surely that was for the best.

N'est-ce pas?

Even if the test had the barest, most infinitesimal possibility of endangering the child's very existence?

CHAPTER THIRTEEN

'YOU'RE very quiet.' They were crossing the Seine en route to *chez Laraine*. 'Was it all too much? Are you feeling well?'

'Sure. I'm feeling great. Just—thinking, is all.'

Thinking about what an idiot she was. Why had she done it? She'd set up a trap and walked straight into herself. She didn't *want* that ghastly test unless the doctor specifically recommended it.

It only served her right for angling for reassurance. And how useless that had been. If a man wasn't in love, he wasn't and nothing would ever make it happen.

At least he wasn't lying to her. She supposed she should respect his implacable resistance to swearing undying love he didn't mean.

With a sick feeling she realised that if she didn't take the test, Luc would assume she was scared of the outcome.

'This may not be the best time for you to go to lunch when you have had such a strenuous morning,' he said apologetically, 'but on any normal day I'll be at work. I'm not sure you're ready to visit Maman on your own. What do you think?'

Shari glanced quickly at him. *Her*? Visit Maman on her own? Had he been eating the wrong mushrooms?

'You may be right,' was all she said. But her mental cogs were whirring like crazy. Was this to be her lot from now on? Regular visits into the jaws of hell? Not that they were unkind to her there. It was just that her status with them was so uncertain. She wasn't quite a cousin, nor yet a *fiancée*. Perhaps she was a girlfriend, although surely Frenchmen loved their girlfriends.

'What am I?' she said.

He looked sharply at her. '*Comment?*'

'How do I explain myself to your family? I mean…it's hard to know where I stand there. Am I a friend of the family?'

'Of course you are a friend. You are—*my*…' Seemed he too had trouble finding the word. 'It will be easier for you when you learn more French,' he said suavely. 'Everything will be easier.'

After twice making an exhibition of herself before his entire family, she seriously doubted that. It would take some magnificent achievement, like saving France from invasion, or reconstituting Napoleon, to correct the impression she'd made.

'Exactly how much does your mother know?' she said lightly as he backed the Merc into an impossibly tight space in the vicinity of the building.

'She knows nothing. Or…' He lifted his hands from the wheel. 'She is Maman. She could know everything.' He flashed her a grin.

Great.

'Think of it this way,' he said smoothly, urging her up his mother's garden path. 'Now you are staying in Paris you will need to know some people. When I am at my office all day, you might need a friend to talk to. Here are some people who are willing to know you.'

Shari broke into a laugh. Her heart warmed with love for the sweet man. At least he was thoughtful about her loneliness. And his excitement about the baby was a fantastic relief.

Fortunately, this visit was less nerve-wracking than the first. She'd done everything humanly possibly here to dispel the notion she was Rémy's woman on her first visit, and today it paid off. No urns were on display, and the assembly around the lunch table treated her with kid gloves.

She guessed that those who hadn't been present the first

time she visited had been apprised of her dive into the twilight zone.

Strolling in with Luc, she tried to look reassuringly normal and joyous. Certainly, after the visit to the doctor, some joy must have still been hanging about her because it kept trilling through her spirit. Nothing too terrible could touch her with Luc's enthusiasm for their shared secret wrapped around her heart like a shield.

'*Alors*, Shari, how are you today?' people said after the exchange of kissing. 'Are you well, *ma chérie*? Are you eating your food?'

Laraine herself, dressed in a lovely linen suit, was very attentive to Shari's comfort. Shari wondered if it was an accident the decanter of mineral water had been positioned near her place setting. How was a woman able to be so charming, so intelligent, so pleasant and discreet all at the same time, and still be so formidable?

At least Shari felt more confident about her clothes. She was wearing her floral dress, heels, and had wound her hair into a chignon to show off some aquamarine earrings Luc had surprised her with in honour of their first consultation.

She'd drawn a caterpillar on her collarbone, but felt pretty sure it would only be visible if she leaned forward, or had to twist about.

Laraine's cast of characters had expanded. There was a new couple, Raoul and Lucette. Lucette had a baby in a high chair she was feeding while attempting to eat her own food. Every so often Raoul interrupted his conversation to amuse the baby or assist in the production of shovelling food into his little rosebud mouth. Whenever Raoul looked on them a softness touched his eyes.

He loves him, Shari thought, trying not to stare. Really loves him. And he loves her.

Tante Marise was late to arrive, and after she'd kissed and been kissed by everyone she exclaimed to Luc, '*Again*, Luc.

nd so soon. We are honoured, *hein*?' Then she turned to Shari,
her blue eyes so genuinely kind Shari felt warmed. 'I am so
happy you are here, Shari. When do you return to Australia?'

Shari felt Luc's quick glance. 'Not yet. Not for a while.'

'*Oh, là*, but where are you staying? Not in an 'otel?'

'Shari is staying with me,' Luc said, taking up a ladle and
turning to Shari. '*Tagine, chérie*?'

All eyes sparkled and flitted between Luc and Shari. After
a polite nodded 'Ah' from Tante Marise, conversations about
half a dozen random subjects broke out while the family di-
gested the information with their *tagine à l'orange*.

Chickpeas and lentils in a mildly aromatic sauce.

Delicious.

Shari felt a pleased glow. She could have kissed the man
right there. A public acknowledgement of their relationship,
however discreet, was a breakthrough.

Laraine seemed to take the news in her stride. She merely
nodded, as if her son was confirming something she'd suspected all along. Her glance at Shari continued warm, curious,
a little amused, and Shari felt it often.

She supposed mothers worried about who was birthing their
sons' babies. By some feat of witchcraft, Laraine had already
guessed she was in the family way. How soon would be tactful
to fill the matriarch in officially? Not understanding how things
worked between mother and son made the territory chancy.

Until Luc was ready to declare his paternity to the world,
Shari couldn't feel any real security. And how likely was he
to announce it loud and clear unless he knew for certain he
was the father?

By the time they were through the salad course, Rochefort
and were embarking on the *mousse aux framboises*, Rémy's
name hadn't been mentioned once. The family were making
an effort.

Maybe a day would come when she would feel relaxed with
them all and stop worrying about every little thing. But after

she and Luc had said their farewells, kissed and been kissed, the burning question had crystallised in her mind.

When would she return home? Would she *ever*?

'It wasn't quite so scary this time,' she said to Luc afterwards.

'It was good you remained conscious,' he agreed, smiling.

'And the earrings helped.'

'*Tu étais belle*. Soon they will love you.'

Her heart panged. Would they?

Would he?

She twisted her hands in her lap. 'It feels strange not to know for certain where I'll be in a year's time. Or if I'll be seeing Neil at Christmas.'

He looked sharply at her. 'You'll be *here* at Christmas. With me. On the very brink of giving birth, if not in the hospital.'

'*If* we can arrange the visa.'

'Don't worry about that, *chérie*. You worry far too much. I'm meeting with someone tomorrow, and we will discuss it.'

'Someone in the government?'

His eyes veiled and he waggled his hand. 'A friend.' After a long silence he observed casually, 'You and Neil must be— very close.'

'Well, naturally. He practically brought me up, you know.'

He was silent so long, she turned to examine him. He was far away, a curious twist to his mouth.

'Now who's looking worried,' she teased. 'Lighten up. I'm the one giving birth.'

Eager to fit in, she enrolled in intensive French lessons. Five mornings a week she caught the métro to Saint-Placide where she brushed up on her vocabulary and grammar. It didn't seem to help when she was on the train eavesdropping on people's conversations, but at least she was learning things about French manners and customs that hadn't been included at high school.

Luc was pleased. And she began to notice that, more and

more, he reverted to his own language when they were conversing.

Gradually, words and expressions must have been seeping into her understanding, because often she caught his meaning. Not that she understood *him* any the better, except in the matter of passion, where understanding flowed between them like a tumultuous river.

The first ultrasound scan was an unforgettable experience. The indistinct and everchanging images of a tiny burgeoning person, the brave little rhythm of another heart beating within her had a deeply emotional effect on them both. During the event Luc seemed to lose all power of speech. Shari naturally cried, but glancing at Luc at one point she caught an awed shimmer in his eyes too, though he quickly concealed them from her.

The news was good. The baby was developing well, and growing at the normal rate. The doctor offered to tell them the gender, but seeing a doubt in Luc's shining eyes, Shari said softly, 'I think we'd like to be surprised.'

Before they left, the doctor paused. 'Everything is looking very strong. Your next ultrasound will be in July.' She produced a schedule with all Shari's future consultations listed. The amniocentesis test hadn't been included, to Shari's relief.

Maybe she could just quietly forget about it. Pretend the subject had never come up. But her relief was shortlived when the doctor added, 'I see no need for the amnio test you inquired about. Your risk level is very low. Unless you have some concerns you wish to settle?'

Shari tensed. 'No, no. I just…' She glanced at Luc, who'd frowned. She could feel a blush creep up her neck and into her hair. Admitting to the doctor that the father of her child had ever had the slightest question about his paternity, rightly or wrongly, was harder than she'd even imagined. 'Can we make the decision later?'

Luc scoured Shari's troubled face. He said gently, 'We don't need to have the test, you know.'

The doctor looked from one to the other, her intelligent glance veiled.

'We'll discuss it again,' Shari told her, cheeks blazing. 'I'll let you know.'

'*Bien sûr*,' the doctor said easily. 'I will write it in and we can always eliminate it if we decide to.'

They would decide to, Luc thought, pierced by Shari's blush. Somehow he would persuade her out of it. He thought guiltily back to the day he'd snapped at her in the café. He'd planted that seed of insecurity in her himself with his own careless tongue. Added to the Rémy effect…

Was it any wonder she believed he didn't trust her?

It was a delicate balancing act, keeping a woman happy and secure without making her feel as pinned as a butterfly. How did guys achieve it? With a cold anxious burr it occurred to him that if he wasn't careful she'd be on the next plane to Australia.

And then what?

A flash of his life before she came into it chilled his soul like a sudden arctic breeze. He wouldn't let her go. Not without a fight.

'I wish I didn't have to return to work,' he said thickly out in the street, pausing to shower her face in kisses. 'I want to be with you. I could have you right here against this lamppost.'

'Flattering, but would it be wise, *monsieur*? I'd rather not be arrested.'

He laughed, but, surrendering to her protest, escorted her to the car with his arm around her waist, brimming with positive energy that communicated itself to Shari.

'Now we know we are safe we can begin to tell our friends *n'est-ce pas*?'

Shari nodded excitedly. 'Good. I can't wait to tell Neil. He and Em'll be over the *moon*. But…' She shot him a glance. ' think it might be best for your mother to hear it from us first.

His dark eyes shimmered with some mysterious knowledge. 'Ah, *oui*. Maman will like you to tell her. And we must start some serious planning. We need to research the schools. And you've never said... Do we want a nanny? And I'm wondering if we need to hire a dietician to prepare your meals from now on. What do you think?'

She stared incredulously at him.

'No?' He burst into an amused laugh. 'But I *am* thinking of hiring a car with a driver for you. You shouldn't be travelling on the métro. It's too much of a risk. Anything could happen.'

'Now just hold on there. I *like* catching the...'

Luc stiffened momentarily and the words died on Shari's lips.

A taxi had drawn in behind their car and a woman got out to help another alight. When the second one straightened up Shari saw she was heavily pregnant, moving with the changed gait brought about by the redistribution of body weight. She was in jeans and heels, her enormous bump lovingly outlined by a tightly fitted shirred top. Her hair had been cut in a short, sleek, very chic bob, and she wore minimal jewellery, apart from some bangles and hoops in her ears.

Noticing Luc, she teetered backwards on her heels for an instant, and Luc lunged forward to steady her. He barely had time to touch her elbow before her companion stepped in and took a firm steadying grip of her other arm.

With a sharp pang Shari recognised that face. Who else at her advanced stage of pregnancy could manage to be so elegant? And she was, Shari acknowledged. Truly elegant. With a glowing, luminous beauty.

Luc smiled, though there was a hard glint in his narrowed eyes.

'Ah. Manon. What a magnificent surprise,' he said in French.

The beauty inclined her head. 'Luc.'

'Imagine meeting you here, of all places.' How could such

suave and graceful words be so punishing? 'And looking so—robust. Not bored with America, I trust?'

Manon glanced quickly at her friend, then pushed back her sunglasses. Her gorgeous amber eyes were defiant. 'I could never be bored with America. But where else does one go at this beautiful time of life?'

Her glance flicked sideways to Shari for a bare instant, then back to him.

There was a screechingly silent abyss when no one said anything, then the other woman tugged at Manon and hustled her into the clinic.

On the trip home, the atmosphere in the Merc had a certain explosive fragility. It crept in upon Shari that her situation was really very precarious. It was terrifying to think, but there was a horrible possibility about the man she loved she needed to take into account.

If he was still fixated on Manon, how long would he be likely to stay with *her*? Until the birth? Until the babe was a week old? Three months? And if he left her, would he be content to leave his baby behind?

A familiar claw caught her entrails in a death grip. She knew nothing of French law in the matter of child custody. But how likely was it that a mother—who wasn't even a citizen—would take precedence over the father who *was*?

In one swoop the excitement of the fantastic visit to the clinic was wiped.

'She's very beautiful,' she said, fluttering her lashes to draw his attention to the fact that hers were at least as long as Manon's. 'More beautiful than her pictures.' He made no answer, but she persevered. 'Did you know she was pregnant?'

His dark eyes were cool and veiled. 'I may have heard.'

'It's—quite a coincidence.'

'How is it a coincidence?'

'Well…you and she were together. Now *she's* pregnant, and here you and I are…'

'Life goes on. And...' He turned his head, and said softly, *You* are beautiful.'

Really? If he hadn't been so angry with Manon, she might have let herself believe him. 'Was that her sister with her—some relative?'

'I can't say. I barely looked to see.' He glanced at her, his dark eyes softening. '*Chérie*, don't allow this accident of timing to bother you.'

She smiled. 'It's not. Why would it? I wish you had introduced me, though.'

'Ah. I'm sorry.'

'You could have said, "Allow me to present my pregnant friend, Shari."'

He flushed. 'Yes, I should have, but it was a shock, you know, coming upon her so—unexpectedly.'

'Mmm. I sensed that.' She compressed her lips.

'This is the first time I've seen her in seventeen, eighteen months. The last time I saw her we were...she and I were engaged in mortal combat.'

She could just imagine it. The drama and the passion. Especially the passion. 'Who was the victor?'

'Oh, Manon, *bien sûr*. A man has no chance against a woman with claws extended.'

Her heart pained. How he must have loved the beautiful woman, to feel so bitter. She wished she'd never asked.

'You must miss her,' she observed coldly.

'*Shari*.' His gentle chiding tone made her feel ashamed. Advertising her neediness was hardly the way to inspire a man to love her. She felt her throat thicken, but held back the tears for all she was worth.

The rest of the journey seethed with an unbearable silence. When they drew up in the street before their apartment building, he turned to her, his intelligent eyes alert and at the same time grave.

He hesitated, then took her hand and said firmly, 'I don't

miss her, *mon amour*. I'm with you now. I've moved on. We all have.'

'Sure. Sure we have.'

'Hold the irony, please, Mlle Lacey.' His dark eyes scrutinised her face with tender concern. 'We—Manon and I were over long before our affair ended.'

She lifted her eyebrows. *'Affair?* Oh, that's cool. After seven *years*...'

He shrugged. 'That was what she wanted our relationship to be. No promises, no certainties. More than anything in the world she didn't want to *belong* to anyone.' His mouth made a sardonic curl. 'So she *said*. That was what caused the final crash. She wanted our relationship to stay the same. But...' He opened his palms and said simply, *'I* changed. I wanted—more. I understand now she saw that as a betrayal. At the time I was—angry. Disillusioned. You might say a little bitter. I said some things that were unkind, and she—stormed off to the airport in a fury, never to return.'

'Oh.' So it wasn't just the Jackson Kerr affair that had broken their relationship. Shari hardly dared ask, but the question was burning on her tongue. 'What was it *you* wanted?'

He flicked down his lashes and made a rueful grimace. 'Not a Russian wolfhound. No. I...er...suffered a brainstorm on my way home one evening and thought I wanted to have a child. Imagine that.' He shot her a veiled glance.

Her heart started thumping with a dawning realisation, but she struggled on to extract more of this astounding confession. 'You and Manon? You *wanted* a—a—baby?'

He inclined his head.

'Oh. Right. Well. *Well. So...* Did you—propose to her?'

He shrugged. 'The roses, the ring, the carpet of rose petals, the private room in the restaurant, kneeling like a fool—the whole bloody farce.'

'Oh-h-h.' She winced in sympathy. 'And she said no?'

He gave a sardonic laugh. 'Manon was a little like you in

ome of her ideas. She accused me of being a selfish chauvin-
st determined to cruelly subjugate her to domestic slavery and
revent her from realising her full potential by weighing her
own with children.' From the harsh intake of breath through
is nostrils, some lingering outrage was apparent. 'That was
what she said to the media, among other things.'

She could imagine how bitterly such a rejection had hurt.
Then to see Manon allowing herself to be subjugated by the
next man in so precisely the manner she'd sneered at…

Shari's heart positively ached for him. No wonder he'd been
o cold to the beauty when they'd met. 'That really wasn't fair,'
he said earnestly. 'You may not be perfect, but you aren't
ruel.'

He laughed and kissed her lips. 'Thank you, *chérie*. I am
rying very hard not to be. And the fates must have forgiven
ne, because now I have an adorable…'

'Friend.'

His dark eyes gleamed. '*And* a child to look forward to. I
m the happiest father-to-be in Paris. Do you believe that?'

Meeting his glowing gaze, she did. If there was one thing
he was certain about, it was that. He was definitely in love
with the baby.

'And I'm not really like her at all, by the way,' she said, get-
ing out of the car.

But the concierge called to him at that moment, and Shari
oubted he even heard.

Darkness was approaching when Luc strolled into a bar in a
idestreet tucked around the corner from the Ministry for the
nterior. His elderly friend was already ensconced at a table,
erusing *Le Figaro*.

'Henri.'

'Ah, Luc.' He folded the news sheet and rose to brush cheeks.
Good to see you, my young friend. What are we drinking?'

Henri already had a cognac before him, so Luc signalled the

bartender for the same. Once the courtesies had been observed, enquiries made about health, family and the stock market, the real reason for their meeting was subtly addressed.

'I'm afraid the news is not good for your friend with the *fiancée*.'

Luc's heart lurched. 'No?'

'There are some laws made of steel. They cannot be bent in the slightest. I'm sorry, my friend, but what can one do? This is the new world. The law is implacable on immigration matters. However…' Henri contemplated his cognac. 'Might I suggest a possible solution?'

Luc listened, and his spirits sank. Henri was assuming that this situation was straightforward, the woman like any other.

He endeavoured to explain. 'She is not—I *believe* from what my friend says—she is not the sort of woman who wishes to be pinned down. Forever is not a phrase in her vocabulary. My friend is concerned that if he sets a foot wrong she'll be fleeing to the airport in a snap.'

Henri arched his brows and laughed with frank amusement. 'Ah, Luc. Tell your friend he is an idiot. He just needs to find the right inducement.' He made a suggestive, masculine gesture. 'In the end they all want to be pinned down.'

Luc grimaced ruefully. 'Not all.' He rose, thanking Henri before leaving and walking slowly back to the métro, a heavy weight constricting his heart. 'No. Not all.'

Shari spent some of her afternoon engaged in research. It was a risk, it could have been self-defeating, but knowledge was power.

Unsurprisingly, there was little of recent date to find out about Manon. The grand passion seemed to have dropped altogether from public sight. As Shari had noticed as far back as Sydney, it seemed that once the scandal had been milked for every last drop the media circus had moved on. The tabloid

ites were no longer swamped with sightings of Jackson Kerr
nd his new woman.

Just a view here or there of Manon spotted in Beverly Hills,
lways shying away from the camera. Manon sunning herself
n Jackson's private beach with a friend.

Was it possible they'd split up? Was this why Manon was
ack in France to have her baby? Shari was ready to bet LA
vas dotted with fabulous clinics for celebrities. Surely the
merican ones would compete with the best in the world.

She studied some of the old images from the time Manon
ad worked for the glossy. How could Manon have even
reamed of exchanging Luc for a butterfly like Jackson Kerr?

Scrolling back to the Malibu image, she enlarged it so she
ould get a clearer view of the friend. She could have been the
ame woman who'd been with Manon at the clinic.

Jackson might have been off on location somewhere. Shari
oped he wasn't seducing another leading lady. He already had
few notches on his belt in that direction, if the celeb spotters
vere to be believed.

That would certainly explain why Manon had come back.
Maybe she needed to call on friends and family for support.

When Luc arrived home Shari noticed a change in his mood.
Ie tried to conceal it, but she sensed there was something on
is mind. As if that over-the-moon excited guy in the street
utside the clinic had plummeted to earth and it had gone hard
vith him.

She examined him carefully. 'Is everything fine? At work?
'our family?'

Anxiously she contemplated the meal she'd cooked. Her
alad—she was leaving the vinaigrette dressing to him—the
amb cutlets with the Shari Lacey version of ratatouille instead
f a sauce. It was Luc's turn to make the dessert.

His handsome face lightened. 'Everything is good. No need
o worry.' He smiled, but she couldn't help wondering. And
vorrying.

He partook of the meal she'd partly prepared with apparent appreciation, but, as she'd noted before, he was a courteous guy. She made the resolution to take some lessons in French cuisine just as soon as she had the chance. Definitely.

Over the next week or so he often seemed deep in meditation. Once or twice she caught him looking at her with an expression she couldn't interpret.

Well, she *was* starting to show. Her waist had thickened a little, and there were definite signs of a bump. To compensate she started making sure she looked beautilicious when he arrived home. Pretty clothes, underwear. She even had her hair cut and foiled and bought a straightener. At one point she succumbed to ironing a tee shirt.

In the bedroom she felt driven to experiment in ways that surprised even her normally inventive self. Was it hormones, rivalry or sheer insanity? Every time he looked gloomy, she felt challenged to distract him in some new and sensuous way.

She was at risk of turning herself into a femme fatale.

Luc came home early one afternoon when she was working on her book. The dining room's light with its romantic view of the rooftops and chimney pots of Paris had made it the obvious choice for her workplace. To spare the furniture, she'd spread a sheet over the table for her paints and paraphernalia, and pinned up some paper to protect the silken walls from splashes.

'*Ça va.*' He kissed her, tasting of coffee, the city, man and desire.

'You're early.'

'*Oui.*' He noticed her painting and bent to examine it, exclaiming, 'Aha. The carousel in the Luxembourg. You know my papa used to take me there when I was a little kid.'

'Oh, did he? It's so beautiful there. It must be the best gig in the world for a juggler.'

'But I don't see your owl,' he said, searching the picture.

'Ah. No. I've abandoned him until I'm in Australia again.'

He frowned, as he often did when she mentioned Australia.

ia. She guessed the reminder of Rémy's business shenanigans here still stung like crazy.

'See?' Shyly, she showed him her initial sketch, and some beautiful old posters she'd unearthed from the famous Cirque d'hiver. 'I'm still working on the face. It's not so easy to do he juggler.'

He compared them with her painting, exclaiming about the little telltale signs she'd used to make the setting obvious to Parisian children. 'It's so good. It's…exceptional. *Magnifique.* You are a great talent.' Glancing about at her protective measures, he indicated the room with a sweep of his hand.

'Maybe you'd like to change all this. Find a new look for he apartment. Make this a proper studio.'

'But that would be so much trouble, wouldn't it, when we don't even know how long-term my stay here will be? I'd hate to cause you all that expense for something that might well turn out to be temporary.'

'*Shari…*'

She looked enquiringly at him. He looked almost pained, hen his jaw hardened. He threw out his hands. '*Chérie*— There s something— I have something I must discuss with you.'

Clunk. For some reason her heart hit a pothole. She picked up a cloth and wiped her hands.

He took her shoulders and looked gravely at her. 'I have had news. Your visa can't be changed from within France. I'm sorry, *chérie*, but the laws here are very strict. If you wish to apply to be a resident, you must do it from Australia.'

'Oh.' It was a shock. 'You mean—go home? *Already*?' Disappointment, and a zillion obstacles flashed through her mind. Being with him. Their life. Her hopes and dreams. Her French lessons, her clinic appointments. Leaving him. Leaving *him*.

He lifted his hands. 'The immigration and visa laws have tightened here as everywhere. This is why…' his dark lashes screened his eyes '—I am suggesting—to spare you the trip— we should get married.'

Her brain spun for a giddy minute or so. When it slowed down she noticed a certain rigidity in him. A waiting stillness. Then the full implications of the words hit.

Pain sliced her heart like a knife. 'Oh. Oh. *Married*. Heavens, has it come to that?'

His eyes glinted. 'It may look like an extreme solution, but in your condition… Surely a long flight wouldn't be advisable?'

'Oh, that's just…' She smiled bitterly and shook her head. 'Pregnant women can fly right up until the thirty-sixth week.'

'Are you sure? How do you know?' His voice sharpened. 'Have you been checking?'

'Emilie. She wanted to come for the… Anyway… Anyway…' She laid her palm on her forehead. She felt flummoxed and prickly, as if all her fur had been horribly ruffled and she might just burst into tears. 'If I go home, who knows how long I'll have to wait for a residential visa? I'll just have the baby there, I guess.'

'*No*. No, Shari…' He made a sharp movement but she turned away from him. 'Don't think of leaving, *chérie*. No need to give up. The marriage ceremony is nothing. Just a formality. A banal, bureaucratic formality.'

'Look, I just need to think for a while. Excuse me while I go for a walk.'

She grabbed her bag and almost flew out of the apartment. Down on the ground floor she rushed blindly past the concierge's office, then headed to the nearest métro. The closest station to the Luxembourg was only one stop further on from Saint-Placide where she travelled for her lessons. Several times already she'd walked from there to the gardens to help her story cook.

Naturally, like the thoroughly emotional woman she was, she cried on the train. Then she cried on the way to the gardens, which was silly because she bumped into people and some of them were quite rude.

Then she walked past the children's garden, past the carouel, all the way to the fountain where she'd first told Luc she was expecting. As a coincidence, it was late afternoon again, not many people about.

She sank into a green chair and sat with her head in her hands. These last few weeks she'd been living in a bubble, she realised, and now it had burst.

But if you loved someone, what did it matter? A marriage proposal was a marriage proposal. She probably didn't deserve roses and pretty words and kneeling on the ground. The alternative was to leave him and fly home. Leave him without his baby? How could she even contemplate such a thing?

If she did make that long journey, would she ever come back? Would he even *want* her back?

So he wasn't 'in love'. He was a decent man. Straight, honourable and good. *Gentle*. What was she quibbling about? There were women who would give their eye teeth to be where she was. He'd be good to her, she supposed, since she was the mother of his child. His first child.

She waited for the ache in her heart to ease. Eventually the peace and beauty of the place soothed her enough that she could pull herself together. Then she hauled herself up and caught another train home.

When she walked in she noticed with surprise Luc holding a whiskey in his hand. She'd never known him to drink alcohol, other than with a meal.

He scrutinised her carefully, his eyes burning strangely in his taut face. 'Did you walk far?'

'I—went for a stroll in the Luxembourg. Thought I might as well check on something while I was in the mood for roaming. Oh, and about that other thing. Okay. I'll marry you, if you insist. But let's not make a fuss about it, eh? No white dresses and all that palaver. Just regular old clothes.'

Frowning, he looked at her uncertainly. 'Are you sure?'

She half turned away. 'Well, it's just a formality, isn't it? Let's do it without a fuss.'

'*Chérie...*'

Whatever he'd been going to say, he thought better of it.

They avoided each other's eyes after that, and there was a strain during dinner.

In their bed that night, she lay with her back to him, her heart aching too much for sleep. While Luc's breathing was steady and regular, a certain tension in him made her aware he was awake.

She tried to cry silently, until she felt his touch on her thigh and a burning, treacherous tingle ignited her blood. Desire and resistance warred in her flesh, until with a groan he reached for her and pulled her into his arms, murmuring, '*Chérie,* don't be sad. Everything will be all right.'

And once again he was the most virile, passionate and demanding of lovers. He rode her, he owned her, he possessed her like a king. Then he changed tack and became the warmest, the tenderest, the most considerate.

In his powerful arms she melted, she surrendered, she showed him all the love blazing in her soul. And from the tenderness in his embrace, anyone would have thought the man truly loved her.

CHAPTER FOURTEEN

'I'M NOT so sure about wearing old clothes to our wedding, *chérie*.'

Shari scowled. Until this moment she'd been enjoying her breakfast. Until this moment croissants and toast had never tasted so good. She was doing her best to be gracious over the travesty of a wedding she was forced to settle for, but that didn't mean she should have to discuss it when she had serious things on her mind.

Things like wilfully endangering her baby just to pander to some totally unfounded suspicions. Sure, it had been her suggestion, based on an insane and quixotic impulse, but the fact that Luc was going along with it *even after* he'd thoroughly read that pamphlet, interrogated the doctor to within an inch of the poor woman's life and researched the whole question on the Internet ad infinitum spoke for itself.

He still didn't one hundred per cent trust her.

And if he didn't, how could he ever love her? She knew from her own bitter experience the end of trust meant the end of love.

In this case, love had never begun.

Despite all his affectionate words and gestures, his concern for her well-being, his apparent pride when he introduced her to people, he'd never once been tempted to say he loved her, when she, on so many occasions, had only just managed not to embarrass him with heartfelt outpourings of eternal love by severely restraining herself.

Oh, there'd been moments in the heat of passion when he'd come on pretty strong about how he adored her, she'd changed his life, et cetera, but she knew the difference, and so did a sophisticated guy like him.

He couldn't even claim it was a cultural idiosyncrasy at work. Everyone knew the French were renowned for their passionate declarations. For heaven's sake, hadn't they invented the language of love?

Even in Australia, where men feared to string more than two words together at a time in case of being thought female, they managed to say deep and soulful things to their lovers in private. Behind closed doors. With the blinds down.

This whole amniocentesis thing was another symbol of her failure to inspire love in a man. It was shaming to think some women were forced to go through the procedure for very urgent and genuine reasons, while she'd signed on for little more than as a test to prove herself.

To prove she wasn't a liar. How sad was that?

Paradoxically, she suspected Luc wasn't comfortable with the idea himself. But it had become another of those things they didn't talk about. Like love.

'It occurs to me…' he said, casually spooning double cream onto the jam he'd spread inside his croissant. How could the man stay so lean and fit? *His* abdomen was as flat as a washboard. '…That our witnesses are likely to use the occasion of our wedding as an excuse to strut their finery.'

'Well, then, it's a pity we can't choose witnesses who aren't *prone* to finery. Like perfect strangers walking along the street.'

Though his dark eyes shimmered, his face continued grave. 'Yes, that is a shame. Strangers would have been perfect. Unfortunately, the law has spoken. Perhaps we can strike a compromise. Suppose tomorrow we take a stroll through the boutiques? There must be something in Paris you could enjoy wearing to your wedding. A suit. A dress.'

'I doubt it.'

The truth was, any control she'd had over the event was fast slipping away. Already she'd been forced to give in on the witness question.

The law was stacked against her. During several visits to the *mairie*, her situation in regard to her Australian birth and the inadequacy of her visa had occasioned some terse comments from the *conseiller municipal* who was to perform the ceremony.

Could she prove her relationship with Luc was genuine and not just an attempt to marry a French citizen by devious means? Could she *prove* she had genuine links with France and deserved special consideration?

The doctor's certification that she was pregnant, and had certainly been pregnant before she left Australia, possibly coinciding with Luc's documented visit there, only went part of the way to assuage official doubts. Even the dozen or so Australian documents she'd sent home for, along with Luc's documents, were held as doubtful.

Her relationship by marriage to Luc's cousin Emilie was counted as helpful. Even more helpful would be the endorsement of other members of Luc's immediate family.

Though Luc argued fiercely with the officials about the ridiculous red tape and bureaucracy that was strangling France and its citizens, he accepted the ruling.

Shari wasn't sure how regretful he truly was when he announced they were forced to invite two members of his family to be their witnesses.

'What can I say?' he'd raged when he broke the news, striding up and down and flinging out his hands. 'We live in a paranoid society in which citizens are considered guilty before being proven innocent. I'm so sorry, my darling, but our hands are tied. This is why I'm leaving it to you to decide who we should honour with the role.'

Shari frowned. 'Two?'

'*Bien sûr*, the law requires two.'

Two of his family. It wasn't that she disliked his family. They'd been very kind on every occasion. Since their announcement of the baby, both the Sophies had invited her to go shopping with them, Raoul and Lucette had invited her and Luc to dinner, and Laraine had called by to drink tea. During the visit the gracious woman had expressed her sincere condolences about all the yellow silk.

'It doesn't suit every complexion,' she'd said sympathetically. 'I'm not sure it even suited Manon. And it can be very wearing on the nerves. Probably on relationships, I wouldn't be surprised. Make a couple a little irritable, *hein*? I know my son has always detested yellow. In your case, *ma chérie*, a warm white, pale cream, perhaps even a *très, très* watery shade of blue could be to your advantage.'

Laraine was right about one thing. Yellow was irritating.

In fact, ever since Luc had made the proposal, if anyone could call it that, things that hadn't bothered Shari before bothered her now. That was one good reason why this so-called wedding didn't deserve to be classed as a celebration.

She tried not to look at him, all crisp and fresh in his city suit, his handsome jaw cleanly shaven while she was still a classic frump in one of his old tee shirts and straggly hair. It wasn't fair that a man should always be beautiful.

He was absorbed in reading his tablet, but every so often he remembered she was alive. 'Have you thought any more about the witnesses, *chérie*?' he said absently. 'We will have to give them some warning.'

'I'm not sure who in your family would have the *time* for such a banal formality. It's hardly a social event. Merely the signing of a contract.

Behind their dark lashes his eyes glinted. 'It shouldn't be impossible to find two who are willing. I dare say everyone in my family would *like* to witness my wedding.'

She glanced at him, but his face was entirely innocent as he perused *Le Figaro*, making occasional stabbing gestures with his forefinger at articles that infuriated him.

'Well…' She studied her toast, which could have been improved by a very thin smear of Vegemite, if only the French knew it. 'I suppose it would be nice to ask your mother.'

There was a moment of silence. Then, 'You think?'

She said gloomily, 'Though if we ask her, we can't possibly *not* ask Tante Marise.'

He nodded. 'Although Oncle Georges would be overjoyed to be included. Still, it's difficult with only the two. But what can one do? Papa is in Venice, but even he might feel he has a claim…'

She could see the crack widening in the dam wall. ' I *suppose*…one *could* invite some of them as guests.'

He glanced up, his face illuminated with a sudden devastating smile that wrung her heart. 'Only if you would feel comfortable with that, of course.'

She shrugged, gracious in defeat. At least he could be happy. 'Oh, sure, sure. Invite them all. And the children. *And* their dogs. But you know what that means, don't you?'

He was smiling at his iPad. 'What?'

'Printed invitations. Flowers. Photos. Receptions. All that stuff. Stuff I know nothing about arranging.'

'You can leave all that to me. What about Neil and Emilie?'

'Are you kidding? The twins are barely three months old. Em won't want to travel with them. And she's breastfeeding so she can't leave them behind, even if she wanted to. No, I'm doomed to go it alone.'

'Tsk, tsk. So depressing. At least on Saturday we can see about your dress. That will be something beautiful to think of, *n'est-ce pas*?'

She heaved a bored sigh. 'Whatever. Choose what you like. Just so long as it's yellow.'

She could tell she'd made some impact with that. He looked at her long and hard.

But it gave her no real satisfaction. Did she want to disgruntle him and send him off to the office looking stern for another day of terrifying his employees? No, she wanted him to be happy. She wanted him to have everything in the world he wanted. Even if it wasn't her, all that much.

Of course, once she had proved her case about his paternity, he might see her in a different light. If she didn't throw herself off the Pont Neuf first.

After he'd kissed her goodbye, then strode off to catch his train, she drifted around for a while, half-heartedly tidying things like a nineteen fifties housewife and feeling miserable about the whole damned thing.

It was lowering to know that a man would never have dreamed of marrying you if you hadn't been pregnant. And just to underline that fact couldn't even be bothered to dress up his proposal with a few flowery words.

Lately, she'd even given up the effort to dress herself up. Most days she mooched around in shorts, shirts and sandals, her hair in a daggy ponytail. Occasionally she'd drag on a skirt for the shops, but that was her biggest concession.

She felt Luc's gaze on her often, anxious, troubled, but she didn't feel like explaining. If he couldn't work out that a woman liked to feel at least *equal* to his ex in his regard, what was the point?

There was an evening when Luc was taking her to a reception at the Turkish embassy. When she emerged from her boudoir in a shortish skirt and a vest top, Luc stood stock still, gorgeous in his evening suit, surveying her quite sternly. Then he steered her back into her dressing room, stripped off those clothes and pulled out her good black dress.

'Put this on,' he commanded, then added smoothly, 'They will be going to some trouble for us. We have to consider their feelings too, *mon amour*.' Though gentle, there was unmistakable steel in his demeanour.

She knew she was sulking like an angry, disappointed child,

but that was because she was an angry, disappointed woman, with a child inside. While she capitulated in the matter of the dress, in a bold act of defiance she painted a fly on her cheek.

Luc simply smiled and said, 'Enchanting.' And to further destabilise her, he introduced her to all the dignitaries at the reception as his future bride with apparent glowing pride.

The rift stretched between them as wide and cold as a frozen sea.

Her blue mood persisted until the day of the amnio test. On the morning of the test she was jumpier than a cricket. Since her appointment at the clinic wasn't until early afternoon, she killed time by going to the market.

In an effort to crush down the jagged rocks in her chest, she visited her favourite art-supply shop first, and purchased some gentian blue and vermilion. Then she wended her way through the market, collecting sundry fruits and vegetables for the household supply. Shopping was easier now she could ask for things in French.

She was just gazing wistfully into the window of a patisserie she knew she should avoid when a voice she vaguely recognised accosted her.

'Shari, is it?'

She turned. Like an apparition from her worst nightmares, Manon was standing there, smiling a little uncertainly, an elegant tote bag hanging off her wrist.

'Oh. *Bonjour.* How are you? I mean you...you look very well. Beautiful, as always.'

Manon laughed. '*Beautiful.* I feel like a whale. My back aches, my ankles are swelling, and I'm hot. I've only just arrived and already I need to sit down. Shall we go inside?'

Shari only just managed not to drop her jaw. But why not? Why refuse the elegant woman?

'How close are you to your time?' she enquired over the tiny sliver of gateau that she'd allowed herself. No added cream. Even on a horrible day some lines had to be drawn.

'Three days past. My waters could break at any second. Does that give you an uncomfortable feeling?' She grinned and Shari allowed herself to relax and laugh. 'I'm not supposed to go out but I needed to escape. My partner would be cross with me if she could see me now.'

Shari pricked up her ears. Well, well, well. Here was an intriguing turn-up. She wondered if she should tell Luc that he and Jackson Kerr had been supplanted by a woman.

'Was that her at the clinic that day?'

Manon nodded. '*Oui*, that was Jenny. And are you and Luc still living around the corner?'

'Yep.'

'I enjoyed living there. Such a wonderful part of the city.' She smiled across her strawberry mousse.

Shari lowered her gaze. 'Mmm. I love the views.' And the man. So much. Too much.

'*Vraiment*. So pretty. I still think of my peaches and lemons sometimes. It was Luc's maman who whispered Luc's favourite colours to me.'

Shari lifted her brows. 'Really?'

'*Oui*. I could never really grow used to it. And after all my effort I was never even sure he noticed. *Men*. What can we do about them?' She gave a Gallic shrug, then winked. 'I have found my own way.'

Shari looked searchingly at her. 'And—you're happy?'

'Never happier.' The glowing radiance of her smile was undeniable. 'Life is too short not to be as happy as you can be.'

Shari agreed with that philosophy with all her heart. Though why did other people's happiness always make the heart twinge? 'Do you mind if I ask something?'

'*Mais non*. Ask away.'

'Did you have the—amniocentesis test?'

Manon nodded. 'I needed to. We had some concerns at one stage about spina bifida, because it is in my family genetics.

But…it seems there was no need to worry, after all. It's good to know our baby escaped that terrible thing.'

'How bad was it? Taking the test?'

She waggled her hand. '*Comme ci, comme ça.* A little scary. Everything is scary when you've never done it before. But in the end—not bad. It gave us peace of mind.'

'Of course.' If only *she* had peace of mind. She was beginning to doubt that a test would deliver it, when all was said and done. Feeling Manon's curious gaze, she hastened to change the subject.

'Is Jackson Kerr as gorgeous as he looks on the silver screen?'

Manon laughed. '*No.* He looks hot, but that's where it stops. He's selfish, his breath smells like a drain, and he thinks about nothing except his beauty, his personal trainer, and football. Always football. And his *mother.*' She shuddered. 'Luc is a much sweeter, smarter guy.' She added softly, 'But not the one for me.'

Heartsore on that subject, Shari lowered her lashes.

Manon scraped the bottom of her glass with the spoon. 'Someone has told me you are an author of children's books?'

'Oh, well…' Shari certainly didn't want to boast, but, under duress, she admitted it.

It was an illuminating conversation. Perhaps because they didn't need to be rivals, Manon was warm and genuinely friendly. After they'd canvassed pregnancies, partners and partners' mothers thoroughly, Shari saw her into a taxi and turned for home.

Somehow during that forty or so minutes she'd reached a decision. Cruel though it was to face the truth, she saw with clarity that clinging to a man in the hope some day her love would be returned in full measure was a fool's game. Experience had shown her that pain would only escalate with time. And life was short. Take Rémy, for instance. Here one day, gone the next.

Luc, beautiful man that he was, had done his best to do the honourable thing. He deserved a chance to find a woman he could prize as he'd prized Manon.

Somehow she'd allowed her Rémy period to sabotage her confidence and her belief in herself. The damned fool test was a case in point. How an intelligent person could have tied herself up in knots over it was nothing short of amazing.

On the walk home, she phoned the clinic and cancelled her appointment. Back in the apartment, she booked her flight to Australia, then started to gather her things. She was in the kitchen unpinning her sketches from the fridge when she heard Luc's key turn in the door, far earlier than expected.

'Shari? Are you here?'

'In the kitchen.' She braced herself, her heart thumping like a big bass drum.

When he walked in, his dark eyes were serious and unexpectedly stern. Her heart skipped a beat. What was it?

'Ça va,' he said, kissing her. He continued to hold her arms firmly, his eyes intent on her face. 'Shari, I can't let you do it.'

She started. '*What*?'

He shook his head. 'I'm sorry, my darling. I know you feel this is important for *us*, but nothing about us is as important as this little one in here.' He patted her bump tenderly.

'Oh, the test. Yes, I know, and that's exactly—'

'No, *chérie*. I need you to listen. I know you've been driving yourself crazy over this. Why are we doing it?'

She was winding up to explain her change of heart, but he went on regardless.

'It isn't necessary. I *know* you are not a liar. I've always known—what you are. Who. Who you are to me. And I won't let you leave me.'

'*Comment*?' A guilty blush heated her cheeks. Had the guy inherited his mother's terrible clairvoyance?

His face tautened. 'I—I only agreed because I wanted you so much to stay, but as far as we know it's not a medical necessity, is it? Some people need to go through this thing, but we've already decided to go ahead and have our baby, whatever the test uncovers. We said that, didn't we?'

'I know, we did. I only suggested having it in the first place because I've been feeling so insecure. Anxious.' She flushed a little. 'It was ridiculous. I couldn't be certain you trusted me. But I decided today that you'll just have to take my word for it, and if you *can't*...'

His eyes sharpened. 'But of course I take your word. And in the end,' he added hoarsely, 'who cares who our baby resembles or what selection of genes she has? Or *he* has? We'll love her, or him, because he belongs to us.'

'Oh, Luc. Oh, my darling, darling man, that's so wonderful to hear.' Tears sprang into her eyes. She put her arms around his neck and kissed him passionately, long and deep.

She could feel his hard body pressed against her, his big heart thumping with the force of his emotion. Her own was thundering fit to burst.

'I don't think you know how much I love you, Shari Lacey,' he said gruffly when they at last surfaced. 'And how I—need you.'

'Honestly?' she breathed, hardly able to believe her ears. Her heart swelled.

'*Bien sûr.*' He held her face between his hands, his brows earnestly drawn. 'You have warmed my life.'

'Oh.' Thrilling with a tremulous, painful joy she blinked madly to hold back the tears. 'Is that really true?'

He searched her face. 'How can you not know?' He spread his hands in rueful amazement. 'You won't believe it, but I used to consider myself a hard guy. Cynical, even. With you I've turned into a—a *putty*. I don't recognise myself. I've become dependent on the sound of your voice. Your—face in the morning.' His voice cracked slightly. 'At work I—I find myself thinking of you, worrying you won't be here when I come home. Even today I...' He shook his head, then looked firmly

at her. 'Listen to me…' He was breathing rather hard, and his
eyes grew stern and serious. 'Don't dream of walking out that
door. I won't *let* you. I'll hunt you down, if necessary. I'll chase
the plane you leave on. I'll pursue you to the ends of the earth.'

While she contemplated this exciting scenario, he muttered
to himself, 'All along I've been so scared of losing you, I've
been agreeing to crazy things like a—a madman.'

She had a fleeting vision of the time he'd raced to the Ritz
at midnight to pick up some buttery scrambled eggs, but dismissed that as an example. Any man would have done the same.

She gave a gurgle of laughter through her tears. 'Oh, I
wouldn't say *madman*.'

'*Oui, oui*. It's true. Every time we've disagreed over anything I've held my breath for fear you would run for the airport.'

'Oh, my poor darling.' Her heart ached with love and remorse, and a degree of guilt. 'My poor Luc. Why would you
think that?'

'*Why*?' His handsome face softened. 'Shari, chérie, I've
heard it in your voice. Seen it in your eyes. How you miss
Neil… How you long for Australia. I understand how cold it
feels in a strange country with only me to cling to.'

She gazed at the gorgeous hunk of man through her tears.
'Well, you are something worth clinging to, you know,' she
said shakily. 'You don't need to worry about Neil. Of course I
miss him and Em, but you…I'm in love with you. Isn't it obvious ? You're all I've ever wanted. You're the kindest, the most
sexy, the hottest, the most…'

His voice thickened. 'While you are the most desirable, the
most confusing, clever, adorable, darling woman…'

Joy was such a powerful aphrodisiac. This was a precious
moment, a solemn, soulful moment when hearts were open
and truth was on the table. The most thrilling words she would
ever hear in her life were being spoken to her by the most gorgeous man in the world, yet in her delirious state of sunshine
and supreme happiness she was feeling aroused.

So inappropriate. And so fantastically promising.

'I know I've been difficult,' she breathed. 'So emotional. Even now I'm feeling far too passionate. Is there any way I can make it up to you?'

'Yes,' he said fiercely. He swept her up in his arms and carried her to the bedroom.

Afterwards, when passion was for the moment in abeyance and she was lying with her head on his chest, contemplating the incredible fact that she'd misinterpreted so much about him, she said, 'I should have told you sooner how I felt. But I was afraid you were still in love with Manon.'

'No. Though I admit I felt—hurt, or something. We were over long before we split. I didn't really even understand that until the day in the café when you asked me about her. That day I brought you home and *you* nearly ran away as well.'

She squeezed his bicep. It didn't even leave a dent. 'Were you surprised when she took off with Jackson Kerr?'

He grimaced. 'Hardly. The guy's a stud. Isn't that what you women think?'

'He might well be for all I know. He *is* cute. Nice abs.' She laughed. 'Sorry. Just teasing. No, actually...' She took a deep breath. 'You may get a bit of a shock at what I'm about to tell you.'

She related the story Manon had told her in the patisserie, about falling in love and knowing it was the right thing for her.

Luc sat bolt upright as if electrified. 'What? Are you serious? She *told* you this?'

Shari nodded. 'She did. She told me things you wouldn't believe.'

'What things? Things about me?'

'No, no. Other things.' Realising she'd come close to saying too much for any macho guy to take on board at one time, she gave him a womanly glance to warn him off sacred ground. 'What we call in Australia secret women's business.'

'*Comment*?' His brows bristled with intrigue.

'Put it this way.' She hesitated, casting about for words. 'Her affair with Jackson Kerr was just a flash in the pan. Doomed to extinguish itself while she was working herself out.'

'Ah.' Luc's brows zoomed high and he looked keenly at her, his eyes glittering with an intense light as he tried to conceal his excitement. 'So… Are we saying…? Does this mean that er…sooner or later Manon would have left me regardless of how much of an insensitive *voyou* I am?'

Shari could hardly restrain a grin. He looked so chuffed to be off the hook.

'I dare say. Although she deserves a medal for how long she hung in there with all this ghastly yellow.'

He gave her a playful punch. 'She wanted it.'

She smiled. 'Yeah?'

Maybe she did. And maybe she didn't.

CHAPTER FIFTEEN

THE wedding was a glorious affair. There might have been
Parisian couples in the past who'd outshone the Valentins, but
most of those had been royal.

The ceremony in the *mairie*'s office was purely a bureaucratic formality, though the room had been decked with pink
and white roses and a red carpet laid for the bride and groom.
The real ceremony came afterwards, at the Eglise St-Eustache,
a sixteenth century church with exquisitely stained glass.

The service itself was austere and beautiful.

Shari had forgotten Luc's connections in the air industry, or
she wouldn't have been so surprised to discover that a friend
of Luc's had volunteered his private jet to transport Neil and
Emi, their children and two nannies to Paris for the festivities.

As it was, Shari was overjoyed.

Strangely, Neil and Emi were not as totally astounded by
her and Luc's falling in love as Shari might have expected,
though their approaching parenthood had come as a surprise.

As well, an elderly gentleman from Venice made the journey. When he'd first strolled into the *mairie's* and sat down beside his wife, Shari glimpsed a sudden rare shimmer in Luc's
eyes.

A magnificent reception was held at the Ritz, one of the
Hotel's last great events before it shut up shop for renovation.
Everyone Shari and Luc knew in Paris was there, including
some friends Shari had made at her language class.

Even if Neil hadn't been able to come, even if Shari hadn't been wearing a Valentino original, cut specifically to reveal the blue bird of happiness on her shoulder, just seeing her lover's joy would have made the day fantastic. As it was, it was sheerest heaven.

After the dancing, the toasts, the love and bonhomie of family and friends, Luc whisked his bride upstairs for one last splendid night in their favourite suite. Then in the morning, after a long and leisurely breakfast, he flew her to Italy for their honeymoon, where they planned to explore the Amalfi Coast for some weeks while their apartment was being renovated.

This time in palest ivory trimmed with softest aquamarine and a pale, pale, very watery blue, shades Shari knew suited her complexion perfectly.

It was a beautiful time of life.

EPILOGUE

'HERE,' Luc said. 'Give him to me. We don't want him to catch a chill.'

They were strolling together in the Rue Montorgueil. It was late in the day, and Shari felt the sudden cool snap in the breeze.

Although their baby boy was dressed well, the air could turn frosty in a second. Luckily Luc was wearing his padded jacket.

Shari handed the precious bundle over and Luc positioned him carefully inside his coat while Shari drew up the zipper.

'Not too far, now,' his father warned. 'Let him see out.'

Shari laughed as Luc-Henri chortled and his eyes, brown now and growing darker by the day, opened wide at the sudden change in his circumstances.

'There, now, isn't it lovely being held in Papa's arms? I quite like it myself.' Luc laughed with her, then she noticed him glance up at a passer-by and wave, his face alight with pride and pleasure.

Shari looked at the stranger. 'Who's that? Do I know him from somewhere?'

'Remember? He's the *boulanger* from the bakery near the fruit market.'

'Oh, of course. I know. How nice of him to wave. He must have noticed that ours is the most beautiful babe in Paris.'

'*And* he has the most beautiful *maman*.'

She smiled and planted a kiss on his bristly jaw. 'Thank you. That reminds me. Have you ever read *The Outlaw Earl?*'

He lifted his brows. 'I don't believe so. What happens in it?'

'Well, this beautiful lonely maiden is kidnapped from the home of her greedy parents by a wicked, but really hot earl.'

'Ah. And then what?' His eyes gleamed with a piercingly sensual light. 'Tell me.'

* * * * *

MILLS & BOON®

Why shop at millsandboon.co.uk?

Each year, thousands of romance readers find their
perfect read at millsandboon.co.uk. That's because
we're passionate about bringing you the very best
romantic fiction. Here are some of the advantages
of shopping at www.millsandboon.co.uk:

* **Get new books first**—you'll be able to buy your
  favourite books one month before they hit
  the shops

* **Get exclusive discounts**—you'll also be able to buy
  our specially created monthly collections, with up
  to 50% off the RRP

* **Find your favourite authors**—latest news,
  interviews and new releases for all your favourite
  authors and series on our website, plus ideas for
  what to try next

* **Join in**—once you've bought your favourite books,
  don't forget to register with us to rate, review and
  join in the discussions

Visit **www.millsandboon.co.uk**
for all this and more today!

MILLS & BOON®

Why not subscribe?

Never miss a title and save money too!

Here's what's available to you if you join the exclusive **Mills & Boon® Book Club** today:

- ✦ *Titles up to a month ahead of the shops*
- ✦ *Amazing discounts*
- ✦ *Free P&P*
- ✦ *Earn Bonus Book points that can be redeemed against other titles and gifts*
- ✦ *Choose from monthly or pre-paid plans*

Still want more?

Well, if you join today, we'll even give you
50% OFF your first parcel!

So visit **www.millsandboon.co.uk/subs**
to be a part of this exclusive Book Club!

MILLS & BOON®
By Request

RELIVE THE ROMANCE WITH THE BEST OF THE BEST

A sneak peek at next month's titles...

In stores from 7th April 2016:

- **His Most Exquisite Conquest** – Elizabeth Power, Cathy Williams & Robyn Donald

- **Stop The Wedding!** – Lori Wilde

In stores from 21st April 2016:

- **Bedded by the Boss** – Jennifer Lewis, Yvonne Lindsay & Joan Hohl

- **Love Story Next Door!** – Rebecca Winters, Barbara Wallace & Soraya Lane

---

Available at WHSmith, Tesco, Asda, Eason, Amazon and Apple

Just can't wait?
Buy our books online a month before they hit the shops!
visit www.millsandboon.co.uk

These books are also available in eBook format!